I ILLIAN GERDES

MW01003086

Montana Courage

Also by Caroline Fyffe

Montana Courage

A McCutcheon Family Novel

Book Nine

Caroline Fyffe

Montana Courage
Copyright © 2017 by Caroline Fyffe
All rights reserved by the author.

www.carolinefyffe.com

Montana Courage is a work of fiction. Names, characters, places, and
incidents are either products of the author's imagination or used fictitiously.
Any resemblance to actual events, locals, or persons, living or dead, is wholly
coincidental.

No part of this publication can be reproduced or transmitted in any form or
by any means, electronic or mechanical, recording, by information storage
and retrieval or photocopied, without permission in writing from Caroline
Fyffe.

Cover design by Kelli Ann Morgan
Interior book design by Bob Houston eBook Formatting

Proudly Published in the United States of America

ISBN# 978-1-944617-03-5

To all my dear friends and colleagues from the twenty years I spent in the horse show world as an equine photographer; this book is for you. Photographers, owners, competitors, and trainers—you are all very close to my heart.

Chapter One

Heart of the Mountains Ranch, early January, 1887

"**W**inter," Shadrack Petty grumbled through frozen lips, the wool scarf around his face offering little protection. As he approached the ranch, he gazed across the snow-streaked brown plains to the distant purple mountain range, some mountaintops already coated in white. The blue sky gave no hint of the breathtaking cold. A storm was coming; he could smell the sharp crispness on the wind.

He halted in front of the bunkhouse hitching rail, noting how the desolate ranch yard resembled a frosty ghost town. His arms and legs felt like frozen blocks of wood. With effort, he swung his leg over the saddle, stepped down to the rock-hard earth, and tossed his reins over the wooden bar, eager to be inside. The ranch buckboard sat nearby. A large tan oilcloth covered the contents and the harness hung from a sideboard, ready to be hitched to the unfortunate team that would have to pull.

Someone's going somewhere—but that someone ain't gonna be me.

Walking stiffly past the horse bits and branding irons displayed on the outside wall of the building, the tall Wyomingite pushed into the warm, musty room smelling of wet leather, smoke, coffee, and fresh-baked bread. The familiarity did little to gentle his growing agitation. He'd postponed speaking with the boss long enough. He'd need to corral Luke, or another of the McCutcheons, today.

Let the chips fall where they may.

He went directly to the fireplace, spreading his gloved hands before the sizable blaze, purposely leaving on his wool-lined coat. He glanced over his shoulder at the men eating their noontime meal.

Francis, his thick brown hair in need of a comb, promptly got up and started for his coat. His bulky wool shirt hung loose at the tails, hiding the young man's muscular chest and body.

"I'll see to your horse, Shad."

"Appreciate that, Francis. Any grub left for me?" The prickly hole in Shad's belly was beyond painful. Hot food, and plenty of it, was the only cure.

As he spoke, Lucky Langer, the bunkhouse cook, stirred something in a pot on the stove. The other men didn't even lift their focus from the plates in front of them.

"'Course there is," Lucky barked. "Does a whale have blubber?"

"Don't know. Never seen a whale."

The cook limped over to hand him a steaming cup of coffee. "It does, and lots of it. Now, guzzle this down till I fill your plate. Any snow falling in the upper pastures?"

"Naw, just colder than skinny-dipping in a snowbank. But the high country got some dusting last night, from the view on the plateau. I think the storm's coming our way."

Setting his cup on the wooden mantel of the fireplace, Shad peeled off his damp gloves and tossed them to the hearth to dry. He retrieved the cup. The heated porcelain between his icy palms felt like holding the sun.

He momentarily closed his eyes. "Night watch never gets any easier, I swear."

"Quit your grumbling," Smokey said with a chuckle. A wrangler, he'd been a permanent fixture at the ranch for years.

Finished with his meal, the bowlegged, weather-beaten, happy-faced cowboy stood and ambled to the kitchen area to deposit his dish and utensils into the wash bucket. Smokey's red cotton long-john shirt was tucked into a pair of well-worn jeans. If the cowhand felt the cold, he didn't let on. A moment later, he was at Shad's side.

"Seniority does have its advantages. Ain't that right, Uncle Pete?" he called over his shoulder. "You and me been here 'bout since the dawn of time."

The cowhand at the table grunted and waved an affirmative hand in the air but kept eating.

"You'll get there someday—*if* you're tough enough," Smokey added with a grin, grasping Shad's shoulder and giving it a shake. "How're the cattle up at Covered Bridge?"

"Good as can be expected this time of year. Acre upon acre of frozen earth as far as the eye can see. Found one carcass brought down by wolves. I opened the frozen waterholes and checked the pole barn. Hay's still high and dry in the loft. I found a few unbranded strays."

"Well, warm up and then get some grub. It's tasty."

Shad slugged down half his cup as he took in the table. John Berg, Bob, Uncle Pete, Ike, Hickory, Pedro. The atmosphere still felt a little off without Roady Guthrie in the bunkhouse. The foreman had married around the time Shad hired on, and moved to a cabin a short ride away. Although Roady didn't live in the bunkhouse any longer, he was usually around, keeping tabs on jobs and giving orders. Shad could go to him with his problem, but Guthrie would just have to speak with the bosses. Might as well start at the top.

He winked at Hickory sitting next to Pedro. The top of the kid's head barely reached the Mexican's shoulder. "Hey, what about school, Hickory?" he asked. "You skippin' just 'cause it's cold? I rue all the days I sneaked out, gettin' into all kinds of mischief. Schooling's important."

Lucky straightened, a frown pulling his mouth. "Skip school? Not in my bunkhouse."

The orphaned boy Luke had brought home from Waterloo glanced up at the mention of his name. His dripping spoon, heaped with the gooey gravy fare, stopped midway to his mouth.

"Teacher got sick yesterday, Shad," he said over a mouthful. "School's out till she's better, which I'm hopin'll be next month."

"Hickory!" Lucky said, admonishing the boy whose wide grin looked like a raccoon's.

Shad took notice of the others' plates, but couldn't discern what they were eating. "What'd Lucky concoct today?"

"Chicken and dumplings," Smokey replied. "Two whole crocks full, plus lots of bread. Good and hearty."

Lucky set Shad's plate at his normal spot.

Smokey gave him a nudge. "Go on. Fill your belly."

"Don't mind if I do." Shad got comfortable between Hickory and Pedro.

They both gave a sideways glance without coming up for air. When Lucky prepared something especially good, the fellas ate fast so they could get a second helping before it was all gone.

"After I eat, I'm gonna roll up in my blankets and sleep until tomorrow morning," Shad mumbled, swallowing down a hot mouthful. "Nobody better wake me, neither." He glanced sideways at Hickory to be sure the boy was listening. "And that means you. I need my beauty rest."

"I won't wake ya, Shad. I'll be quiet."

"Yeah, well, we'll just see about that." He held back his teasing smile, then took another spoonful and chewed and swallowed, thankful to be home. "What's with the loaded buckboard? Someone going somewhere?"

Uncle Pete opened his mouth to answer but before he could get the words out, Luke McCutcheon came through the door. The boss's sheepskin-lined coat was pulled up about his neck, sweat-stained chaps lined with wool wrapped his denim-clad legs, and the new black leather gloves the boys had chipped in for a Christmas present protected his hands. He looked around and nodded to Shad before addressing the men at the table.

"Faith has a box of things she'd like to add to the buckboard before you pull out," he announced. "Be sure to swing around and give a knock on the front door. It'll be ready when you are. I'm riding over to Roady's for a few hours," Luke went on. "If you need Flood, he'll be in his office all day. Matt and Mark are at their own homesteads." He shook his head and gave a happy whistle. "With the two newest McCutcheon boys making their appearance in November and December, my brothers have their hands full."

Lucky ambled up close, and Shad noted the tenderness brimming in his eyes.

"How are the little tykes," the cook asked. "Amazing how Miss Rachel and Miss Amy birthed 'em so close together. They'll grow up more like brothers than cousins. Can't wait till we get ta see 'em." He chuckled. "And it's about time we got some more boys."

"If the weather was warmer, I'm sure Matt and Mark would have already brought 'em by the bunkhouse," Luke replied. "They're about ready to burst their buttons with pride. Especially Mark. A man will get like that over his first son."

"When's the next one for you, Luke?" Shad swilled down the last of his coffee. He set the mug on the table and pinched a coffee ground off the tip of his tongue. "You don't want to get left in the dust."

"Our hands are adequately filled to overflowing with the little ones we have, Shadrack. But that doesn't mean I won't be plenty happy when another one does come along." Luke strode to the door but stopped and turned back. "You finished eating, Hickory? Colton's riding with me to the Guthries'. If you don't mind the cold, you're welcome to come along."

Hickory's eyes grew large at the prospect.

Seeing how much the boy idolized Luke wasn't difficult. The few months since he'd been living in the bunkhouse he'd gained weight, did his reading lessons every night, and often visited Luke and Faith.

"Want to go?" Luke asked again.

Hickory jumped up and practically ran his empty plate over to the dish pail filled with water. "I sure would. I'll go saddle Punk."

"We won't be ready to ride for a good ten to fifteen minutes," Luke said. "That gives you plenty of time to layer on more clothing." He nodded at Lucky. "Be sure he's covered head to toe. It's cold out there. And don't forget his gloves."

"You think I was born yesterday?" Lucky frowned and jammed his hands on his hips. "Hell, I was making sure you had your gloves not that long ago."

Luke chuckled. "Guess you were. Hey, Hickory, heard tell Sally is making a cinnamon cake today. Let's hope she did."

If the kid even heard Luke's last remark about the cake was debatable. The boy was moving faster than a roadrunner with a coyote on his tail feathers. He yanked on another heavy shirt, an extra pair of socks, wound a wool scarf around his neck, and then went down on hands and knees to look under his cot for anything else he might have forgotten.

Shad felt his eyelids drooping. The warmth of his coat, a full belly, and the fire were making him sleepy. "Who's goin' where in the buckboard? No one ever said."

"Me, *amigo*," Pedro replied. "To the Blanchard farm." Finished with his meal, the Mexican withdrew some cigarette papers from his front pocket, along with a skimpy pouch of tobacco, and began to roll a smoke. "Taking supplies out to the widow."

"Never know when a big snow will hit," Luke said. "Wouldn't want to see her get snowed in without the things she needs. Since Behemoth killed her husband, Mrs. Blanchard has only made a handful of trips to town. Faith and the other women are worried about her. The least we can do is make sure she has food and firewood."

Uncle Pete stood and stretched. "I'm going along too. And Jonathan. She'll have some chores that need doin'. The three of us can get 'em done quicker than one." He grinned, giving them a nod. "I surely don't mind her company; I can tell you that. She has that certain way of looking at a man…" His words drifted away.

Pedro lifted the rolled paper filled with tobacco, wetting the length of the seam with his tongue and then twisting the ends. He struck a match and looked over the small orange flame at Shad. "That bear mauling her man has her a bit touched in the head." He moved the flame to the end of the cigarette hanging from his lips. "Not good for a woman to be alone much. *Comprendes?* Not with winter knocking at her door."

"Not good at all," Shad agreed.

Rosalind Blanchard was quite the widow. Any whisper of her name brought the bunkhouse to life. Seemed all the cowhands had a secret hope of catching her eye. Uncle Pete had all but said as much a moment before.

Everyone except me… and maybe Francis, since she's too old for the lad. I enjoy my bachelorhood too much to ever settle down. When I get lonely, I head into town. Fancy Aubrey's sass and flash is more my type. The saloon girl avoids any ties that bind, just like I do.

As Luke opened the door to leave, Shad stood. "Wait up, boss," he called, quickly following him into the biting cold.

Luke stopped and turned. "Petty? Something on your mind? Wouldn't you rather talk inside, where it's warm?"

Shad ignored the cold that zipped through him, bringing back the gooseflesh he'd only recently gotten rid of. Best to get this discussion done quickly.

"This is a private matter." Shad hoped now was a good time to bring up the request. He hadn't worked at the ranch all that long, although he'd like to be a permanent fixture. He liked living here. Could see himself settling in for good. "Everything's fine with the beef, Luke," he said in response to his boss's wrinkled brow.

"Good to hear. Then what's on your mind?"

Shad swallowed. He'd started the conversation, and now there wasn't anything to do but finish. "My brothers. I got a letter about a month back. They didn't say much, except they were on their way here from Wyoming. I'm expectin' 'em any day now. Was hoping you'd hire 'em on."

Luke's lips pulled tight, and in the quiet yard, his deep sigh was evident. "We don't usually take on men this time of year, Petty. You should know that. We have winter to get through."

Shad shuffled his boots. Yeah, he did.

"If we need extra hands, we hire in the spring."

Disappointment weighed heavy. With his years of ranching experience, Shad had expected that answer. Still, he'd been watching out for his two brothers since his grandma Girdy passed on some twelve years back. Keeping them on the straight and narrow, so to speak—as best he could. Times were tough. Work was scarce. If they hired on here, they'd get the stability he'd found at the Heart of the Mountains. He couldn't give up just yet.

"They're good workers, Luke," he added, trying not to sound desperate.

Luke held his gaze. "Chance Holcomb just hired a man a couple weeks ago. Said with Evie so close to delivering, he wanted the freedom to stay close to the homestead. Too bad we didn't know sooner."

Shad nodded. "Yeah, I heard about that myself. It's a shame. Well, thanks, anyway. My grandma used to say it never hurts to ask." He turned to go.

"Hold up, Petty. How old are they?"

"Nick is twenty-four, and Tanner twenty-three."

"Any experience in the saddle?"

"Plenty. Just like me. They're good hands. Honest." *Although, Tanner's a bit of a hothead…*

Luke gave him a nod. "Tell 'em we'll hire 'em on half-time until spring. When we begin work on the new barn at Matt's place, they can go full-time. That's the best we can do at the present. They can live in the bunkhouse just like everyone else."

"Thank you." Shad thrust out his hand. "That's darn nice of you."

Luke smiled and shook his head. "Nothin' nice about it, Petty. Business is business. Now, get back inside and get some sleep. You've earned time off. Tomorrow, you'll be back out in the cold. I want you to ride out to the Holcomb ranch and the Preece farm."

"For?"

Luke looked up at the sky.

Shad followed suit. In the distance, foreboding black clouds hung low to the ground. He shrugged deeper into his coat. "Those weren't there a half hour ago when I rode in."

"Exactly. That's why we're sending men out to every homestead within ten miles of town, just to be sure everyone is ready. Flood and the rest of us are feeling a mite gun-shy since the early snowstorm that caught Roady and Sally unaware in the mountains. We've been expecting snow—but since then, it hasn't come."

"I'll deliver your message first thing after tasks tomorrow."

Without a glance back, Luke lifted a hand and clamped down his Stetson as he strode toward the ranch house. A sudden gust swept past, setting the evergreen branches dancing and scattering aspen leaves across the frozen dirt.

Shad grasped his coat lapels together and started back for the bunkhouse, thinking of the hot fire burning inside, the great weight lifted from his shoulders.

Tanner and Nick had jobs. His first obstacle conquered.

The black clouds in the distance caught his attention once more. Shad stopped and stared, the satisfied feeling in his belly pushed away all too soon by disquiet. Now his brothers just had to arrive in one piece. The sooner they did that, the better he'd sleep.

Chapter Two

Relaxing in Sheriff Brandon Crawford's large desk chair, newly hired Deputy Justin Wesley scanned last week's three-page Sunday *Herald* for any tidbit he might have missed. After a few disappointing moments, he looked away from the printed page he'd read ten times and sighed.

Y Knot wasn't Denver. He'd only been deputy sheriff a little over a month, but he hadn't taken long to decide he'd enjoy living in Y Knot—even if there wasn't much news to read about. He'd already adjusted to the quiet streets, and knowing each and every person he encountered.

But he had a quick mind. He needed to keep his thoughts occupied, or else he found himself in trouble. He added subscribing to the *Rocky Mountain News* on to his mental list of things to do. The news would be old by the time the daily arrived in Y Knot, but old news was better than no news.

With a satisfied grin, he took in the fruits of his labor. The jailhouse was spotless. Not a thing on the sheriff's desktop was out of place. On one corner, recent correspondence was stacked in order by date. At the top center was the coffee cup filled with pencils. On the other corner, Crawford's two large law books were stacked one on top of the other, along with the official journal where the town's daily happenings were faithfully recorded.

Justin wanted to show Crawford he was up for the deputy job, which wasn't just about hunting outlaws and upholding the law. In the short time he'd been in Y Knot, he'd gotten an earful about Jack Jones, the previous deputy. How the place was always a mess. Neatness was one of Justin's best qualities, and he aimed to show Crawford he'd hired the right man.

His gaze drifted to the basket and jar of apple butter in the middle of the desk at the same time hoofbeats thudded on the icy ground outside.

Francis, the McCutcheons' ranch hand, stepped into the building. The tall young man was bundled against the frigid weather, his hat pulled down tight. He closed the door and smiled when he spotted Justin sitting behind Crawford's desk.

"Howdy, Francis." Justin stood and came around the desk, extending his arm, and they shook hands. "What brings you to town on this downright chilly afternoon?"

"Errands," Francis replied, eyeing the ten-foot-long bullwhip attached to Justin's left hip opposite his pistol. He moseyed over to a chair in front of the desk and sat.

Justin reclaimed his warm seat and neatly folded the newspaper.

"You always carry that whip?" Francis asked.

"I do." He shrugged. "Feel naked without it."

"Brandon around?"

"Nope. Not much going on here, so he rode out to Matthew McCutcheon's, or maybe Mark's. I'm surprised the two of you didn't pass. Charity's been out there a good month, helping out with the new babes. Brandon's dog-faced because of it. Misses her, I guess."

Francis removed his hat and tossed it behind him to the long bench under the window before pulling the scarf from around his neck. He peeled off his gloves, eyeing the place. His lips inched up in amusement. "I would too if she were my wife."

Justin pushed the wicker basket toward Francis. "Brandon made these before he left. Help yourself, if you're hungry."

Francis's eyebrow winged high. "What are they?"

"Biscuits."

Francis reached forward, flipped back the cloth, and stared.

Justin chuckled. "Go on, they're not rattlesnake eggs."

"Yeah, but Brandon made 'em. Any good?"

The one Justin had choked down sat in his belly like a stone. "Not bad with coffee," he mumbled. "Have some." *So they'll be gone by the time Brandon returns.* "They'll warm you up." Tossing them out wouldn't be right. He'd like to report how others had enjoyed the sheriff's cooking.

Francis scooted his chair back an inch. "Naw, Lucky's spoiled me for others."

"The spread make 'em even better." He pushed forward the jar.

Clearly against his will, Francis reached in, retrieved the top biscuit, and took a large bite, crumbs falling everywhere.

Seeing the mess, Justin frowned but kept his comments to himself.

Francis swallowed and stuffed the remainder in his mouth. "Not as bad as I thought," he said over a mouthful, dusting his hands over his lap. "But nothin' like Lucky's." Finished, he stood, dropping everything on his lap to Justin's clean floor, and went to the stove for a cup of coffee.

Justin sighed.

"Sure looks good in here since you were hired," Francis said. "When Jack Jones was deputy, the place looked like a twister passed through—every day." He chuckled. "Brandon tried to keep up, but Jack messed things faster than Brandon could clean."

"A place for everything and everything in its place," Justin replied. He wasn't all *that* fussy, but he did like to find things when they were needed. His first day, he'd washed the front windows and cleaned out the jail cells. "Anything new out at the ranch?"

"Quiet out there too, now that we're back from the stockyards. For the first time ever, we drove about three thousand head of yearlings and two-year-olds to Miles City and sold 'em mid-November."

"That's right. Charity mentioned something about that."

Francis got comfortable in the crumb-strewn chair. "We still have the cows and bulls, of course, and the horses, but the place is bare bones for the amount of stock we've usually got around to look after. Feels nice not to be worrying over the young animals."

Curious at this news, Justin sat forward. Over the years, he'd worked at his grandfather's ranch in Colorado and knew the cattle business as much as the next ranch hand. "That's an odd time to push a herd. Usually you wait until spring, when there's plenty of grass along the way. By the time they reach market, they've gained weight and are worth more per hoof. Taking them in the fall is no way to make money." He shrugged. "Seems strange to me."

Francis nodded. "Miles City is only about a sixteen-day trip if nothin' happens. Not long enough to lose much weight. The McCutcheons are wary after last year's harsh winter, followed by the long dry summer and fall. Better to sell now and lighten up."

"Sounds reasonable."

"I can tell you, the ranch hands are liking it." Francis grinned, took another biscuit, and then stood. "More readin' and poker time on days too cold to be ridin'. I better get moving. Things to do; people to see."

Justin stood and walked out with Francis, watching his new friend head toward the Hitching Post Saloon. His chuckle died in his throat. The slate-gray sky overhead had an ominous feel. Snow was on the way.

Chapter Three

The following day, Shad, content with his life, loped down the long, winding lane leading to the Holcomb ranch. He'd pretty much fallen into a vat of chocolate when the McCutcheons hired him on. They were fair, the bunkhouse was comfortable, and Lucky cooked as if he'd been born with a spatula in his hand. The help was paid on time, and town was an easy ride away.

The Hitching Post poured good whiskey, and Fancy Aubrey was sweet on him—and just about every other cowboy in town, he reminded himself. Just depended on who was sweet-talking her at the time. But that didn't matter. When she came close in the saloon, she made him feel like a king.

Dexter, Chance Holcomb's dog, raced out to meet him, and Shad slowed riding into the ranch yard. A fellow he didn't recognize came out of the barn, bundled from head to toe.

"Howdy," the fellow called.

Shad glanced at the house, and then back at the man. "Afternoon."

When he dismounted, the fellow hurried forward. Of medium height and build, he was about as average as they came except for a nickel-sized birthmark on the right side of his chin that resembled a heart, of all things.

"I'm Andy Lovell," he said, reaching out his hand.

"Shadrack Petty, from the Heart of the Mountains. I heard a new man had signed on out here." They shook hands. "Chance around?"

"Sure. In the house."

Warmth sprang to Shad's face. He'd hoped to catch Chance outside. Evie was in a delicate way, and he didn't want to intrude. His chest tightened, thinking about the baby to come. Chance might have a son soon—or a daughter. A stone dropped into the pit of Shad's stomach at the memory of that fateful day in Virginia. Then again in Colorado, the moment he'd gotten "the news." Melancholy pricked inside.

"Mrs. Holcomb is close to her time. You think they might not want to be bothered?"

Andy wrapped his arms around himself. "She's not due for another month. She was gathering eggs in the henhouse only ten, fifteen minutes ago."

"In this cold?"

"That's right. There's no stopping Evie."

Shad nodded his thanks and tied his horse. Taking the three tall porch steps, he knocked lightly and the door opened. Expecting to see Evie or Chance, he was taken aback at the very businesslike older woman before him who held the door, waiting. He heard a scraping chair and saw Chance stand from his place at the kitchen table.

"Shad. Come in," Chance called. "Good to see you."

Shad entered slowly, edging his way around the woman, who stepped back to give him room.

With awkward movements, Evie rose from her seat by the fire, placing her hand protectively on her protruding tummy. "How nice to see you, Mr. Petty," she said. "Please, come in and meet my dear friend, Mrs. Margaret Seymour. She was the proprietor of the mail-order-bride business in St. Louis, where I used to work." She blushed as she looked at her husband. "And because of her, I met Chance." Evie smiled warmly at her friend.

Margaret smiled back.

"She also raised me when my mother passed on. I think of her as a second mother *and* a friend. She's come to help in my time of need, and I couldn't be happier. I just hope I can talk her into staying for good." She laughed and shook her head. "My, that was a mouthful. Margaret, this is Mr. Petty. He works for the McCutcheons."

"Ma'am," he said, conscious of holding his hat.

"Mr. Petty."

Something about the woman made him nervous. There wasn't a wrinkle to be found in her military-style blue dress. Her brown hair was neatly swept up on her head with one gray streak at her temple. Even though her tone was quite friendly, her expression still had him cautious, as if she'd like to rap his knuckles with a ruler.

"I'm delighted to make your acquaintance," Mrs. Seymour said as regally as a queen. "Have a seat with Mr. Holcomb, and I'll get you a cup of coffee. I'm sure you could use something hot after being out in such cold weather."

Evie lumbered forward, placing both her hands on the back of the chair Chance had been using. "I was just about to suggest the same thing. And we have crumb cake too, fresh from the oven. I won't take no for an answer."

Chance waved to the table. "You better do as my wife says, Shad. I don't know if you've noticed, but she's bigger than the both of us together. I think she must have three babies in there. We don't want to get her mad."

A second passed before Shad realized Chance was joking, and he let out a laugh.

Mrs. Seymour was already at the sideboard getting an extra cup.

Being a messenger wasn't bad in the least. He could use a cup of coffee and a slice of crumb cake. Even though Lucky had made a three-layer double-chocolate cake last week, Shad wouldn't pass up his chance for more sweets.

Chance picked up his fork and started into the half-eaten portion on his plate. "You meet my new help?"

"I did. Seems like a friendly sort," he said as Evie set the cake before him.

"He is," Chance said. "And a hard worker. We're lucky to get him for as little as I can pay." His appreciative smile colored his wife's cheeks when she refilled his coffee cup. "Thank you, darlin'," he drawled.

Evie looked past her time, when in reality, Andy had said her baby would come next month in February—a bitterly cold time in Montana.

Shad forked in a large bite and took a sip of coffee. "This is mighty tasty, Mrs. Holcomb. Thank you."

"My pleasure. Margaret and I set to cooking today. That's why the kitchen is a mess."

"And also why the air smells so good," Chance said with a grin. "You can understand why I decided to stay inside."

"I do, indeed. I'm glad Luke picked today to send me out. I'm sure your crumb cake won't last long."

Evie laughed. "You're right about that. Now that we have Mr. Lovell to feed as well, things are finished more quickly. Nothing goes to waste."

Chance chuckled. "Did they ever?"

Mrs. Seymour had taken a cup and sat by the fire, listening and smiling. Shad supposed she wasn't as imposing as he'd first thought.

"What's the news?" Chance asked.

"Not really news. Luke and the rest are just making sure everyone is duly set with supplies and such for whatever weather might be coming."

Chance dabbed at the crumbs on his plate with his thumb. "I'm well aware of the seasons. I only had three steers to sell this year. I sent them early when the McCutcheons drove their herd to Miles City. Besides that, we're stocked up and ready."

"Luke figured as much, but wanted me to stop by anyway and say hello. See if you had any news for them. I'm headed to the Preece farm next."

"I'm glad you did," Evie said, leaning on Chance's chair. "Staying in touch is good. I haven't been to town in two months. Cabin fever has set in. I wanted to have a big welcoming party for Margaret when she arrived, but with the holidays and the weather…"

"And with you being very near to your time, a party is definitely not needed," Mrs. Seymour sternly added from her chair by the hearth. "I'm just happy to be here. I'd planned to arrive sooner, but a dear friend was sick and needed me. I stayed until she was better."

Evie shook her head. "We'll have a party with all the brides and their husbands just as soon as we can. In town, at the Biscuit Barrel."

"You have a baby to deliver," Mrs. Seymour insisted. "Your thoughts should be on that—and only that. Anything else is just foolishness."

Chance caught Shad's gaze over the rim of his cup.

His friend seemed happy and would soon add another to his household, something Shad would never be able to do. He cut away his gaze, but it landed on Evie's hand resting on Chance's shoulder.

Shad swallowed and looked at the crumbs on his plate. Give him his horse, a herd of cattle to tend, and open country. He'd be content with his lot.

Chapter Four

Prancing down the stairs of her sister and brother-in-law's two-story farmhouse, Poppy Ford felt on top of the world, as well as invigorated from her nap.

Since she'd ventured to Montana, she'd become a different person. Happy. Carefree. She and Kathryn hadn't been this close in years. Getting reacquainted away from Boston and their father's continual attempts at sabotaging their relationship was refreshing. Why he acted that way, she didn't know. It was puzzling, to say the least. Last night, she and Kathryn had stayed up until all hours reminiscing, laughing, and clearing the air on years-old grievances.

Kathryn Ford Preece was a remarkable woman. Even though she had been raised as opulently as any princess, she'd actually learned how to milk a cow, churn butter, preserve food, and cook—all within a few short months. Poppy didn't know how she'd done it. Since becoming a mail-order bride and marrying Tobit Preece, her sister was a changed woman, a caterpillar that had transformed into a beautiful butterfly. She was happier and laughed all the time. Poppy had no trouble seeing Kathryn loved her husband with all her heart, even though he was only a farmer.

Poppy couldn't keep the smile from her face, and she didn't want to. She really didn't understand this magical feeling inside her heart. She finally felt free, with a mountain of hope that nothing could hold her back. Her one regret was that she'd allowed Oscar Scott to accompany her.

When Ossy, as she and Kathryn called him, had discovered her intentions to travel to Montana Territory, he'd begged to come along so he could see to her safety. The long train ride followed by a stagecoach trip wasn't something a beautiful young woman should attempt on her own, especially as late in the year as she was planning. He argued he'd traveled to Y Knot in July, knew the route and the routine. When his idea was rejected, he hinted that perhaps her father wouldn't be pleased if he knew about her plans. To him, Kathryn was dead.

Besides all that, Poppy was enrolled for next semester's art course in Paris, at great expense. Something she'd been pleading for from her father for three years. Perhaps he'd renege on his promise when he found out her plans to sneak to Y Knot.

Ossy had threatened, and she'd complied. Indignation pushed up at the man's meddling. She wouldn't think of him now, not on a brand-new afternoon that held all kinds of possibilities. He was keeping to himself and mostly staying in his room.

At the bottom of the stairs, Poppy stopped at the front window and looked out across the yard toward the large barn. The air here in Montana was so clean and fresh. The land stretched as far as the eye could see until it butted up to a large stand of purple-blue mountains. She would never have believed she could feel this way about the wilderness.

Well, Y Knot wasn't quite wilderness. The small town had a handful of charming stores and a throng of well-meaning citizens. But it wasn't Boston. Or London. Or Paris.

As crazy as it sounded, after three weeks here, she understood completely how Kathryn could trade everything from her former life to wed and stay. This morning, Poppy would bundle up and venture out to the barn with a handful of carrots from the root cellar. She loved the way the bunnies' noses twitched as they chewed. Their long ears flopped forward and back. And she adored their soft coats. She didn't like the fact that Tobit raised the darling creatures for their meat and fur. That was unthinkable.

I'd like to take the whole lot home with me when I return.

If I go.

The thought hit her out of nowhere. She lifted a hand to her throat, knowing her staying here would kill her father. But she liked the slowness of life on the farm. The lack of judging eyes and critical comments was appealing.

Sounds from the kitchen drew her attention. She hurried forward, thinking that a cup of tea would taste so good. Placing her palm on the swinging door, she was just about to push in when she heard her name spoken.

Poppy jerked to a halt. Dropping her hand, she moved back a step, then slowly turning, she placed her shoulder to the door and her ear to the crack. Tobit's harsh tone had her breath lodged in her lungs.

"Please, Tobit, be reasonable," Kathryn begged softly.

Kathryn and Tobit. Discussing me? Fire rushed to Poppy's face, and her stomach pitched forward like it had on the stagecoach ride to Y Knot.

"Kathryn, you know I don't mind your sister showing up unannounced. I love Poppy."

His tone didn't sound like he loved her at all. In fact, the exact opposite sounded true. The long, strained silence cut Poppy to the quick.

"I do, Kathryn. You know I don't lie."

He's trying too hard to make Kathryn believe his words. His tone isn't natural.

"If that's the case," Kathryn went on in a whisper, "I wish you'd just drop this whole conversation and start over. Do it for me."

"I can't abide the way she measures your every move. Calls out your mistakes. Finds ways to undercut your confidence."

"She's just being playful, Tobit," Kathryn replied.

Poppy pictured her older sister's supplicating outstretched hand. Kathryn had done enough groveling in her dealings with their father.

"She's young, high spirited. I don't mind. She's finally finding her way, and I'm so thankful for that. I promise you; she doesn't mean any harm."

The mountain scene painting across from where Poppy stood wavered in and out, and her heart shuddered.

Tobit doesn't like me.

What Kathryn said was true. Growing up, Poppy had sometimes piggybacked on their father's critical ways. She hadn't meant any harm…

Hogwash. I'm snippy and arrogant. But I can't seem to stop myself. It's who I've been for so long, I don't know how to be any different.

"What you say may be true," Tobit bit out. "But bringing Oscar Scott along was thoughtless. I can't abide that intolerable windbag. He's pointed out everything on our farm that needs fixing, and the shortcomings of our home compared to Boston. Living under the same roof with him has my gut in a knot."

"Tobit, please."

"You said you'd written to Poppy, told her everything that transpired with him before we married. How he'd tried to use your amnesia to *trick* you into marrying him. She *should* have known better. Surely she didn't think we'd welcome him with open arms."

I thought about those facts briefly and promptly disregarded any problems his appearance might cause. I was only thinking of myself. Worried over what Father would do about my Paris trip. I couldn't chance it.

"He's a cheat and a liar," Tobit went on. "I've been patient and hospitable. Endured his backhanded insults. Tolerated how he looks down his long nose at everything only because Poppy said they were staying three weeks and would leave before Christmas. If you haven't noticed, it's January eighth."

"I know, Tobit, I know. But Poppy and I have been having such a fine time, the days got away."

"You say that now to defend her, but whenever she 'teases' you, it pains me. You're my wife, and I love you. I'm angered each time I see it and don't speak up in your defense. I don't like anything or *anyone* who hurts you. That's just a fact of life I can't change."

"I'm sure they'll only stay a few more days."

"If the snow starts in earnest, they'll be stuck. Here. In this house, for months." Tobit's granite-hard tone was brutal.

Stuck? Paris flashed before her eyes.

"They will? Why?"

"The stage can't go through deep snow. Surely you know that. And in Waterloo…"

Tobit must have paced the length of the kitchen and turned his back, because Poppy couldn't hear the tail end of what he'd just said.

Her insides crushed with hurt, thinking how much she'd taken to Tobit when they'd met. He was handsome, young, and so very nice. She had a brother-in-law, the only one she'd ever have. Like a brother. And what a man he was too.

She could understand how Kathryn had fallen so deeply in love, even though that meant living and working on a farm, something Poppy knew little about. Kathryn's life was very different from the way they'd been raised with nannies, cooks, and servants to do their bidding. Still, Poppy had never heard her sister utter one word of complaint.

"I'm begging, Tobit. Please be patient a little longer. The situation isn't all that bad. I'm thrilled Poppy came to see me. She'll be overseas all of next year. Who knows when we'll be together again? To tell you the truth, I'd thought she'd forgotten me completely."

Poppy pushed her palm to her lips, holding back the anguish that almost slipped out.

"Every time I see Oscar looking at you, sweetheart, I want to go another round with fists, like we did at Ina's—"

"Please lower your voice. I'd hate for Poppy to hear. She's only eighteen."

"Ha! That's a grown woman. And if you remember, she can't hear me. She's upstairs getting her *beauty rest*."

Shame heated Poppy's face as she recalled her egotistic words from this afternoon. She'd laughed and patted her hair as she said it. *How horrible.*

"She won't be down for a good hour," Tobit went on. "Eager for her supper. And leaving all the cooking and cleanup to you—as usual."

Help cook? Help clean? Those thoughts had never crossed her mind, Poppy realized shamefully.

"You've been helping, Tobit. I've enjoyed that very much."

"You're missing the point. *She* should be helping, shouldering some of the responsibility. She's taking advantage of your good heart. To be sure, Scott won't be down before it's time to pour himself a pre-supper whiskey. What does he think this is? We don't have cooks to churn out five-course meals every night, but he never tires of telling you how much better everything is in Boston."

That was true. Ossy had been insufferable to Tobit, even in her estimation. The man had grown up more a brother to her and Kathryn than the son of their father's friend and business partner. Poppy took Ossy's words with a grain of salt—but now she knew Tobit hadn't. She bossed Ossy around and couldn't care less what he thought. But that didn't mean Tobit would.

She should have told Ossy to go to her father if he wanted. Laughed in his face, and her father's too. Mostly, she should have thought of her sister and her new husband, instead of being concerned about herself. *How selfish I've been.* Kathryn's letters had mentioned the man's shenanigans in Y Knot, but Poppy hadn't paid that much attention, too busy gallivanting around the countryside with their aunt Alice.

Just one more example in the ever-growing list of how she was thoughtless and unfeeling. Hearing clomping on the front porch, Poppy stepped away from the door. She pushed her pain deep inside and put a smile on her face. Waiting, she knew who would be entering any moment.

The door opened and Isaiah, bundled from head to toe, stepped inside. He yanked off the wool hat that protected his bald head and then peeled off his gloves, tossing them on the floor. He shrugged out of his coat and hung the worn garment with shaky hands. When he saw her, his eyes lit with pleasure— almost bringing her to tears.

"It's dang cold out there, missy. I suggest you stay indoors until spring." His old eyes twinkled as he made his way slowly across the room.

Kathryn and Tobit stepped out through the kitchen door. They both pulled up when they saw her.

"I didn't know you were up," Kathryn said, her brows crunching down. "Did you have a nice nap?"

Unable to answer, Poppy nodded.

"How're the animals, Grandpa?" Tobit asked a bit gruffly. "The critters doing all right out there?"

Tobit had yet to meet her gaze. His mouth was set.

"Oh, you know how it goes, Grandson," Isaiah said, his gravelly voice loud because of his deafness. "Them animals don't feel the cold like we do. I had a hard time getting Billy into the barn. That goat is as cantankerous as I am." Isaiah laughed at his own joke. "If he keeps testing my patience, he'll end up in this Sunday's supper pot—you mark my words."

"But you did get him in, correct?"

"Said I did, didn't I?"

Tobit crossed his arms. His overalls were clean since there wasn't any field work to be done on the farm these days, as she'd been told. During planting season, Kathryn had shared he'd return from plowing covered in dirt from head to toe.

Poppy had a hard time imagining that picture. On any other day, that thought might make her smile. But not today. Not now. Knowing what her brother-in-law really thought of her was like a bucket of ice water over her head.

"What about Blue Boy and Sergio?" Tobit asked.

"Them horses are munching away in their stalls." He eyed Tobit suspiciously. "You haven't checked up on me this much since you first arrived and didn't know I was plenty capable. I ain't senile yet."

Tobit's gaze caught Kathryn's.

He's rambling because he doesn't know what else to say.

"I've been running this farm far longer than you have, boy." Isaiah squinted and leaned toward his grandson. "If'n somethin' is eating ya, speak your piece."

"Nothing's eating me," Tobit bit out. "I'll do the milking and other barn chores tonight after supper."

Isaiah scratched his head and lifted a shoulder. "Just like you always do. You sure are talking queer. Thanks for letting me know." He pushed past his grandson and started for the kitchen. "What do I smell cooking in there?" He winked at Kathryn. "Is that pork roast?"

"It is, Isaiah." She rubbed his arm affectionately as he walked by, and Tobit followed. "Should be ready around four o'clock."

Was what Tobit said about the stage closing down true? Poppy had lost track of the days. Would she and Ossy be stranded in Montana until spring? Her ship's passage was booked for April. She'd been begging her father for this chance for years. She wasn't a great artist, but that didn't matter. Her return to France had been her utmost dream, until she came here.

And now Poppy was a strain on her sister's six-month marriage. She needed to pack her belongings and get to town. Catch the next stage to Waterloo, and on to Boston. Money wasn't an issue. She had plenty of funds to do whatever she liked. Maybe that was the problem. She *was* spoiled, just as her friends used to tell her. Her father had indulged her all of her life. She'd never wanted for a single thing—except this art class—and he'd finally given in.

"What is it, Poppy?" Kathryn asked softly, coming to her side. "You look as if you've seen a ghost. Are you feeling well? Is something wrong?"

Gazing into Kathryn's eyes, Poppy willed herself not to cry. When she was young, she'd looked to Kathryn as her shield. Her sister hadn't stopped protecting her as they grew older until Poppy had asked her to in a not-so-nice way.

She pushed away another round of shame and hardened her heart. She could never be as compassionate and caring as her sister. Everyone knew that fact. Charity wasn't her virtue, and why Kathryn thought so highly of her, she didn't know.

"Nothing at all. I think I just woke up a little too soon. My head feels woozy. I'll be fine as soon as I have a cup of tea."

"Oh yes. I was just about to suggest that."

Kathryn hooked her arm through Poppy's and headed for the kitchen just as their dogs, Duke and Duchess, set to barking. Both girls turned back toward the front door.

"Someone must be coming. It can't be my piano student," Kathryn said. "It's much too cold for Lael's mother to bring her out. Saturday is her usual lesson day, but still." She went to the window and peered out. "No, I see a single rider. I wonder who it could be?"

Poppy swallowed down her hurt and followed her sister to the window. A tall cowboy sat his saddle like a king as his horse loped easily forward.

She'd met more than a few people when she'd ventured into town with either Tobit or Kathryn, but she didn't remember this fellow. To her, all the cowboys looked the same. But as he got closer, something about his face drew her, the pull, the attraction, and it wasn't his high cheekbones, reddened by the cold, or his strong chin.

Seeing him look at the house made her take a small step back.

It was his eyes. Poppy was positive she'd met this man somewhere before. She'd have remembered him if they'd met in town. Any woman would.

Chapter Five

Shad had lingered at the Holcombs' far too long, enjoying three cups of coffee and two slices of crumb cake. On his way out, Evie asked him to drop off a healthy slice to the ranch hand in his living quarters in the barn. Lovell had a cozy room that he and Chance added to the back of the barn when he was hired, complete with a woodstove, a window with a view of the back pasture, and corncob insulation.

Riding into the Preece farmyard, Shad spotted Tobit's two large dogs bounding out to meet him. They barked and circled his horse, excited to have a visitor. When one sniffed too closely at his gelding's hind fetlock, his horse, no lover of dogs, kicked out missing the animal by a few inches. Frightened, he let out a yip and jumped back, unhurt.

"Let that be a lesson to you," Shad said as he dismounted, a cold shiver going up his spine. His words came out in a puff of frosty breath, his boots crunching on the frozen earth as he tied his mount.

Mounting the steps, he rapped on the front door, his leather gloves muting the sound. A burst of wind whistled around him. He hunched his shoulders against the dropping temperature. The wind from the north was picking up.

Kathryn Preece opened the door. Her light brown dress matched her eyes and reminded him of the hot cocoa Lucky sometimes made as a treat. Shad knew her less than he knew Evie Holcomb, but he remembered they'd both been mail-order brides from St. Louis. He'd met Kathryn in town and enjoyed her Boston accent, so different from Tobit's soft Southern drawl.

When Mrs. Preece smiled, two dimples appeared, taking him by surprise, as much as they had the first time he'd met her. For a moment, he lost his train of thought.

"May I help you?"

He whipped his hat from his head as fast as he could move his cold arm. "Uh, yes, ma'am," he said, feeling a drip forming in one nostril. The wind had taken its toll. "I'm Shadrack Petty from the Heart of the Mountains." He pulled out his handkerchief and wiped his nose. "Is your husband here?"

"Of course. I thought I recognized you, Mr. Petty. Please, come in." She stepped back, holding wide the door.

The rush of heat felt good on his face. He shuffled inside to the aroma of good cooking thick on the air.

"Tobit's in the kitchen. I'll get him."

Her soft voice was like a warm blanket. From the corner of his eye, he was suddenly aware they weren't alone in the room. Mrs. Preece hurried away, and Shad chanced a glance to his left to see a shorter, younger version of Mrs. Preece regarding him. He nodded politely and used his handkerchief again to blow his nose. Some things just couldn't be helped.

Why the young woman looked familiar was a mystery. Surely this was Mrs. Preece's sister, and most likely from Boston too. They'd yet to meet.

"Excuse me, sir, but I feel I know you."

She speaks with her sister's accent. Nice.

The swinging kitchen door opened and Tobit strode through.

"Shad. Good to see you," he said, a welcoming smile on his face. Behind him came his wife and grandpa. "I see you've met Kathryn's sister, Miss Poppy Ford."

Shad hastily stuffed his handkerchief back into his pocket and took Tobit's hand in greeting. "Well, sort of." He gave the young woman a smile and a nod. "Good to see you, Tobit. I have a short message, and then I'll be on my way. Wind's picking up and a storm's blowing in. Had a few snow flurries on my way over from the Holcombs'."

Mrs. Preece's hands clapped together over her bosom, or thereabouts, but Shad tried not to notice.

"You were at the Holcombs'?" she said, her voice filled with emotion. "How is Evie? Her delivery date is approaching, and I know she's been feeling the effects quite profoundly. Did you speak with her, Mr. Petty?"

"She's fine, ma'am. Lumbering slowly, but seems in good spirits." He snapped his mouth shut when Isaiah chuckled. He hadn't meant to say that.

"That's wonderful."

"She also wanted me to pass along that as soon after the baby as possible, and with weather permitting, she intends to have a welcoming party for her houseguest, Mrs. Seymour. Said you'd know who I was speaking of. She wants it to be real special. That you, her, and Heather Klinkner owed the woman a lot."

He shrugged. He liked the stern-looking female well enough, but he didn't feel the excitement about her he'd heard in Evie's voice or the delight written on Kathryn's face. She surely must be someone extraordinary.

"Oh yes, we do, Mr. Petty, we all do. She found us our husbands, and made meaningful matches."

Tobit cleared his throat.

Kathryn laughed. "Well, Evie made her own match, so to speak. After I heard through the grapevine Mrs. Seymour had arrived in Y Knot, I've been tempted on several occasions to stop in unannounced. But the weather has been chancy. Tobit wouldn't let me go. I wish I had now, since the weather is turning. I don't want to wait until spring."

"It'll be sooner than that, sweetheart," Tobit chimed in. "You're not that experienced with the wagon yet. And the horses get spooky in the wind. Everything in its time." He turned his attention back to Shad. "What brings you out today?"

Another stranger came down the stairs to stand by Miss Ford.

"The McCutcheons sent out all the hands, making sure everyone is set for winter. Seeing if anyone has any special needs we can help with. Luke didn't think you would, but wanted me to look in just the same." Shad took this opportunity to glance around and take a longer look at Kathryn's sister.

Tobit and Isaiah exchanged a look before Tobit spoke. "We're as set as we'll ever be. Just a bit surprised the snow has held off this long."

Isaiah harrumphed. "Last year this time, I was shoveling the path to the barn. It weren't no picnic."

Tobit nodded. "Isaiah's right. Hopefully, this year will be easier. But we're as set as we'll ever be. Stocked with plenty of food and fuel to burn. I appreciate you asking." He waved his arm toward the kitchen door. "Now that you've relayed the message, can I invite you to join us for a meal? I'm sure you've noticed that rich pork roast scent hanging on the air."

Indeed, he had. And his mouth had been watering since he stepped through the front door. He had about a twenty-five-minute ride to town and another thirty-five to the ranch. The invitation was awfully tempting...

"We insist, Mr. Petty," Kathryn said. "You can get to know my sister Poppy and her friend Oscar Scott." She motioned to the two.

Poppy, flanked by Oscar, had the same cocoa-brown hair as her sister, but her eyes were ice blue. Shad had seen her before, but couldn't place where. Something about that frisky little tilt to her lips.

Mrs. Preece tipped her head. "Mr. Petty?"

"That's real neighborly, ma'am. Don't mind if I do. Thank you."

"Wonderful." Her dimpled smile reappeared.

"Follow me, Shad," Tobit said. "I'll show you where you can stable your horse." He shrugged into his coat and then wrapped a wool scarf around his neck. His gaze cut to the other fellow. "Want to come along, Oscar?"

The man sniffed with disdain. By his expression, there was no love lost between him and Tobit.

"I'll stay here, thank you."

"Suit yourself," Tobit replied, grasping Shad's shoulder. "Let's get this taken care of while the women see to supper."

Shad nodded. Still dressed in his coat and gloves, he took one more secretive glance at Poppy to find her watching him.

For some reason, he was hit with a surge of discomfort—and then embarrassment—but had no idea why. Was Kathryn's sister the reason? That seemed more than a little strange.

Tobit led the way out the door, and Shad was only too happy to follow.

Chapter Six

Leaving Ossy standing in the front room, Poppy followed Kathryn into the warm, good-sized farmhouse kitchen. Before her sister could open her mouth, Poppy hurried to the cupboard and took down a plate and carried it to the dining room table.

"Thank you, Poppy." Kathryn followed her with silverware and a napkin. Tobit and Isaiah's places were at each end. To either side of Tobit were Kathryn and Poppy's spots, with Oscar next to her.

Poppy circled the table to set the plate next to Kathryn. She kept her gaze trained on what she was doing.

"That was kind of Tobit to invite Mr. Petty to stay," she said, working her voice to rid any emotional quaver. Every selfish thing she'd ever done ran through her mind like a locomotive. She'd love to skip supper and retire early to pack and plan, but doing so would definitely hurt her sister's feelings.

"Tobit likes company. His generosity is one of the things I adore about him."

Not like me.

Kathryn circled the table, moving a knife here and fork there, making everything perfect. The plates sat a half inch from the edge, the water glass at one o'clock. Just like the servants did at home.

Could I ever be like Kathryn? Even if I wanted to? She doubted it.

Kathryn reached out and lovingly traced a graceful finger made for playing the piano around the edge of one plate. "These dishes belonged to Isaiah's wife, Lori. Every time I set the table, I feel the love they nurtured through the years. Aren't they beautiful? I'm privileged they've been passed down to Tobit and me."

Poppy took in the tiny yellow flowers on the blue ceramic. She'd noticed the colorful dishes her first evening here and thought them pretty, but she hadn't said anything, believing they were too rustic for someone of Kathryn's standing. *Sickening.*

"You sure put a lot of stock in where our thingamabobs go."

Poppy's head snapped around to see Isaiah watching them.

Kathryn smiled. "I do. Setting a proper table shows respect for one's guests." She examined the settings one more time. "There, everything is perfect. You hungry, Grandpa?"

"Aren't I always?"

"Indeed. With good reason. You're a very hard worker." She moved closer and touched his hand. "Tobit would be lost without you. This place is much too large for one man to run on his own."

"That's why he has you when I pass on. You and the young'uns ta come."

Kathryn shyly dropped her gaze. "Yes, someday. I don't know how you managed for as long as you did."

Isaiah chuckled good-naturedly. "The place was falling down around my ears when Tobit showed up. He wrangled things into shape. You and him both. But there's still some wrangling ta do. It's not finished yet."

Kathryn put her arm around the old man's shoulders and squeezed. "Maybe not, but now it's time for me to mash the potatoes and cream the peas. The men will be in any moment."

Poppy sighed inwardly. Suppertime in Boston was a lot easier. All you had to do was sit down and the food appeared.

"What can I do?" She followed Kathryn into the kitchen and glanced around. If she knew how things worked, she'd find a chore herself. She was so limited in knowledge of meal preparations.

Kathryn's head whipped around, and she stared. "You're a guest, Poppy. You don't need to help. Go out and entertain Oscar. I'm sure he's probably wondering where you've gone off to."

"Not tonight." She straightened her spine. "I feel like cooking. Just tell me what you need, and I'll do my best."

Thirty minutes later, the group settled into their seats. Isaiah offered a blessing and the food was passed around. Not until everyone had a few bites did the conversation begin to flow.

Poppy hadn't told Kathryn yet she planned to leave in the morning. The trip wouldn't be easy. Temperatures continued to fall. For the first time ever, the thought of saying good-bye brought on a strong surge of emotion that had her blinking back moisture.

Before long, the meal had been polished off.

"Poppy is an accomplished equestrian," Kathryn said to Mr. Petty over the warm chocolate cake she'd just served. "You should see her ride."

Seeing the pride in Kathryn's smile directed her way hurt, and Poppy sucked in a breath.

The ranch hand had been speaking about how the horses at the McCutcheon spread were bred for working cattle. "Is that right?" he responded. "She looks much too petite to ride a big ol' horse."

The sparkle in his eyes caught Poppy off guard, and she lifted her fork.

"How long have you been riding, Miss Ford?"

She took a moment to pat her lips with her napkin. "Since I was eight years old. But I ride English, and in particular, I foxhunt. Although I abhor if the prey actually gets caught. I'd like to change that aspect of the sport. Do you know the discipline, Mr. Petty?"

"Two years ago she was invited to the most prestigious hunt in Virginia," Oscar added pompously. "In the Piedmont."

Seriously, Ossy? In the Piedmont? As if Mr. Petty will know where that is.

Mr. Petty was just taking a drink from his glass when he sputtered water across the table, hitting Oscar in the face. Poor Mr. Petty grasped his napkin from his lap and furiously wiped his mouth.

"What the devil?" Oscar shouted. He jerked up his napkin and wiped his face.

"'Scuse me," Mr. Petty blurted, keeping his gaze on his plate. A scorching red line crept up his neck and continued to his face.

He looked so miserable, Poppy wished she could ease his discomfort.

"No harm done," Kathryn said quickly. She nibbled her lower lip as she glanced at Ossy, who was still outraged over the incident.

Tobit looked to be struggling with laughter. "Not to worry, Shad. Mr. Scott was due a bath in the next day or two, anyway. Now you've saved him the trouble."

Oscar drilled Tobit with a hateful stare before sliding it to Mr. Petty.

"No big deal." Isaiah chortled. "Ain't the first time, and I'm sure it ain't the last. We're all almost family, been living together long enough."

When Mr. Petty lifted his gaze, he sought Poppy first.

His embarrassment seemed overly exaggerated. Why would a rancher care so much over such a blunder? This was a family supper in the Montana Territory, not a Christmas Ball in New York. The hand holding his napkin quivered before he moved it under the table, as if he were in shock over something important.

She felt a burning need to put him back at ease. "Please, Mr. Petty, no real harm was done, I assure you."

He glanced at his empty dessert plate and stood. "I'm sorry I can't stay to help you clean up, Mrs. Preece," he said sincerely to Kathryn before glancing out the window. "That coal-colored sky is about to unleash. I better hit the trail if I don't want to be caught in a blizzard." Seeing Tobit move to stand, Mr. Petty held out a palm to stop him. "You just stay put. I can see to my horse and be down the road in three minutes. Thank you again for the tasty meal."

In silence, they all watched him stride out of the dining room without a backward glance.

Poppy stifled the urge to run after him, wondering about her concern over this new acquaintance, so different from her usual attitude. What had they said that caused his shock? She thought back but couldn't figure it out.

But somehow, some way, she longed to make him feel better before she left Y Knot, never to return.

Chapter Seven

Shad rode into the ranch yard after dark, the easy stride of his horse doing nothing for his agitated mood. The moment he'd heard Poppy Ford had been in Virginia—*the Piedmont*—the same time he'd been there, the memories he'd worked so hard to forget came rushing back. She'd seen everything. He remembered her now. That coincidence felt like a bad dream.

The Turner Hill Farm foxhunt had coincided with his arrival at the magnificent Southern spread known for breeding the best livestock around. He was there with the Texas ranch he used to ride for to pick up Redbud, an Angus bull, notorious in the county for his nastiness.

Shad rode directly into the open barn doors, forcing Whiskers, the barn cat, to dart out of the way of his horse's hooves. He unsaddled in the dark.

He'd put the accident behind him long ago. There was no changing the past or its outcome. Once he had been released from his recuperation, he'd pulled himself together and lit out for other pastures. No one knew about the damage the bull had done, not even his brothers, who had been working farther north.

Who would have thought my shame would follow me here?

Now, as fate would have it, Poppy Ford had been one of the onlookers. She'd seen what had happened. Someday, she might even ask about it.

A group of equestrians, finished with the hunt, had gathered in the gazebo on the lawn just off the cattle barn. Several servants served refreshments to the dandies in their tight-fitting, uncomfortable-looking breeches, red coats, and tall black riding boots. There wasn't a spot of mud on any of their silly attire.

The women, dressed in black riding skirts and tailored jackets, had long since removed their netted top hats as he and his group of "real men" struggled to get Redbud from his paddock to a waiting wagon. Some of the younger cowboys smiled and waved at the women, to the disgruntlement of the fops.

He recalled Miss Ford's inquisitive blue eyes regarding him keenly. Not only that, he remembered her laughing face after Redbud, not liking what was being asked, lunged away, swinging his head in anger and catching Shad by surprise, knocking him off his feet.

Not realizing the severity of the mishap, he'd scrambled quickly to his feet and jumped away from the menacing animal. For some odd reason, the accident struck Miss Ford as amusing, as well as the rest of the women.

He turned his horse into one of the empty stalls, fed him, and headed to the bunkhouse. By now, most hands would be wrapped in their blankets, reading or staring at the ceiling in contemplative thought. Entering, he removed his coat. A good number of pegs were empty when he'd normally have to hunt for space. He looked around.

"Where is everyone?" he asked quietly to anyone who felt compelled to answer.

Lucky was already shut away in his room, but Francis, sitting on his blankets, had his back to his pillow against the wall. A thick Mexican wool throw wrapped his shoulders. He glanced up from the book in his hands.

"Luke received a telegram from the boys who went over Pine Grove way to take supplies to Widow Blanchard. Old Sheriff Huxley saw 'em passing through town when they were finished at her place. Seems they're a bit short on manpower, and he wondered if they'd give him a hand for a day or two. Said he'd clear it with the McCutcheons. Being the workload here is light since we took the yearlings and two-year-olds to Miles City last month, they agreed."

Thankful he'd snagged Roady's old bunk by the fireplace, Shad stripped off his shirt. Still good for another few days, he hooked the garment on a knob on the wall. While he untied the bandanna around his neck, he took stock.

Smokey, already in his covers, dealt out a game of solitaire on his blankets.

Bob slumped in a chair in front of the fire, his feet stretched out to the flames, his big toe pushing through a large hole in his sock.

Ike sat on the side of his bed, sewing something by the light of his lantern.

And Hickory was already sawing logs, his small form barely a bump in his blankets.

Shad swallowed and forced his gaze to his own bunk. Something about Hickory had him feeling sentimental tonight. He'd not have a son, not today, not this year—*not ever*. Or a daughter. Redbud had taken care of that two years ago.

Chapter Eight

Around nine the next morning, Oscar met Poppy in the upstairs hallway, a cup of coffee in his hand.

"I wish a newspaper was delivered to this home," he grumbled. "I dreadfully miss the opinion page with my coffee. Returning to some civilization can't come soon enough. If I see another cow, goat, or pig, I'll scream."

Poppy noted his disheveled appearance. He'd let himself go, probably believing no one here needed to be impressed. His haughty attitude rubbed sensitive her already-raw nerves.

"I'm glad to hear you say that, Ossy."

He stared. "You are?"

"We should arrive home by the end of next week. Is that soon enough for you?" She opened her bedroom door to show him her packed trunk, making his eyes go even wider. He was so predictable. "We're leaving today."

"What? Why didn't you say something sooner? Last night?"

"I wasn't sure of anything until yesterday. So, now you know." She went to push past him.

He caught her arm. "What's gotten into you? At dinner last night and now. I've never seen you so—"

"What?" She was interested in what he would say.

"Subdued. Your attitude is troubling."

"I'm not subdued." *I'm sick at heart for my childish and hurtful behavior.* "I'm just anxious to be home, as well. I have several things to accomplish before April. I can't believe we've stayed so long."

"Amen to that."

How she wished she hadn't brought him along. Seemed everything he did reminded her of past mistakes. After quietly packing and then tossing back and forth most of the night, all she wanted was to have this emotional roller coaster over with and be on her way home. Civilization couldn't come fast enough for her either.

After descending the stairs, she pushed into the kitchen to find Isaiah and Tobit at the table and Kathryn at the stove, spatula in one hand and a ladle dripping with batter in the other.

Her sister looked up and smiled. "Ready for something to eat?" Her red polka-dot apron covered a warm cape she wore over her light blue dress.

Poppy still had difficulty seeing her sister in such a domestic role. "Yes, thank you, but I can get it."

Before Kathryn could set down what she was doing, Poppy went to the cupboard and took down a plate. Still shy of Tobit after what she'd heard through the door, she kept her gaze safely on the window. "My, the clouds seem much darker this morning." She chanced a glance at her brother-in-law.

Tobit nodded, setting his coffee cup back in its saucer. "They are. I think the weather has finally arrived."

"Since it's not begun snowing yet in earnest," Kathryn said, "I thought today, when I'm finished cleaning up, we could take that walk to the ridge, see the far fields we plant in wheat. We keep talking about it but never seem to accomplish getting out there. Tobit and Isaiah are taking the buckboard into town, so now would be a good time."

"You better dress warm," Isaiah grumbled around a bite of toast. "It's colder than you think. Can be deceiving."

This was her chance. Poppy hadn't known Tobit had planned to take the wagon into town, but the timing couldn't be better. "I guess that outing will have to wait for my next visit."

Kathryn swung around and met her gaze. "Oh? Why?"

"If Tobit will be so kind as to let us hitch a ride, Oscar and I are leaving today."

The flapjacks forgotten, Kathryn took a quick step in her direction. "What's this? Why? You haven't mentioned anything before."

Poppy forced out a small, self-centered-sounding laugh. "You know me, Kathryn; I come and go on a whim. This farm is closing in on me. I feel the need to get back to Boston and take care of a few loose ends before my voyage in the spring. You don't begrudge me that, do you?"

Frowning, Kathryn searched her face. "Surely, you're joking. You haven't let on for a second that you were thinking of leaving. I won't let you."

"You must. I've had just about as many peaceful vistas, colorful sunsets, and silence-filled nights as I can stand. I need some interaction, some beautiful restaurants, some excitement. I'll only be young once, Kathryn." She gave a flourishing twirl to punctuate her empty-headed statement, to be sure her sister, or anyone else, would think better of trying to stop her.

Tobit stood, went to Kathryn, and placed a protective arm across her shoulder. "Of course I'll give you a ride. I'm sure you didn't think I would refuse."

His fed-up tone almost made her turn and run.

"It's Sunday," Kathryn said. "What can you get done today?"

"Nothing. But I'll be ready nice and early for Monday. The hotel never closes." Poppy brought her empty plate to the stove and picked up the forgotten spatula, scooping out two golden-brown pancakes, nicely crisped around the edges. She raised the plate to her nose. "These smell delicious. Thank you for taking such good care of us during our visit."

She couldn't look into her sister's face. They'd become so close the last few weeks. She hadn't known what an exceptional person her older sister was until this visit. Kathryn was brave, courageous, and smart. Poppy would miss her with all her heart.

Tobit gently cleared his throat.

"Oh," Poppy said, truly surprised, almost dropping the plate. "These are yours, Kathryn. I wasn't thinking."

Mortified with herself, she acknowledged that she really *was* self-centered. She hadn't even given a thought to Kathryn and what she was to eat. Treated her like one of the servants back home. She thrust the plate toward her sister.

Kathryn shook her head and picked up the bowl. She stirred the batter a few times, and then ladled several large spoonfuls into the sizzling butter, the hotcakes growing wide. "No, those are for you. Go sit and eat, and then I'll talk you out of this crazy idea."

"I'm going," Poppy said. "There's nothing to talk about. Please, don't be angry."

"I'm gonna be mighty disappointed if you do," Isaiah said, finished with his breakfast. He wiped his mouth on his napkin and set it on the table. "Won't seem the same around here without yer bonny laughter, missy." He looked at Kathryn. "My granddaughter has been happier than I've ever seen her since her baby sister arrived. She's gonna miss ya when you go."

That statement was almost Poppy's undoing. She didn't think anyone would miss her once she was gone. Why would they? She was a burden and a sassy pants. Sincerity was not her forte.

Chapter Nine

Finished with his morning coffee, Luke stood from the dining room table at the main ranch house and walked to the living room window. The view of the yard, and the bunkhouse set back a good hundred feet, was serene. With the freezing temperatures, the ground was dangerous and as slippery as a wet sheet of ice—and made the going slow. A dusting of snow lay on top, but nothing was falling at the moment.

His parents joined him at the window. Esperanza clearing the breakfast dishes from the table was the only sound in the room.

"What's bothering you, son?" Flood asked, still carrying his coffee cup. "It's just another cold January day." He grasped Luke's shoulder. "You look troubled."

"Don't know. Nothin' specific."

"You should be thankful you have a quiet house," Claire said with a small laugh. "Your brothers are both in the throes of new babyhood. You remember those days, don't you? Holly isn't that old."

He glanced down at his mother, dressed nicely and ready for a new day. "I remember just fine. Poor Faith never gettin' any sleep, wet diapers overflowing the pail, crying baby, the house looking like a whirlwind had just passed through. I'm not envying Matt and Mark right now. No sir, not at all."

Claire rubbed her hand down his arm. Her face was free of strain, and she looked rested. A few more wrinkles this year, but it was amazing how she grew more beautiful as she aged.

"It wasn't all that bad, and you know it."

He chuckled and wrapped one arm around her. "Pretty darned close. I'm not ready for another one quite yet."

"You will be when the time comes," Flood added. "Each one enriches your life. You'll change fast enough when Faith utters those special words."

His mom pulled away and slipped over to Flood. "You're right about that, husband."

He laid his arm over her shoulders. "I was gettin' jealous."

"I know. I could feel it." She hugged Flood close.

Keeping his gaze trained outside, Luke once again thanked the heavens for such a strong family. He couldn't have gotten to where he was today without their unfailing love and support.

Francis came out of the bunkhouse, followed by Hickory, and both youths disappeared into the barn. Feeding had been done hours ago, and now the boys would muck the stalls.

Well, Francis wasn't much of a boy any longer, but Luke struggled to stop thinking of him in that way. He'd grown tall, strong, and put on weight. Would he spread his wings someday and leave the ranch? Flood had found him as a child, and as he'd done with Hickory, brought him home, gave him a roof over his head and a job, as well as a place in their family.

"What's Faith up to today?" Claire asked, now using her husband's chest as a backrest. "Anything interesting?"

"I'll say. She and Dawn are making apple pies. They were setting up this mornin' when I rode out."

Flood smiled. "That sounds tasty. And will keep the kitchen warm."

"And the rest of the house," Luke added.

Flood nodded matter-of-factly. "What about Colton? I expected to see him with you."

"He rode out with me, but he veered off the trail and went over to Matt's. Wanted to see Billy and Adam. That boy is so smart. He really is." Luke puffed out his chest. "I'm proud of him."

His mom patted his arm. "You've done a fine job raising him, Luke. No one could love him more than you do."

"That's a fact… the loving-him part, I mean. He'll be twelve this year. Time the two of us went off for a week or two, camping and hunting. Like Pa used to do with us when we were old enough, one boy at a time. I learned a lot on that trip."

He turned and looked at Flood, the man who had generously raised him as his son, even though Luke had been sired by a Cheyenne Indian.

Flood met his gaze, his expression full of meaning. "You remember that?"

"Of course I do. That was the trip I got my first buck, without the help of anyone tracking for me. I can still feel the thrill of that day. You were so proud of me, I almost busted out of my shirt."

"That was after I got over my anger at you sneaking off before sunrise with that rifle that was almost as tall as you were. All I could think about was how mad Claire would be if you went and shot yourself. Afraid I'd never be out of the doghouse if you did."

Claire whirled on him. "What? You were not."

He laughed and pulled her into a hug. "'Course not. The minute I discovered Luke's bedroll empty, fear gripped my soul.

But then my good sense kicked in and I reminded myself that *my* boy had been hunting many times, he was good with his rifle, and that he had a sensible head on his shoulders, as well as an uncanny mentality far beyond his years. There was never a time I can remember when Luke was just a happy-go-lucky kid. He's been a deep thinker since the day he was born."

Luke scoffed. "Ha, then you didn't know me that well."

"I think I did—and do."

Not liking the sinking feeling in his belly that lingered, Luke ambled away from the window. No need for it. All was well. Nothing but getting through the winter months—like they did every year—and have the spring to face. The workload on next year's cattle drive would be light since they'd taken a good majority of their stock to market. What could be better than that?

He took a deep breath. As in a poker game where his good luck had just gone south, he felt a need to get up and move. Trouble was, he was already home. Everyone here was safe and sound.

Chapter Ten

"What do you mean, the stage can't go to Waterloo? Of course it can. That's how I arrived here not all that long ago."

At the sound of distress in Miss Ford's voice, Justin lowered the newspaper he was reading to watch the exchange at the Cattlemen's Hotel counter. Relaxed against the soft cushions, the deputy had been enjoying some company in the warm lobby when the easterner had entered a few minutes ago. Her traveling companion was nowhere to be seen. Because of Oscar Scott, Justin hadn't gotten past small talk with Kathryn's younger sister. Seeing the dandy had staked his claim wasn't difficult. He wanted every able-bodied man to keep his distance.

That was fine with Justin. He'd heard Poppy Ford was strong-willed, uppity, and had plenty to say about everything under the sun.

Poor Miss Hildy Hallsey, the hotel clerk, was doing her best to calm the Bostonian. "Almost a month has passed since your arrival, Miss Ford. Christmas has come and gone. New Year's, as well."

"Yes, yes, I know," Miss Ford replied. "I was enjoying myself so much that—"

She must have felt his gaze, because she slowly turned to find him watching. He smiled and lifted the paper to block his view.

"I'm sorry, Miss Ford," Hildy said more softly. "But this is Montana. I received a telegram last night. Snow is falling in Waterloo something fierce. And the storm looks to be headed this way. In all actuality, the stage has run much longer than any of us expected. If you really must go to Waterloo, check with June Pittman at the livery. She has a sleigh she rents out once the snow gets deep. I've even heard that she's taken customers over that way a time or two. Not this year, mind you. But if you're desperate, you—"

Miss Ford's anguished whimper silenced Miss Hallsey midsentence.

"Miss Ford?"

She softly cleared her throat. "Please, go on."

"If you do get to Waterloo, that won't guarantee the train will still be running. Most all transportation shuts down when the winter sets in. The schedule is different every year."

Justin couldn't stop himself from peeking over the newspaper one more time. Hildy had placed a comforting hand on Miss Ford's arm, and amazingly, she hadn't pulled away.

"It's going to be all right, miss," Hildy crooned.

Miss Ford's shoulders pulled back. "Of course it is."

He recognized her steely tone. This Miss Ford he was better acquainted with.

"This is just a tiny setback," she went on. "Nothing for me to get upset over."

He didn't miss Hildy's wary expression. Seemed he wasn't the only one who walked carefully around Miss Ford.

"That's exactly right. Would you like to take a room, or will you be returning to your sister's?"

Several moments slipped by. "I'll take a room, thank you. And we'll need another for Mr. Scott. Do you have two available?"

Hildy straightened her shoulders and her nostrils flared. "Mr. Oscar Scott, you say?"

"Yes, do you know him?"

"Indeed. He stayed here on his last visit." Hildy began writing in her ledger. "For one night, or more?"

Miss Ford just stood there.

"Miss Ford?"

She softly batted her fingers on the counter. "I don't know. You'd better make them for a few days. I'm not sure yet what we'll do."

"Very good. You already know about our restaurant. It opens each morning at six. If you'd like coffee earlier than that, I usually have a pot brewing in my office just under the stairway. You're welcome anytime."

"Thank you."

She handed Miss Ford a key. "Would you like Mr. Scott's key, as well?"

"No, you can leave it here, and he'll check in with you when he returns." She turned and looked at her trunk, a rosy pink coming up in her face.

Hildy came around the counter. "I'm sorry, but Sunday is when Harold mops the mercantile—you know, when the business is closed. As soon as he's back, I'll have him bring your trunk up to your room."

A golden opportunity.

Justin folded his paper and stood. "I can get that for you, Miss Ford."

Surprised, she blinked a couple of times. "Deputy, I couldn't ask that of you. I don't mind waiting."

She was avoiding his gaze. Probably didn't want him to see her watery eyes.

"No problem at all." Squatting, he hefted the heavy trunk by the handles on each end and started up the stairs. "What floor?" he asked over his shoulder.

Miss Ford followed behind. "The third."

Justin bit back a groan and re-hefted the cumbersome object more firmly in his arms as he rounded the staircase on the second-floor landing.

"Across from the bridal suite, I believe, Mr. Wesley," she added in a soft voice.

At the top, he stopped, and she hurried past him to unlock the door before stepping inside.

"Brr, it's quite cold up here." She hugged herself as her gaze landed on a small fireplace and a stack of wood opposite the bed. "I wonder if I'm the only occupant up here."

Justin placed her trunk on the floor by the window. He turned around, feeling self-conscious. "Sorry. I wouldn't know."

"Thank you, Deputy. I can't tell you how much I appreciate your assistance."

"I'm happy to help, miss. I overheard you're headed home to Boston."

"I'm trying." A sad smile appeared on her lips. "We'll see how things play out. For now, the stage line is stopped because of the weather. But I'll get there one way or the other. Things always seem to work out for me."

Poppy Ford was attractive. She looked like her older sister, except her eyes were a vivid blue—and quite striking. At the moment, she gazed out the window, a faraway expression on her face.

She turned to him. "It's surprising, really."

"What?"

"I think I'll miss this place much more than I ever believed I could."

Justin chuckled, even though she sounded sad. "Y Knot does have a way of growing on you. I haven't been here long myself, and I find the town already feels like home."

Hildy Hallsey knocked on the doorjamb of the open door. Her dark blue skirt, simple striped blouse, and warm wool shawl were a contrast to Miss Ford's fine-quality clothes.

Justin liked Hildy. She was levelheaded, nice, and quick-witted. When there wasn't anything to keep him in the sheriff's office, more often than not, he found himself relaxing in the comfortable chair of the hotel lobby. Why not? The place was right next door to the jail.

"I've brought you some things, Miss Ford." Hildy came into the room and placed two folded towels on the bed. "I hope everything is to your liking." She crossed the rug and opened the doors to a large wardrobe set against the wall. "Pegs are here to hang your cape, if you wish."

Miss Ford ran her hand over her fur cloak. "The air is much too cold yet, thank you."

"That's true. I'll have Harold build a fire as soon as he returns." The clerk wrung her hands as she glanced at him, and then back at Miss Ford. "If you'd rather, I can move you down a floor where you're closer to the restaurant's kitchen stove. I thought you'd like this larger room, but perhaps you prefer another."

"This will do nicely, Miss Hallsey," Miss Ford replied. "I don't intend to be here long."

"Look," Hildy exclaimed, pointing out the window. "The snow's falling in earnest. I can't help but be excited. I dearly love the way the white flakes float down from the clouds. Isn't it pretty?"

Justin came to the window where Hildy and Miss Ford looked out on Main Street and the Hitching Post saloon across the way. With the on-again, off-again dustings that Y Knot had experienced the last few weeks, he'd begun to believe they would skate right through the most difficult months without much of a problem.

Now, by the blackness of the clouds overhead, Mother Nature was about to prove him wrong.

Chapter Eleven

After six hours of heavy snowfall, Shad began to think this storm was going to be a whiteout blizzard. Snowflakes were coming down hard, and the temperature was falling. The talk in the bunkhouse turned quiet. All the cowhands had lived through bad winters before, and accounts of losing loved ones, animals, or appendages began to come out.

Hickory sat by the hearth wrapped in a heavy blanket, his long hair braided down his back and a cup of hot cocoa between his palms. The young fellow had learned to wait quietly for his turn to speak.

"And that's how I met the woman I was gonna marry. Yes, sir. I can remember the day like it was yesterday," Smokey drawled. "While I helped dig out her pa's prairie schooner axle-deep in the snowbank, I had time to do a little wooing. She sure was a purty little thing, even with her apple-red nose and purple lips. She thought I hung the moon, and said so six times."

"What was her name?" Ike asked. "You never said."

"Can't remember."

A howl of laughter went up. Shad shook his head and smiled.

"Really?" Hickory's eyes had gone wide. "That don't seem right."

Smokey winked at the boy. "The incident was a long time ago, son."

"What happened to her?" Hickory asked. "How come she ain't here?"

A shadow of sadness crossed Smokey's face. "Her pa didn't think I hung the moon. No sir, not at all. Made sure the wedding never happened."

A few murmurs sounded.

Lucky crossed to the door and went out on the porch. Within a few moments, he returned. He clicked the door closed and then rubbed both hands up and down his arms.

"How's it looking out there?" Shad asked.

Lucky scanned the faces around the room. "I don't recall a time I ever seen so much snow fallin' unless it was up in the high country. There's at least six new inches already. It's piling up quicker than dirt behind Hickory's ears."

"That right?" Ike slung his arm across the mantel as he leaned around the fire. "That's pretty fast. The cattle'll be hard-pressed to find enough grass to eat these next few months."

Lucky nodded. "And the wolves are howling."

Francis sipped from his cup. "Can't blame 'em much. Could be they're hungry too."

"Shouldn't be," Shad added. "The carcass I found up at Covered Bridge was a new kill. Still had plenty to scavenge."

Lucky ambled away toward the kitchen. "They've been quiet for the last ten years. The long, dry summer had the rodents and small animals out searching for water, easy kill for them. Years have passed since we thinned 'em out." He turned and looked at the men. "Anyone need anything more before I turn in? My old bones are feeling the cold."

The bunkhouse was quiet.

"Fine then," Lucky said. "Get some shut-eye. Come tomorrow, I'm sure we'll have plenty of work shoveling out to the house and barn."

Shad, still rolled deep in his warm blankets, glanced at the window when he heard the bunkhouse door open and close. Murmured voices brought him more fully awake. The sky was dark and cold. Who would be coming in at this time of the morning?

By the light of a single lantern burning low on the dining table, he saw Luke and Roady in the doorway, shaking off a coating of white. He sat up and rubbed a hand across his face. The cold air brought gooseflesh to his arms, even through his long johns.

"What time is it?" he asked quietly. In the wintertime, when no one needed to head out to the pastures, Lucky rose at five instead of four. The cook was still in his room.

Luke crossed the floor and lit a second lamp on the mantel. "Four thirty. Snow's still falling."

Most men were now awake and dressing.

Roady went to the kitchen and began loading wood into the cookstove. Finished with that, he pumped water to fill the coffeepot. "I'm moving Sally over to the main house on invitation of the McCutcheons," he said quietly as Shad met him in his stockinged feet. "I won't leave her alone at the homestead—not in weather like this."

I wouldn't either.

Shad pulled on his boots, coat, and hat, and made a mad dash for the outhouse. The McCutcheons had been talking about bringing indoor plumbing to the place soon, but it couldn't come soon enough to suit him. Freezing wet snow slipped down his coat neckline. Hunching against the howling wind, he kept a tight hold on his hat.

For some odd reason, thoughts of Miss Poppy Ford jumped into his mind unbidden. He'd made a fool of himself last night when he'd sputtered water into Oscar Scott's face. The memory taunted him. He felt his face heat, despite the howling wind.

At the outhouse, he quickly did his business and hurried back inside. Luke and Roady wouldn't be here this early unless there was a good reason.

Lucky now moved around the kitchen, whipping up some grub.

"What's going on?" Shad asked, wanting to get to the bottom of why his two bosses were here so early.

"We've had twelve inches of snow in twelve hours, and the snowfall doesn't look like it'll be letting up anytime soon," Luke said. "With the new babies, Matt and Mark will remain at their places, but we want to send out men to circumvent any problems. Ike and Bob, you ride over to Matt's homestead, check on things there, and then go over to Mark's. If everything's fine, come on back to the bunkhouse. I'll help Roady move Sally to the main house with my parents. Hickory, get some things together. I'm moving you into the main house too."

"But, but," Hickory sputtered, looking around at the others. "Is Lucky staying here?"

"No buts about it." Luke's tone was hard. "Just follow my orders. I've paired up men so nobody will be riding anywhere alone. We've had several reports about the wolves. If we get caught off guard, we'll have no one but ourselves to blame."

Shad glanced to Francis and Smokey. What would their orders be?

Roady, now with a cup of coffee in his hand, turned to the group. "Shad, Francis, and Smokey, you three ride into Y Knot.

Check the road along the way and make sure no one was taken by surprise. Mrs. McCutcheon wants you to check on Brandon too. Charity, who you all know for the last month has been taking turns at Matt's and Mark's to help the women, is worried about him. Wants to know that he's safe. When you're finished, come back to the ranch."

"What about the livestock?" Shad asked. He'd thought they would be sent out to the pastures.

Luke's stern face was answer alone. His shoulders tensed and the coffee in his hand looked forgotten. No one liked the thought of the cattle suffering in a storm like this.

"Nothin' we can do for 'em now." His voice was low, his tone grave. "Once the snow stops will be soon enough to check 'em out. For now, we have people to worry about."

Shad guzzled down half a cup of black coffee and waited as Lucky filled their plates. A full belly was prudent when venturing out into a blizzard like the one buffeting the walls. At times like this, cattle weren't the only things to worry over. Every man stepping through the bunkhouse door had danger to face.

He glanced around the stern faces. Seemed everybody else realized that too.

Chapter Twelve

Hickory crept down the large staircase in the main ranch house, feeling completely out of sorts. He wasn't used to living upstairs in Luke's bedroom. He liked the bunkhouse, Lucky, and the men. His cot, next to Francis's, was his castle. Whiling away the hours with his books or sketchbook was easy.

Here, he was like a tadpole in sand. Mrs. McCutcheon was very kind, and Esperanza, the maid, hovered over him like a mother hen. He was a ranch hand—not a son, or guest, or a kid— and he didn't want to be treated like any of them.

He wished he'd been sent to town with Francis, Shad, and Smokey to check on the others. Punk had forded his share of snowy roads. Besides, Hickory enjoyed spending time at the sheriff's office, playing checkers with Brandon, filing papers, or sweeping the floor.

When Hickory had first come to Y Knot, he'd been frightened of Brandon Crawford, the tall, serious-faced sheriff, suspecting him to be like the lawman in Waterloo, always out to blame him—the town's homeless waif—for whatever bad happened in the town. If something turned up missing, everyone immediately assumed Hickory had taken it. Didn't matter that they rarely found anything in his dugout. Not to say it never happened, but he wasn't the only one scraping out a living on the streets—just the one they could easily find.

Hickory gave a mental shrug. That was done and past. His thieving days were over. Luke had seen to that, making him take an oath to always be honest and truthful. He'd done his share of stealing in Waterloo, but this new leaf he'd turned here in Y Knot felt good and honorable. He'd not mess up the fortunate hand he'd been dealt. No, sir.

"Hickory, did you get your things settled?" Mrs. McCutcheon asked from her seat by the large living room window. She pulled her gaze from the snow falling outside. The lantern burning by her chair cast her in golden light like an angel.

"Yes, ma'am."

"Good. If you're hungry, Esperanza is in the kitchen. Since it's hours until suppertime, she won't mind if you venture in there and ask for something to eat. I know little boys are always hungry. Billy, Colton, and Adam like the high stool by the warm kitchen stove. She spoils them rotten." Mrs. McCutcheon laughed and shook her head.

He could tell her warm smile was the result of some memory.

"I don't know where the years have gone." She gave Hickory a wink. "Go on; I promise she won't mind. And if you're not hungry, surely you'd like a cup of hot cocoa. That's always available in this house."

Although he wasn't hungry, because he was missing the bunkhouse, Hickory nodded obediently and shuffled toward the kitchen door. He knew his mistress, but not like he knew Lucky, Francis, and the rest of the boys. Being singled out to come into the main house where he'd be safe from harm felt like a prison sentence. To sit and do nothing when work needed to be done was torture. And he didn't like it one bit.

At the kitchen door, he stood silently, watching the slim Mexican woman scrub the leathery-looking potato she held in her hands. She rinsed the spud in a bowl of water, and then scrubbed some more. Why anyone cared so much what the outside of a potato looked like was a mystery to him. Lucky surely didn't.

On the counter by the windows were two golden-brown pies, most likely baked this morning for tonight's supper. Thank goodness Roady and Miss Sally would be staying here too. He'd not like to be the only one singled out for special treatment. At least the burden of conversation wouldn't fall solely on his shoulders.

Esperanza straightened at the faint howl of a wolf. Her gaze darted to the window. She mumbled something unintelligible, then crossed herself before going back to work.

Hickory took a small step into the room.

"*Chiquito*, come in," she said when she saw him. Her smile widened, and she reached for the nearby towel on the counter.

She was soft-looking, her shiny black hair pulled back and braided down her back.

"Come into my kitchen and I'll feed you, *sí*? Anything you like. What can I make for *mi chiquito* Hickory? Scrambled eggs, meat sandwich, leftover enchiladas? Anything you want, *cariño*."

He wished she'd stop calling him *little one* and *sweetie*. Luke had translated on a bark of laughter when Hickory had first come to the ranch. Since then he heard *chiquito* this and *cariño* that. Didn't she know he was a ranch hand?

"Hot tortillas with melted cheese?" she asked, her gaze darting to the ice box. "That is a favorite of the young *señores*. They only take a minute and keep you filled until suppertime."

He'd better think of something quickly, or else she would have him eating a five-course meal. "Hot cocoa, ma'am. Please."

She gave a nod of her head. "Ah yes, a favorite of *señores* Billy, Adam, and Colton. And that of their fathers, especially on a snowy day. You sit here by the stove and stay warm."

Hickory climbed up on the stool she'd indicated and got comfortable.

The woman set to work, filling a small pan with milk. She put it on the hot stove top.

He glanced around. A multitude of pots and skillets hung from a rack above the sink. On the far wall, the icebox, where she kept things like meat, cheese, and milk, as well as a mountain of leftovers, stood next to a butter churn.

Colton had showed him the night after Thanksgiving. The kitchen had been cleaned, Esperanza gone to her room, and everyone else was nowhere to be found. The two boys had stuffed themselves on leftover turkey and pumpkin pie.

Hickory shook his head at the memory. He could have survived a month in Waterloo from the many covered crocks and jugs of eatables she always had stored away.

From a basket by the side of the stove, Esperanza took a log and reached for the oven door, a dish towel protecting her hand against the hot metal.

"I can do that for you, ma'am," he said softly. "I don't mind."

She put the last two small logs into the stove. "Oh no, *chiquito*. That is my job. I like what I do."

Hickory hopped down anyway. He was meant to do, not be done for.

"Then I'll fill the empty basket." His gaze challenged hers as she was about to say no.

Esperanza gave a laugh. "You are a small man in size, but large in heart. You may fill my wood basket if you'd like. I will not rob you of that task." She winked. "You and I are much alike. But you should first put on a coat."

"I'll be out and in before I get cold," he said with a smidgen of pride. "I fetch wood for Lucky every day. It's one of my jobs." He lifted the medium-sized basket and hurried to the kitchen door. He'd seen the logs stacked very close to the wall, making the job of fetching wood in the winter simple.

The wind howled inside when he opened the door. A freezing-cold flurry hit him in the face as he worked, robbing his breath. Esperanza grasped the back of his heavy wool shirt and hauled him inside, closing the door. He'd had just enough time to get four logs into the basket.

"Much too cold for you. Besides, the storm has made darkness fall more quickly." Her uneasy gaze darted to the door. She seemed as if she had more to say, but held her tongue.

Sensing her skittishness, Hickory lugged the basket to its spot and climbed back on his stool, now thankful to have the heat from the stove to chase away the blast of cold that had all but frozen him in one strong gust. He rubbed his palms together several times, thinking how fast his skin had turned icy.

How were the ranch hands faring, the ones singled out to ride into Y Knot? Perhaps, instead of holding a grudge at Luke for sending him here, he should be grateful. At least he was warm, and soon he'd have a nice hot mug of cocoa to enjoy. If things got too boring, he was close enough to the bunkhouse to slip away and go see Lucky for a little while without being missed.

"Here you are, *mi chiquito*."

Esperanza handed him a filled-to-the-brim mug. Holding it carefully, Hickory blew on the top of the liquid.

Now that he thought about it, that was a darned good idea. Mr. McCutcheon was closed away in his office. Perhaps Mrs. McCutcheon would go upstairs, leaving him on his own. He thought of how surprised Lucky would be to see him. At first he'd be annoyed, but then Hickory would get to help him in the kitchen.

No matter the falling snow, or even the wolves, Hickory was fast. Nothing could catch him in a dash to the bunkhouse.

Chapter Thirteen

Shad's five layers of clothing did little to ease the biting cold of the howling north wind as snow accumulated on the shoulders of his long leather duster and hat. The hot coffee, biscuits, and gravy in Shad's stomach were not keeping him warm.

Francis rode between him and Smokey, the group picking their way carefully through the two feet of snow on the road as they watched for possible victims. The day was dark, even though sunrise had arrived some thirty minutes ago. Each man had his sidearm, as well as a loaded Remington in his saddle scabbard. They weren't expecting trouble, but if it arrived, they'd be ready.

"What's that?" Smokey lifted an arm and pointed twenty feet ahead to a lump of snow larger than a horse. "Ain't seen nothin' along this stretch of road before. At least, nothin' that big."

"Don't know." Francis had yet to say a word since they'd headed out of the ranch yard.

"Let's check it out," Shad replied. They were now only ten feet away. The snow-covered object looked too angular to be a person or animal, but still they were curious.

Shad's mount snorted and shied away. Using leg pressure, Shad pushed the unreliable gelding forward, encouraging but insistent when the animal hesitated. One of Shad's specialties was finishing newly broke horses; that's why Luke had hired him on. He'd yet to start a new batch of colts, so until then, he'd been riding the less broke mounts. Putting on miles, making them dependable.

This particular gelding hadn't settled in as expected and was avoided by most of the hired hands, which made the problem even worse. A mount like this needed miles, and lots of them, especially in every sort of condition, as the weather was today. Shad had chosen him for the ride into town, thinking the snowstorm would be a good training day. He hoped he wouldn't regret his decision.

With a light touch on the thick split reins, Shad gave a gentle pull, which brought the gelding's head around by way of his snaffle bit to face what was spooking him instead of letting the horse turn away. Horses were animals of flight. As soon as they perceived danger, whether actual or not, their instincts told them to bolt, to put space between them and the threat. That was, unless you trained that impulse out of them. This leggy chestnut had good breeding and was built well, but had the brain of a peanut. He wasn't going to learn the lesson in one day.

Smokey rode right up to the scary-looking snowbank with branches sticking through white. "It's just two saplings. One broke off and made a bridge, enough branches to catch all the snow." He leaned forward and brushed away some snow, then gave a tug on one of the limbs. Chunks of snow dropped away, and the intact tree snapped up straight.

The burst of motion made Shad's horse almost drop to the ground in fear.

Francis cut his frowning gaze to Shad. "Jeez, Shad, did ya have to ride that spook today?"

"Guess it wasn't such a great idea. Wanted to get him some experience. He just might leave me in a snowbank."

The howling wind and snow stole away his words. Didn't even know if anyone heard him, but it didn't matter. They were almost to Y Knot. He'd welcome a cup of coffee in Brandon's office.

Shad hitched his head and they ventured on. A quarter mile out of town, he pulled up and pointed to the road ahead, which until this moment had been a beautiful undisturbed bed of white for the whole ride out.

"Tracks," Francis hissed. "A hell of a lot of 'em."

They rode closer in silence. The sight made a tingle of awe tickle up Shad's back. He'd never seen so many wolf tracks in one place. The evidence didn't bode well.

"How many you think?"

Smokey shook his head. "That's some pack. I'd say twenty or more."

The scent of the predators made Shad's mount paw the snow nervously, so Shad reached down and patted his horse's sodden neck with a moist leather glove. *Here's something you* should *be afraid of, boy. I won't tell ya no on this.*

They all should be troubled. A hungry wolf pack was nothing to trifle with. Single wolves could be a problem when their bellies had been empty too long. He didn't like to think of twenty or more.

"Come through not long ago," he hollered into the wind. "Tracks are still visible. By the looks of it, a fairly large male is leading 'em. I don't remember seeing a paw print that size before."

The falling snow was already covering the sign of the menace lurking in the trees. As if on cue, all three men glanced around uncertainly.

"Let's get to town," Francis said. "I'm getting colder by the second. Won't be long 'fore you'll have to pry me out of this saddle with a crowbar. Knowing you two, you'd leave me on my horse without a backward glance."

Nudging their mounts, they moved along slowly as the visibility grew worse. Shad was hard-pressed to see his horse's ears.

He didn't like the thought of Nick and Tanner traveling in this storm. Surely his brothers would hole up somewhere and wait out the weather, even if that took three months, wouldn't they? They were smart men, and he shouldn't worry. But anyone could get turned around in a whiteout like this. More than a few stories existed about grown men getting lost on their way to a barn or outhouse.

Empathy for the cattle filtered through his mind. Going into this winter, the grass had been scarce from the hot, dry summer. With the frozen earth, many would go hungry. The thought rattled his nerves. The ranch horses too, the ones that stayed out. At least the McCutcheons had some hay stored. The feed in the pole barn at Covered Bridge would help, but maybe not long enough.

Poppy Ford's smiling face appeared in his thoughts on the wall of white in front of him, chasing away his concerns for the livestock. More than the animals could be at risk. City dandies too.

"Almost there," Smokey called out.

They rounded the corner into Y Knot, and as expected, Half Hitch Street was deserted. The freezing, howling gale had already whipped the snow high against buildings. Not a person was in sight. A window in the butcher's shop glowed from within, but other than that, the places were dark.

"We should take the horses to the livery before we go to the sheriff's." Smokey pointed down the street. "We may be here a while. Then, if Brandon and Justin haven't done it yet, we'll go from shop to shop to make sure no one is missing."

"Sounds good," Shad replied, hunching against the cold. Getting out of this weather sounded darn appealing. A body could withstand this cold only so long. "Let's get this done."

Crossing Main Street, the three arrived in the undisturbed snow out front of June Pittman's large barn that served as Y Knot's livery and forge. Shad glanced down the street to Lou and Drit's boarding house, hoping to see a light or two in the windows there. He had a special love for Lou's beef stew and hoped she had a large pot simmering on the stove. When lunchtime rolled around, he'd be sure to check that out.

They were close enough now to see a light flickering in Brandon's office.

"Whoa," Shad crooned to his frightened horse.

He swung out of the saddle, barely able to clench his fist around the stiff leather rein. Shouldering open the livery's large wooden door, he stood back to let Francis and Smokey ride inside. Once they passed through, he pushed the door shut, blessedly closing out the howling wind. The quiet felt good, although he still felt the imaginary snow beating against his back.

"Welcome, boys," June Pittman called out as she strode up the barn aisle, pitchfork in hand. Her shoulder-length brown hair was a mess sticking out of her wool hat. She was a different sort of woman, a breath of fresh air. Her mischievous glance said they must look a sight.

Morgan Stanford followed at her side, his distinctive limp pronounced by the cold.

The scent of the hay, mixed with the lamp oil, was welcome. Shad took a deep breath, relieved to have arrived in one piece. "You have room for our horses?" Every stall looked occupied.

June nodded. "We'll make room. They'll have to double up, but that can't be helped. I'll feed and water 'em, as well."

Morgan watched as the three began unsaddling. "What brings you into town in a blizzard like this?"

"Just thought we'd go for a little stroll," Smokey said sardonically. He lifted the saddle from his horse's back and slung it onto a nearby sawhorse. He laid out the wet blanket on top, and then crooked a wet eyebrow at Morgan. "Actually, Luke sent us in to check the road. Make sure no one was stranded. Don't take long to lose your fingers and toes from frostbite."

"Let alone your life," Shad added.

"That was good thinking," June said, receiving the reins of Smokey's gelding and leading him away. "Seems we've been waiting on this storm, but now that it's arrived, feels like it dropped on us out of nowhere." She turned and gave them a look.

Her uncharacteristic expression caught Shad off guard. He'd seen fear, and something else, etched on her face.

She opened the gate to the second stall and pushed back the horse that was interested to see what was going on. She clucked her tongue.

"Get on back, boy," she said patiently, pushing the horse back with a hand to his chest. "Go on. You're getting a little company. No kickin'." Smokey's horse went inside eagerly to meet his new companion. "There may be a little ruckus at first," she said. "But they'll wise up soon enough."

After repeating the process twice more, the five stood around the stove in the front area, the three ranch hands shivering from their wet clothes.

"Everything in town is closed up tight," Morgan said.

"Have you moved into your upstairs living quarters?" Francis asked.

Morgan nodded. "I have. I miss Lou's cooking at the boarding house, so I still take most my meals there."

"You're not cookin' for him, June?" Francis asked, surprised. "He's your fella, ain't he?"

She raised one eyebrow at him.

Smokey turned to Francis with a smile. "Never miss a good chance to shut up."

June crossed her arms over her chest, plenty comfortable to stand boot toe to boot toe with any man. "Cook for him? I say he needs to cook for me. That's what's holding up this wedding."

Chapter Fourteen

In the quiet of her cabin home, Sally Guthrie, dressed in her thick coat and wool scarf, gazed into her small travel trunk, debating on what she'd need at the McCutcheons'. Roady hadn't said how long they would stay, only that he couldn't leave her here alone when a good possibility existed he could get snowed out. Besides, in this brutal cold, he had no way to keep this cabin as warm as he'd like in her delicate condition. She smiled over his protectiveness. At the moment, he was at the McCutcheons', but he'd be home soon enough. Before the road became impassable for the wagon, he'd said.

Taking another dress from the wardrobe, she folded the garment and placed it in the half-full trunk. Her life had changed since venturing to Montana last September. A warm glow heated her face. God had blessed her and dropped into her lap a savior in the form of a loving husband.

She recalled the first few weeks after she'd discovered she was with child. She'd been an unwed mother without a future. Despair had almost crippled her after the attack that had changed her life. Mr. Greenstein, her boss at the St. Louis newspaper, might have forced his advances, but he hadn't destroyed her. After realizing she was the only person who had control over her fate and could direct the outcome, she'd picked herself up, given herself a stern talking-to, and made some plans.

As I best do right now before Roady returns to find I'm not ready. He said time was of the essence.

Hastily, she chose one more skirt and petticoat, folded both, and set them inside. Finished for now, she went to the window. The large, delicate snowflakes falling from the sky reminded her of rosettes, the German delicacy Aunt Tillie liked to fry on holidays. Her mother's younger sister often made a large batch, all dusted with powdered sugar so fine that sometimes it melted into the warm, greasy goodness before anyone had a chance to consume them.

Sally glanced out the window. The pines, covered in a white blanket of snow, looked larger, almost touching the sky. The tracks Roady made earlier to the barn were long since gone. Everything was still, white, and quiet.

She pulled her shawl tighter. As much as she tried, she couldn't get warm. Even with the fire blazing and the cookstove loaded with as much wood as it would hold, her hands felt like two blocks of ice. She'd be glad when Roady returned.

The dancing snowflakes reminded her of a ballet performance she'd once seen in St. Louis. Since the tickets were much too expensive for her family, her oldest brother, Travis, had bribed someone to leave the alley door of the theater ajar. Even though she, Heather, and Anita had to take turns peeking through, the night was one of the most exciting of her life. Melba, her youngest sister, had only been five. Much too young, and her health too fragile. She'd had to stay home.

Realizing she missed home, Sally sighed. That didn't mean she regretted marrying Roady, or that she wanted to go back to St. Louis. Just that she missed seeing her beloved family. Her mother wasn't getting any younger, and that was a fact. And

Melba, always on the verge of going to the angels, had only so long to live.

Movement on the edge of the forest caught her gaze. Nothing now, though. Her contemplation wandered to the barn. Another dark flash brought Sally's gaze back to the timberline. Had she seen something move or had it been the wind in the trees? A coyote? Or maybe a stray steer from the main ranch? Impossible to say.

Her skin prickled, and she let her hand fall to her ever-growing middle, thinking of the little one nestled inside. She was being silly. As long as she stayed indoors, nothing could hurt her child.

Two riders appeared out of the wall of white. Both men, hunched in their saddles, their shoulders and hats covered in white, rode without talking through the snow that almost reached their horses' knees. Close enough now, she recognized her husband and Luke. The men entered the barn without dismounting.

Excited, she kept watch. Roady soon appeared, and on his way to the cabin, he looked up and caught her watching. He smiled and waved. Eager to get to the ranch this morning an hour before dawn, he hadn't taken time to shave, and stubble now shadowed his jaw. She admired her handsome husband, and then laughed when a gust of wind almost took his hat.

The ride to the McCutcheons', although short, would be plenty cold, but she was looking forward to the adventure. Sally hurried to the door and greeted him when he stepped in.

He looked at her and then down at the doorknob. "Didn't you lock the door when I left?"

"Yes, I did. I guess I forgot to re-lock it when I went out on the porch for wood." She helped him out of his thick winter coat covered in white. She took it from his hands and hung it on a peg.

He patted her backside. "Be more careful."

"That's some storm out there," she said, affected by his looks and the warm thoughts she'd been thinking.

Now divested of his snow-covered outer garment, he wrapped her in his arms and pulled her close. "Warm me up, darlin'. I'm cold."

All too happy to oblige, Sally rubbed her hands up and down his arms, and then pounded his back to get the blood flowing. "You've been out there a long time—too long."

They kissed, something they did often.

He chuckled. "You're right."

"How's that feel? Warmer?"

"Not yet." He nuzzled her neck. "But gettin' there."

His frigid face sent lances of cold down her frame. She gasped and pushed him away.

"Fine. If you don't want me, then I'll have to find my kisses elsewhere," he said playfully.

"And your goose will be cooked, if you do."

He placed one more final kiss on her lips, his hands cupping her face, and stepped back. "Unfortunately, we don't have all the time in the world. The snow hasn't let up a bit, and the temp is still falling. I just wonder how I'll keep you warm on the ride over."

She glanced at the door. "Where's Luke? Isn't he coming in?"

"Nope, he's hitching the wagon. We don't have time to spare." He glanced to their bed and the trunk. "You packed and ready?"

Sally nodded. "Your things, as well."

"Good girl." He looked her up and down. "Have on all the layers you can under that coat?"

She held out her arms. "Can't you tell?"

He nodded. "Hickory will be there too."

She smiled. "Wonderful. I'll take along some of my favorite books, and we can work on his reading." She went to her small bookcase, pulled out a few titles, and set them in the trunk.

Roady went to the window, looked out, and turned back to her. "Have a surprise for you."

She felt her eyes go wide. This man was a wonder. He never stopped trying to make her happy.

"Francis was in Y Knot yesterday and went by the mercantile." A smile drew across his face in pleasure. "Picked up a letter for you from Mr. Simpson. As usual, it arrived a while ago, and he had it filed in someone else's box. I hope it's not important."

"Every letter is important," she said on a gasp. Over a month had elapsed since she'd had any word from home. A letter now felt like Christmas. She also worried about Melba. "Can I have it?"

He glanced out the window and shook his head. "Here's Luke now. Grab several blankets off the bed while I put on my coat and get the trunk." He quickly checked the stove to see the door was latched tight, and then made sure the screen was in front of the fire.

"Did you see who it was from?" Most likely the author was Anita, or perhaps Melba. Her mother didn't have much free time to write after working to keep food on the table.

"No name, just a street address. From St. Louis, but not your home."

She followed Roady to the bed and did as he asked with the blankets after he'd closed the trunk and hefted it into his arms.

No name? How strange. "I guess I'll have to wait a little longer." Sally pulled the door closed after Roady exited, locking it with the long silver key.

"Wait here until I load this," he said, crunching down the steps. "The ground is slippery. I don't want you to fall."

Wrapping herself in her arms to ward off the cold, she wondered about the note. Her excitement about the visit to the McCutcheons' was now overshadowed by something she couldn't put her finger on.

"Morning, Sally," Luke called out. "Everyone's excited for your visit."

"Good morning, Luke. I am, as well."

He laughed with good mirth. "And the warmth?"

"Absolutely the warmth. But your mother's companionship most of all. I've missed her."

Roady was back, and when Sally went to take his hand, he lifted her into his arms.

Burying her face into the crook of his neck, she tried to dispel her growing anxiety. Nothing was wrong. This was just a typical snowstorm. And the letter from home brought good news… not bad.

Chapter Fifteen

Poppy huddled under her blankets, shivering and wishing for the lovely radiators back in Boston. She'd passed the night fully dressed, rising every hour to feed the fire from her dwindling stack of logs. She'd have to see the wood supply was replenished today, or she'd not make it through another night. Stretching her leg across the frigid sheets, she searched for the bed warmer with her sock-covered toe.

Nothing. As cold as ice. She stifled a sob of misery.

A slow squeak just outside her door made her lower the coverlet from her face and listen, everything else forgotten. Except for the amber glow of the coals, the room was pitch dark. What was the time? Difficult to tell, because the window was gray and all was quiet. The squeak came again. Was someone up here on the third floor with her?

Don't be silly. This is a hotel. Of course, someone may be checking in, or cleaning a room, or—waiting to kill me.

She listened to the quiet, trying to quell her overactive imagination. A scratch somewhere in the hall, and then creaking…

The hair on the back of her neck prickled. When had she turned into such a fraidycat?

The moment I moved in up here—all alone.

She glanced at the dying fire. It needed more wood, and she only had three logs left. Her stomach pinched from hunger. She'd have to get up and descend the stairway if she wanted any breakfast. Even a cup of the coffee Hildy had spoken of would be welcome. Oh, how she dreaded stepping into the frosty air.

Rolling to her side, she reached for the small box of matches she'd left within easy reach, and a lonely twang pulled at her heart. What was Kathryn doing? She prayed her sister's house was cozy and warm. Surely, Tobit would see that Kathryn was taken care of.

Poppy pictured her sister in her red polka-dot apron, serving Tobit and Isaiah a platter of hot buttermilk biscuits slathered with fresh-churned butter and sweet blackberry jam. The men would compliment her cooking, and her face would turn a rosy pink. A smile producing both dimples would appear on her face.

She has so little compared to Boston but is actually happy in Montana. No, more than that. She's in love. Poppy had a difficult time understanding such an emotion.

Enough analyzing. She had sufficient worries of her own right now without getting sentimental.

She fumbled the matches. With perseverance and shaking fingers, she lit a match and touched it to the lamp's wick.

Light.

Standing, she pulled the quilt from the bed and wrapped it around her body before shuffling to the window. A wall of falling snow blocked the view. The sun had indeed risen, but was hidden behind the clouds. She could barely see the street below.

Pushing onward, she sat on the side of her bed, pulled on her boots and laced them up, all the while gripping her jaw to keep her teeth from clacking like a skeleton's. She found the water in her pitcher frozen as slick as the skating rink back home.

Blast.

She'd have to take care of her ablutions downstairs. After putting her toothbrush in the pocket of her skirt, as well as her hairbrush and pins, she pulled her warm beaver cape more closely around herself. She opened the door a few inches and peered out into the dark hall.

Nothing.

No ghost. No vampires. And no light.

Why hadn't Miss Hallsey, or someone else, thought to light the lamps up here? Two unlit lanterns sat on the landing table. Surely, the clerk knew how dark the third floor could be. Poppy would be sure to mention the oversight. She glanced at the door of the vacant room across the way. Plenty of places for monsters to hide.

Something smacked the hallway window, making Poppy cry out. She slammed her door shut, her heart almost leaping from her chest as she stood like a statue, unable to move.

What should she do? She had to eat. She had to get down to where it most certainly would be warmer. She glanced at her lamp. Should she bring it along? That must have been a bird, or squirrel, *or something else*. But in case she had to run, she'd leave the heavy, cumbersome light behind. No sense in weighing herself down.

She blew out the lamp, exited, and locked her door. Taking a deep breath, she felt her way along the wall to the stairway. Each step felt like ten feet. Sensing an eerie stare on her back, she glanced over her shoulder and trembled. She'd never been frightened of her own shadow before. What had happened to her gumption?

It has flown out the window with the warmth and the light.

The narrow stairway cast in darkness didn't help. Every few steps, a loud squeak announced her progress. A lamp was burning on a hallway table on the second floor. *How thoughtful.*

Spurred on and feeling a little better, Poppy proceeded. When she reached the painting of the frightful old woman she'd noticed yesterday as she'd checked in, she kept her face averted. Yesterday, the hag's eyes, swallowed up in a crinkled old face, had caught Poppy off guard as the old woman's murderous stare seemed to follow Poppy's every move. She wouldn't look again, she told herself as she hurried past.

With a huge intake of breath, Poppy arrived in the lobby. She halted on the last step. Only two lamps flickered, leaving the place in shadows. The meager light in the vacant room reflected the ever-falling snow outside.

Sounds echoed from the dining area.

Relief washed through Poppy. She'd made it down alive. She rushed on, eager to speak with someone, anyone, perhaps even Oscar.

"Here you are, miss." Lenore Saffelberg approached, holding a tray with two coffee cups and spoons. She stopped midsentence and looked Poppy up and down. The rail-thin woman's chin actually elevated. She was bundled in her coat, although her apron hung out the bottom. Her nose was red.

"The water in my room is frozen solid," Poppy said, in explanation of her disheveled state of dress, smoothing down one side of her hair. "I couldn't clean up, even though I tried." She resisted leveling the complaint how in Boston, or even other less prosperous places, establishments provided light, heat, and water.

"Cook has a pot of warm water on the stove for that purpose. Would you like that now, or after you eat?"

"Now, please." Poppy glanced into the dining room where a few tables were occupied—but no Oscar.

"Very well. Follow me."

Ten minutes later, cleaned up and sipping a cup of dark coffee, Poppy relaxed in her booth. An older couple in a table on the other side of the room held hands across the tablecloth and spoke in hushed whispers. The dining room was a bit warmer than upstairs, but not by much. She wrapped her cape more firmly around herself, wishing for several pairs of wool socks. Her toes felt like chunks of ice.

Would she really be stuck in Y Knot all winter? Maybe even in this hotel? The possibility had sounded farfetched the first time she'd heard it, but now? And where was Oscar? She'd expect him to be here eating while reading a newspaper, outdated or not.

Miss Saffelberg arrived with a plate of scrambled eggs, potatoes, and toast. "Here you are."

"Thank you." The food on the plate looked delicious. "Can you tell me why it's so dark in here?" She gestured around to the tables. "There are many more lamps you could light."

"We have a limited supply of oil. Without the stage to bring in more, we have to be prudent and make our stock last."

Heavens! This *was* the Wild West. "Please tell me you have plenty of food."

The waitress nodded.

Poppy clenched a handful of white tablecloth. "And firewood—lots of it?"

Impatience crossed the woman's narrow face. "Yes. Wood shouldn't be a problem."

"Thank goodness for that. I need more in my room. I used most I had last night."

Miss Saffelberg looked down her nose, an easy thing to accomplish since she was standing and Poppy was sitting, but somehow, she made her feelings known. "That's something you'll need to tell Miss Hallsey. I'm only a waitress and seldom leave the dining area. She takes care of the guest rooms and anything that needs doing."

"Oh yes, of course. Miss Hallsey." Poppy felt at the mercy of this hotel, as she never had before to anyone in her life. A port in the storm, so to speak. "Is Miss Hallsey here yet this morning?"

"Somewhere. She lives on premises. Her room is just past the office."

That's handy. "Thank you. I'll find her," Poppy said, glancing past the woman's formidable barricade of garments to the shadowy room beyond. The place loomed larger than it had in the happy burning lamps last night at supper.

Watching Miss Saffelberg walk away, Poppy picked up her fork. Although the fare was only simple eggs and potatoes, it tasted like a feast. She took her time spreading butter on the toast, followed by jam, savoring every bite.

A window on the wall faced out to a small building and an open lot behind. The day had lightened some, but the storm had not let up. Judging by the tree trunks, the snow must already be two feet deep. Snowstorms in Boston never mattered much because their Georgian mansion had everything anyone could need for years, as well as a staff to cook, clean, and fetch.

Poppy blinked back her dismay at finally realizing just how entitled her upbringing had been. She glanced around the quiet room. *This is how real people live. Like Kathryn and Tobit. Like the rest of Kathryn's friends.*

Oscar walked through the doorway, his usually perfectly combed russet hair a mess. He was bundled in his coat and wool scarf. The scowl on his face reminded her all too much of her father. Seeing him spot her, she gave him a little wave.

Giving her a nod, he started over, and Poppy prepared herself for the outburst that was sure to come. He scooted in across from her without saying a word.

This could be far worse than she expected. Oscar Scott, if one thing, was direct when upset. He didn't mince words. By his pained, entitled expression, she knew he was about to let loose.

In no mood to hear his tirade, she put up her hand. "Before you say anything, Ossy, just remember one thing."

He drilled her with his gaze but kept silent.

"You *begged* me to come along. When I told you no, you all but blackmailed me that you would inform my father of my intentions. You have no one to blame but yourself."

"I've been thinking about that all night as I struggled to stay alive. How foolish I was." He cupped his hands and blew into them. "One trip to this godforsaken town should have been enough. I should have learned my lesson. But no, I didn't want any harm to come to you—"

"The hotel's not that bad."

"No? I'm literally frozen." He held out his reddened hands. "I've never suffered as I did last—"

"Hush. Here comes the waitress."

Miss Saffelberg was back. "Coffee, sir?"

"What do you think?"

Poppy gasped. "Oscar."

Miss Saffelberg's tray wobbled in her hands and her nostrils flared. She'd already picked up the full mug she'd intended to set on the table but halted halfway.

"Of course I want coffee." He lifted his face defiantly. "An imbecile would know that, if for no other reason than to thaw out my frozen hands. The water in my room is rock solid, as well. I really must complain."

"You're being rude," Poppy exclaimed. "Say you're sorry, Oscar. Miss Saffelberg can't help the weather or the dropping temperature."

The waitress set the mug back on her tray none too gently, ignoring the liquid that sloshed over her hand. She turned on her heel.

"Wait." Oscar thrust out his hand. "I said I *do* want the coffee. Come back here this instant."

With a ramrod-straight spine, Miss Saffelberg marched into the kitchen.

Poppy glared at him. "Now you've done it."

She was so angry, she felt like stomping away herself, but she didn't have anywhere to go. She had little wood in her room, and at least here she had someone to speak with. Passing the whole day in this booth might be her only option.

"Like it or not, Oscar Scott, you're dependent on these *kind* people. You better watch what you say—as you should, anyway. The world does not revolve around you."

Chapter Sixteen

With the way Morgan was looking at June, Shad thought it best to change the subject. "We appreciate you putting up our animals," he said. "The ride into Y Knot sapped our horses—and us more than a little, truth be told. We're thankful you could make room."

"And that you have your stove burning good and hot," Francis mumbled.

June gave a small laugh, then elbowed Shad in the ribs. She was a playful one.

"You know I always make room for the Heart of the Mountain's horses—and their riders, of course. You're some of the best men I know."

Smokey directed a pointed stare her way, all the while blowing into his hands, his shoulders shivering. "You'd make room for any horse, not just ours."

She grinned as she shrugged. "Guess you're right."

She looked mighty small in her heavy wool coat. Even with her woodstove cranking out the heat, the barn was plenty cold, but at least frost wasn't still streaming out on their breath.

Having June for a sweetheart was sure handy for Morgan. Gave him somewhere to rest his backside during the long winter months. His furniture shop was just up the street a short distance. The business was new, and he was still getting the place off the ground. That would change as more people moved to Y Knot.

Shad had seen Morgan's work. He was good. Enough people didn't live around here to keep him working full time, though. Because of it, he'd kept his job working the lumberyard with his brother-in-law, Hayden Klinkner.

"You know I'm right." Smokey laughed. "If an outlaw stepped through the door and asked for shelter, you'd put him up without question. You're too softhearted, June. It'll get ya into trouble someday."

Morgan slung his arm over June's shoulders as if she were one of the men. "Nothing's gonna happen to June. I'll see to that."

Smokey harrumphed and pressed his hands out to the warmth of the stove.

"I just might stay in here all day," Francis said, quivering like a cornstalk in the wind. "You and Smokey go check out the town." He looked at Shad. "I can tell you honestly, I'm not looking forward to the ride back to the ranch. I can't never remember the temperature being this cold before."

Shad hitched his head. They wouldn't get things done huddled around June Pittman's woodstove. "Let's go see if Brandon's in his office. I think I saw a light in the jailhouse window. Best get things done, and head back to the ranch."

Anxious shouts sounded outside.

Morgan pulled open one door far enough for everyone to see out. The snow was still a solid sheet of white. "What is it?" he asked.

Another couple of shouts came from up the road. Soon, a dilapidated Conestoga appeared. It came slowly, Brandon Crawford at the lines. Justin Wesley, the new deputy, rode alongside, leading Brandon's horse. The two-horse team pulling the wagon looked about dead on their feet.

"Someone caught off guard?" Shad shouted in the wind before jogging out to meet the wagon.

"Can't stop," Brandon shouted back. "Found these folks a few miles out of town, and they need help. They're nearly froze to death. Taking 'em to the hotel."

With that, he slapped the lines over the rail-thin horses that struggled in the harness, and they lumbered forward. The wagon disappeared in the wall of white as it rounded the corner and out of sight.

Shad turned to the others, who'd trailed him outside.

"I'll go for Dr. Handerhoosen," Francis said quickly. The youth, all business now, had a darn good head on his shoulders. "They'll most likely need a doctor."

Shaking her head, June grasped his arm. "Last I heard, Doc's over in Pine Grove. No telling when he'll return."

Trouble had arrived even without them searching. Was this the last, or would they find more unsuspecting people stranded in some snowbank? If there were, they wouldn't live long in this cold.

Shad glanced at the worried faces. "Whatever needs doing, we'll have to do ourselves. We best get moving. Brandon and Justin need our help."

Chapter Seventeen

At the Holcomb ranch, Mrs. Seymour paced the front room, waiting for Evelyn to come out of the bedroom. Now that her goddaughter was getting so large, she'd complained she was finding sleep difficult, and so wasn't able to rise when she normally would. Margaret stopped at the window, the sheer volume of snow that had accumulated overnight sent chilling thoughts through her mind.

I'm not qualified to deliver Evelyn's baby. I've only been to one birthing—and that poor darling creature died. That's why I've been so eager to arrive. Make sure Chance knows how important it is to have a doctor present when the time comes.

She swallowed nervously, gazing at the snow. Evelyn had been born three weeks early. Because of it, Margaret had missed her delivery altogether. *Nothing bad will happen to my Evelyn. I'll make sure of that.*

Earlier, she'd cooked breakfast for Chance. His attempts to quell her nerves had fallen on deaf ears.

He'd assured Margaret they'd get Evelyn into town days before the baby arrived. They still had an entire month to go before the birth. There wasn't a storm in Montana that could last that long, he'd said, and insisted he'd carry his Evie the whole way himself, if he had to.

The hired hand, Andy Lovell, had come in too, since he took all meals with the family. They'd eaten, bundled up, and headed outside, leaving her in the quiet to her disturbed thoughts.

"Good morning." Evelyn stepped through her bedroom door, bundled in a warm robe. She ran a hand through her abundant blond curls falling freely around her shoulders. When she glanced at the clock, her eyes widened. "My. It's almost ten o'clock. I'm sorry for leaving you to do all the cooking for the men. Have they been gone long?"

At the beautiful sight of her, Margaret felt her frown dissolve. "Good morning, Evelyn. An hour or so, but you know I enjoy cooking. Makes me feel young again."

Evelyn laughed. "You're not old at all."

Today, worrying over the baby, Margaret felt every one of her forty-five years. "You already know what I think of your fine husband, but I'm coming to admire the young hired hand, as well. Much can be said for the school of hard knocks. He's very polite and appreciative."

Evelyn went to the teakettle and poured hot water into the cup Margaret had earlier prepared. "I agree. From the moment we met, Chance took to him. Me, as well. He's been a great help. Chance has much more time to spend with me. The strain has left his eyes. And with the baby coming next month, I'll appreciate that even more, I'm sure."

Margaret pulled out a chair at the table. "Now, sit." She went to the counter and took a yeasty roll from the stack and placed it on Evelyn's plate, and brought it to the table. "You can start on this while I scramble your eggs." She opened the stove and, with a folded towel, withdrew a plate that held a few strips of bacon, then set that on a trivet in front of her.

Evelyn eased into her chair. "This looks delicious."

"It's just bacon and a roll," Margaret answered. "Nothing fancy. Remember the soufflés Dona used to make every Sunday morning back in St. Louis?" She closed her eyes in appreciation. "*Those* were delicious."

Evelyn slipped a portion of bacon into her mouth and chewed. "How could I forget? Yes, they were delicious, but this is too." She held up what was left of the bacon. "As hostess, I'm supposed to be waiting on you, Margaret, not the other way around." She picked up the roll, broke it apart, and took a bite. "Mmm, just like Dona's."

"You don't think the brides-to-be were the only ones taking note of her instructions, do you?" Margaret couldn't hold in a sentimental laugh, thinking about her beautiful Victorian house, the large-boned woman who acted more like an army sergeant than a cook, the array of mail-order brides, and all the fun they'd had.

Evelyn took another bite, a sound of admiration escaping her throat. "Ina taught me to make a mean biscuit, but I'd be indebted if you'd show me how to make these." She slathered the second half with butter and jam, and it disappeared into her mouth.

Margaret glanced over her shoulder as she stirred the eggs in the hot butter. Evelyn was the daughter of her heart. The daughter she'd never had. She'd do anything for her... anything except deliver her baby. The risks were just too large. So many horrible things could happen.

Pushing the eggs with her spoon, she blinked away the fear she'd been trying so hard to ignore. "Of course I will, Evelyn. Today, if you'd like."

Chapter Eighteen

At a clamoring noise in the lobby, Poppy jumped from her dining room seat, her meal forgotten. Voices shouted, and men called out. Without waiting for Oscar or Miss Saffelberg, she hurried down the hall to where the deputy held open the door to the blustering storm.

The sheriff came through carrying a very young child, a girl, whose eyes were closed.

Fear ricocheted through Poppy's chest. *Poor little thing. I hope she's not dead.*

A woman staggered inside next. Her arms were wrapped tightly around her thin body, and ice had crusted her face. Poppy ran over, and with an arm around the woman's waist, helped her toward the lobby stove.

A cowboy she didn't know, carrying a little boy, was next. And then Shad Petty, the cowhand who had taken supper with them two nights ago at Kathryn's. In his arms was a replica of the other little girl Sheriff Crawford had set in the chair. Her matted hair was pressed against Mr. Petty's large chest, her hands outstretched as if waiting for something.

Poppy left the woman by the stove and dashed over, remembering in that moment that he was the cowboy she'd seen in Virginia. The one who'd been hurt by the bull. *What a small, crazy world.* The incident felt like a different lifetime ago. The way she and the woman had carried on that day brought an embarrassed blush to her cheeks, and a prick of shame heated her face.

"Give her to me, Mr. Petty," she said, reaching for the little thing. As he handed her over, cold zipped through Poppy's layers of clothing. She hugged the child close and hurried to the warmth of the woodstove now surrounded by people.

Finally, a large man stumbled inside with the support of the deputy. The reek of whiskey filled the room.

Mr. Petty stepped forward as Poppy pushed closer, her precious cargo nestled quietly in her arms. She worried over the other children and glanced around. Miss Hallsey held the girl that had been in the chair, and Miss Saffelberg the boy.

"What should we do?" Poppy asked, knowing instinctively time was of the essence.

"See to the children first," Brandon Crawford barked. "Remove their wet clothing and wrap them up the best you can. Justin and I have to go back out. The fella mumbled something about others lost in the storm."

The man he spoke of lay on the floor, unaware of what was happening.

Brandon looked around the room. "Any volunteers to help?"

All the men in the room stepped forward.

"Good. I was hoping you would. Smokey, Francis, Morgan, get mounted." He looked at Mr. Petty. "Can you handle things here?"

"I can. But I think I'd be more help to you."

The sheriff was already heading for the door. "No telling when we'll make it back. I'm putting you in charge. I've never seen a storm like this. A man needs to stay here, be in charge."

Brandon's intense gaze sent shivers up Poppy's spine. This was bad, very bad.

He glanced at the window and shook his head. "We don't have time to lose."

Poppy thought of Oscar. Where was he? He could help.

Mr. Petty ran a hand through his hair. "Fine, then. I'll handle it."

"Good," Sheriff Crawford said. "We'll be back as soon as we can."

"I'll tend to their horses," June said, still wearing her coat. "The pitiful things are so thin, they might drop in their tracks."

"Be sure to go with the men, June. It's easy to get turned around in a whiteout. We don't want to lose anyone today." Brandon's tone was ripe with meaning.

Poppy hugged the tiny girl closer, unconsciously rubbing her back as she worried about Kathryn. Tobit and Isaiah would keep her safe, wouldn't they? Sure, the men had experience living in Montana, but as the sheriff said, not much was needed to get lost in a whiteout.

Glancing at the window agitated her thoughts. These poor, half-frozen people testified to the fact the situation at hand was much more dire than she'd ever imagined.

"Francis, keep your wits about you," Shad called, feeling responsible for the younger lad who reminded him all too much of his brothers. "I don't want to hear you've gotten yourself lost."

"I've been riding these snowy hills a lot longer than you have, Petty," Francis shot back, heading for the door.

Shad recalled his statement earlier about staying in the livery all day and getting warm. Not much chance of that happening now. Didn't seem like any of them would be warm today. Or for a long time to come.

After the door closed behind the last man, Shad glanced around. Lenore Saffelberg, Hildy Hallsey, Cook, and an old couple he didn't know.

Miss Poppy Ford was here. She'd been the one who'd taken the child from his arms. Her hold on the little ragamuffin was gentle as she rubbed her back. He supposed her friend Oscar Scott was here, as well—somewhere.

"All right, listen up. We need to warm these people up slowly. That means one blanket, in a heated room, but nothing more."

Miss Ford stepped closer, shifting the child in her arms. "Shouldn't we soak their hands and feet in hot water? I've heard that's what one does for frostbite."

"No. Slowly warming their core is best. Don't rub their hands and feet. Be careful with their skin. Keep them quiet and handle them gently." Coming from Wyoming, he had plenty of experience with snow and extreme cold. He looked at Miss Hallsey. "Pick one of the guest rooms and stoke the fire. Put the children and their ma into the bed to share body heat, get them some bed warmers, and cover them with one blanket. Go on now, get moving."

"What about the man?" Hildy asked. "He's their pa."

Shad had a strange feeling about the liquored-up fellow. *What father, or what man, took to drinking in a situation where his wife's and children's lives are at stake?* "Put him on a pallet on the floor. He's stronger. He'll be okay."

Hildy rushed to the stairway, followed by Lenore and Poppy, helping along the mother. The cook headed back to the restaurant, as did the old couple.

That's when he saw the easterner watching from the shadows. "Scott," he said in his no-nonsense tone. "There's wood stacked out back. Bring in plenty to the kitchen and lobby."

The man's shoulders snapped back. "I don't work here," he replied stiffly. "I'm a guest."

Shad could feel the scowl on his face. "Not anymore. No telling how long this storm will last. We need as much wood inside as possible. As a matter of fact, take some to each occupied room and stack it outside the doors to make things easier."

"I'll do no such thing."

As Shad came closer, Scott's eyes bulged. "I guess you won't be needing any of that wood yourself. Or sustenance. Either pitch in, or get out."

The corner of Scott's left eye twitched several times before he replied, "When you put it like that, I don't have much of a choice now, do I?"

"No, you don't. Get moving."

Shad turned on his heel and followed the women with the children, leaving the man passed out on the rug. Shad would deal with him as soon as the others were seen to. The drunk had enough rotgut inside to keep him out for hours, but the others didn't.

Chapter Nineteen

In the upstairs bedroom of the Heart of the Mountains, Sally unpacked her travel bag, thankful to be out of the storm. Once Roady had seen her safely delivered into the ranch house and Claire's capable hands, he'd left with Luke, eager to get back to work.

This storm seemed to have everybody rattled, not just her. The men weren't letting on, but everyone she encountered had a furrowed brow, and worry lurked in their eyes. Claire had invited Sally to tea as soon as she had her things settled.

Being in the same bedroom she'd used right after she and Roady had married brought back many memories. Sweet, anxious, and ones where she'd thought her life would never turn out right. The comfortable chair in the corner was the same where she and Roady had gotten to know each other. Many hours were passed there, along with the other chair he'd brought in from across the hall. They'd married as strangers but soon they'd became friends, and so much more. After setting the last of her things in the dresser drawer, she carefully pushed it closed.

Earlier, she'd set her unopened letter against an empty vase on top of the highboy. She studied the post for several seconds.

She had no idea about the handwriting and should open it. Find out. Put her fears to rest—but Claire McCutcheon was waiting.

"Hi, Miss Sally."

Turning, she found Hickory standing in the doorway. The boy's lopsided grin always pulled her heartstrings. "Hello, Hickory. I heard you'd be here, as well. I'm delighted we'll have some time together."

He ducked his head.

"I didn't get a chance when you visited last Friday to ask you about school. Do you like it?"

"I guess it's all right. I'm learning a lot." He lifted one shoulder. "I don't like it when the older boys make fun of me, though."

She came forward and crouched down to his level. "What do you mean? Not Billy, Colton, or Adam, I hope."

"Naw, none of them. They're nice enough. Other boys. They don't like my long hair. Call me a little girl. But I ain't gonna cut it."

Sick at heart, she straightened and beckoned him inside her room. He slowly came forward.

"Of course you're not." She went to the bed and sat on the edge. He followed her over. "You can't worry about what other people say. My mother used to tell me it's when they stop talking about you that you should worry. They're just trying to get attention. If you ignore them, even though that's difficult, your newness will eventually wear off, and they'll leave you alone. Do they ever hit or punch you?"

"Not since Billy busted the ringleader's lip."

Sally stifled a smile. Seemed the McCutcheons took charge, no matter what age they were. "I see. Well, good for him. Some children are hardheaded and need a bit of encouragement to straighten up. If you're ever being punched or hit, you let someone know. You shouldn't have to put up with that. You can come to me anytime."

He squared his small shoulders, his expression earnest. "I can take care of myself, well enough. Been doing so for a long time. I was ready to do something about the troublemaker before Billy stepped in."

Hickory smiled, but she could see the hurt in his eyes. No one liked to be bullied.

"Oh, look." She went to the dresser for the book she'd laid on top and handed him the volume. "Scary stories. Perfect for a snowy afternoon. Let's read some a bit later, after I have tea with Mrs. McCutcheon. Would you like that?"

His gaze was fixed on the skeleton drawing on the cover. "Scary stories? They're my favorite."

"Mine too. Most children like them. The majority aren't really that scary, just unusual. I thought they'd be fun while we're snowed in. It also has some very interesting drawings. Go ahead and take it to your room. Mrs. McCutcheon is waiting for me in the living room, and I'd like to freshen up. When I'm back, we'll read some together."

Hickory looked up into her eyes and smiled.

Back on the large bed Hickory would be sleeping in tonight, he thumbed through the pages of the heavy book. The drawings were done in great detail. He didn't try to read any pages; the words looked much more difficult than anything he could handle. He was more interested in the art. His father had liked to draw, and his mother had said many times that his father should try to sell some of his work. That was before they'd ventured west, and Hickory had lost his family to sickness.

Filled with memories, he slowly traced the straight line of a barn roof on a hill overlooking a cornfield. He missed his family. With them, he hadn't been a misfit needing charity to survive. He liked the McCutcheons just fine. They were plenty nice and caring, especially Luke. Nevertheless, he'd been a part of his own family once. And the thought that he'd never see them again always shut down his heart.

Hickory gazed at the drawing. Something about it made him uneasy. The way the cornstalks swayed in the wind, almost looked as if faces were peering out between the golden-brown stalks.

He flipped the page. The stories were short, just a page or two. Here a sheepdog watched a flock of sheep by a pleasant river in the sunshine. That was appealing, considering the unrelenting snow hadn't stopped since yesterday. Hickory clenched his cold fingers as a shudder moved through his small frame. What could be scary about this story, he couldn't imagine. Maybe he and Miss Sally would read this one.

Skipping to the back, he came upon a drawing that filled both pages. It was a night scene, with a cave illuminated by the light of a crescent moon. Several wolves sat at the entrance of the den. On the opposite page, a crouching man waited behind a hedge as a rancher walked from a barn toward a dilapidated house. The hunkered man had hairy arms and legs, and large pointed ears. His eyes were just slits. The wolf man's fangs made Hickory shiver. Three other wolves sat beyond the house, howling at the moon. Two frightened children peered from the window.

Unnerved, he slammed shut the book.

"Hickory, is everything all right?" Sally stood at the door.

"Thought I heard Mrs. McCutcheon callin' me."

"Really? I didn't hear her." Her gaze took in the book on the bedspread. "I hope those drawings didn't frighten you. Some are pretty creepy, but not all."

"No, ma'am."

Scooting by, he ran down the hall, not wanting her to discover he was a scaredy-cat. For several years, he'd lived alone on the streets of Waterloo. He'd not let some silly drawings get under his skin.

He wondered what Colton was doing today. He wished Luke had taken him there, to be with someone his own age.

Arriving on the upper landing, he stole down the large staircase without making a sound or drawing Mrs. McCutcheon's attention. At the bottom, he made a sharp turn into the small reading library and went straight to the window. His deep breath whooshed out onto the glass.

The tall pine trees outside, now covered in white, loomed tall at the clearing's edge, making the side yard look very different. The wolves must be plenty hungry. He'd heard the men talking. This year everyone was warned to be on alert.

Chapter Twenty

"There you are," Claire McCutcheon said as Sally descended the stairs. Claire's chair was pulled close to the fire. On the table beside her were two cups, a pair of spectacles, and a six-inch cross-stitch hoop with an unfinished breakfast scene done in colorful ribbon. "Did you get settled?" she asked.

"I did. Thank you. It's lovely to be back. The room aroused a flurry of nice memories."

"Some unsettling ones too?"

How did Claire do that? The woman seemed so in tune with everyone. She must have been thinking about the talk she'd given Sally those first rocky days when she and Roady were just coming to terms with their hasty marriage, the misunderstandings, and some hurt feelings. Unmarried and with child. What would she have done without Roady then? He'd come to her rescue.

"Yes. The interval hasn't been all that long since our hurried wedding." She gave a small laugh. "And now I'm a happily married woman." Claire hadn't known about the growing babe inside her. She hadn't known how much Roady had sacrificed to help her.

"And now you're expecting." Claire patted her heart. "I can't wait to hold that little one. I have a feeling you're going to have a boy."

Sally nodded and touched the front of her skirt. "Yes, I think that, as well." For some odd reason, Sally's thoughts flew to the unopened letter sitting on the highboy. Why hadn't she taken one moment and at least opened it? Who was it from? No one could hurt her now, or her little one.

I didn't want to keep Claire waiting.

Not so, her conscience whispered. *It's something else. Something is in that letter I don't want to read.*

"Well, sit and drink your tea. It must be cold by now. I can take it into the kitchen and get some warm water, if you'd like."

Sally made herself comfortable, enjoying the heat of the fire on her face. "Oh no, this is fine. I like my tea lukewarm anyway, so this will be perfect."

"While you were getting settled, Flood stopped in. All the horses have been divided between the ranches and put in the barns." Claire picked up her stitching and began to work. "Next year, when we build another, we won't run into this kind of problem. That will be a blessing."

Taking a sip of her tea, Sally listened. She had a lot to learn to become a proper rancher's wife. They'd put the horses inside. What would happen to the cattle that had to stay out?

"I've been thinking about my sister Heather. I hope they were prepared for this storm. I wish there was some way to contact them. Having a telephone would be nice, like some do in large cities. Can you imagine just calling someone up and asking?"

"I know what you mean. But don't worry. The Klinkners have lived in Y Knot for years, and they know how to weather a Montana winter. They're snug enough in their house. All you need to do is rest and relax, and anticipate the coming of your little one. How is Roady adjusting to married life? Every time I see him, he has a smile on his face."

"I believe he's satisfied with the way things are," she said, taking another sip of the warm brew. She hoped he was. He said he was, but could he say different if that weren't the truth?

Claire smiled and snuggled deeper into the blanket on her lap. "I thought as much. Have you heard from home? How's your family? Your sister Melba? I know you and Heather are concerned for her fragile health."

"The last I heard, she is still doing well. Before I came out, she said she would be the next one to venture to Y Knot. This coming year, in fact. I don't believe my mother will go along with that idea, but my little sister can be very persuasive when she wants to be."

"Perhaps our mountain air will be just the thing to get her completely well." Claire's brows lowered. "How old is she?"

"Going on sixteen."

"That's plenty old enough. You should encourage her visit. I was a married woman by that age." Claire's eyes twinkled in the firelight, a silly expression pulling at her lips.

Sally couldn't imagine Melba a married woman. For that matter, imagining herself a wife and mother-to-be was difficult. Where had the time gone? She wouldn't trade her life for another, if she were offered. As long as things stayed as they were now, with her and Roady, and the little one to come.

Again, the letter moved into her thoughts. This was silly. She needed to open it and put all her fears to rest. And she would. Just as soon as she ventured upstairs.

Chapter Twenty-One

Exhausted, but happy with the progress of the cold, frightened children, Poppy made her way up the squeaky stairway to the third floor, intending to change out of her damp dress and clean up. She'd gone into the kitchen and retrieved a pan of warm water, which she balanced in her grasp along with a candleholder and lighted candle.

The hallway was dark and cold. Although as leery with her surroundings as a cat in a barn full of dogs, Poppy was too worn out to worry overmuch about the painting of the hag on the second-story landing or anything else. Keeping her gaze glued to the steps so she wouldn't stumble on her hem, she slowly climbed the stairs.

She, Hildy, and Lenore had stripped the three frail children of their damp clothing and bundled them into garments they'd gathered from their own belongings and donations from other guests. The attire was much too large but would work to warm the children up. Then they'd put them in one large bed together and laid a blanket over top while Mr. Petty brought the fire to its capacity.

The poor befuddled mother could do little more than sit in a chair, shiver, and wipe the tears that never stopped. When they'd offered her dry garments, she'd refused, saying she'd be fine now that they were out of the storm.

The heavyset fellow was a different animal entirely. Poppy didn't like him. She'd seen his kind before, down at the Boston docks. Drunken, coarse, with a gaze as sharp as a knife's edge, even if he was inebriated. To endanger his family as he had was unforgivable. The children were lucky to be alive. He was in the same room, sleeping on a pallet close to the fireplace.

At the third floor, Poppy stepped onto the upper landing, noting someone had come up and lit one of the hall lanterns. She jerked to a halt when she saw Shad Petty stacking wood at the foot of her door. Startled, she glanced around the dim landing. Outside the window, what could be seen of the sky had darkened, even though it was yet midday. The snow had not let up.

"Mr. Petty, I didn't expect to find you here."

"Well, I expected you. I heard you squeaking up the stairs from the first floor." He smiled.

Her heart gave a small squeeze. His clothes, rumpled from the last hour of work with the rescued family, looked almost as bad as her own.

"Just wanted to make sure you had wood to last. I told your friend, Mr. Scott, to bring some up, but just as I thought, he hasn't gotten around to the chore yet." He glanced to the window. "Now that you're here, if you open the door, I can stack it inside."

"I can do that." She glanced at her full hands. "No need for you to—"

"Nonsense. We all need to pull together. Actually, seeing you here today was a surprise."

"I was trying to get home to Boston, only to find the stage has stopped running."

His eyes met hers with a look of amusement. "I'm afraid you're stuck for the time being. After lunchtime, you should stay down in the dining room where it's warmer, just until the storm breaks."

The long frigid hours of last night had been agony. She set the candleholder on the small table and cupped her hands around the warm pot of water. "I suppose you're right. What about the others? The men who went out searching in the storm? I'm worried about them. Shouldn't they have already returned?"

His brow furrowed. "Yeah, I expected them back too. A body can't stay out too long in this. I suspect they've holed up somewhere else." He strode to the hall window, even though there wasn't much to see but white. "Herrick's Leather Shop, the mercantile, maybe back at the livery or the sheriff's office by now. Just as soon as I'm finished here, I'm going out to take a look."

Mr. Petty glanced down at her since she'd followed in his tracks. He didn't look all that confident.

She resisted the impulse to lay her hand on his arm. "You should eat something first, to keep you warm." Seeing his expression in the shadowy hallway was difficult, but she thought she saw a small smile on his lips.

He shrugged. "Do you know where your friend has disappeared to?"

"My friend?"

"Mr. Scott. Everyone needs to pitch in. He didn't bring the wood upstairs, so I'll take him with me when I go. No telling what we might find. I may need some help."

"I'm sorry, I don't. But he's never been one to help. I think you'll be disappointed."

Mr. Petty straightened, and his mouth pulled down in a frown. "He'll *learn* to follow my orders and pitch in, or he can find somewhere else to live. I don't care who he is. Sheriff Crawford put me in charge. Scott won't be treated differently than any other man."

With no defense for Oscar, she turned, set the pot of water on the table, and fished in her pocket for her room key. After unlocking the door, she took up the candle and pot and stepped inside. "No, I wouldn't think so." She glanced over her shoulder and had to look up to see his face.

He waited at her threshold. "You mind if I bring in the wood?" He gestured to the pile of logs he'd deposited by her door.

"Not at all. I appreciate your help very much."

Not wasting any time, he stacked the wood by her fireplace and soon had a fire burning.

Ice crystals had formed on the inside of her window and her mirror. The air was so frigid, you could store meat anywhere you'd like.

"It's darn cold up here. I think it best to ask Hildy to move you downstairs, where it's warmer. Not much heat reaches up those stairs."

"I'm fine here, thank you."

"What's going on?"

Poppy swung around to Oscar's angry voice. He stood in the doorway, his hands fisted at his sides, his face a picture of jealousy.

In a swift movement, Mr. Petty stood. "What the deuce does it look like, Scott? I'm doing your job. You've had plenty of time to get the task done, and yet not a single room has the supply it will need for tonight. Where have you been, and what have you been doing? Hiding out to avoid work?"

Disdain oozed from Oscar's expression. "I don't answer to you."

"You sure as hell do."

Poppy put out her hands in an effort to calm the situation. She didn't want things to get out of control.

Oscar's chin jutted. "I don't like you in Miss Ford's room."

"Oscar, you have no right to speak to Mr. Petty that way. And you have no authority over me or to speak for me." She pointed a finger in his face. "I demand you leave this instant."

"I'll do no such thing while he's still in your room. Your father would be appalled to think that you're—"

Poppy threw back her shoulders. "What? Trying to stay warm? Trying not to freeze to death? I don't think Father would fault Mr. Petty for watching out for me, do you? For bringing me firewood when you refused to?"

Mr. Petty straightened his rumpled shirt, stained with grime. "Question is, Scott, what're *you* doing up here? I don't see any wood in your arms. And you never answered my question. Where have you been hiding out for the last few hours? I checked your room, but it was empty."

Oscar's lips curled, purpled by the cold, and his shoulders shivered. His eyes widened when the cowboy stepped closer. "I was in the kitchen."

"Helping? Or eating and making a pest of yourself?" Mr. Petty's voice held a mountain of disbelief. When Oscar didn't answer, he said, "Just hanging out in the warmest place available, but ducking out of sight when I came around? How fitting for a man like you. Question is, what are you doing up here? Your room is on the second floor."

Without another word, Oscar glared at Poppy, then turned on his heel and stalked away.

Mr. Petty followed to the door and called after him, "I'm going out to check on the others. You're going with me!"

Poppy was still in disbelief. What did Oscar expect of her? That she'd just fall in line? They'd never had a relationship like that. He was supposed to marry Kathryn from as far back as she could remember. She and Ossy had just been pals, never anything more. Was he angling to find a place in their family, one way or the other?

"He's a pleasant one," Mr. Petty said once they were alone. "I can see why you like him."

Poppy couldn't help laughing. What else could she do? He was right. The flames were building, and she looked forward to cleaning up. Lenore had said Cook would be serving meat and potatoes anytime they were hungry.

He glanced around the room and then lifted a shoulder. "Is there anything else you need?"

"No, thank you."

"Fine, then. I best get back downstairs."

"Will you be staying here, Mr. Petty? In the hotel, I mean? Do you need to go back to the ranch?"

"Under the circumstances, I won't be going anywhere for a while. The McCutcheons will know we got stuck here, I'm sure. They sent us to do what we could for the townsfolk, and that's what I'm doing." He gave her a shy smile. "I'm staying on, at least until we can get around town without too much trouble."

Relief washed through her. Poppy hadn't realized how much she was depending on his presence and his help. She trusted him.

"You're very good with the children," she said, delaying his departure. The fire felt good; she moved closer and held out her hands to the crackling flame.

"I have two younger brothers I practically raised when our grandma died. Mothering just comes natural."

She could see that. He'd been easy and calm with the youngsters today, and they'd clung to him like a lifeline, although not so with their own mother.

"I envy you. Kathryn is my only sister. We were close when we were young, but then we went our separate ways, it seems. I'm not really sure why."

They'd grown up in that big, empty house, playing with nannies and housemaids. Given everything except what really mattered most. She sighed, sorry that he would soon leave.

He ambled to the door, looking eager to be away.

"Go on; I'm fine. I'll see you downstairs for the noontime meal."

"Miss Ford." He tipped his hatless head and was gone.

Poppy closed the door and rested her back against the barrier. The room felt a bit cozier with the fire. A few flecks of heat were melting the inside ice crystals. Now that Mr. Petty was staying on, watching out for them all, she could relax.

At her dresser, she discovered the pot of water had gone tepid. She dipped in her washcloth and washed her face. Once the snowfall ended, they could shovel a path to the mercantile, and perhaps the telegraph office. Things wouldn't be bleak for long, and for that, she was thankful.

This was the adventure she'd been craving—and she should make the most of her time. Before long she'd be back in Boston, and then on her way to France, on a slow-moving steamship enjoying unimaginable luxuries. Just think, the trip of her dreams…

Still holding her washcloth, she moved to the window to see the flakes had become smaller and she could now make out a building or two. The wintery picture before her eyes was serene. Yes, she was looking forward to home and going abroad. Why then did the thought of leaving bring such a hollow feeling to her heart?

Chapter Twenty-Two

Fifteen minutes later, after consuming two large helpings of meat, potatoes, gravy, and biscuits, Shad layered on clothes by the light of a single candle. It wasn't as tasty as Lou's, but it sure filled his belly in a good way.

He could wait no longer. He needed to find out what had happened to the others. While the rest of the hotel occupants took their noon meal, he'd head out, being careful not to get turned around in the thick-falling snow. Shrugging into his waterproof leather duster that reached almost to the floor, he pulled on his hat and exited the small first-floor room Hildy had given him.

The lobby was empty. A few soft-spoken voices lilted out from the dining room. Almost at the door, Shad paused as a loud squeak from the staircase announced someone's arrival.

"Mr. Petty?"

He turned. Poppy Ford had changed and looked as if she'd layered on a few more garments as well. Her hair was pulled back instead of piled on her head as he'd seen it before, matching nicely the color of her expensive-looking beaver-skin cape. Wrist-length leather gloves covered her hands, and she held the candleholder he'd seen before.

She hurried forward. "What're you doing?" she asked in alarm. "Aren't you taking Oscar?"

"Decided I can cover more ground without him."

"But that's dangerous. Sheriff Crawford said so himself. You could get turned around."

Impatience moved him a step closer to the door. "I'm only going to inquire up and down the street. I won't get lost. If I have to go farther, I plan to come back and get *your friend.*"

When her mouth pulled down, he couldn't discern what displeased her more—his situation, or him calling Scott her friend. But he couldn't stop to wonder right now. The others had been gone too long, and he could feel the minutes floating down around him as quietly and relentlessly as the snowflakes in the storm outside.

"I see." The candleholder quivered in her hand.

"You go on and get some grub, and then stay in the kitchen or dining room where it's warmer. I don't expect I'll be back for some time, maybe an hour."

Her eyes widened.

"I won't be out in the storm the whole time. I'll be checking at the businesses. If I don't come back, don't come looking." He narrowed his gaze. "Just means the task is takin' longer than I thought. Or I've run into someone who needs help. You understand?"

Miss Ford nodded, looking like she didn't want him to go. He breathed deeply, pushing that warm thought away.

"I just checked on the little tykes," he said. "They're sleeping, and their hands don't look like frostbite set in. You did a good job."

"Thank you, Mr. Petty. We were just following your orders. As soon as they wake, I'll feed them more hot soup and tend their fire."

He nodded and started for the door. Funny, a couple of nights ago, out at the Preece farm, she didn't impress him as the kind of girl who would take to children—especially little ragamuffins who needed a good scrubbing—but that's exactly what she'd done. Trying not to think too long on that fact, he secured his scarf over his nose and mouth. When he pulled open the door, a pile of snow fell into the room. He glanced back.

"I'll get that," Miss Ford said softly. "Be careful."

With his head into the raging storm, he stepped high and then sank up to his calf. Under the overhang, the snow wasn't as deep as it was in the street. Dry, stinging snow slapped him in the face, and a bitter chill pricked around his eyes. Turning to make sure the door was securely closed, he saw Miss Ford watching at the window. With great effort, he plowed through the snow, intending to check the sheriff's office first.

Shad counted eight steps as he made his way into Brandon's office door. Thankful to be out of the wind, even though only seconds had passed, he glanced around the empty room. A lantern burned on the desk.

"Anyone here?" he called, thinking someone might be in the back. Wind whistled around the building. He strode to the woodstove and placed his hand on top. Barely warm. No one had been here for a while.

Opening the iron door, Shad fed a few logs into the fire. With no time to stand around, he pulled his hat down and stepped out into the storm. He crossed the street and pounded on Berta May's front door, leaning close to the wood. With the howling wind, she might not hear him.

After a few seconds, he tried the knob, which was locked. He pounded again and a second later, the door opened.

Berta May's face split into a smile. "Shad. Come in." She grasped his arm and dragged him into the fabric store, unmindful of the snow he brought along, and slammed the door closed. Same as at the sheriff's office, only one lantern illuminated the room. "What on earth are you doing? My goodness."

"Checking on you."

"That's mighty kind," she said, her voice softening. Just like Miss Ford, she was wearing layers of garments as well as a heavy coat.

"You have everything you might need for a few days, Berta May?" He blew hot breath into his gloved hands. "Food and firewood?"

"I sure do. No need to worry about me. Have you ever seen such a storm? At first, I was glad the snow had finally arrived, but now…" She shook her head slowly. "I don't know what to think."

"It'll let up soon. I'm looking for Brandon, Francis, and a few others. They went out searching for some people that are believed to be stranded."

"And you're getting worried?"

He nodded.

"I'm sorry, but no."

Disappointment descended, and he was anxious to be off.

"I haven't seen a thing," Berta May added apologetically. "I've been working on my needlepoint upstairs in bed under the covers. But what about Charity?" She stiffened. "Is she stuck alone in their little house behind the jail? I hate to think it."

"No. She's been out at the ranch for some time. Helping Rachel and Amy with the new babies."

"I see. That's a good thing, to my way of thinking," she muttered. "Better than to be snowed in here."

Shad turned for the door. "You have any problems, Berta May, you hang a piece of red fabric out your upstairs window. I'll see it. I'm staying at the hotel for the time being. You're welcome to join us, if you want."

"Thank you, but I'm fine here. Knowing you're across the street gives me some piece of mind, though." She touched his arm. "Be careful. Doesn't take long for life to be sapped out right through the skin."

Back outside, he passed Y Knot's small bank, the windows dark and empty. At the saloon, he gladly stepped inside.

Abe looked up from his stool behind the bar.

"Abe, you the only one here?" Shad glanced around, and then toward the upstairs rooms.

"Just little ol' me," the bartender replied, swamped in his clothing with a blanket wrapped around his shoulders. "You better come have a drink." He set a shot glass on the bar with shaky hands and reached for a whiskey bottle. He filled the glass to the brim.

"I like how you think."

Shad clomped forward as Abe refilled his own glass. Trying to stay his shivering, he reached for the glass and tossed it back. Whiskey had never tasted so good.

When the fiery heat finally left his throat, he asked, "You see Brandon or anyone else today?"

"At daybreak is all. Been only me since then."

"Fancy upstairs?"

"Yeah."

"I'm making the rounds up and down the street. Tell her to get a few things together. On my return to the hotel, I'll stop in and fetch her back with me, and that goes for you, as well. I'm sure she'd rather be with a few other folks at a time like this." He glanced back up the stairway. "Besides, her room can't be all that warm with this one measly stove down here to heat the whole building."

By Abe's expression, the bartender had taken offense. "I provide for us well enough. I have ta stay here and guard my whiskey. If I leave, I might get looted."

"Suit yourself. I'll be back for Fancy."

"Won't people mind?" Abe's mouth pulled down. "You know, living in the presence of a soiled dove."

"Don't care if they do. The hotel's a big place. If they take offense, they can stay in their room."

Abe picked up the coffee cup sitting next to his shot glass and took a sip. "Guess you're right. I'll tell her." He reached under the counter again and brought up a flask. "You better take this along." With difficulty, and an abundance of alcohol wasted on the bar top, Abe trickled whiskey into the small hole of the flask.

Shad nodded his thanks and stuffed the offering into his inside coat pocket. "Good of you."

Back outside, Shad leaned into the dry powder and kept the brim of his hat pulled down, shielding his face. Pushing through the snow that had accumulated on the boardwalk and up the sides of the buildings, he pressed forward, being careful not to slip or fall.

A building loomed up in front of his face. He tried the door. Finding it unlocked, he went inside.

"Tracy, you around?" he called out toward the stairway leading to the telegraph operator's upstairs living area. The dwarflike man was nowhere to be seen.

"Who's asking?" came a reply.

"Shadrack Petty. You doing all right?"

"Oh, Shad. 'Course I am. Come on in and warm yourself."

"Can't. Have things to do. You see Brandon, Morgan, Francis, or Smokey recently?"

"Did earlier," Mr. Tracy hollered back. "Leaving the hotel after that wagon unloaded. But nothing since then. Them people gonna live?"

"I 'spect so," Shad answered. His unease over the whereabouts of his friends was growing stronger. "I'm staying at the hotel. You have any problems over here, or need help, you hang something out your upstairs window."

"Something? Like what?"

"You got a bandanna?"

"Oh, sure."

"I gotta move on."

"Thanks for stopping in."

Outside, Shad stuck his head briefly inside the quiet bathhouse to find it empty. He glanced across the street. A light burned in the leather shop window. Good thing Trent Herrick had come home a few months back to look after his elderly father.

Lou and Drit's boarding house was next. Wasn't it just a few hours ago he was dreaming of Lou's hearty beef stew, a warm woodstove, and some friendly conversation?

With both hands, he worked the short gate forward and back a few times to get it open enough against the buildup of snow for him to get through, then proceeded up the walk. Before going in, he dusted off the best he could before making a beeline for the warm stove.

Lou, sitting on the couch, looked up when he came in and smiled. "Why, Shad, I'm surprised to see you. You come by for a bowl of stew? I have some cooking."

"Not today, but thank you kindly. I was thinkin' about your stew on my ride in, though. Everything all right with you?"

She nodded. "Sure."

"You see Brandon, Morgan, and the rest? I'm looking for 'em."

She stood, wrapping the plaid wool blanket she'd had on her lap over her shoulders. "Why, no, I haven't. The sheriff came by this morning to check on Drit and me. You don't think something has happened to 'em, do ya?"

No, he didn't, he told himself firmly. But being sure would ease his mind.

"Not exactly. Brandon and Justin brought in a wagon of people with some children. The fella was drunk, but Brandon thought he'd mumbled something about others. I stayed back in the hotel to see to things there, and Francis, Smokey, Justin, and Morgan went out searching. Don't know if they split up. Freezing temps are hard to take for long."

She stepped forward, wringing her hands. "You got that right. Drit said he saw a large wolf pack a week ago on his ride back from the sawmill. Was pretty rattled by the size. Now we got that to worry about too."

Shad nodded. "We saw signs on our ride in."

"The Lord's watching out for our friends," she said softly. "They'll be fine."

And my brothers as well...

She rubbed his arm. "Quit your worrying. I'll be praying. Now, let me get you some hot coffee before you venture back out. You must be frozen."

"Thanks, Lou, but I'll catch you next time. By the way, how many boarders you got staying?"

"One fella named Ned Thompson, who took a room last week. I don't know his business, but he's riding cross-country with a couple of mules. Haven't heard a peep from him today, though. The place is pretty quiet."

"Just keeping track of who's who and where they are. I'm at the hotel for a few days, if you need anything."

"Thank you. If anyone turns up, I'll send Drit down to let you know. He's gone across the street to Lichtenstein's for a few things—lamp oil the most important. Should be back soon."

"Maybe I'll see him. I just have the Biscuit Barrel left before I cross over."

Shad sucked warmth into his lungs before heading back out. He wondered if Reverend Crittlestick was up at the church. Maybe the storm took him by surprise, as well. If it had, the preacher would really be in a tight spot since the building had no living quarters. No harm in checking before starting back up the street. If not, he'd wonder all day.

"You stay safe," Lou called. "The stew's always on for you, Shad, and you know it."

And he did. He hoped Nick and Tanner were waiting out the storm someplace safe and warm. They'd like this town, if they got here in one piece.

When Shad opened the door, the wind, whistling under the porch, buffeted his hat and face. They were fine, he told himself. He'd accept no other option.

Chapter Twenty-Three

Sally paced the length of the living room worried about Roady. His safety was foremost in her mind. Growing up in St. Louis, she'd experienced snow, but not like this. Here, the wind bent the trees sideways as the tempest raced around the house with howling screams.

"I think I'll go and check on Hickory," she said when Claire reentered the room. "He looked a little lonely when I left him."

Actually, he looked scared. Perhaps her time would be better spent reading with the boy.

"That's a good idea," Claire said. "I've invited him to join us, but he's still very shy. Feels most comfortable with Lucky and the men. Still, I insisted Luke bring him here. Little ones are easy to misplace in times like this."

Sally hurried to the library, the last place he was headed when she'd come down for tea. From the hallway, she glanced into the dim room. Two lanterns were burning, but she didn't see him.

"Hickory," she called. "Are you in here?"

A small sound drew her attention to the large leather footstool. With his back to the furniture, he sat on the floor facing the window. He looked like a caged animal that longed to be set free.

"There you are." Sally approached. "I'm sorry I took so long to return. Time just slipped away."

He regarded her with an earnest gaze. The look reminded her of the first days after Luke brought him home from Waterloo.

"Shall we go into the front room where it's warmer? The fire's going strong." The air was downright cold in here. She wondered how he stood it.

"Naw, I like this room. Don't want to get in anyone's way."

"I see." Sally got comfortable on a small couch. "Did you bring the book I lent you?"

He shook his head. "Naw, I've been thinking, is all."

That's a long time for a boy to be thinking. What could possibly be on his mind?

He came and sat by her side. "You ever heard of werewolves?" he finally asked, studying her face.

"Werewolves?" she repeated, surprised. Then she remembered the last story in the book. She hadn't meant to cause him alarm. "Of course I have. But they're just made up to scare people. They're fictional."

"Fictional?"

"Pretend. Have you heard the wolves howling outside?"

He nodded, his anxious gaze slipping over to the window.

"Don't worry, Hickory. You're safe here. No wolves can get inside."

Esperanza poked her head in the room. "The meal is almost ready."

"Thank you, Esperanza. We'll be right in." When the woman left, Sally turned her attention back to Hickory. "Shall we go wash up?"

He nodded and climbed to his feet, his gaze straying for a moment to her growing belly.

Even though she had no appetite, she'd be sure to consume a good portion for the baby. Just last week, she'd felt a slight movement. The feeling reminded her of the swish of a feather against her skin. The sensation had taken her by surprise, followed by a great surge of love. Love for a tiny babe conceived in an act of violence.

Protecting him or her was utmost in her mind. Sally would never want her child to know, to hurt, to feel different.

Chapter Twenty-Four

Finished with her noon meal, Poppy carried her dirty dishes into the cramped kitchen and glanced about for a place to set them. The area was messy but warm, just like Mr. Petty had mentioned.

Lenore stood at the counter, speaking with the cook. As Poppy approached, the waitress sanctimoniously lifted her brows and gestured with her chin to the sink.

Feeling the fool for not even knowing this small fact, Poppy deposited her plate and teacup into the water and dusted imaginary crumbs from her palms.

"I could have gotten that, Miss Ford," Lenore said.

Her taciturn tone grated on Poppy's nerves. Oscar had fixed things so the woman would never forgive them.

"I don't mind. And actually, I came to get the food for the children. You said their plates would be ready when I was finished with my meal. I'd like to look in on them. Would that be all right with you?"

I need to walk softly; do what I can. And in all honesty, the behavior feels like the right thing to do.

Despite the cold, Lenore's forehead was shiny from cooking and serving the few lunches that had been needed today. "The staff can deal with that, as well. No need to trouble yourself."

Poppy smiled, feeling a need to win over the cranky woman. Just because Poppy had had a privileged upbringing didn't mean she couldn't pitch in and help wherever she could.

"I want to be of service, Lenore. Please, let me help. To lighten your load."

Make up for all the years I took Kathryn for granted.

A vision of her sister churning butter in her farmhouse kitchen danced before Poppy's eyes. Poppy was still getting used to seeing her older sibling doing for others. At first, Poppy had been repelled—a Ford acting like a servant just wasn't natural. Then, as her stay at the farm continued, she'd begun to feel differently. See things in an altered light. Kathryn fairly beamed when Tobit complimented something she'd cooked or done. The feel of her country home was far superior to what they'd grown up with in their Boston manor.

"Mr. Petty expects us all to pull our weight, including me. He told me that himself. If you don't want me to take the food to the newcomers, show me how to wash the dishes. Or maybe Miss Hallsey can give me another project. Is she around? I haven't seen her since this morning."

Lenore took a plate from the cook and set it on a tray, followed by two more. "If you insist on helping, this is for the children and their parents. A plate for each adult, and one for the tykes to share. If you need more, just let us know." She marched over and handed the large tray of food to Poppy.

A job. Good. Purpose filled her chest.

Two cloth napkins, two cups of what looked to be tea, as well as the three plates. One bowl of soup. The tray was heavy, but she worked to keep it level.

"Thank you," she mumbled as she walked out, concentrating not to spill or drop anything. "I appreciate it."

What would Father think? Her thanking a domestic for letting her help. How fast her circumstances had changed. Normally, she'd be in her hotel room, huddled under her blankets or in front of her fire, expecting a servant to bring her lunch.

As she slowly started up the stairs, a gust of wind hit the lobby window with a smattering of snow.

Where was Mr. Petty? Had he found the sheriff and the others? This was no joking matter. She remembered what Sheriff Crawford had said about getting turned around in the snow. Mr. Petty might be lost, stumbling around on the open prairie by now. The thought of him suffering in any way brought an unfamiliar lump to her throat.

Why was she worried about Mr. Petty in particular? She felt no affinity toward the others. The thought was strange. Although, he *was* in charge of them now, until the blizzard subsided, and she was grateful for that. Was she only thinking of herself again?

On the second floor, she stopped outside the appropriate door, wondering how to get in. Poppy glanced at the tray in her hands and then up and down the deserted hallway. She dared not set her burden down for fear everything would spill.

Hildy appeared out of a room on the opposite side of the hall.

"Hello," Poppy gushed in relief. "I'm glad to see you."

The hotel clerk tipped her head. "Checking on the Grants," she said in explanation. "What're you doing with that? Where's Lenore?"

Poppy's arms strained, and the tray wobbled. "In the kitchen. With dishes to do. I volunteered. Would you mind getting the door for me?"

Hildy sprang forward. "Oh, not at all."

She opened the door to a rush of warmth. Poppy followed her in and glanced about.

The man slept on his pallet by the fire. Perhaps he was used to sleeping on the floor. The woman was huddled in bed with the children. Her eyes, still wary, clamped on the tray of food.

"Miss Ford brought you some lunch," Hildy said. "How're you feeling?"

The woman nodded.

Poppy realized they'd yet to learn their names, or why they'd been caught off guard in such a storm.

The children scrambled up into a sitting position, their eyes large and shining.

"Bread," the little boy whispered, glancing guardedly to where the man snored. "C-can I have some?"

"Yes, of course," Poppy replied. "That's why I've brought it. I'm sure you all must be ravenous."

The boy's head bobbed up and down, and the twin girls mimicked his movement. Placing the tray on the end of the bed was a great relief.

"Now, be very still until I can distribute this food."

Poppy handed the woman her plate and utensils, and gave the boy a slice of toast, and a half each to the girls.

"Eat this while I cut the meat." She glanced at the woman. "How old is he?"

The woman's gaze darted to the sleeping man and then back at the boy. "'Bout six," she finally mumbled. She forked in a chunk of beef and fried potatoes. A heavy sigh moved her chest. Her face was weather-beaten and her hair disheveled.

Poppy moved her gaze back to the two little waifs that were her daughters.

Strange how the mother stumbled over such an easy question, but perhaps the cold still had her befuddled. If the boy was six, the girls must be one and a half, or perhaps two. They watched the proceedings but made no move to get any of the food themselves.

Poppy handed the woman her cup of tea and set the man's on the dresser with his plate. "Do you want to feed them, or shall I?"

The woman shrugged. "I don't mind if you do the feeding."

Again, strange. Well, maybe not for what she's been through.

Determined to be friendly, Poppy smiled at the woman. "I'm Miss Ford, of the Boston Fords. May I ask your name?"

"Sanger," she muttered, looking away.

Well. That hadn't gone so well. Poppy began cutting the children's meat. She handed a couple of pieces to the boy, who'd finished his toast but waited patiently, even though she'd heard his stomach grumble loudly.

"Here you go," Poppy whispered, placing another piece into his hand. "And what's your name?"

His chewing sped up, and then he swallowed. "July, ma'am." His lips curled into a small smile.

"And your sisters?"

"April and May."

Poppy gave a small laugh. "I should have seen that coming."

His steady voice was much too composed for someone so young. He impressed her. She glanced again at their mother, who seemed to be lost in thought.

"Can the girls eat this, July?" she asked, feeling a fool for knowing so little about young children. "Did I cut the meat small enough?"

July nodded. "Sure. They eat most anythin'. They're not persnickety."

Poppy set the plate of diced food, along with a fork for July if he was interested, between the three.

The girls, who were still working on their toast, looked at her for several seconds. With a start, Poppy realized they waited for permission, so she nodded. They reached out and each stuffed a handful of the meat into their mouths.

They did have teeth, thank goodness, and quite a few, so Poppy felt certain they wouldn't choke.

The woman had wolfed down her portion and eyed her husband's plate on the tray.

"Would you like that? I can get more when your husband wakes up."

"Yes'm," the woman answered. "Richard won't come 'round for a while—hours maybe. No use letting good food go ta waste."

"No, of course not."

Poppy retrieved the plate and swapped it for the empty one. Something was suspicious about this poor, ragtag family but she didn't know what. She couldn't put her finger on it, just something peculiar. When Mr. Petty was back, she'd be sure and mention her qualms to him.

Now that they had some sustenance in their tummies, April and May were bouncing slightly on their knees as they chewed another handful of food. Their golden curls moved in the light of the fire and lamp, and their eyes twinkled.

Poppy reached out to gently push up the cotton fabric of their undershirt sleeves, and felt each little arm with the back of her wrist. They weren't warm yet, but their bodies were much warmer than they'd been when the sheriff brought them in. She thought they were out of danger of frostbite, but she was no doctor.

"I'd like you to eat this soup before it cools too much. I'll help."

They swallowed what they had in their mouths and then let her spoon in a portion for each, just like little birds. How sweet.

When was the last time they had a hot meal? Or a bath? Or some attention?

Their mother didn't seem to be interested. She was more concerned with consuming everything within reach.

Poppy tried not to judge. Perhaps she'd act the same if faced with similar circumstances. Maybe she would, but she didn't think so.

"There, that's everything," she said, scooping the last spoonful of soup and giving a little to each. With the napkin, she wiped April and May's tiny lips, noticing the girls looked sated now that they were full. She handed the napkin to July.

"Can we come with you, ma'am?" he asked, gesturing to his sisters before glancing at the door.

"Oh no. Your room is the warmest in the hotel, and you all still need to bring up your temperatures."

Mrs. Sanger's face tightened. "Don't you be bothering this fine woman, July," she snapped. "You know better than that. Your pa would be angry if he heard you pestering."

July's gaze darted to his still-sleeping father, and he slowly nodded.

"He's not a pest," Poppy heard herself say before she thought better of her interference. "As a matter of fact, as soon as you're able, July, I'll take you out to the lobby, and we can play a game of checkers by the woodstove. Would you like that?"

She slid a secretive glance at Mrs. Sanger to see a scowl on the woman's face, just as she suspected. Some people were very protective, but that didn't feel like the case here.

"Yes'm. As long as my sisters can come too."

"Of course they can. Now, you all snuggle back in bed and stay under the covers. I'll return a little later to check on you."

The woman nodded but kept her comments to herself.

For some odd reason, Poppy had taken a disliking to the mother. She shouldn't have. Mrs. Sanger was a victim, just as the children were. All five family members had almost died.

After putting all the dirty dishes on the tray, she stood and tucked April, May, and July in tight, making sure the blankets were up to their chins. She placed a kiss on each forehead with the tip of her finger. They reminded her of the baby bunnies out at Kathryn's farm. She took one last look at their snoring father, trying not to feel disgust.

"Sleep tight. I'll be back soon."

Poppy stepped out into the chilly hallway, wishing her room were a bit closer to the children. As silly as that sounded, it was true.

I must be going through some sort of transformation here in Montana. She carefully descended the stairs with the cumbersome tray. *As soon as I'm on that ship to France, I'll be back to normal—won't I?*

Chapter Twenty-Five

The Biscuit Barrel was locked up tight, as was the church and Morgan's woodworking shop, Stanford Fittings. As June had predicted, Dr. Handerhoosen's place was dark when Shad looked in the windows and tried the locked door.

Each step he took was more difficult than his last. He could no longer feel his fingers except for the shooting pains that had replaced the chill, and his toes felt as if ice was wedged between each one. In his right fist, he gripped his coat collar around his neck in an attempt to keep out the snow.

Only two more stops and then he'd cross over and fetch Fancy back to the hotel. Brandon and the rest must have taken shelter at the mill or someplace else. They were too smart to get stuck out in such a storm.

Stumbling onto the boardwalk in front of the mercantile, Shad tried to ignore the pricks of stinging ice on his face. He shouldered his way into the front door of Lichtenstein's, thankful the place was unlocked and a lantern burned a welcome. He could barely hear the voices in the back room over the inexorable clattering of his teeth.

"Hello?" he called, feeling like a snowman that had just tumbled down a hill. "Lichtenstein? Mr. Simpson? Who's back there?" Unmindful of the snow falling from his clothes and boots, he trudged over to the woodstove and got as close as he dared.

"Shadrack."

Finally. He recognized Brandon's voice. That was one worry gone.

Boots on wooden floor tromped toward him, and soon all his friends, as well as Mr. Lichtenstein and Mr. Simpson, were gathered around the stove.

Francis looked as if he'd been dragged through a snowbank by a team of horses, and Smokey didn't look much better. Brandon's hat was gone, and his wet hair stuck to his head. He wrestled a kerchief from his coat pocket and blew his nose. Morgan's coat looked soaked through, and his face was cherry red. Lichtenstein and Mr. Simpson appeared almost ready for bed in layers of nightclothes, several pairs of thick socks, and stocking caps on their heads.

Shad held back a chuckle at the sight.

Brandon took hold of Shad's shivering shoulder. "Has something happened at the hotel? How long have you been out?"

"Long enough to know better," he said through rattling teeth. "Got worried about you not coming back. Didn't want to discover you all as clumps of ice tomorrow. You find anything new? Any signs of more people like that fella said? Where're your horses?"

"In the back alley where they'd have a little protection. Didn't find any people. No tracks either, of course. No wagons. I think his words were just drunken ramblings."

"Thieves hit us here, though," Mr. Lichtenstein barked, pointing to the back room from where they'd all come. "I did not discover until one hour ago, but someone jimmied the back lock during the night. The thieves stole the last of my lamp oil, all of the staples such as flour and sugar, dried fruit, and canned food. Already my supplies were low, since the stage has not been coming regular for reasons of weather or sickness in other towns." The portly German's eyes flashed with anger. "Those robbers, they do not leave one clue behind. Maybe those greenhorns you found this morning are responsible." His eyes narrowed suspiciously.

"They didn't have much in the way of food, and certainly not your supplies," Brandon said to the proprietor.

Morgan started for the front door. "I'm headed back to the livery. Don't want to leave June alone longer than need be."

"Wait up," Smokey said, striding with Morgan. He glanced at Shad. "You ready to ride, Petty? We need to head back to the ranch before we lose our chance."

Still heating his hands an inch from the stove, Shad shook his head. "I'm staying behind. Watching over the hotel. You two'll be fine if you go now. Just watch your back trail. Lou said Drit saw wolf sign too, and close to town, out by the sawmill."

He thought of Miss Ford, Fancy, Lenore, Miss Hildy, and the others. Oscar Scott, one elderly man, and the drunk Sanger wouldn't be much help if this storm went on longer than they expected. They couldn't count on Brandon. He had the whole town to look after.

"I appreciate the help, Shadrack," Brandon said. "Justin and me both. One less place to worry about. I'm sure my father-in-law will understand."

Smokey nodded. "We'll make sure he does."

"Where's Justin?" Shad asked, just now realizing the young deputy wasn't with the bunch gathered in the mercantile.

"We left him out at the Klinkners'. Ina was on edge that Norman wasn't feeling well. They have Hayden, but that's a big place."

"What about my property?" Mr. Lichtenstein demanded. "The town will need the lamp oil now more than ever. The food too. I keep the surplus locked away in a cabinet in the back for the lean months of winter. Now that it's gone, I won't be able to open my doors."

"Ain't good a'tall," Mr. Simpson mumbled under his breath. "Who'd do a blame thing like that? I don't like ta think of the children going hungry."

Brandon glanced out the front window at the wall of white. "We're not quite there yet, Mr. Simpson. I'll do my best to find the missing supplies."

Seemed Old Man Simpson had aged a hundred years. The elderly man looked beaten and bewildered.

"Until we do," Brandon went on, glancing around the group, "everyone will have to conserve. Use candles instead of lanterns whenever possible. One meal a day, plus one snack. We can't hunt in conditions like this for some time." He glanced at Smokey and Francis. "You best get moving, boys, the light's dwindlin' fast." His cautious tone reminded them all this wasn't a laughing matter. "Like Shad said, keep an eye on your back trail... and your front."

Shad needed to get moving, as well. He had Fancy to pick up and deliver. With a heavy heart, he watched the men leave, staving off the impulse to shake each of their hands and tell them they'd been a good friend. In conditions like these, one never knew if that was the last time in this world you'd see your comrade.

Chapter Twenty-Six

Unable to stay her ragged nerves any longer, Poppy took her book to the lobby and dropped into the vacant chair across from Oscar. Mr. Petty still hadn't returned. Had the tall cowboy lost his way, sat exhausted by the cold and gone to sleep for the last time in his life? The horrible thought sent a chill up her already-cold backbone.

Oscar stared out the window straight-faced, his blank expression mirroring his foul mood.

She knew him well enough to guess what he was thinking about. Taking the lap throw from the back of the chair, she wrapped it around her legs and tried to ignore the shooting pains tormenting her freezing fingertips.

When she felt Oscar's stare, she turned to look at him. "What?"

"I was just thinking this situation could be really bad," he said. "Much worse than anyone thinks."

"Don't be silly. Snow like this happens every year. Hildy said as much to me not an hour ago. We just have to sit back and be patient."

His lazy gaze dared to sweep her countenance.

"Don't look at me like that, Ossy! I didn't ask you to come along."

"That may be so, but I'm glad I'm here." He leaned forward in his chair, and she pulled back. "To look after you. I know the trouble you tend to find without even trying. You should thank me for coming along. I could have gone to England with my father, but I gave that up for you."

The audacity of him. Was there no end to his arrogance? No wonder Kathryn couldn't bring herself to marry him. Poppy surely wouldn't.

"I wish you *had* gone to England. Then I wouldn't have to worry about you offending everyone here. Would you please think before you speak?"

"Are you referring to that horse-faced woman, Lenore Saffelberg?" He gave her a dismissive scowl. "She's just a waitress in this no-name hotel in this godforsaken town. And she always will be. She means nothing to us. You shouldn't worry yourself over her, or what she thinks."

"Oscar!" Poppy quickly glanced around to be sure no one was within hearing distance. "Lower your voice. If you don't have anything nice to say, don't say anything at all. My gosh, have you no heart, sense, or manners? I used to think Kathryn was making up things about you. I stuck up for you, always came to your defense." *I brought you to her home without asking.* Shame filled her anew for her thoughtlessness. What must Kathryn think? And Tobit? "I thought of you as someone special, *a brother*, a confidant to all my secrets. This trip has opened my eyes."

Jerking back, he hit his head on the back of the chair. "A brother! Surely you don't think of me like that. I've always *loved* you, Poppy. Right from the very start. Since we were old enough to know there was a difference between us."

The way his eyes alighted on her person, filled with some sort of suggestive invitation, made her stomach squeeze with revulsion. Had he been fantasizing about her all these years? Her skin prickled with disgust.

He put out a hand in supplication. "I was only going along with our fathers' wishes to marry Kathryn to make them happy and keep the peace. Given a choice, I'd have picked you. I still plan to make you my wife."

"You've lost your mind," she spat back.

Anger warmed her for the first time since the snowstorm had begun. She'd use no kid gloves here. She needed to quash his crazy idea right now. Make sure he knew exactly where he stood with her. Nowhere!

"We will *never* marry! Ever. Read my lips. Engrave the words on your heart. Never, Oscar. Ever, ever, ever—"

"All right. I hear you loud and clear." He sprang to his feet and stood there, glaring down into her face.

Poppy was so incensed by what Oscar had presumed about them, she hadn't heard anything over the pounding of her heart. When the front glass door opened and a gush of frigid air rushed into the room, she stood and whirled around. She took a moment to recognize the tall, snow-covered Mr. Petty. She didn't know the smaller person standing by his side and clutching his gloved hand. Whoever it was, she was greatly relieved to see the cowhand back and still alive.

"Here you go, Fancy," he said, speaking with much familiarity and affection. He stood there shivering as he brushed snow from the woman's shoulders and back. "Keep your cape on for a while." He glanced over at Poppy. "Like Miss Ford."

Instantly, for something to do, Poppy ran her hand over her own heavy cape.

The woman looked around with interest as if this was the first time she'd ever been in Cattlemen's before. She seemed content to stay by Mr. Petty's side.

Poppy found her voice and closed the distance between them. "Mr. Petty, I'm relieved you've returned. I was beginning to get worried." That was an understatement. She'd begun her worry the moment he'd stepped out the door. "Who is this?"

She felt Oscar shuffle up to her side and wished he'd just go to his room and stay there.

Before Mr. Petty could answer, the woman smiled and pushed back the hood that covered her head, revealing a bounty of long hair the color of sunshine. She peeled the gloves from her hands, exposing elegant fingers, only to brush away several snowflakes that had stuck to her abundant lashes. She gazed back in amusement.

"I'm Fancy Aubrey," she said, her voice sounding as warm as the scotch whiskey Poppy had once snuck from her father's tumbler. "You must be Miss Ford, Mrs. Preece's highbrow sister from Boston. Shad has told me all about you."

"The saloon tart," Oscar snapped angrily. "What's she doing here with respectable people?"

Mr. Petty stepped toward Oscar, his eyes gone hard. "She's waiting out the storm where it's warm." His voice escalated with each word. "Just like the rest of us. If you have a problem with that, Abe has a vacant room for you down at the Hitching Post. Upstairs where it's cold. Don't let the door hit you on the way out."

How does Ossy know this woman? And Mr. Petty too?

The bravado left Oscar's face. He shook his head and dropped his gaze to the floor.

Hildy came hurrying out of the hallway and halted abruptly in front of the group. "What's going on out here? I could hear your angry voices all the way from the kitchen." When she recognized the saloon girl, her eyes widened but she didn't say a word.

"I'm checking in Fancy. You have a room somewhere, private like, where she won't be disturbed?"

Hildy chewed her bottom lip for several seconds. "The top floor is the most quiet. Maybe she'd like to go up there."

"It's warmer on the first and second floors," Mr. Petty said, and then looked at Poppy.

I shouldn't be jealous. He tried to move me down.

"Did you want to move, Miss Ford?" Hildy asked.

Feeling flustered for no obvious reason, Poppy glanced between Mr. Petty and Hildy, all the while aware of Oscar breathing down her neck. "No, I'm situated nicely. And I've settled in. The cold hasn't been too bad."

Mr. Petty's lips quirked up.

For some reason, she was glad she'd answered the way she had. "I'll stay in the room I have." *And I don't mind the saloon girl moving in,* she thought, but kept the statement to herself.

Shad nodded. "The third floor—"

"Will do just fine," Miss Aubrey finished for Mr. Petty, throwing him a playful look. "And from now on, I can speak for myself, Shadrack." She turned to stare at Oscar, not intimidated in the least. "You liked me before, Oscar," she purred, and jiggled her shoulder. "You remember, don't you? Last weekend? I had no idea you thought me such a vile creature you couldn't stand my presence."

When Oscar sputtered in objection but didn't come up with a coherent response, Poppy fought to hide her smile. Seemed he could be bested by a saloon girl with ease.

Hildy turned on her heel and headed for the counter. She took a key from a slot and smiled at Fancy. "I'll show you to your room now, ma'am."

"No ma'am here. Fancy is fine," Miss Aubrey said.

Mr. Petty picked up the duffel bag he'd dropped at their feet when they entered the lobby. He glanced around. "I can do that. And afterward, everyone should meet in the restaurant. Gather all the guests that are able to come. We have things to discuss."

Poppy couldn't help but admire his forthright way. He seemed so different from the cowhand who had eaten supper at her sister's home those few nights ago. The one who had sputtered water in Oscar's face. She fought the urge to lower her gaze when he looked her way.

"Will you be available then, Miss Ford?" he asked as the two made their way toward the stairway.

Hildy lit a candle and handed the candleholder to Miss Aubrey.

"I'll be here, Mr. Petty," Poppy said. "Would either you or Miss Aubrey like a cup of tea when you return? I can ask Cook to heat the water. You must be very cold."

Oscar let go a disgusted harrumph.

Mr. Petty smiled. "That sounds mighty good. Thank you."

With that, Poppy watched the two ascend the wooden stairway, feeling a warm glow growing within. Perhaps being stranded in a hotel would prove to be entertaining... and maybe even more.

In the next moment, she shook the crazy thought from her mind. She had plans to go to France this spring, and nothing would stop her now. Not after all the years she'd been dreaming about the school and begging her father to let her go.

She glanced at Oscar, who also watched Mr. Petty and Miss Aubrey disappear into the darkness, a strange expression on his face. She'd keep an eye out, for more reasons than one.

Chapter Twenty-Seven

A half hour later, Shad paced back and forth in front of the dining room window that looked over the rear of the hotel. He had changed into dry clothing but had put his coat back on.

Hildy and Lenore sat at a table, talking quietly over cups of something he presumed was tea. Miss Ford sat in a booth by herself, and Mel and Bonnie Grant, the old couple he'd just met, sat nearby.

Cook was still working in the kitchen and told Shad to call when he was ready to commence. The family Brandon had brought wasn't present, but Shad didn't expect them to be. He'd explained everything to Fancy when he'd lit her fire and got her settled in. They both thought it best if she stayed put as much as possible. No surprise, Oscar Scott was the only one absent.

Shad ambled over to Miss Ford's table. "We're waiting on your friend. Is he coming?"

Her chin popped up. "I don't know. Let me go to his room and see." She quickly glanced around, then got up and hurried away.

Watching her go into the darker hallway, he realized he shouldn't consider her Scott's keeper. They weren't married or engaged.

A moment later, he heard footsteps. Miss Ford preceded the tall Bostonian into the room and resumed her seat. Scott sat opposite.

"Thanks for showing up, everyone," Shad said, taking stock. He leaned his head toward the kitchen. "Cook, we're starting," he called out in a loud voice. "You may want to come out here."

The round man ambled out, wiping his hands on a dishcloth, and stood next to the door.

"I called you here for a reason. We have no way of knowing how long this storm will last. Could be a day, or it could be a week—or longer. That being said, someone broke into Lichtenstein's last night and made off with much of the supplies he keeps back for the lean months."

A soft gasp sounded, followed by several concerned murmurs.

"We'll have to conserve our resources. That means everything. Beginning with the lamp oil. You'll notice only one lamp is burning in here now. Miss Hallsey, how are we situated with candles?"

Hildy straightened when he singled her out. "Plenty to last months."

"Good. Everyone is to switch to those. We'll allow one lamp to burn in the lobby at all times, and one lamp in here when we take our one meal. Other than that, use candles in your rooms and for going up and down the stairs. But be careful."

"Oh my," the elderly Bonnie Grant said to her husband, so loudly everyone heard. "This visit started off nice, but now I'm scared."

Her husband reached over and took her hand. "No need to fret. We've been through hard times before—many, if my memory serves me correctly. We'll be just fine."

Shad sent her a calming smile. "Your husband is right, ma'am. Nothing to worry about." She reminded him of his grandma, who had raised him and his brothers. "No need to fret." *Yet.* "If we conserve, we'll be fine. Food was also stolen from the mercantile. Staples, canned goods, jarred fruits and vegetables. Dried hams. All the things that make surviving through a harsh winter possible."

"Does Brandon have any clues as to who may have done it?" Lenore asked.

"I'm afraid not."

"We'll watch to see who's staying fat while the rest of us wither away. If this snow keeps up, we'll be in trouble." Lenore's eyes were hard and angry.

"That's why I called this meeting. The hotel restaurant is shutting down on a demand basis, and food will be rationed. A noon meal will be the only one served, then a light snack in the morning and again before bed. The pantry has flour and shortening, so bread shouldn't be too much of a problem. We have ten adults to feed and three children." At Bonnie Grant's distressed look, he felt compelled to add, "But if the weather clears up, I'll be able to check around town for provisions others may have to share. All is not lost, not in the least. And there's hunting too…"

"So knowing all this that you just dropped into our laps, you still brought in another mouth to feed?" Scott blurted. "And a saloon girl, at that. I say we send her back to the Hitching Post. I'm sure Abe can support her better than we can."

The old couple were looking around with interest, as were Lenore and Cook—the few people who didn't know that Fancy was upstairs.

"Saloon girl?" somebody mumbled. "Where is she?"

"Yes, a saloon girl." Shad straightened and glanced around at the confused looks. "Fancy Aubrey is upstairs. The Hitching Post is poorly insulated and cold. Only one woodstove heats the whole building. Every room here in the hotel has a fireplace. I'm sure none of you, with the exception of Scott, would deny her."

"Oh no, we would not, Mr. Petty," Mrs. Grant called out, frowning at Scott. "We're all God's children. A lady of the night upstairs is the least of our worries."

Rubbing the smile off his face, Shad glanced around the room with an affirmative nod, liking the spunky old woman more and more. "Good. I couldn't have said it better myself."

Everyone besides Scott was smiling. Shad hadn't meant to paint such a rosy picture. He'd spoken with Cook privately, and the cupboards were pretty much picked clean already. The already frail children came to mind. He'd make sure they had something in their stomachs, even if he gave them his own portion.

Chapter Twenty-Eight

A little after three in the afternoon, the ranch house door opened and Roady stepped inside, stamping off the snow. The grounds outside were blanketed in soft white drifts, the dark trees sugared with ice crystals. The scene was peaceful and clean, just like the images Sally had admired in paintings in St. Louis. The snow, almost three feet deep, dumped into the door, and Roady pushed it out with his boots.

Filled with relief, Sally rushed to his side, helping him out of his heavy, sodden clothes.

His lips were blue and his teeth chattering. "I'm fine, darlin'. No need to fret. We go through this every year. Only now that I'm married, I get to stay in the big house with you instead of the bunkhouse with the men." He winked.

Her heart warmed. After a day of worry, Roady was back, and the situation was as if nothing had happened. "You don't fool me. I know you'd much rather be in the bunkhouse with the men. You're not one to crave luxuries. You like hot grub, a fire, and the camaraderie."

He turned and pulled her into his arms, her growing tummy intimately cradled between them. "But I crave you, and here you are. I've been thinking about you all day."

Roady's lips found hers for a freezing kiss that made her shiver. Enjoying the feel of being in his arms, cold or not, she didn't pull away as she gazed up into his eyes. She brushed some snowflakes from his eyebrows and a frozen drop from his cheek.

"I know, darlin'; I'm a mess. But it couldn't be helped." He chuckled. "Actually, the snow's so dry it's gettin' blown away by the wind. And that's a blessing. Keeps it from piling up too high."

"Dry?"

"Because of the cold temperature. If it were warmer, the snow would be wet and sticky." He tweaked her nose playfully. "You have a lot to learn. Anyway, what have you been doing to pass the day?"

"A little of this and a little of that. Hickory's been beating me at checkers."

"Sounds invigorating."

"Not as invigorating as your day."

He chuckled. "I would hope not."

They glanced toward the doorway at the sound of footsteps.

"Here you are," Flood McCutcheon said as he came into the room. He hunkered down to stoke the fire. "'Bout time you got back. I could feel Sally's anxiety growing as the hours passed. And you're just in time for an early supper."

Sally smiled and gave a small laugh. She liked Flood very much.

"Good. I'm hungry."

"What's the news?" Flood asked, turning away from the flames and standing.

"Everyone's tucked up tight. Luke went home after we moved the horses. That was about two o'clock. Smokey, Francis, and Shad haven't made it back from town."

Claire McCutcheon came down the staircase with Hickory on her heels. "What's this?"

"Roady was just saying the three men that we sent to Y Knot have yet to return." Her husband rubbed his chin thoughtfully. "But that was about the time the snow started dumping."

"That's right," Roady agreed.

Claire's brow drew down and she glanced at the darkened window. "Anything to be concerned about?"

Roady crossed the room to the fireplace. "I don't think so. If they can't get back, they'll hole up someplace. Most likely in town."

"I see." She patted Hickory's back when the child stopped by her side. "Who?"

"Francis, Smokey, and Shad."

Esperanza came into the dining room, her hands full of a heavy cast-iron pot. She set the container onto a trivet, a secretive smile on her face.

"Tortilla soup, Esperanza?" Flood asked, a quiet awe to his voice. "You know I love that on snowy days."

"*Sí*," she said and hurried away. "I will bring the tortillas. Sit, or they won't be hot."

"Yes, ma'am," Roady replied playfully, escorting Sally to the table.

Now that he'd returned safe and sound, she could relax. The afternoon had passed slowly as she contemplated all the things that might happen out there in that storm. Roady was home and they could eat in peace.

"Thank you, Esperanza," Claire replied, pulling out one of the large dining room chairs for Hickory. "The soup smells delicious. Flood was telling me he hoped you remembered your tradition for the first big snow of the year."

Sally sat beside Hickory, and Roady took the seat on her other side. Flood was at the head, as usual, with his wife to his right.

All quieted as Flood bowed his head, and everyone followed suit.

"Thank you, Lord, for this food, this family, and your blessings." He paused, his worried gaze tracking to the dark window. "And we ask a special blessing for all the animals left out in the cold." He cleared his throat. "And the men we still have in Y Knot. Amen."

"Amen," they echoed softly.

Sally didn't miss the quaver in his voice. Why did Western men shelter their women? They were more worried than they were letting on. She glanced at Roady, who wore the same troubled expression.

With a cloth protecting his hand from the heat, Flood lifted the heavy lid and set it to the side. He filled his wife's bowl first with two scoops as Esperanza appeared with a large plate of tortillas, covered with a napkin.

The unopened letter upstairs strayed into Sally's thoughts.

"Something wrong, sweetheart?" Roady whispered close as he reached for the bowl being passed his way. "You look troubled."

"No," she whispered back, forcing a smile. "Not now that you're home, nothing worries me."

At least, I hope that's the case. I better not go looking for trouble. As soon as supper is over, I'm going up to open the letter and face whatever news it brings.

Chapter Twenty-Nine

A quiet knocking on Margaret's bedroom door brought her out of a restless sleep. She couldn't see past her drawn curtains, but something inside told her the snow was still falling, as it had been when she'd finally blown out her lantern at eleven o'clock last night. Something about the quiet, and the peace.

"Mrs. Seymour? Margaret? You awake?"

Chance.

"One moment," she called and sat up in bed.

The air was bitterly cold. As quickly as she could, she lit her lantern, and then pulled on her wrap over her heavy wool nightgown and socks. Chance had never woken her before. She rose at her own time—early, yes, but never as early as him.

Please don't let this be about Evelyn. But why else would Chance wake me up at, she glanced at her watch, *four o'clock in the morning? Something must be wrong.*

She opened the door to Evelyn's tall husband waiting by the kitchen table, a lantern's golden glow making it possible to see. His hair was mussed from sleep, but he was fully clothed.

"What is it, Chance? Is Evelyn feeling all right?"

"Yes. She's still asleep. Andy was just here. Said there's been an abundance of wolves prowling around the barn all night."

Her shoulders sagged with relief. Even in the wan light, she could see the concern in Chance's eyes.

"A lot, even for this time of the year."

Wolves. How frightening. "But wolves are common, aren't they?"

"Yes. But this pack seems unusually big." He pulled on his thick coat. "In large numbers, they're bolder. They smell the cattle and the chickens. I don't want you or Evie leaving the house for any reason whatsoever."

The look in his eyes sent a jolt of fear through her. "Of course. I'll make sure she minds me when she gets up."

His chin dipped. "Thank you. I'm not too proud to say I'm mighty thankful you're here to help. Evie was fitful last night. Tossed and turned. Needed water, then the chamber pot. The baby is kicking her something awful. I wouldn't be surprised if she slept in until noon."

"I'll be sure to be quiet. She needs her rest. But, Chance, her time isn't until late February." She swallowed against a dry throat. "You don't think her discomfort is because she might be starting labor?"

A smile finally appeared, and he rested his hands on the back of a chair. "No, I'm not thinking that at all. She's just uncomfortable. My heifers do the same thing. There's plenty of time to get her into town where Dr. Handerhoosen can assist."

"I'm relieved to hear you say that. Now, go on and do what you must outside, and I'll keep watch in here."

Margaret noted that he'd started a fire in the hearth and had a pot of coffee perking on the kitchen stove. Soon the chill would be gone, and she'd take up her reading where she'd left off last night.

"Is the snow still falling?"

He pulled on a thick pair of gloves. "Sure is. But the storm has to let up sometime."

"I would think so. When will you be back inside? I'll have something hot prepared for you and Andy."

They all were on a first-name basis and wanted her to do the same. Margaret preferred to be proper, as she always instructed her brides when she'd had the mail-order agency, and had held out for almost three days until they'd worn down her resistance. She smiled to herself. Everyone had insisted, so she had complied.

When Chance finished with his gloves, he wound his wool scarf around his neck and set his hat on his head, pulling it down tight. He buckled on his gun belt and then glanced her way.

"Around eight, I'd think. There's one advantage of having a small herd."

"Oh? What's that?"

He started for the door. "They all fit in my barn, every last one of 'em. There's not much room to spare, but they're thankful to be enclosed."

Needing to be helpful, she hurried past and opened the door. Snow blasted in as he ducked his head and slipped out.

"Be careful," she called as she watched him disappear into the swirling white. She wondered if he'd heard.

The sharp fangs of a wolf shimmered in her mind. They all had to be careful. This was the Montana wilds, where survival trumped all cards.

Chapter Thirty

Sally stretched lazily, lifting one arm over her head, but quickly drew it back under the covers when the cold air bit into her skin. Something had awakened her. When the bed dipped, she forced her eyes open, even though she was loath to leave the goodness of her dreams.

"Good mornin', darlin'," Roady whispered, and leaned down and placed a soft kiss on her mouth. "You were smiling in your sleep."

Other than the bedside lantern, the room was dark, quiet—and frigid cold. Her husband, half-dressed for the day, leaned in closer until she could see a crooked smile on his face.

"Must have been thinking how much I love you," she whispered back.

She lifted her hand from beneath the protective warmth of the blankets and quilts, and caressed his muscled chest. The nubby, well-worn cotton of his undershirt beneath her fingertips made her imagination run wild. When his muscles responded to her light touch, she wished he had awakened her before deciding to get ready for the day.

"Roady, you're the air I breathe," she added, needing him to know just how much he meant to her. "Be careful today. The circumstances are dangerous. Three days of snow, and—"

He put a finger to her lips, halting her words. "I liked it better when you were telling me how much you loved me. No need to worry, sweetheart. The boys and I are fine. Mostly hanging out in the bunkhouse."

"That's not true. I heard you went out with Smokey and Ike yesterday. Opened up some of the watering holes. With the wolves and weather, every time you step out the door, you risk your life."

"That's true enough, but it's my job, and something I've been doing for years. We have to look after the animals. We ride in twos and threes, never alone." He pulled the covers up to her chin and made sure no air was leaking in below.

Worrying did no good. She couldn't protect him. She'd keep him in her love and prayers and wait for his return around three or four. "What time is it?" She glanced to the darkened window.

"Going on seven."

He was usually up and out by five. "The sky is still so dark."

He chuckled. "It's still snowing. You never told me what you were smiling about in your sleep. Do you remember? Sure was a pretty sight." He leaned down and briefly kissed her again.

"I remember now. I was dreaming about the baby."

"Well? Was it a boy or girl? Don't keep me in suspense."

"A girl. And we named her Gillian with a *G* instead of a *J* to look nice with Guthrie."

She waited to gauge his reaction. Was he hoping for a son? A boy to start his family? Men always seemed so partial to that. A male to carry on their name. Her heart squeezed. But the child wasn't *really* Roady's son or blood. Did that truth bother him? He never let on.

"She was very small and as bald as a pumpkin." Sally couldn't stop a small laugh from escaping.

"Gillian's real pretty. Sally and Gillian. I like the sound of that. Is that the name you've chosen?"

She ran her hand along his forearm and noticed his gaze intensify. "I'd never choose a name without consulting you. That's something we should do together. Besides, it was just a dream. I'm sure my imaginings didn't mean anything, and I'm having a boy."

"Who knows? Maybe it's a sign."

"You don't believe in signs, do you, Roady?"

His thumb caressed her cheek. "What do you think?"

"No. You're levelheaded. You think things through on your own."

Sentimentality began to rumble around inside her. His marrying her, even though the baby wasn't his. Taking them in and giving them a home. So very much indeed. Everything they'd been through in the past few months proved Roady was reliable and loyal—to a fault.

He chuckled and stood. "I see you're getting emotional—as usual, these days. No one ever warned me about that."

The floorboards in the hallway squeaked as someone walked by.

He pulled on a thick wool shirt and began buttoning from the bottom. The amber light of the lantern made his face shine gold, like an angel, or like melted caramel candy she ate at Halloween. He reached for his thick wool scarf and, with deft fingers, wound it around his neck. When he turned back from the dresser, to her surprise, he held the unopened letter she thought she'd hidden away.

"I'm surprised you haven't opened this yet. With all your thinking about the baby, did you forget about it?" He held out the battered envelope.

She took it in her fingers. At first, something about the handwriting had her spooked. As she remembered back, she was sure she didn't want to know, and should have thrown the post away where Roady wouldn't find it.

"Sally?"

"I—I, uh, I believe I know who it's from, and I don't want to read anything he has to say."

Roady's gaze jerked up to her face. "He?"

Even in the dim light of the lantern, she saw Roady's smile fall away. His eyes hooded, and he sat on the bed next to her.

She couldn't hide much from her husband.

"You think it's from *him*?"

She did. She couldn't pretend any longer. Why he'd write was a mystery, which made her stomach roil with disgust.

A heated frown slashed Roady's face. "Give it to me." He reached out.

She gasped and held it away. "No. I'll read it. Now. With you here. You shouldn't have to be the one."

Sally swallowed and placed her finger under the flap. Before pulling the paper from the envelope, she scooted up in the bed and put her pillow behind her back. The growth of her tummy was impossible to miss. For the first time ever, she noticed Roady jerk away his gaze.

How stupid. Why hadn't she taken care of this in private? Maybe she was wrong, and the letter was from someone else entirely. She'd made a mess of the whole awful situation, making it even more difficult for her husband.

She opened the note and glanced at the name at the bottom of the page. A wall of emotions slammed into her when she saw she'd been correct. She stared at Mr. Greenstein's signature for several moments, gathering her courage as she began reading aloud.

Dear Miss Stanford,

I've recently learned that congratulations are in order. I happened to be traveling down your street when Anita spotted my buggy. Since we had worked together for some time, she kindly invited me in and shared your news. Your mother was there, as well as Melba and Peter. Everyone is pleased that you've married.

Sally briefly closed her eyes. *Thank God they didn't tell him I am in the family way. Surely, he would put two and two together.* The familiarity of the note, as if nothing had transpired between them, made her want to retch.

I couldn't learn of this occurrence and not send you a little gift for your wedding to help you start your home. Also to thank you for the good work you did for me and my father at the newspaper. I've enclosed a banknote. Anita told me your husband is a cowboy, so I'm sure you can use this small token of my admiration.

With shaking hands, she picked up the envelope and looked inside to see what she'd missed. Daring a glance at Roady's stone-cold expression, she drew out a banknote and unfolded it. One hundred dollars, a huge and inappropriate amount of money from a former employer.

Roady took the banknote from her fingers, looked at the amount, and stood, tension filling the space.

Was he leaving? She hadn't finished the letter.

"The hour's getting late. You stay in bed until the house warms up downstairs."

The edge to his voice cut her to the quick, belying his concerned words. She watched as he set the banknote on the dresser and then pulled on an additional shirt and another pair of socks. His boots, gloves, and overcoat were downstairs where they wouldn't get the house dirty.

"Roady?"

"I'll be back at supper time, if not before." He stepped to the door as if he wasn't going to give her his usual good-bye kiss. He stopped, turned back, and kissed her on the forehead before reaching for the doorknob.

"Be careful." She barely got the words out before he was gone, and certainly before she was able to say *I love you*. As much as Roady's tone had fear rippling through her body, the thought of that monster speaking with her mother and sisters at her house frightened her even more.

In despair, she crumpled the letter in her hand. Anita and Melba were in danger. Something had to be done before the unthinkable happened. She just didn't know what that something was yet—but she would. And she needed to do it fast.

Chapter Thirty-One

The high-pitched whistle under the third-story eaves stirred Poppy from a fitful sleep. Too cold to even turn over, she lay in a semi-awake state shivering, her arms clamped tightly about herself.

Three long, agonizing days had passed since the storm descended. The snow had not let up for even an hour. The mood in the hotel was one of quiet despair. No one was out on the street. No one dared.

Poppy had never seen so much snow. People's nerves were on edge. The occupants of Cattlemen's Hotel crept around like sleepwalkers, speaking in whispers and avoiding interaction whenever possible. The rooms were dark and cold.

Abe, the bartender from the Hitching Post, had joined their ranks last night. He'd locked the saloon and then carefully made his way down the street, bringing with him a gunnysack with several cans of beans, one salted pork hip, three cans of prunes, and a jar of turnip snips. Not much, but no one begrudged him admittance. That brought the number of people to feed to fourteen.

As the cupboards emptied, Cook began keeping a list of their provisions, not explaining why but everyone knew. No one was to take any food without permission. Even Lenore seemed different. The usual down-curve of her lips had straightened out. She kept her biting comments to herself. Everyone was concerned.

Thankfully, Sheriff Crawford or his deputy stopped in once a day with news of others in town. So far, everyone still had a supply of wood and something to eat. Old Mr. Herrick was a concern, as were all the older people of Y Knot. He'd developed a deep cough and a rattling chest. For now, he was doing well staying under his piled covers.

Berta May was staying busy with a new quilt she'd started in the long hours of the day. She extended an invitation to any woman interested that as soon as the snow let up and crossing the street safely was possible, everyone was more than welcome to come help.

Despite the storm, Mr. Tracy said the telegraph lines were still operational. The whole of Montana Territory had been hit with this blizzard, as well as Wyoming and much of the plains. They were not suffering alone.

No one talked about the poor livestock, or the fact that they must be suffering horribly. Their plight was just too heartbreaking to think about.

When Poppy had questioned either lawman about the Preece farm or the Holcombs' ranch, they said they hadn't heard anything yet but assured her that wasn't unusual. People didn't come out in blizzards. They burrowed in their homes to wait out the worst.

Still, Poppy couldn't help but worry about her sister. What was happening? Was she safe? A mantle of responsibility weighted Poppy's shoulders. Why had their father treated Poppy so much differently than Kathryn? Growing up, she'd taken his benevolence toward her for granted. Now she wished she'd stood up to him, asked why he belittled Kathryn so.

Unable to endure the frosty air a moment longer, Poppy crept from her covers and lit her candle with shaking hands. The tiny amount of light wasn't much, but enough to help her maneuver her way to the fireplace without stubbing her toe. She stirred the bed of ashes and added three small logs. Leaning forward, she gently blew on the base of the wood and the tiny cinders, hoping a few coals were still hot enough to catch the wood. She'd used her ration of kindling for the day and would need to replenish it come morning.

Blowing hard brought dizziness. Her head ached painfully from the little sustenance in her belly. She'd never gone any length of time without three substantial meals a day, a tea tray at four, and warm milk and cookies before retiring for the night. Now, one meal and a few morsels of bread felt like a prisoner's rations.

One small ember glowed. Poppy was cold, and her stomach burned painfully. She wanted to go home. The warm, bountiful kitchen in Boston filled the spurts of sleep she was able to acquire when she wrapped herself into a ball under her covers. She never realized that an empty stomach would keep one awake, no matter how tired they were.

It's no use. This fire isn't going to start.

Her mother's two letters tucked away in her trunk came to mind, but burning them didn't feel right. She had a novel, but who knew how long they'd be stuck here? She'd better save that for later.

Home? Would she ever see it again? Was there a possibility they'd all perish in this storm? The warm tear on her cheek brought her to her senses. She angrily brushed it away. She needed to straighten her shoulders and lift her chin.

Hildy seemed to be handling the situation just fine. She didn't whine or complain.

On the other hand, the Sangers refused to leave their room and never let her take the children out. The place was becoming quite rank.

Fancy, the saloon girl, stayed hidden away in her room across the hall.

Thank heavens for Mr. Petty. He fed the lobby stove all night, as well as the one in the kitchen, making sure the hotel stayed as warm as possible.

She scowled at the cold embers that refused to light. Chills pricked her feet through the heavy socks Mr. Petty had given her last evening.

The lobby. She'd go there for some warmth. No matter the time, she'd make herself a cup of tea and let her limbs thaw out. Tea was one staple they had plenty of, and the patrons were welcome to consume it at will. For water, all they had to do was scoop a pot of snow. She'd learned hot water seemed to stave off the pains from a completely empty stomach.

Decided on her course of action, Poppy lifted her cape to her shoulders, noticing the garment had gotten much heavier in the passing days. Or had she just become weaker from the small provisions? She fastened the hook and eye at the base of her neck, and then took up the candleholder. The hallway was completely dark, since they weren't allowed to burn any lanterns and it wasn't safe to leave a candle unattended.

She crept down the narrow stairway, feeling like a thief. Necessity had emboldened her. The painting of the ugly woman didn't bother her in the least. Still, she longed for her home with the mansion's beautiful furnishings, the light, the warmth, the food, and the servants ready to do any bidding at all. Her parents.

She stilled, halting on the landing between the second and third floors. She hadn't thought of her parents at all. She did miss them, but she never thought of them happily together.

A sudden gust of frigid air zipped up the stairway and went up Poppy's ankle-length nightgown under her cape. She shivered, thinking of the stories she'd heard of ghosts passing in a cold rush of wind. Spurred into action, she took the last few steps into the lobby. As she knew it would, a lantern burned on the counter, and a modicum of heat touched her face.

Blowing out her own candle, she set the candleholder on the table at the foot of the stairs. Hurrying to the iron stove, she spread her hands before the blessed heat. Would she ever feel warm again?

The front window was dark. Across the street in Berta May's shop, a small light flickered.

At the sound of footsteps, she turned. Mr. Petty advanced with an armful of wood from the kitchen hallway.

Now the burst of cold air on the stairs made sense. It wasn't a ghost, but their guardian seeing to their needs. She smiled.

Mr. Petty stopped momentarily when he saw her, and then resumed his approach. Without a word, he hunkered down and rolled the logs from his arms on top of the stack alongside the wall. Stepping to the stove, he grasped the handle, opening the door to the fire within. Once that was done, he glanced over his shoulder and caught her gaze.

"Couldn't sleep?"

His deep voice brought a new, different type of awareness to her nerves.

She shook her head. "No. And I couldn't get my fire restarted."

"Best not to let it burn down completely."

Feeling self-conscious, she lowered herself into one of the French needlepoint chairs that someone had brought close to the heat. "I know. I dozed off while thinking I should add a new log." She ran her palms over the soft fur of her cape. "Don't you ever sleep, Mr. Petty? Whenever I'm down here, I see you're here too. Loading wood, tending the lanterns, checking outside."

"I'm used to working, I guess. Riding for the McCutcheons means we take night shifts several times a week when the weather permits. This is no different."

She felt her eyes go wide. Night shifts in the wilderness? "Really? Why?"

A deep chuckle rumbled in his chest. "Keep watch for wolves, bears, rustlers, or other dangers to the cattle. Settling a herd *before* they spook or stampede is best."

"All night?"

Once he had the fire built to his liking, he stood, then sat opposite her in the matching chair. He crossed his arms and hugged his chest. "You bet. The night passes quickly when you have things to do."

"Don't you get tired? How do you stay awake?"

He glanced away.

"Mr. Petty?"

"Singing to the cattle."

A warm glow started in Poppy's heart. She imagined Mr. Petty riding through a large herd of cattle, relaxed in his saddle, singing low. If his singing voice was anything like his speaking voice, she knew the sound would be beautiful.

"Will you sing a cattle lullaby now? I'd love to hear one, and maybe I'll get sleepy."

He tugged his gaze from the stove's closed door to her face, a silly grin pulling his lips. "I surely won't. Cattle are my usual audience, or the boys in the bunkhouse."

Sadness settled inside. "What will happen to the cattle, Mr. Petty? Nobody ever really says. All this snow? And cold? I don't like to think about how they must be suffering."

Any teasing that had been in his face vanished. "No, I don't like to think of 'em either. I hate to say it, but I fear a great many will die. Not so much from the snow, but the frozen layer of ice above the grass, or what's left of it." His brows lowered over his troubled eyes. "This year, a good many days of below zero occurred before the storm hit."

He tented his fingers and brought them to his face, resting his whiskered chin on his thumbs, his fingers touching his lips. After a moment, he reached forward and held a hand toward the heat. Quiet descended like a thick blanket.

The reality was awful. She'd hand-fed some cows on Kathryn's farm, the ones they kept to milk. She'd been enchanted by their large brown eyes and sticky nostrils. They were sweet. They'd be safe in her sister's barn.

"We'll hope and pray for the best," he said low, barely over the crackle of the wood he'd added a few minutes before. "The outcome is out of our hands."

Without anything to say that might help, Poppy nodded. "I'm putting on some water for tea. Can I make you a cup, Mr. Petty?"

He glanced up, his face still troubled. "I'd like that. Thank you."

Between her shivers, she smiled. "Very well, I'll be back in a few minutes. Please save my seat from the crowd."

A smile appeared on his face.

Poppy went to the stairs, relit her candle, and started for the kitchen. She was glad she'd decided to come downstairs tonight.

She was beginning to enjoy Mr. Petty's company very much. He wasn't condescending like Oscar. And he didn't want anything in return. He seemed to put stock in the things she had to say.

Was she changing? Or were the others around her changing?

Chapter Thirty-Two

Without giving it much thought, Shad followed Miss Ford into the kitchen. She smiled when she saw him, and then went about as if she'd been working there for years. Amazed at how well the socialite had adapted to the rustic conditions of the snowed-in hotel, he worked to keep a smile from his lips, knowing she wouldn't like him thinking of her domestic skills.

Having already stoked the kitchen oven a little over an hour ago, he guessed the water in the kettle was hot. As much as he'd like to carve large strips of meat from the ham they'd eaten last night and add several scoops of cold beans, he knew he couldn't.

Hopefully, the weather would break soon. Then he could get out and restock their shelves from others who had food to share. If he had to, he'd make a trip to the ranch for supplies. Until then, they all had to play by his rules—including him.

Finished with her preparations, Miss Ford handed him a warm mug.

"Thank you," he said, looking at the tan-colored water and wondering why women cottoned to it so much. He'd much rather pull out Abe's flask and take a swig to warm his belly, but wanting and doing were two different things.

"You're welcome." She gripped the warm cup in her hands. "This feels so good. I've never experienced such c-cold." Her last word stuttered out from her shaking jaw.

Shad didn't miss how her gaze darted away from his as soon as he looked at her. He remembered her from Virginia and how arrogant she'd been, how she'd treated the servants as pets, and him, as well. Apparently, she didn't remember the incident, for she'd never said a thing.

"How is Fancy Aubrey getting along upstairs?" Miss Ford asked. "I never see her. I wouldn't mind if she came down and ate with us. Plus, doing so would save Hildy from carrying a tray to the third floor."

He took her measure for several moments. Was she being sincere? Why would she care? "The scene your friend made when she arrived is the reason. She's biding her time in privacy. She has some pride too."

Miss Ford took a sip of tea. "Oscar should have held his tongue." She looked directly at him. "And I'm sure she does have pride. She's very beautiful."

"Nobody would dispute that," he said, holding her gaze.

Miss Ford set her mug on the counter and traced the rim with her fingertip. "I'm worried about the Sanger family," she said, her brows pulling together in the middle. "Why won't they come out of their room? Their behavior is odd. Mr. Sanger won't say a thing, and just watches me if I go in to read to the children or take them their tray. April and May are so adorable and sweet. And July." She shook her head and laughed softly. "That boy has stolen my heart. The things he comes up with are astonishing. I'll miss them when we finally get out of this mess."

Shad was amazed at the tenderness and passion brimming in Miss Ford's eyes. "I know what you mean," he replied quietly. "Their mother never says a word and practically ignores the children. Nothing we can do about the situation now but keep an eye on them. I've had my doubts for a while about Mr. Sanger."

Miss Ford's chin jerked up, and her mouth opened. "You think he's dangerous?"

"Don't know. I've mentioned it to Brandon. He'll send some telegrams."

"Sheriff Crawford? Do you think Mr. Sanger is an outlaw?"

Shad didn't miss the waver in her voice. "You don't have anything to fear. I won't let anything happen to you. Or the others. You're safe."

She released a deep breath and picked up her tea. The alarm left her eyes at his declaration.

Suddenly, he had the urge to take her in his arms. Despite her heavy cape, the kitchen stove, and the warm cup between her palms, the girl was still shivering. The temptation was too great. He set his cup on the counter and opened his arms.

"Come here. You're cold. Let me warm you up just for a moment."

Miss Ford's eyes widened, but she didn't say no. Her gaze went from his face to his chest, and then back up to his eyes. The candle on the opposite shelf flickered as she set her cup on the counter.

Slowly, as if weighing her actions very carefully, she inched forward in the quiet of the room, shadowy and dark. He wrapped her in his arms, his chin resting above her head. Her warmth was heavenly, but so were her curves beneath her fur cape. He imagined the thumping of her heart as she wrapped her arms around his middle and placed her cheek upon his chest.

Should he say something? Should she? For some peculiar reason, his heart was pounding as if he'd just sprinted up a steep hill.

"You're warm," he whispered low. "I didn't expect that."

She nodded. "You are too."

Her whispery voice sent a tickle around his chest. She wasn't judging him as a cowboy right now, but as a man. The thought brought him a measure of well-being.

A few feet away, scraping sounded on the back door. Poppy pulled back and looked up into his face. "What was that?"

Being he always wore his gun on his hip, Shad was fairly confident they weren't in much danger. He gently set her away, pulled his Colt, and moved to the door. He twisted the lock and inched the door open.

"H-help…"

Shad jerked the door wide to a flurry of wind and snow.

Hunched over and barely able to stand on his own two feet was Harold, who lived in a small cabin behind the hotel. He made a living by mopping the businesses around town.

Shad had thought Harold had been staying with the Herricks above the leather shop since the onslaught of the storm. Grasping the young fellow under the arms, Shad dragged him inside.

"Who is it?" Miss Ford asked, crowding in. She unwrapped her cape and slung it around Harold's body.

Shad hurried into the restaurant and brought in a chair, setting it next to the warmth of the stove.

"Thank y-y-you," the boy stuttered through his clenched jaw.

"What were you doing out there this time of the night?"

"I've been staying with Trent and his pa for the past few days. Why I decided to go home today was stupid, but I did. Took me hours to dig myself back into my cabin, but the place was freezing and I couldn't warm up even after I changed my clothes. I only got one coat so I kept it on, even though it was wet. After shivering for hours, I finally realized that if I didn't get into this hotel tonight and warm up, I'd be dead. Didn't expect ta find the door locked."

Shad removed Miss Ford's cape, then stripped off Harold's wet coat, replacing the cape even though she was shivering like a windblown leaf. "Lichtenstein had a break-in and was robbed. Since then, we've been locking the doors."

"Yeah, I heard about that. That's why I went home. Herricks' food was getting pretty sparse. They was good to take me in, but I didn't want to be a burden." The boy practically hugged the stove.

The time was nearing five o'clock, and Cook would be up soon. He'd been serving biscuits with a small scoop of oatmeal, which was getting smaller and smaller each day.

Shad went to his room, stripped the blanket off his bed, and brought it to Harold, giving Miss Ford back her cape.

"Have you met Miss Ford, Harold?" Shad asked. "She's Kathryn Preece's sister from Boston."

"No. But I've seen her from afar." He shyly ducked his head. "I'm pleased to make your acquaintance, miss. If you need any cleaning done, don't be afraid to ask."

"Thank you," she responded without missing a beat, as if she met strange wet boys every day at four thirty in the morning. "Please, take this. It'll warm your insides." She offered him her cup.

He greedily gulped down the warm tea and didn't come up until the whole cup was drained. "Any more where that came from?" he asked, wiping his mouth with the back of his arm.

Miss Ford handed him Shad's cup. "I'll make some more right now. In a bit, we'll have breakfast." She sneaked a quick glance at Shad.

Was she as disappointed as he was that they'd been interrupted? The way her gaze warmed, he thought perhaps she was.

"And I'm sure you're very hungry," she said softly, still holding his gaze.

"I admit that I am. But so is everyone else. Do you think I could stay here for a few days? I have some food to share. I can retrieve it now, if you want."

"There's plenty of room for you," Shad replied. They wouldn't turn anyone away. Everyone was welcome, as far as he was concerned.

Cook stumbled into the kitchen, wiping a hand over his sleepy face. His eyes lit with pleasure when he saw Harold. "I've been worried about you, boy. When did you show up?"

"Just a few minutes ago. If Shad hadn't unlocked that door, I would have froze to death on your doorstep."

"That's a good point," Miss Ford said, searching his face. "Maybe we should leave the doors unlocked for whoever else might need to get inside."

Shad nodded. *I should have thought of that before.* "I agree. From now on, front and back doors are to stay unlocked. I'd rather tangle with a thief than let one of our friends die. Cook, you'll have to start sleeping in here to keep the food safe. And I'm always in the lobby."

Cook began banging around, putting on a pot of coffee and gathering snow to melt for the oatmeal.

Shad turned to Miss Ford. "You warm enough to make it back to your room? Sleepy yet?"

"Actually, I am now."

Her smile was doing funny things to his insides. Seemed they had a secret they shared.

"Do you need me to walk you up?"

"Heavens, no," she said on a soft laugh. "You get this poor boy settled in a room. That will make me the happiest."

"Fine, then." He wanted to thank her for the conversation, but that might sound stupid. "Good night, Miss Ford. We'll save your breakfast for when you awaken." Now he was sounding like some nursemaid, the kind of person she was used to.

She glanced back as she left the room. "I appreciate that, Mr. Petty, and for the fine conversation we shared."

Shad felt the questioning looks of Cook and Harold. Let them wonder; he had no explanations to give.

Chapter Thirty-Three

That night, when Roady skipped supper and sent Francis with a message that he'd eat in the bunkhouse with the men, Sally tried not to take the news to heart. He was working through the problem in his mind, the way he always did. When he finally came in, they would discuss the situation and make a plan.

In her chair by the window, Claire worked on a piece of cross-stitch. Flood read an outdated newspaper he'd pulled from a wicker basket next to the fireplace. Sally sat across from Hickory at a small table, the chessboard between them forgotten.

"Your move, Miss Sally," the boy said softly.

The atmosphere in the room was strained, as if everyone had picked up on her disquiet.

"Oh." Sally reached forward to move her knight. She didn't miss Flood's fretful glance to the dark window. He wasn't worrying about Roady, but his cattle and stock.

Claire got up and crossed the room to his chair, setting her hand on her husband's shoulder. Both their faces were drawn with grief.

"Nothing more we can do," he said low.

Sally waited. It wasn't her place to ask, but since yesterday, the tension had grown. Roady had told her the cattle, as well as any stock left out of shelter, were in peril.

Claire massaged her husband's large shoulders. "Sending that herd to Miles City was a wise decision. At least those cattle won't suffer."

He reached up and laid his hand on hers, his mouth pinched tight.

The anguish on both their faces made Sally want to cry. With the way it felt inside, she couldn't imagine trying to stay alive out in such a storm.

"Will the snow stop soon?" Hickory asked after moving his rook and taking one of her pawns.

Flood reached for his pipe when his wife went back to her chair. "I wish I knew the answer to that, son. Only the Good Lord knows." He struck a match and held it to the tobacco, puffing a few times before smoke came out with his breath. He shook out the match and set it in a small copper ashtray.

The front door opened, and Roady stepped inside. He glanced around the room as he went about stripping off his snow-covered coat and removing his boots.

"Sorry I missed supper," he said, avoiding Sally's gaze. "Sometimes a lot of problems get solved around the bunkhouse supper table. I needed to stay. Francis said he gave you my message." His expression said nothing along those lines had been accomplished.

Sally stood and went to his side.

"He did, and we understand," Flood responded. "No need to fret. Right now, the ranch takes priority over sensibilities. I'm sure your pretty wife didn't mind at all."

"Of course I didn't," Sally hurried to respond. She wanted to help Roady with his layers, but no task was left to do.

He looked down into her face and then around the room. The buffeting of the wind had turned his cheeks to leather, and his teeth still chattered from the walk from the bunkhouse. "You don't mind if I turn in right away? Didn't seem like today would ever end."

"I'd expect nothing less," Claire said. She stood and smoothed her skirt.

Sally laid her hand on Roady's arm. She missed their easy manner, and had been pining for him for hours. "I asked Esperanza to warm water for a bath and light the stove in the bathing room. I can have it ready in moments, if you'd like."

He touched the tip of her nose with a frozen finger, and she smiled. His attention was the first sign she had that things were going to be all right.

"That was considerate. I'd like that very much."

"I'll run up and fetch your sleep shirt and some clean socks, and meet you there."

Under normal circumstances, she wouldn't have spoken so intimately in front of the McCutcheons, but she had no choice today. She knew once he got upstairs and rolled into bed, there would be no getting him out.

Roady nodded and ambled into the downstairs hall.

Halfway up the stairs, she stopped and turned. "Sorry, Hickory. We can finish our game tomorrow, if you'd like."

On the upper landing, she rounded the corner and went into their room, gathered the things Roady needed, and returned to the bathing room. She gave a tentative knock and waited. In their own cabin, she often helped him scrub his back in their small wooden tub, but tonight she was feeling shy.

"Come in."

She pushed open the door and set his things on the small pine table where a candle burned. The woodstove in the corner had the room nice and warm. A kettle sat on top for when they wanted a quick reheating of the water.

Roady was stretched out in the coffin-sized tub, the water halfway up his body, his eyes closed. "This water feels mighty good," he mumbled, opening his eyes. A ghost of a smile pulled at his lips.

At that moment she knew—whatever transpired about the baby, and its father, they would get through it and be fine. Roady wouldn't throw away what they had because of bruised feelings and pride. He'd told her often that he didn't care that he hadn't actually fathered their child; he'd love it as his own. It took a big man to declare that.

Had she really been afraid he'd go back on his words? Gazing into his eyes now, she couldn't believe it.

"I'm so glad. I took a hot bath earlier. It's the only way to get some warmth down to your bones."

His eyes glittered. "Want to join me? You can always take another. If I move over here," he splashed to the side, "there's plenty of room."

Sally knew he was kidding, but appreciated his willingness to reach out and put her feelings first. This was his way of making up for how he'd left things this morning, leaving her to worry and brood over his actions. But she didn't care about that now. She was just glad to have him back.

"No, I don't, thank you very much. You must be remembering me before I looked like a pony. There isn't room for us in there now, and you know it."

"What?" A deep longing crossed his face. "That's the most far-fetched statement I've ever heard. You're more beautiful today than when we married."

She picked up a folded cloth from the table, dunked it in the water, and began soaping it as heat from his compliment suffused her face. "I don't feel beautiful. But I promise, if the tub were larger, you couldn't keep me out."

His eyebrows waggled. "I'll keep that in mind when I add on to our place next year. Our bathing room will have enough space for a bathtub to fit two. You can bet on that."

She giggled. "Just think how much water we'd have to warm to fill it."

Sally pulled the short stool around to the back of the tub. He leaned forward and let her lather his wide shoulders. For several moments, she worked in the quiet.

"Are you ready for more hot water? I can get the kettle off the stove."

"Mmm, no thanks, darlin'. Just keep doing what you're doing on my back, and I'll never complain. That feels good."

"After today, I'm relieved to hear I'm still your darling," she replied, dipping the cloth in the tub and picking up where she left off. The tangy scent of the soap tickled her nose. "When you left this morning, you were upset. I'm so sorry about the letter."

Roady glanced around, his face shiny from the heat of the room and the bath. "You'll always be my darlin'. I'm sorry about leaving the way I did. I shouldn't have. Things that happened weren't your fault. I was a horse's butt, acting the way I did."

Sally caressed his shoulder.

He took the cloth and washed his face, arms, and legs. "Look out now. I'm gonna rinse."

She moved back, resting her hands on the edge of the tub.

He dipped under the water and came up with a chuckle. "You've gone and tamed me good."

He looked to the clean, folded towel on the table, and Sally promptly handed it to him. He stood and dried until his skin was a rosy pink.

"Like what you see?"

Roady was never this bold. She didn't quite know how to answer. She'd been admiring his beauty, but now dropped her gaze to the lantern. For the few months they'd been married, he'd encouraged her to speak her mind.

"You know I do," she whispered, feeling a smile tug at her lips.

"Then why are you being so shy? I feel like we've gone back to the start."

He stepped out of the tub, wrapped the towel around his waist, tucked in the end to keep it in place, and then gently lifted her chin with one finger until she looked into his eyes.

She swallowed nervously. "We haven't."

He lowered his face to hers, kissing her sweetly. The moment lingered. A small sound as if he were eating a piece of cake made her smile. He always had a way of lightening a moment.

Reaching for his nightshirt, he slipped the garment over his head before he removed the towel and pulled on his robe, the garment he only wore to get from the bathing room to the bedroom. Sitting on the stool, he undid the thick pair of socks rolled together in a knot and drew them on one by one.

"But we do need to talk, Roady," she said. "As much as the letter makes me sick, and I wonder why in the world that man would contact me after what he did, I can't stop thinking of something else. And I'm not sure what to do."

He straightened, all playfulness gone from his face. "Your sisters?"

Shocked, Sally felt her eyes open wide. She and Roady were so much alike sometimes, the realization astounded her. She nodded. The room was still quite warm from the woodstove. She felt moisture on her forehead and behind her neck.

"I'm worried he'll use me to get to Anita and Melba." When an unstoppable shiver rippled through her, Roady reached out and smoothed his large hand down her arm. "He might go visit. Gain their trust. Tell them how smart they are and perhaps possibly offer to help them in some way." She swallowed back her revulsion, remembering how Mr. Greenstein had slowly reeled her in, an unsuspecting innocent. "How can he do that, Roady? He's married and has children of his own. As much as I detest what he did to me, I can't help but feel sadness for them. Why would he do it? I don't understand a man like that."

Roady stood there, looking down at her, but she could tell his thoughts were miles away—in St. Louis, confronting her attacker. His flared nostrils and hardened expression made his face look like a slab of granite, unmovable and certain of what he wanted to do.

"That's because he's not a man, he's an animal. You need to remember that. Any repercussions that fall upon his unsuspecting family are *his* doing, not yours."

Roady gave her a direct stare, a hard look that she dared not argue with, or even comment upon. And she didn't want to. To have such a champion on her side relieved her of the crippling weight she'd felt on her shoulders for the last few months. They needed to warn her family. That was one thing she was certain of.

Leaning forward, he briefly pressed his lips to hers. "As much as we wanted to keep what happened a total secret," he said next to her lips, "I don't think we can any longer. Actually, I've been thinking about this for a while now, but didn't want to upset you." He reached down and gently caressed the growing bump that had once been her flat tummy. "This is my son or daughter. But we've moved on. I trust you with my life, and I think you trust me the same way."

She nodded, spellbound by the man who held her whole world in the palm of his hands.

Roady tucked a strand of wayward hair behind her ear. "Tell you the truth. Now that we know nothing can hurt us as long as we don't let it, keeping the past a secret doesn't feel as all-fired important as it did back when I first learned the truth. I do want to protect and shield you and the babe, but for me, I really don't care who knows."

Sally's throat burned with emotion. She ran both her palms up the thick cotton fabric covering his solid chest. "Thank you. To hear such words from you is a salve to my heart."

"Surely, you've known that's how I feel, haven't you?"

She nodded. "Yes. But hearing you say the words makes the feelings real. Do you have a plan?"

"I do. And just as soon as you're upstairs under the covers getting warm next to me, I'll share it." He turned, opened the stove, stirred the fire with the iron poker, and then shut the door tight. Outside, the wind whistled around the house, unrelenting.

Sally's heart swelled. She followed Roady out the door, down the hall, and around the corner. Everyone else had retired to their rooms, and the flickering flames in the fireplace provided the only light.

Roady paused at the bottom of the staircase and reached for her hand. Everything would be all right. Somehow, they'd send warning of the dire situation before it was too late.

A quick glance to the window, and the storm beyond, almost made her foot falter. How would they send a message if they couldn't get to Y Knot? Every moment counted. Until the letter arrived, she'd been certain that monster would never show his face to her family, but now she knew different. He already had. He'd begun laying the groundwork.

Something had to be done… and quickly.

Chapter Thirty-Four

"Sorry, Sanger, you're fit enough to come out of this room now and eat with the rest of us," Shad bit out, holding tight his anger. Brandon was still waiting for a return telegram about him, and Shad hoped it arrived sooner rather than later.

The sullen man sat in the chair by the fire, his mouth twisted in an angry knot.

He enjoyed being lazy, there was no other explanation to why he'd want to stay holed up in a room with his wife and three children since they'd arrived. His only trip out was to the outhouse. The setup was extra work for Hildy and Lenore, and both the women were weak from the small rations. The parents would come out of this room or go hungry, if it were up to him—and it was.

"From here on out, you eat in the dining room with the rest of us, or you don't eat."

Mrs. Sanger and the three children huddled under the blankets as they listened to the one-sided conversation. The plates on the tray Hildy had delivered half an hour before were licked clean.

"And your young'uns could use some cleaning up," he added angrily.

When he saw July's expression fall, he wanted to kick himself. It wasn't the boy's fault. The girls were too young to understand what he'd just said. Even as a boy himself, and in charge of his two younger brothers, Shad did a better job tending to them than this couple did looking after their own children.

"How do we do that?" Mrs. Sanger asked, her eyes downcast with embarrassment.

"You bring Cook the snow and he'll warm it up, enough for a bath if you want. But he's not going to fetch it and do everything. We could also use another man's help keeping up with the firewood needed in each room."

Mr. Sanger had yet to respond.

"You hear me? I'm not joking about this."

"I hear ya," the man snarled out, causing the little girls to cuddle together, their eyes large.

"Let me take the children. I'm happy to give them a bath and save you the trouble," a female said from behind him.

Recognizing Miss Ford's voice, Shad turned. She looked fetching in spite of what they'd been through the last few days. Little food, little heat, and less-than-perfect living conditions. The girl had spunk.

July's eyes went wide. "I ain't taking no bath with April and May."

Shad noted the worried glance Mrs. Sanger shot to her husband. What were they hiding? "I think that's a good idea, Miss Ford."

Encouraged, she stepped in next to him. "July, you won't have to bathe with your sisters. You can go first, by yourself. Does that sound good?"

"That ain't possible," the bulky man responded. His stubble-covered jaw jutted out in challenge as he climbed to his feet, the first time Shad had seen him standing.

"That's too bad. We're all stuck here together. Shouldn't your wife be making the decisions about the young'uns? Miss Ford is being helpful."

Mr. Sanger's glance darted back and forth. If the man had a gun, Shad felt sure he'd try to use it. His whole family was afraid of him.

"Fine," he finally said. He stomped forward and narrowed his eyes at July, causing the little tyke to shake like a leaf.

Anyone could see this father ruled with an iron fist, something Shad couldn't tolerate. The man better not try beating his children or wife while he was staying here, or he'd get a taste of his own medicine.

"Behave yourself, July," Mr. Sanger said, and then smiled. "You remember your manners, or there will be hell to pay. You got that?"

The boy nodded. "Yes, sir. I do… and I will."

Miss Ford smiled at Shad. "Thank you, Mr. Petty. I'll go gather the snow and put the pots on the stove. I'll have a tub ready in no time."

"Have Harold help you," Shad said, still feeling the effects of Miss Ford's pretty smile. "He'll be happy to." He chuckled, never seeing someone so happy about bathing children. *To each his own*, he thought as she hurried away.

Scanning the room, Shad decided he'd stick around until she returned for July and his sisters. Mr. Sanger's expression smoldered with anger, although the man was too much of a coward to say any more.

Shad didn't want the woman or children to be the recipient of any anger directed at him. Going to the side of the room, he eyed the pile of belongings they'd never taken the time to put away. He looked at Mrs. Sanger, still lying in the bed.

"Any clean clothes in there for the children?"

"Sure," July said.

"Hun-gy," one of the twins said as her eyes filled with tears, whether April or May, Shad wasn't sure as he couldn't tell them apart. The other's bottom lip wobbled.

July was the most responsible of them all. He bounded off the bed and hurried over to sort through some belongings. "I'll find some clean duds. For them. And for me."

Before long, July had two small shirts, two pairs of tiny pants, two sets of holey long johns, and four socks that looked better suited to be rags. All the garments appeared to be hand-me-downs from the boy's own clothes.

"Those are for the girls?" Shad asked. "They look like your clothes."

"They was, but I grew out of 'em. They're still good, though. See?" He tugged one pair of pants at each leg, but the garment didn't rip.

"I believe you," Shad said, embarrassed.

July snagged a pair of blue overalls and a shirt out of the mangled pile. "Here's for me." He smiled up at Shad, eager to please.

These children were as different from their parents as lambs were from a wolf pack. Something was amiss, and Shad aimed to figure out what.

He ruffled July's hair. "Good job."

Miss Ford was back in the doorway. "Everything's ready, July. Come along with me. I'll show you the way. As soon as the first bath is finished, I'll be back for your sisters."

The boy stuffed his clean garments under his arm and then looked at the bed where April and May watched. "I'll take 'em along now, so they don't rile Pa. He's tired." He held out his arms to his sisters, a loving smile on his lips.

"Fitting will be a tight squeeze. The bath room isn't all that large," Miss Ford said, slanting a conspiratorial look at Shad. "But I guess we can make it work. Everyone will be as clean as a whistle when we get through."

Mr. Sanger looked like he wanted to object, but rightly held his tongue. Mrs. Sanger just watched complacently.

"Hun-gy," one cherub whimpered softly.

They'd already had the noon meal, and it would be hours before their bedtime snack. Perhaps a few exceptions could be made for the little ones once they were out of this room. Their father always complained he wasn't getting enough to eat.

Shad couldn't stop his gaze from cutting to Miss Ford. Her expression said she was thinking the same thing. He sent her a surreptitious wink, and she gave him a slight nod.

"No more food until bedtime," he stated bluntly for the parents' benefit, but followed the four toward the kitchen. The bath room sat opposite.

Miss Ford stopped in the hall and turned, one little girl in her arms and the other holding July's hand.

"I'll see you in a few," Shad said, tipping his head toward the kitchen.

"I hope so, Mr. Petty," she answered in a self-satisfied tone. "Thank you for taking the appropriate action. I believe we have much more to learn."

"Let's just tackle one problem at a time."

She glanced at the grubby little face so close to hers and placed a gentle kiss on the child's chapped cheek. "I think that's good advice."

Shad lingered several seconds, admiring the view before slipping into the kitchen. Cook wouldn't begrudge a few bowls of oatmeal for the little tykes.

Were he and Miss Ford on to something important about the children? He thought yes, but only time would tell.

Chapter Thirty-Five

"What happened?" Luke shouted as he ran out the door and made for the bunkhouse.

The men had shoveled a path from the ranch hands' living quarters to the barn, corrals, and house. His boot hit an icy spot. He slid but caught himself before he fell and kept going. An unfamiliar sleigh careening into the yard and up to the bunkhouse porch had caught his attention from his father's office window, but not until he recognized Pedro and John lifting a body wrapped in blankets out of the conveyance was he spurred to action.

Who was it? Was he dead, or just hurt? Pedro, John, and Uncle Pete had been detained in Pine Grove when they'd gone to check on Widow Blanchard. The two black horses hitched to the sleigh were covered in sweat. Steam lifting from their hot bodies mixed with the snowflakes.

Luke was right behind the men as they carried the person through the door, held open by Lucky. The cook's face was stricken with grief.

Pedro and John were fine. That meant that the person in the blanket had to be Uncle Pete.

On the way in, Luke grasped Ike's shoulder. "Go get Pa. And Roady."

Ike ran out the door.

Francis and Smokey crowded beside Pedro who, along with John, gently laid Uncle Pete on his cot. Lucky gimped into the group of men huddled around the bunk.

Uncle Pete. Badly injured. Luke's chest pinched with regret. He went to the head of the bed and dropped to one knee to examine the damage. The gashes were difficult to look at. He turned and glanced over his shoulder, noticing Pedro had also sustained some wounds to his hands.

"What happened?" Luke asked again.

Hickory must have followed in Luke's footsteps from the house to the bunkhouse, because the boy stood wide-eyed at the foot of the bed.

"Wolves." John's word weaved quietly through the room.

Each man stared at their wounded comrade, their mouths pulled down, their eyes dark. Every day was filled with danger and the possibility of meeting your end. But reality never ceased to shock.

"On our way back to the ranch, we decided to make one more call on Widow Blanchard, make sure she was still doing all right since the snow had begun to fall. Uncle Pete was tending her stock in the barn. When he started for the house, he was attacked."

"Attacked? But it's the middle of the day," Francis said, his gaze never leaving Uncle Pete.

John rubbed a large hand over his face. "Didn't make no difference. They were bold as brass. Pedro was restocking wood on Widow Blanchard's front porch and didn't see anything until he heard the noise, since the barn is shielded by the side of the house. When he pulled his gun, it was too late. They were too quick. He started for Uncle Pete, hollering at the top of his lungs. He fired and grabbed the ax on the way over. When I heard the commotion and got outside, I saw him swinging away at the snarling knot of animals, trying to get them off Pete. As soon as I seen what was happening, I emptied my gun, killing as many as I could before the others run off."

Finished with his story, John slowly shook his head. "I ain't never seen nothin' like it before. Never."

Luke swallowed slowly. Things didn't look good for Uncle Pete. Skin was torn from his face, and rips through his coat and pants showed the skin of his arms and legs slashed and bloodied.

When Francis moved up and took Uncle Pete's hand, the cowhand's eyes opened to slits. "Pa? That you?"

Francis glanced around nervously. "No, Uncle Pete. It's me, Francis."

"What happened?"

"You're hurt. You're back in the bunkhouse."

A low moan slipped through Uncle Pete's lips. "That's right. The wolves." A shiver ran the length of him. "Where's Pedro and John? They make it through?"

"I'm here, Pete," John said, his voice laced with sorrow. "Pedro is too. He's gonna be all right."

"I appreciate—you... bringing me home," he said in a raspy voice broken in pauses where none should exist. "Back to the Heart of the Mountains. Didn't want to die nowhere else, not after all these years." He dropped his hand to the edge of his bed and fingered the blanket, his chest lifting in a deep sigh. "Been my home a mighty long time." He coughed and then grimaced in pain.

"Can I get ya anything, cowboy?" Lucky asked, the huskiness of his speech making Luke's eyes sting. "Anything. You name it; I'll cook or bake whatever you want."

"You're a good man, Lucky. Thanks, my old comrade, but ain't no time for that—not now." Uncle Pete glanced around the room. "Flood here?"

"Not yet. I am, though," Luke said, drawing the man's gaze.

"So you are. Right here close." He gave a weak chuckle. "Now that I'm on the ranch, I can let go. I'm anxious ta meet my maker. I'll put in a good word for y'all."

Was there anything they could do, Luke wondered. How would Doc Handerhoosen tackle all these wounds? Uncle Pete's face was chalk white from all the blood he'd lost. He was weak. Luke couldn't imagine he'd last more than a few minutes. His father best hurry.

Luke couldn't remember how long the man had worked at the ranch. He'd been just a boy when Uncle Pete had signed on. From that very first day, he'd instructed all the children to call him Uncle, and the handle had stuck even as the children grew into men and women.

"Don't be in such a hurry, Uncle Pete." Luke took his shoulder gently and met Uncle Pete's gaze. "You've been a loyal hand. Thanks for making us your family."

Luke glanced around the faces. Hickory chewed his bottom lip. The boy would be an easy target for a wolf pack. He'd followed him across the ranch yard unattended and could have easily met the same fate. He'd have words with him later.

Roady bounded through the bunkhouse door just as Luke had without a coat or hat, his eyes frantic. He hurried to the side of the bed. "What happened? I saw the sleigh from the upstairs window and heard Ike in Flood's office but didn't stop to ask. Someone hurt? Whose sleigh is out…"

The men parted until he could see Uncle Pete lying quietly on the bed, his clothes just rags on his body. Roady's eyes jerked wide, and he skidded to a halt.

"Widow Blanchard's sleigh, *señor*," Pedro whispered, his hands now wrapped in cloths to stop the bleeding. "She offer to help our *amigo* so we can get him home. He too hurt to put on horse."

Luke's eyes filled. He blinked and cut his gaze away from Roady. His friend knelt on the opposite side of the bed, his expression one Luke rarely saw.

"I'm dying, boys," Uncle Pete whispered. "I don't mind, truly. Not now that I made it home." He stopped to take a breath, the crackling fire the only other sound in the room. His gaze slowly traced the faces of the men gathered around. "Ike here?"

Lucky touched his boot. "He's gone for Flood. They should arrive any second."

"If I don't last that long, tell him I want him to have my gelding. He's always liked Cutty. He's strong and steady, even if he does still think of himself as a stallion. Has plenty of rides left in him, for sure. Be sure Ike lets him run from time to time, or he'll get cranky."

"We'll pass on your wishes," Lucky said. "Every word."

Uncle Pete weakly lifted his arm and ran a trembling hand over his face. "And today I went without a shave. Don't that just beat all. You be sure an' take care of that for me before I'm buried, Lucky."

"'Course I will."

A smear of blood covered one side of Uncle Pete's face, almost hiding the whiskers he was worried about.

"Francis, you take my saddle. It's old, but comfortable. If you don't want ta keep it, I won't take offense if ya put it up for sell at Herrick's and turn a little profit. You've been a good lad, assisting with our horses all these years. I appreciate all you've done."

"I'm honored," Francis mumbled as he shook his head. "I won't sell it. I'll ride it, so all the men can think of you."

"That's mighty good to hear." Uncle's Pete's eyes slowly closed.

All the men leaned in, and when he opened his eyes again, Luke let go his breath.

"Luke, I have a message for Flood," Uncle Pete wheezed out. "Tell him I'm mighty grateful he gave a man with a past a chance to change his life. To make some good after bad. He gave me a go when no one else would. I ain't never forgotten that."

This was all news to Luke, and he was sure none of his brothers or Charity knew what Uncle Pete was referring to. Only his father. The truth had stayed firmly hidden, justly giving the man a new start.

"Will do, Uncle Pete. Don't you worry about that at all." Luke's gaze caught Smokey's, and he hitched his head.

Smokey made for the door to go see what was keeping Flood.

A funny little smile curled Uncle Pete's bloodstained lips. "Where's Hickory? I don't see the boy."

John nudged Hickory forward, and the boy moved close enough for Uncle Pete to see him.

The mauled cowhand held out a shaky hand. "You know where I keep my nickel-plated harmonica?"

Hickory nodded.

"Thought as much. If I give it to ya, you promise to practice? A little every day?"

A big lump went up and down on the boy's throat. He nodded again.

"It's yours, then," he said softly. "I'd appreciate it if you'd mind it with good care. I've had it for more than thirty years."

Uncle Pete's countenance brightened as his gaze moved around the rafters, a strange expression on his face. With great effort, he lifted his arm only a few inches, but his finger was pointed.

"Well, I'll be," he said on a chuckle. "Look at all them purty faces…"

Flood barreled through the door, followed by Ike and Smokey. The men parted to allow Luke's pa to come closer.

The man who'd raised Luke went down on one knee, taking Uncle Pete's bloody hand in his own. "Pete," he said in an anguished voice. "Pete, talk to me."

But he arrived too late.

Uncle Pete's sightless eyes gazed up at the rafters, a small smile on his lips.

Chapter Thirty-Six

Thank God, the snow had finally stopped. The wind had died, and several stars could be seen in the blackness above the hotel.

Frosty puffs of crystals streamed from Shad's mouth each time he breathed out. He glanced toward the livery, and then past Berta May's and in the direction of Klinkner's mill. The temperatures were still below freezing, but he'd needed some fresh air on his face. He couldn't see very far in the darkness, but remembered the sight of the heavy snow layered on top of each building.

Somewhere, a dog barked. In response, and closer than he'd ever heard, a wolf responded, the deep howl foreboding.

They'd been hearing wolves for days now. He'd seen the tracks when he'd ridden into Y Knot with Smokey and Francis. Everyone who stepped out of the protection of walls was on high alert. Hayden Klinkner and Drit had sighted several, and many more reported tracks around their buildings. The pack, or maybe it was more than one, were larger and stronger than any they'd faced in these parts before.

Shad stuffed his gloved hands into his armpits, knowing he shouldn't stay outside too long, but yearning for the open space of the prairie made him restless. This time of night was his only opportunity to think. Everyone was asleep.

A small smile pulled at his stiff lips. He'd cooked up a good portion of oatmeal, enough that the Sanger tykes all ate their fill after their bath.

Miss Ford swore July to secrecy, which wasn't hard to do.

If he had to, now that the snow had stopped, Shad would head out of town, track a deer or elk, or even some ranchers' stray beef. The folks in his care might be hungry now, but no one would starve to death.

Lifting his shoulders, Shad wondered what was troubling him. He'd been in tight spots before. They'd get through this rough patch without any casualties.

Tonight, the fate of his brothers occupied his thoughts. Had they taken shelter? Or had they been surprised somewhere along the way? They'd be riding cross-country with their mounts, not traveling any other way. But their last letter said they were anxious to get here. Surely, they'd watch the signs of the season. See the danger of the approaching storm. Hopefully, they didn't do anything foolish.

Shaking his head, he looked back up at the sky. Tanner and Nick were unpredictable. Shad couldn't guess, even if he tried. Best not to speculate. At least he knew they were riding together. That was a consolation, even if a small one.

Across the alley to his left, Brandon stepped from the sheriff's office where a light burned in the window, a beacon for anyone in trouble. The place didn't have a porch and overhang like the hotel and most of the businesses on the street. Presumably, Brandon or Justin had shoveled out the doorway.

Brandon cupped his mouth. "Everything all right over there?" he called in the white, frozen stillness.

To cross the alley from his doorway to the covered boardwalk in front of the hotel meant forging through a three-foot depth of snow. Neither of them wanted to get wet all over again.

"Things are fine over here," Shad called back. "Just needed some air." Even in the darkness, he caught Brandon's nod.

After patting his arms for a moment, the lawman stepped back into the sheriff's office and closed the door. He must have been very relieved Charity, his young wife, was safely housed at her brother's homestead.

Intending to go back inside himself, Shad returned to the building. Reaching for the door, he caught movement as a dark shadow slunk out of the alleyway between the hotel and Lichtenstein's mercantile.

Wolf!

The moon gave off just enough light that Shad could see the silver tips of his coat glisten as the tall, rangy animal lunged through the snow into the center of the street. A pack of about twelve followed in his path.

Shad sucked in a breath. They were bold, wild, and dangerous. Several smaller wolves stretched out on the snow. Another yipped when bitten from behind by one of his comrades. The first wolf that had appeared, the largest in height and weight, must be the lead male. The animal glanced his way, unconcerned that Shad was watching them. He was making a statement. Anyone who thought a wolf had no intelligence hadn't spent any time in the high country. They were cunning and sharp.

This beast's golden eyes glittered as he lowered his head and exposed his long, yellow teeth in a guttural growl.

A rifle report rent the still night, and a wolf on the edge of the pack dropped in the snow. The two that had lain down leaped to their feet and bounded away with the pack.

Shad cut his gaze up the street. Trent Herrick's head and rifle stuck out of his second-story window. He cocked his weapon and fired again, but the pack had already scattered.

The door behind Shad flew open, and Miss Ford stood in the doorway.

"Mr. Petty. What's happening? Who's shooting out there?"

He came in, closed the door, and crossed the lobby to the woodstove, craving the heat.

"Trent Herrick, the leather worker. He killed a wolf in the street."

She gave a small gasp. "In the street? They came that close? I know wolves are around these parts, but I was assured they avoid people and never come into town." The bodice of her cape lifted with her frightened breaths.

With his hand, he gestured to the chair by the stove. Their nightly meetings had become a habit. If he were honest with himself, he looked forward to their talks. During the day, Oscar Scott was usually never far from her side; he took the noon meal with her, and walked her to her room at night. Even with all the easterner's attention, Shad got the distinct impression she couldn't stand the man.

"That's true enough, in most cases. I've never seen them before in town or out at the ranch house. Could be, the leader feels empowered by the fact we're snowed in. He has the advantage, but we have guns. As long as you stay inside, Miss Ford, you're in no real danger." He glanced at the darkened window. "And I don't see that changing anytime soon, even though the snow has stopped."

She sucked in a breath. "It's stopped?"

"You haven't looked outside?"

"I was so worried when I heard the rifle shot I didn't notice." She left the stove and went to the window. "This is good news. Soon I'll be able to check on Kathryn."

She turned and looked at him over her shoulder with such adoration and trust, her gaze made his stomach tighten into a constricted ball. He had to remember he had nothing to give her. Nothing.

He'd been rendered infertile by Redbud. The blow of the bull's head to Shad's midsection had crushed some reproducing things inside. The doctor had given the long, unpronounceable names of what exactly, but Shad had been so miserable, he'd put them out of his mind. At the time of the accident, the pain had been excruciating but he'd gotten through, helped away by two comrades bearing his weight. Not until he'd been examined two weeks later had the real pain started.

"Might be a while before you can get out to the farm. Don't start planning yet," he replied gruffly, seeing the light in her eyes dim. "Brandon and Justin will make rounds just as soon as they're able. You leave that to them."

Looking grumpy, she made her way slowly back to the lobby stove and lowered herself into her chair.

He chastised himself. It wasn't *her* chair or *his* chair, as he'd begun to think of them. They were the lobby chairs, and soon life would be back to normal.

"You're touchy tonight, Mr. Petty. Did you drop a log on your toe or something?"

Miss Ford's voice had turned sugary sweet, like she used to speak. Perhaps he'd been a little heavy-handed.

"Just don't get your hopes up about getting out there too soon. It's darn cold, difficult for horses and people." He chanced a glance in her direction and almost smiled. She was using him for imaginary target practice.

"Hildy told me the livery has a sleigh to rent. Why can't I take that out to the farm? The distance isn't far."

"Who'll drive you?"

"I'll drive myself."

Right. Shad tamped down his growing annoyance. "We're in the middle of a hellacious winter storm. Just because the snow has let up for the first time in days doesn't mean it's cleared away."

"I see. Well, I guess we best change the subject." She gave him a smug smile. "We don't have to agree on everything, you know."

He knew that very well. He thought about the soft feeling he'd experienced for Miss Ford a few moments back, and almost laughed aloud. "That's true. What do you want to talk about?"

"I don't care. Anything."

Let her be peevish. Shad stretched back in the chair and closed his eyes. The late hour was closing in on him. The fire was stoked and pumping out the heat.

"I wonder if your employer misses you," she finally said. She pulled her feet up under her cape and got comfortable in the chair.

"I'm sure they have enough on their minds not to be worrying over me. But I wonder about you and your parents. Are you expected home?"

Now, why did I ask about her? I don't want to know any more than I already do. She is Kathryn Ford Preece's sister.

He remembered the expensive gown Tobit's wife had worn to the harvest party held in Lichtenstein's store a few months back. Whooee… The dress probably cost more than a cowboy's yearly salary. And Oscar Scott had dropped enough information the last few days to fill in what a pampered life Miss Ford had led up until they'd arrived in Y Knot.

Now Shad had gone and opened the floodgates. He glanced at her. Or had he?

She hefted a deep sigh.

"Something wrong?" he asked, again against his better judgment. He couldn't believe she hadn't seized the opportunity to use his question for a chance to brag about her mollycoddled existence. Still, he couldn't stop picturing her walking down the hotel hall with the little cherub, April or May Sanger in her arms, and the other two Sanger siblings at her side.

"By now, my father is furious with me. I have plans to go to France in April, and a good possibility exists, after my visit to Kathryn and my delayed return, he may renege on his promise to send me. I would be deeply disappointed if he did."

France! The disparity between them was worse than Shad had imagined. He didn't know how to respond. He didn't even have the ability to conceive how privileged her life really was.

He pulled his coat tighter. "It'll work out," he mumbled from the side of his mouth.

"Pardon me? I didn't hear that."

Irked with himself, Shad straightened. She'd been doing and fetching around here just like Hildy and Lenore. She'd helped cook, serve, and even bathed the Sanger children. In all of her efforts, he'd forgotten she was practically royalty. An image of Miss Ford in Virginia after the hunt, laughing with the other women as he and his men fought with Redbud, made him scowl.

"I'm sure it'll work out just like you want it to, whatever your plans. That is, *if* you get home by April." *Now that was downright mean.*

Her forehead crinkled and she bit her bottom lip. "Do you think it's a possibility I won't? Father will be fit to be tied. I can't imagine that happening."

"Anything's possible. Why're you going to France? That's a long way away, you know."

"Yes, I know." She gave a small laugh. "I've been there already, and other places in Europe. However, I want in the worst way to attend an art school there. I've been dreaming about it for years, and I've been after my father for about that long to let me go."

"You mean pay your way."

Miss Ford smiled as if that was obvious. "Of course I mean pay my way. Isn't that what fathers do?" She lifted her chin. "Plans and reservations have been made, most of them nonrefundable."

"So, you're an artist too? Why aren't I surprised?"

"You're very sarcastic tonight. The smugness doesn't suit you."

"Really?"

"You're mocking me."

Shad rubbed a tired hand over his head, suddenly feeling exhausted. Why did everything she say hit him like a personal attack? She had no idea how spoiled she was, and he'd never be able to explain it away.

"Sorry. Your circumstances are not of your making."

"Circumstances?" she said calmly. "What're you talking about? Have I been behaving badly around here, wanting special favors, putting you out? I've done my best to do my share and not be a burden. I think you've painted a picture of me of how you *think* I should act, not as I have." She smiled and took a sip of her tea.

Was Miss Ford right? Was he judging her so unfairly just because he felt his own inadequacies up to his ears?

Chapter Thirty-Seven

As Poppy sipped from her cup, she studied Mr. Petty from under her lashes. He'd not get her goat, not in this lifetime or the next. She had lots of practice dealing with her father. Her face wouldn't give away one iota of her feelings.

The fact that her attempts to fit in had gone unnoticed by him, and probably everyone else, hurt. She might as well take to her bed and demand Hildy and Lenore wait on her hand and foot. What difference did her behavior make? She'd never change their perception of her.

Well, she wouldn't think about the situation right now. She looked forward to these times alone with Mr. Petty. She didn't want to spoil tonight by being angry. They didn't have many nights left.

"Thank goodness the snow has stopped. I never knew the clouds could hold so much." She glanced at him.

"Safer ground?"

"Yes."

No more snow meant the sooner she'd be able to check on Kathryn. She knew Tobit would take good care of her sister, but until she saw that fact with her own two eyes, the seed of doubt never quite left her mind. Kathryn had changed so much in the few months she'd been married. Or perhaps Poppy had just never had such a private opportunity, away from her parents and the household servants, to get to know her properly. Maybe they could have more of the same.

A bud of unfamiliar happiness stirred in her chest. *Amazing.* She liked the feeling very much.

"Something tickling your fancy?"

Mr. Petty's deep voice drew her gaze from her cup back to his face. In the dark, quiet lobby, the cowboy, as well as the rest of the world, seemed so different. They were comfortable with each other's company. Her mother would be mortified, and her father would have forbidden her to speak to him.

"I was thinking about Kathryn."

"Are the two of you close?" he asked quietly.

She thought the question was mostly just to pass the time, but when he looked into her eyes, she realized he was sincere. "No, not really. At least, we weren't until this trip. Growing up, we were very different. I liked to travel, and my father encouraged me. Not so with Kathryn. I wondered why, but never asked."

"Now you feel differently?"

She gave a small laugh. "Are you sure you're a cowboy? You seem to have the knack for asking just the right questions. I'm amazed."

This time it was Mr. Petty's turn to smile. "I was responsible for my two younger brothers when we were all boys. I learned to dig deeper. Usually when they were telling me one thing they really meant something else."

"And where was that?"

"Wyoming Territory. We lived with my grandparents for as long as I can remember." He took a sip from his cup. "You were saying about Kathryn and this trip."

"We did grow closer. At least, to me it seemed we had… and I'm glad. She appears genuinely interested in me and my future. I admire her. How she left a pampered life to make something more meaningful of her own. She abandoned everything for an unknown future. That takes courage, Mr. Petty. Much more than I would have, I'm afraid."

He crooked a brow, and the gesture made her smile.

"I'll admit I was more than skeptical when I heard she planned to be a mail-order bride. People of our standing don't do that. I shuddered at the thought, but now that I know Tobit, I'm ashamed of myself. He's a good man, and she's very happy. Happier than I've ever seen her in my life. She's in love."

"Different doesn't have to be bad."

"And so I've learned, although Oscar doesn't agree. He thinks her the utmost of fools."

"Consider the source."

Poppy couldn't stop a quiet laugh. "I even chastised Kathryn when she went against our father and refused to marry Oscar. He and I have always been friends, but he was pledged to Kathryn since they were both very small children."

Again, the sardonic expression. Mr. Petty was holding back to spare her feelings.

"Go on," she said. "You can say it. My family is quite strange."

He twisted in the chair to glance at the window. It wouldn't be long before the sun rose. "I didn't say a word."

"But you were thinking it."

"Maybe so. But most families aren't what they appear on the outside. Everyone has their secrets."

Shame for acting so immature the first time she'd seen him in Virginia brought heat to her face. Her actions had been childish—*and wrong*. Did he remember? If he did, he never let on.

Should she clear the air? She felt dishonest remembering and not saying anything. If she apologized, perhaps she wouldn't feel so guilty. *And* it was the right thing to do, she lectured herself.

"Mr. Petty," she began and stopped, still uncertain. She didn't want to ruin their friendship. "Do you mind if I call you Shad?"

His lips twitched. "Not at all."

"Thank you." Was this right? She didn't want to embarrass him. "I remember why you seemed so familiar when we met at Kathryn's. Actually, I remembered a few days ago. You were in Virginia. With a group of cowboys."

The pleasant expression faded from his face, and his gaze shuttered. He was like a completely different man sitting across from her.

"Am I correct?"

"That's right."

The gruffness of his voice surprised her.

"We were picking up a bull named Redbud. He was a mean cuss better suited for a bullet in his brain than breeding."

"That's horrible!"

Maybe that wasn't nice to say, but that animal had changed Shad's life forever. Bulls were smart creatures, but not all were calculating man-killers. In his way of thinking, he wouldn't pass that bloodline on for nothing. No matter how large the bull's offspring grew or how fast they matured. The McCutcheons had a handful of bad-tempered bulls, but none tried to get you in a corner and smash you to death. The pain of that fateful day rippled through his thigh and lower body, making his skin heat with anger and remorse.

"I can see you haven't lived out west long enough to know— animals have their place. They aren't cuddly creatures for pleasure, like you spoke of the bunnies at the Preece farm. Those rabbits are raised to sell to the butcher. To feed people, hungry people, and to earn money. By now, your sister knows that, but most likely didn't want to tell you."

Poppy straightened. Her pretty, kissable lips were now white in anger. She didn't like what he'd just proclaimed. Well, that was just too bad.

"Thank you for correcting me. I guess I'm just naive. I hope Redbud didn't hurt you. I saw a scuffle down at the corrals, and some of the women were talking about going down to watch. Then we were told one of the hands had gotten hurt."

"I did. But not badly." *At least, not on the outside.*

"I just want to say how very sorry I am. The whole episode was juvenile." She chewed her bottom lip. "When I remember back, I'm mortified at myself. I hope you will forgive me."

He shrugged. "Sure. All's forgiven." Actually, her words did bring a sort of calming.

Now that he'd given her absolution, she brightened.

"But what a small world we live in, don't you think? I'm from Boston, you're from Wyoming, but we first meet in Virginia, then again in Montana. What are the chances of that happening? It's almost like destiny brought us—"

A deep rumbling above made them both glance up at the staircase. The vibration caused Poppy to drop her cup to the floor, and a loud groan was followed by the snapping of boards.

Shad jumped to his feet, but Poppy grasped his arm, halting him.

"What was that?" Her large eyes looked to him for answers.

"Stay here," he commanded, and took the stairs three at a time. He approached the second-story landing where Lenore met him, bundled in her nightclothes and coat.

"What's happening?" she asked, her voice wavering with fear. "It sounded like the roof buckled."

"That's exactly what happened," he called over his shoulder. "Stay put until I check it out. More than the roof might be coming down." A gust of frigid air cascaded down the stairway.

What about Fancy? Had she been killed? Shad didn't like to think of her buried under the weighty snow and wood. Wouldn't she have called out if she could?

Everything was deathly quiet except for him clomping to the third floor. When he was almost to the top, a flurry of snowflakes hit him in the face. Looking up, he saw a glittering of stars through the rooftop. Fancy Aubrey was nowhere to be seen.

He cupped his mouth. "Fancy! Where are you? Are you all right?"

No reply.

Sounds from behind made him look over his shoulder to see Poppy following close behind. "What're you doing? Go back downstairs."

"I won't. That's my room up there. Besides, Miss Aubrey needs help."

A blockage of splintered wood, debris, and mountains of snow made going forward impossible. The below-zero temperatures ripped at Shad's face, and he was sure Miss Ford would soon scamper away.

"What should we do?" she asked from beside him. She searched the wall of wreckage as if she didn't feel the cold. Taking hold of a splintered board, she gave a jerk, but nothing moved.

Footsteps pounded to a halt behind him.

"Can we get through?" Harold asked with Cook at his side.

Shad grasped a beam that protruded into the stairwell and pulled, but the weight of the snow kept it firmly in place. He turned to the men.

"Harold, run to the livery and get a ladder. Cook, you round up any tools in this place—shovels, saws, anything—and bring them back here. Get the other men. And be quick about it!"

Harold grasped Shad's arm. "The ladder only reaches to the second floor."

"Then get a wagon to set it in," Shad barked.

Harold shook his head. "That won't happen in this snow. You know that."

"Just figure it out, Harold. Do something!"

Frustration squeezed Shad's insides. If Fancy was injured and covered in snow, she'd freeze to death in a short time.

"We need to get to Miss Aubrey. She may be unable to speak or worse." Again, he heaved the beam with the same result.

Harold and Cook bounded back down the stairs.

"Look here."

He turned to find Poppy on her knees, pulling snow from beneath the blockage with her bare hands. Violent shivers wracked her body, but she kept working. He hauled her to her feet, none too gently. This was dangerous. More of the roof could give way. She needed to get back down where it was safe.

"What are you doing?" she screeched. "I see a small passage. I'm sure I can get through."

"No, you can't. Cook will be back soon with some shovels and the other men." *At least, I hope so.* "We'll dig her out."

"By then, she could be dead."

"She might be dead now."

"Let me try. I know I can do this."

Shouting sounded from below, and Shad turned. Cook, Abe, and Oscar had several shovels and something else in their arms as they clambered up the staircase. Thank God. They could set to work.

"See?" he said. "They're back…"

He turned and when he saw Poppy was gone, a deep fear almost knocked him from his feet.

Chapter Thirty-Eight

Lances of cold fire ripped along Poppy's hands and arms as she dragged herself through the narrow channel of snow and broken boards. She clenched her teeth to keep from crying out. Everything was frozen. The muffled voices behind were undistinguishable. Her cape caught on something stopping her progress.

"Poppy," Shad called in a panicked voice. "Get back here."

She tried to find where she was stuck, but that was impossible in the cramped tunnel. She would die if she didn't keep moving; that was the only thing she knew for sure.

Shad had been right. This was no job for a girl, but she *would* prevail. Miss Aubrey's life depended on it—and so did hers.

Poppy slid her hand down the side of her body and took hold of her cape, tugging hard. Nothing. She'd have to back up. Cold pressed in from all around. Her fingertips felt wet, and she thought they were bleeding. What if the snow and boards on top of her let go? Would her life be crushed away?

Inch by agonizing inch, she slowly backed up. The effort seemed to take hours before she found the place her cape was caught on a nail. How something so small could cause such difficulties was frustrating.

Once she was free, she resumed her forward crawl. She had to hurry. Soon she would be too cold to move. All she could think about was the few times she'd run into the beautiful saloon woman who kept herself tucked away from the rest of them. Her eyes had held such curiosity and humor. Poppy had wanted to start up a conversation, but she'd held back.

"Poppy. Can you hear me?" Shad called out.

The desperation in his voice made her wince. She and Shad must only be a few feet apart, but the wreckage made seeing her impossible.

"Come back. We'll get Fancy. You can't do this on your own. Please," he called now in desperation.

Feeling a gust of wind on her face, Poppy blinked and looked up. She was coming out into the hall. Miss Aubrey's door must be someplace in front and to the right. But the area was dark and difficult to see.

"I'm out," she cried, pure joy filling her. "I'm out, Shad. On the other side. I can see her door."

She tried to climb to her feet, but she was stiff and so cold. Her knees wouldn't bend, and she had to go slowly. The doorknob, still a few feet away, jerked in front of her face from her shivers.

"Good girl!" Shad called back. "Try the door. Is it locked?"

She was so frozen she could barely grasp the knob, but the pride she heard in Shad's voice kept her moving. Her fingers wouldn't close around the cold steel. She had to make this work. She couldn't go back now without Miss Aubrey. With both hands, she gripped the knob and turned. Her heart sank.

"It's locked!" She pounded on the door with her arms, the only thing she had left that would still work. "Miss Aubrey! Please, Miss Aubrey, answer me." Poppy felt crushing disappointment, but she wouldn't let it defeat her. She would save the poor woman, and herself, or die trying.

A weak sound came from within.

"I hear her, Shad! Open the door, Miss Aubrey. Please, open the door."

Clamoring sounds of digging in the rubble at the stairs echoed into the night.

"Mr. Petty— Shad," she called. "It's locked tight." Poppy didn't realize she was crying until warm tears slid down her cheeks. "I—I don't have the key." She felt a moment of despair wedge inside. "I can't get her out."

"Yes, you can. You're smart and strong."

There it was again, the pride in his voice, the awe. She wanted to do this for Miss Aubrey, but also for Shad.

Was there something in her own room that might help? She turned her head. *The sun must be coming up.* The sky above was brightening, and a few beams of light fell upon her bedroom door.

Like a sickly peasant unable to straighten her own spine, Poppy stumbled forward and opened the door she'd left unlocked when she ventured downstairs in hopes of seeing Shad in the warm lobby. Her candle was still burning, much to her shame, but now joy. She couldn't always be responsible. Had that been only an hour ago? The time felt like years.

Her hands shook uncontrollably as the door opened wider. Her room was unaffected by the collapse with the ceiling still intact, and everything neatly in its place. With a numb mind, Poppy glanced around, searching for something she could use to open the door.

In the dim light, she saw her ripped and torn fingernails, bleeding and purple. The sight made her stomach pinch with pain. She had to do something and fast. Time was running out. The giant meat lockers down at the Boston docks came to mind.

Without the key, she was helpless. She blinked to clear her thoughts. She pushed one foot forward, and then another until she was at her nightstand. Taking her own key, she placed it in her pocket and looked around some more. Her eyes landed on the dark fireplace. And then on the few logs still on the hearth.

That's it! She didn't know if her idea was futile, but she couldn't think of anything else. The men's voices and Shad calling to her rumbled in her mind.

Finally with a purpose, she forced her legs to move. With difficulty, she grasped one log in her numb hands and started back the way she'd come.

"Poppy. Are you still there?"

"I'm here now," she replied in a billow of frozen breath. "I was in my room. I'm trying something. Give me a moment."

Extracting the long silver skeleton key from her pocket, she paused. All the concentration she could muster was needed just to get the object in the small hole with her shaking hands. She narrowed her gaze and picked up the log she'd set at her feet. The weight almost toppled her in her weakened condition. Her head swam with dizziness.

I can't pass out. I can't. Keep going. Keep moving.

She had one shot at this, and she couldn't mess it up. *Please, Lord, let this work. I can't do this without your help.*

With the weighty log in her battered hands, Poppy reared back and sent it forward with all her strength, aiming at the key. The jolt sent a shot of pain through her hands and up her arms, causing her to cry out. The log fell to the floor, narrowly missing her feet.

"Poppy!"

Shad, worried for me.

With new determination, she swallowed back her pain. It seemed as if the key might have moved forward, but she couldn't be sure. Was the blow hard enough to break the bolting structure inside the doorknob? She'd never tried to break into a room before. She had no idea if locks were strong or just for show.

Breathing hard, she reached for the knob. "It turned," she shouted with joy. "I'm going inside."

The room was shadowy with the coming sunrise. A cold wind whistled up Poppy's cape and around her neck, numbing her ears and face.

"Miss Aubrey," she called. "Miss Aubrey, where are you?"

"Here," came a weak reply.

Poppy weaved her way across the rug, avoiding the rubble on her way to the bed, but didn't see the woman. Hurrying to the other side, she found Miss Aubrey on the floor. She knelt as fast as her frozen limbs would allow and picked up the saloon girl's hand.

"Miss Aubrey."

The woman opened her eyes. A large lump had formed on her forehead. "M-Miss Ford…"

Poppy pulled on her arm. "You'll have to stand, Miss Aubrey, because I'm not strong enough to lift you." Hearing commotion, Poppy stood and moved to the window.

A swarm of men were below with a ladder that only reached halfway up the building. No wagon was in sight.

She hurried back to Miss Aubrey. "This is up to you and me," Poppy said. She took a firm hold of Miss Aubrey's arm and slung it around her neck. "Just think how good you'll feel downstairs by the fire."

Heaving with all her might, Poppy dragged Miss Aubrey to a stand. How on earth could the woman crawl on her own those few long feet beneath the blockade? She'd have to if she wanted to get out.

They lumbered a few steps. The saloon girl seemed to be getting stronger. The goose egg on her forehead looked painful. They crossed the room and were out in the hall.

"I have her," Poppy called out. "She's alive but has a bad bump on her head. She's wobbly and keeps almost passing out. I don't know if she can crawl."

"We've been widening the tunnel on our side," Shad called back. "If you can get her in, I'll reach as far as I can and grasp her hands. It won't feel good, but I'll pull her out."

Shad pulling Miss Aubrey might work. Poppy quickly unclasped the hook and eye at her throat and laid her cape on the floor, pushing it as far as she could inside, underneath the rubble.

"I'm going to lay you on your belly," she said as she brought the woman down, trying to keep her from falling.

When Miss Aubrey just lay there, Poppy gave her arms a firm shake. "Go on. You need to crawl as far as you can. Try to keep the cape under you if you can. Shimmy forward. When you can't go any farther, hold out your hands and Mr. Petty will take them."

"I can do this," Miss Aubrey said weakly.

"I know you can. You have to."

Chapter Thirty-Nine

Once Shad had a hold of Fancy's icy hands, he pulled her through the opening in one swift swoop. Her face was blue, and a large knot sat on her forehead. As he pulled her out and lifted her into his arms, he noticed Poppy's fur cape beneath her. That was why slipping her out had been easy. Poppy must be frozen. He swung Fancy around and set her in the first arms he found.

Oscar sputtered.

"Go! Put her in Hildy's room. Pile on the blankets, use bed warmers, and feed her hot soup. As soon as I have Miss Ford, I'm right behind you. Have someone build up the fire in *my* room too," he called loudly as Oscar, followed by Abe, Hildy, and Lenore hurried away.

Alone now, Shad waited for Poppy, fear burning his belly. All kinds of things raced through his head. Would she be too weak or cold to crawl back? She'd been gone almost twenty minutes. Should he keep working on the tunnel, breaking it through? Or might that weaken the wreckage and cause it to collapse?

That thought brought panic. He dropped to his knees and crawled in as far as the small hole would allow.

"Poppy," he called. "Poppy? Are you on your way?"

"Um, I—am."

The response was low, shaky, her breathing labored. He pushed in farther. "Put out your hands."

He splayed his fingers to grasp her hands. Once he had a good hold, he shimmied backward, pulling Poppy as he went. The movement was slow, and he felt as if they'd never be out.

Finally lifting her to his chest, he gently smoothed back her frazzled hair as he gazed into her face. "You did good." He was too emotional to say more.

"Sh-Shad, I'm…"

"Shhh," he whispered. "Conserve your energy."

He held her tight to his chest, and then carried her down the steps, being careful not to fall. He went directly into his room, where Abe was hunkered down at his hearth. With one hand, he whipped back the covers and placed Poppy inside, pulling the heavy quilt up to her chin.

He turned. "Bring me all the bed warmers that aren't being used on Miss Aubrey."

"I've had them heating since this began," Hildy said from the doorway and darted off. She returned a moment later carrying several cast-iron bed warmers, each with hot stones rolling around inside.

Two he slipped in next to Poppy's feet, and two more on the far side of the bed.

"Look at her hands," Hildy said. "They should be cleaned and disinfected."

"Not now." He toed off his boots and pulled off his coat and shirt down to his undershirt. "Her body temperature is more important. We'll work on one thing at a time. Are you seeing to Miss Aubrey?"

Hildy nodded.

Without a thought to Hildy or anyone else who might object, Shad climbed into the bed and gathered Poppy's ice-cold body next to his. He cuddled her to his chest and pulled the blankets over her head.

He caught Lenore's gaze. "Until we can board off the third floor, I suggest everyone go to their rooms and climb in bed. Tell the men to bring in more firewood and distribute it around."

"Sheriff Crawford, his deputy, Harold, and Morgan Stanford just arrived with hammers and lumber. They're setting to work right away," Lenore replied. "But I'll tell the women and children what you said."

Now that she mentioned it, Shad did hear voices talking and the sounds of pounding. Bandaging the collapse was one thing he wouldn't have to handle, and he was glad.

"Lenore," he called. "Before you go, can you bring something hot for Miss Ford to eat or drink?"

The woman looked at the motionless lump under the covers. "Is she capable?"

"She will be. And if not, I'll help her."

"Very good."

With the fire now blazing, Abe stood and stopped by the bedside. "Since the snowfall stopped, I'm gonna venture down to the Hitching Post as soon as it's light. Gotta make sure no one has broken in and helped themselves to my whiskey, or anything else. I'll be back ta help with the repairs."

Shad nodded, the cold from Poppy's body seeping into his own. As immobile as she was, he could feel the comforting beat of her heart. "Take a gun and keep an eye out."

The skinny bartender nodded, pulling a derringer from his pocket. "Always do."

In the empty room, the crackling fire was easy to hear. Shad rested his cheek on the top of Poppy's head, the quilt soft against his skin. He closed his eyes, realizing he was exhausted. The fact that nobody had been killed was a miracle.

He tightened his embrace, thinking over a year had passed since he'd held a woman in bed. That brought a smile he couldn't stop. Poppy wouldn't like that. He pictured her eyebrow arching in censure.

Fancy and he talked a good game, flirted up a storm, but that's all their relationship was. Friendship—and a good one.

This little soldier in his arms aroused more in him than thoughts of lovemaking, although she did do that in spades. Poppy brought a peculiar sense of home, one he hadn't felt for a good ten years. Of being a part of something larger than his single life. About working for the good of another person. Giving of oneself. Seeing to their happiness.

An image of his grandmother and grandfather tottering off to bed every night hand in hand, their knitted caps covering their gray heads, filtered through his mind. He heard their whispered words as they knelt together beside the bed to say their prayers. Their hopes and dreams for their grandsons, in a world that held little promise. His grandparents never spoke of his parents, or what had transpired. Shad always wondered if they'd gone bad. Been on the wrong side of the law.

He felt the same way about his brothers as his grandparents had about them. He'd tried, and sometimes failed, to make things better for Tanner and Nick. *Life is a gift*, Grandma Girdy used to say. *Don't waste a second on fleeting whims. Every day is precious.*

Feeling an unusual sense of contentment, Shad chuckled softly, causing Poppy to stir. Had she been sleeping, or just too weak and cold to move or talk? Either way, he was anxious for her to awaken. A deep need to tell her what he thought of her risking her life like she had played upon his mind.

He realized he'd begun to warm up, as well. The bed warmers by their feet were cooling, but still gave off heat. Someone walked by in the hall, passing his half-open bedroom door.

Where had Oscar Scott gone? Was he helping to seal off the third floor? If everyone knew he was warming Poppy in his bed, they hadn't voiced any objections. At least, not yet...

Chapter Forty

Why wouldn't that darned woodpecker stop that racket? The sound was maddening. No matter which room Poppy tried to escape into, he was there. She wanted to scream. She put her hands over her ears to keep out the noise.

Tap-tap-tap.

"Miss Ford? Are you awake?"

Poppy slowly opened her eyes to utter darkness. Well, that wasn't quite true; the room was dark, but not completely. The air on her face was blessedly warm, and she was cuddled up against a solid cushion of heat. She stretched, her hands pressing up against the barrier.

"Miss Ford?" The voice was filled with concern.

Poppy drew the heavy quilt from over her head and blinked at the brightness of the room. She turned to see that her suspicions were correct. Shad was in bed beside her, sound asleep on the pillow.

She remembered now. He'd hauled her out of the rubble and carried her down the stairs, all while she felt like a frozen toad. She'd thought she'd die. And now here she was, untold minutes or hours later, snuggled in a warm bed with the cowboy.

"Miss?" Hildy stood in the door with a tray in her hands. "I'm sorry. If you'd like me to come back, tell me, and I can."

"No," Poppy nearly shouted.

She wanted to vault from under the covers, but hadn't taken the time to see what she was wearing. Perhaps she'd been stripped of her dress and was only wearing her chemise and pantaloons. That would make this innocent situation out to be more than it was.

"I'm sorry to wake you, but everyone seems to think it best if you were to eat this hot porridge, biscuit, and drink some coffee. You know, get your insides working and give you some fuel. The rest of you will warm more quickly with something in your stomach." She softly cleared her throat. "I brought the tray about twenty minutes ago, but you and Mr. Petty were sound asleep, and I didn't have the heart to wake you then. Would you like me to come back? I can keep this warm in the kitchen." She glanced at the bowl on her tray and then back at Poppy.

In the height of her embarrassment, Poppy found her voice. "No, please bring it in. That was very kind of you." She glanced over to Shad, who still slept despite the conversation. A soft snore rippled out between his chapped lips.

Relief crossed Hildy's face. "Fine then, I'll set this right here." She lowered the tray to the nightstand. "Will you be able to manage with your hands? We've yet to tend to them."

Poppy pulled her hands out of the warmth to see that her nails were ripped and broken. The tips of most of her fingers were black with dried blood. The horrifying experience she'd been through came rushing back.

"I'll help her," Shad said in a deep and steady voice.

Flipping the quilt back, he stepped out of bed, slipped into his shirt but left it unbuttoned, and then pulled on his heavy coat.

After carefully replacing the covers to be sure she was completely protected, he went to the fireplace and tossed in two more logs.

Hildy nodded. "I'll just be going then."

The poor girl looked completely out of sorts, and Poppy didn't blame her at all. Shad didn't seem the least bit perturbed to be caught in such a compromising situation.

"Please, wait," Poppy called.

Hildy stopped and turned.

"How is Miss Aubrey?" That was the only thing she could think to ask, and she did want to know.

Hildy smiled and came closer. "Doing better. Sheriff Crawford said we need to keep her awake because of the bump on her head. She's finally warming up, even though she wouldn't allow anyone in her bed to help, not like, uh, well, you know." Hildy shrugged and glanced at Shad. "She's in my room with a host of bed warmers and blankets. She's eaten and is feeling better."

Poppy glanced to the hearth to see Shad listening closely. She fought a twinge of jealousy. He seemed to like the saloon girl very much. "I'm glad to hear that."

Directing her attention to the bowl of porridge, she was suddenly ravenous, even to the point of pain. She hadn't eaten since last night's bedtime biscuit. Her stomach growled loudly.

"Please give her my—our—regards."

Shad nodded and made his way over to the tray with quiet footsteps as Hildy hurried away.

Poppy chanced a peek over the edge of the bed to see his stockinged feet. *My reputation is ruined.*

He smiled at her. "Hungry?"

"Very, but I can serve myself."

She hated to lose any of the wonderful warmth under the covers if she sat up, but nothing could help that. She scooted against the headboard and stuck the pillow Shad had used behind her back, then pulled the covers to her neck. She reached for the bowl.

He beat her to it. "No, you can't. Your hands are a mess. As soon as you eat, that's the next order of business." He scooped a spoonful from the bowl, tested it on the side of his lip, and held it up to her mouth.

The hot goodness slipped down her throat to her waiting belly. The heavily sugared concoction was the tastiest thing she'd ever eaten. Instantly, she was ready for another serving. Soon he was spooning as fast as it took to lower and raise his arm. She stopped only long enough to drink from the mug he held to her lips, all the while aware of Shad studying her face.

"Good?"

She felt cherished, protected, and not too proud to say, "The best meal I've ever had."

The earnest, deep laughter that followed her statement made her smile. Shad was quite handsome, and charming. Warm, languid tingles rippled up her spine that had nothing to do with the hot coffee.

"I can hardly believe that with all the traveling you've done. I'd guess you've eaten in the finest restaurants in the world. The best money can buy, I'm sure. Am I correct, Miss Ford?"

Was that bitterness? She was surprised. She brushed a stray drop of coffee from her chin with the back of her hand and glanced up into his eyes.

"*Please*, call me Poppy."

He smiled and nodded. "If you'd like. Poppy. You're right. Calling you anything other now will feel strange after all we've been through."

A sensuous smile tugged the scoundrel's lips, and he actually looked at the spot he'd just recently vacated on his side of the bed.

"I agree. But I'd still implore you not to tell my parents I just spent the last hour in your bed."

He chuckled again, this time breaking off a small portion of the delicious-looking biscuit and placing the morsel between her lips. "You have my word as a gentleman. They'll never hear it from me."

"But they will from me! You can be sure. The sooner the better."

Poppy gasped and turned to the door where Oscar stood, his face twisted.

"They won't like what you've been up to."

"I wouldn't think any different of you," Poppy shot back. "Of course you'll be delighted to report my doings."

How could she have ever thought him a friend? She was amazed at how stupid she'd been. Had he always been such a hateful snob who held himself in the highest esteem? That seemed impossible.

Shad, sitting on the side of her bed, didn't even look up. "No matter that Miss Ford's"—his gaze cut to hers—"temperature was dangerously low after her brave and daring rescue of Miss Aubrey. That doesn't make a lick of difference to you, or to them, correct?"

"Miss Aubrey didn't need someone to warm her body. Why should Poppy?" Oscar's eyes were narrowed, suspicious slits. "Oh, wait, I know. Miss Ford has a fortune to win. Perhaps that enticed you. Can that possibly be the reason?"

Irritation flicked across Shad's face. He glanced at her and then stood. "Someone should have warmed Miss Aubrey whether she wanted it or not. Body-to-body contact is the fastest and best way to bring someone's temperature back to normal."

The talk made Poppy tug her covers higher under her chin.

"You can bet," Shad went on, "my warming Poppy had nothing to do with her wealth. As a matter of fact, that was the last thing going through my thoughts."

Oscar drew up taller.

"And I have half a mind to shoot you for thinking such a thing."

He wouldn't, would he? Poppy felt her face heat with embarrassment. She wished Shad would stop. Oscar didn't need anyone to egg him on. The situation would only get worse from here.

Oscar took a small step back at the threat. "I'm not saying you're a fortune-hunter, but her father will, I can assure you."

"Nothing happened," Shad said. "He doesn't have to know."

"I think he does."

Shad took a step in his direction and Oscar jumped back, his face full of fear. He always could talk a good story, but when it came to backing up his words, he was a coward.

"I wouldn't expect you to understand, Oscar," she said. "Everything is so black and white in your eyes. I feel sorry for you."

All the fight had gone out of her. She felt weak again and cold. She'd created a scandal… especially if Oscar told what he knew.

Oscar wrinkled his nose and walked away.

Poppy grimaced as her stomach pinched around the warm porridge, feeling her life had just taken an unexpected turn. What would come next, she could hardly imagine.

Chapter Forty-One

Sitting in the bedroom chair, Sally heard Roady a moment before he opened the door and stepped inside. He looked tired, as he had this past week. The weather had taken its toll on everyone.

And now the cowhand named Uncle Pete had been savagely killed. The kind man had been rather shy, but she'd seen the light behind his eyes. He liked to spin a yarn to make the men laugh, and the ladies, as well. He was a favorite with the children, taking time with the boys, always teaching them this or that about ranching or the cattle, or how to tell the difference between a meadowlark and a sparrow.

She stood and met Roady halfway across the room, taking his hands into her own. "How are the men holding up?"

He shrugged. "Seems no one can believe Uncle Pete is gone. It's strange. I keep expecting to see his face or hear his voice. Lucky's taking his death real hard, and so is Ike. I haven't gotten two straight words out of Francis."

She heard what Roady wasn't saying. What she saw in his sensitive dark eyes and tight-lipped smile. His heart was broken too. These men had been together a long, long time. Working, ranching, living, laughing, looking out for each other, praying.

The McCutcheon hands were more like family than comrades. When one hurt, the rest hurt with him.

Reaching up, she straightened the front of his hair, and then softly raked her nails on his scalp as she finger-combed the rest, knowing how much he liked it.

"I'm so sorry, Roady. How are *you*? You and Uncle Pete were good friends. I can't imagine how difficult this must be. Especially thinking about the way he died."

"It's hard, darlin'. I won't lie about that. What makes the tragedy even worse is we can't bury him yet. The ground is frozen solid. Digging a six-foot hole is near impossible. We'll have to wait until spring when the earth thaws."

She hadn't thought about that. How dreadful. "What will…" She brought her hand down to his shoulder, his clothes still cold from the walk from the bunkhouse where he'd eaten with the men.

"They've wrapped his body and placed it in the small outbuilding behind the barn. In this cold, he'll be just fine." Finding her hands, Roady lifted her fingers to his lips and kissed them gently. "Gotta be thankful for each day we have. Never know which will be our last."

With that said, he went to the water pitcher and splashed some into the bowl. He scooped up a handful and washed his face before looking at her in the reflection.

"Water's warm."

"I've been expecting you," she replied, liking the way his loving gaze touched her. His small smile of thanks meant the world.

With a nod, he leaned over the bowl and scrubbed his face vigorously several more times, after which he reached for the towel.

Now was probably not the best time to bring up the letter, and his idea of sending a telegram to her oldest brother, someone whose height and weight might be intimidating to Mr. Greenstein. But waiting was becoming problematic. The walls had closed in and her thoughts ran wild. This course of action should have been done even before she'd run away from St. Louis, frightened, with an unknown future. She never dreamed her former employer would be so bold as to call on her family. He already knew her sisters to some extent, and now, with him visiting…

She blinked and pushed away the horrible thought. She'd *not* let him violate Anita and Melba as he'd done her. Could the man be touched in the head? Maybe he didn't believe he'd done anything wrong. That's how his strangely written letter made his sin sound.

Now that she and Roady had come to a decision on what to do, it was prudent to inform her brother Travis as soon as possible. Being snowed in and unable to send a telegram was torture. Any other time, she would have enjoyed visiting with Claire and staying in this beautiful home, but not now. Time was of the essence. She needed to talk with Roady, make him understand her pressing need to get this done but didn't know how to broach the subject, especially with the recent turn of events. When he'd told her of his plan, he'd said they'd go to town just as soon as they were able.

He finished drying his face and turned. "You're quiet tonight."

Sally shrugged, not wanting to add to his burdens.

Setting the towel on the rim of the washbowl, he studied her. "You're not feeling sick, are you?" His gaze dropped to her stomach, which now resembled a small melon. "You'd tell me if you were?" With the difference in their ages, he often hovered over her like a mother hen.

"I'm fine, husband." She glanced at the dark window, gathering her thoughts. "Just anxious to get to Y Knot, I guess. All this snow makes the house feel like a prison."

"It's barely above zero out there. That's no place for you. Especially in your condition. I'll open this window if you need some air."

He won't hear me with an open mind. Why can't we take that sleigh in front of the bunkhouse? We could be to the telegraph office and back in a few hours—a half day at most. The trip to town can't be all that dangerous.

Shamefully, the dead cowhand passed through her thoughts. Of course traveling was dangerous, and not just from the wolves. Fifty other things could go wrong, and they could be stuck. And the baby would be in danger. She had to think of him or her first, but Anita and Melba needed her, as well.

Before she could tell him not to, Roady unlatched the lock and pushed up the window frame, letting in a frigid gust of sharp, crisp air. Icy cold pricked her face and made her suck in a breath.

"Come on over and get a couple good lungfuls before I shut this. We don't want to let out all our warmth—there's not much to begin with."

She had no other option but to do his bidding. He hadn't caught her true desire why she wanted to go. He'd been adamant when he'd told her a trip would have to wait. She skirted over and stuck out her head, the cold painful. How did anything survive out there? No wonder his face, lips, and hands were punished.

Hugging herself, she backed away. "There. Th-that's enough." She giggled through chattering teeth. "Thank you. I don't know how you stand it. Even your walk to and from the bunkhouse. I'm thankful you brought me over here before the big storm. I hate to think if I'd stayed home, and you were snowed out."

He chuckled and pushed down the window, locking out the winter. "That would never happen, darlin'. I'd get to you somehow, some way. Don't ever think otherwise. Now, tell me what's troubling you. The snow can't be the only reason."

Hiding anything from Roady was impossible. She loved that about him. "I want to send the telegram to my brother like we planned. Each day that passes gives Mr. Greenstein a chance to violate my sisters."

"We've already decided we would, when we can."

"The threat is all I think about, Roady," she answered, wringing her hands as hopelessness filled her. "Or dream about when I sleep. I understand about the weather, but I don't want to wait. I don't think we can."

Roady moved to the dresser on his side of the bed. He shed the last of his outer clothing and took his long wool sleepshirt from the drawer, slipping it over his long johns. After which, he slipped under the pile of covers.

"We've already talked this to death, Sally, and I'm tired. We can't go tomorrow, and possibly not for a week or two. You're just going to have to accept that. I promise you, just as soon as we can, I'll take you to town." He punched his pillow several times and got comfortable. "Or better yet, I'll make the trip alone."

"No. I want to go. And I need to check in on Heather at the mill. Is that all right?"

Sally heaved a sigh, blew out the lantern on the washstand, and circled to her side of the bed. After blowing out the stub of her candle, she slipped off her thick wool wrapper and climbed in.

In a rustle of sheets, Roady lifted his arm. "Sure it is. Come over and warm me up. I've been cold all day."

She slipped under his arm and laid her head on his chest. He'd make things right. She could trust him, and she did wholeheartedly. Because of her baby, she'd always be connected to Eric Greenstein—the monster. He might already know about the baby from her family. Still, he had no way of knowing it was his. When it came early, there would be speculation but no proof.

Over the months she'd been in Montana, the pain of the attack had softened through Roady's love. The land, the air, everything so large and clean. She was thankful for that. She shelved her fear, the pain, the shame, the anxiety. Eric would not affect her anymore. *Never again.*

But he could affect her sisters. In the course of ten minutes, they could be changed forever, as she had been. Would he dare?

As if sensing her agitation, Roady slipped his hand downward, gently rubbing her back and soothing her ragged nerves. She shut out the emotional darkness by concentrating on Roady—thinking only of him. All would be well. Soon enough they'd take care of business, and she'd be able to relax.

She stretched her hand over her husband's chest and snuggled in closer. Few things were as wonderful as passing a cold winter night next to the man she loved.

What would happen if Roady ever came face-to-face with Eric? Sally shivered at the thought, and even in his sleep, Roady instinctively drew her closer. To protect her husband from himself, a confrontation was something she'd make certain never occurred.

Chapter Forty-Two

A week later, Poppy sat in the corner of Shad's room—which she still occupied, even over her protestations—in the sturdy blue-cushioned chair by the window. She had only her clothes on her back, and what others offered, since her belongings were sealed away in the boarded-off third floor. Shad had thrown down some blankets next to the lobby stove, saying that was plenty good for him, and warmer to boot. She appreciated his generosity since all the rooms were now occupied.

Hildy had moved in with Lenore, giving her room to Fancy. Everyone was anxious for the snow to disappear, and yet the sky today had darkened, indicating another storm might be brewing.

Outside, everything was still white. Not pretty and fluffy as it had been when the snow first fell. During the day, the temperatures warmed just enough to melt a little off the top, and then at night, the layer refroze into a thin, hard crust. On the road where men tried now and again to get around, dirt mixed in to make it brown and depressing. Poppy was ready for spring, even though they had many months to go.

From her spot, she could see Trent Herrick shoveling the back path to his father's leather shop. His wide, sturdy shoulders moved to a rhythm of his own making. Every once in a while, he'd stop, withdraw his handkerchief from his coat pocket, and wipe his face. The snow, crusted for several layers down, was dense, Shad had said yesterday. To remove any amount took a real effort. For the most part, people were still huddled inside, fighting to keep warm.

Hearing giggles, Poppy turned.

July stood in the doorway with April and May, all smiles, waiting to be invited in.

She nodded and beckoned with her bandaged hands. "Please, come in. I'm lonely. You've showed up at just the right time."

Like a train, July came first, pulling the twins behind, hand in hand.

"What are you up to today?" she asked. "Where are your parents? I'm surprised they let you out alone."

Poppy had come to despise the man who never had a nice thing to say about his children. All he did was glare. And the mother, Poppy couldn't understand at all. If she were ever blessed with such a darling family, she'd shower them with affection and love. The woman seemed incapable of doing little else than eat and sleep.

"We're taking a walk," July responded. "We've been up and down the stairs ten times."

Poppy laughed. "That's a lot of climbing. Your sisters can handle the steps without falling?"

"Yes'm. They're pretty nimble. Just like baby goats."

Poppy held back her laughter. He was so darn cute. And spoke like an adult. "Aren't you tired? Ten trips is a lot of stairs."

July shrugged as he gazed around the room. "Nope."

As usual, April and May's hair was a mess. Their white-blond tresses were little-girl thin, but long enough to brush their shoulders. She suddenly had an urge to fancy them up. "July, can you bring me Mr. Petty's comb from atop the dresser?"

His face brightened. "Sure I can." He crossed the room, went up on tiptoe, and inspected the belongings laid out on the dresser top. He took a few moments to spot the tool. "Here it is." He reached over his head, grasped the comb, returned to Poppy, and placed it her bandaged hand.

Feeling a slight bump, she realized her hands must be almost healed, for they didn't hurt at all.

"Whatcha gonna do with it?" he asked, eyeing her own hair that Hildy had helped fix into a messy bun over an hour ago. "Can you manage?"

She twirled it around. "I can, but I'm still clumsy. I want to comb April's hair."

His eyes grew wide. "She don't like that. You'll make her scream."

"Maybe, maybe not. We'll see, won't we?"

Keeping one step ahead of the children was a challenge. Poppy could see how doing so could take some work—but in a good way. She smiled at the girl she thought was April.

"You're smiling at May."

"Oh, sorry." Poppy held out her hand to the other. "April, may I please comb your hair? It looks so soft. I'd love to make it look like Miss Hildy's."

Hildy Hallsey had beautiful hair that was always brushed to a sheen.

April and May's hair looked as if it hadn't been combed since Poppy had done so after she'd washed it a week ago.

April took a step back, her smile all but gone. She might not talk much, but she understood Poppy well enough.

"No."

July grasped the strap to April's overall as she tried to run away. "That's not polite. Miss Ford wants ta brush your hair. She'll be gentle." He slid Poppy a look much too old for his years.

"That's right, I'll be very gentle. I promise. You'll hardly feel a thing."

April's lip protruded. "Hun-gy."

Leaning against the bed with her thumb in her mouth, May watched.

Poppy's heart squeezed. They'd gotten a few supplies from Sheriff Crawford, but they were still rationing the food. How she wished she could get into the kitchen and try baking something.

"I know you are, honey. I'll talk to Shad as soon as he comes around and see if I can't get some extra biscuits. I'm sure he'll sneak me some if I ask nicely."

April inched forward and let Poppy take her by the shoulder.

No matter what, Poppy would make that happen. She'd get dressed and go door to door begging for food if she had to, to find something for these darling children.

"Turn around, sweet girl," she crooned to the child, who slowly did her bidding. Very carefully, as not to hurt her, Poppy worked at the snarls, for passing the comb through without snagging was impossible. "Very good. We're getting somewhere."

How she'd love to have just a pittance of the food and belongings from her Boston home to shower on the three. Her heart surged, just thinking how their lives could be if she were their guardian. Her hand stilled at the intriguing idea.

Seeing April glance around, Poppy realized she was staring off into space, her hand resting on the child's small shoulder. "Oh, sorry." She laughed softly.

July, standing close, had a sad, wistful expression.

"Wait one second, April." Standing, Poppy picked up July, ignoring the leftover pain in her hands, and set him onto her bed before doing the same with May. "You'll be more comfortable there."

July flopped to his stomach, resting his chin on one palm, and May sat on her knees, still sucking her thumb, a habit that April didn't seem to have.

Poppy returned to her chair and resumed her untangling. "I must say, July, you three have very unusual names. How did you come by them? Did your mother and father tell you?"

"Yes'm," he replied. "I got the name July because I was born on the Fourth of July. Then when my sisters came along on April twenty-second, my ma said the two twos in a row was like a sign—and they should have names one after the other as well. So they'd always be close. May was birthed right after April, so just like the month, that's what they was named." His mouth drew down suddenly, and he began picking at a loose thread on the quilt. "Leastways, that's what she said."

Really? The thought was shocking. Mrs. Sanger's unemotional frown came to mind.

The small boy's voice had trailed off to a whisper, which she had barely been able to hear.

Poppy called his name, but he didn't look up. Instead, a silent tear rolled down his cheek.

"I'm sorry, July, I didn't mean to make you sad."

May gazed at him and then put her arm over his back. "Nuggles," she whispered, moving closer.

"You didn't make me sad, Miss Ford."

"Then why the tear?"

Seeing two more tears slip down his face, Poppy was tempted to cross the room and take him into her arms, but feared that would make him self-conscious. Embarrass him. She didn't want him to avoid her in the future. In this case, less was definitely the best route to take.

He shrugged, obviously not going to tell her why.

"Well," she said. "That's a nice story. And it makes perfect sense."

She smiled, and for the first time, could move the comb from scalp to ends without one catch. She lifted April's locks off the back of her neck with her bandaged left hand and continued combing with her right.

"I was named by my father after he saw a painting in an art gallery of the hills of California. Inquiring about the dark gold flowers covering the coastal hillside, he learned they were called poppies. So, the next month when I was born, I was named Poppy Alexandria Ford. How would you like to be named after a flower?" She laughed and wrinkled her nose.

Was being named by her father strange? After a flower neither he nor her mother had actually seen? *How odd.* Had mother had a choice in the matter?

Poppy had never really thought about how peculiar that seemed. She pictured her parents together, in their usual arguing tones, disagreeing about something. As was often the case, her stomach tightened. They never got along. Their marriage was sad, really. She knew her mother rarely had a say in any matter whatsoever.

"Miss?" July stared at her with questions in his eyes.

"Yes?"

"Aw, nothin'. You was thinking hard again."

"I guess I was." She smiled, then leaned over and kissed April's cheek. "There. You look like the perfect little princess that you are. Now it's May's turn." She stood, picking up April, and set her on the bed next to her brother, exchanging her for her sister.

May was much more agreeable after watching the routine with April, who was now all smiles.

The poppy question rolled around in Poppy's mind as she carefully worked through the knots in the child's mussed hair. The apparent dislike between her parents was so troubling. She'd ignored her home situation for the most part, but now that she had hours to think about things…

This morning, before Shad had bid her good-bye to go do whatever he did every day after he checked in, she remembered the warm goodness that had filled her chest just at seeing him. He didn't even have to speak to create a feeling of sugar-coated butterflies whizzing around inside. She became tongue-tied. She remembered the long conversations they used to have in the wee hours of the morning, wondering how on earth she'd ever thought of anything to say.

True, she and Shad hadn't exchanged intimate words in any way, made any promises, given or received the touch of a lover, but his constant care and the warm gazes he tried so hard to hide had fueled her imagination—and desire. She ached to be held in his arms once again, as she had when he'd carried her down the staircase or when they stood in the deserted kitchen.

Were her feelings some fanciful infatuation because they were snowed in together, or was this attraction something else? She had no idea. She'd never been in love.

One thing Poppy knew for sure—she'd kiss the tall, good-looking cowboy before she left Y Knot for home, or the want of doing so would kill her.

Chapter Forty-Three

In the dim hotel hallway, Shad stopped short of his old room where Poppy was now resting, to listen to the chatter of the Sanger children. Well, mostly July's boyish talk and Poppy, and the girls chiming in now and then with some unintelligible word. They were most animated around Poppy, but quiet in their own room with their parents.

Shad's mood soured when he thought of Mr. and Mrs. Sanger. He had been sure something was fishy with the couple, and if not both of them, the fellow for sure, but Brandon had not found anything. The few telegrams he'd sent came back with nothing.

If there was something to find out, Shad would have to do it on his own. He stepped into the open doorway.

Poppy looked up, her face blossoming with a wide smile.

"Howdy," he said, the warmth of her greeting making him skittish.

He'd made the rounds around town today, checking to be sure others were doing all right. Berta May had given him a dozen oatmeal cookies for the children. Brandon had told her about the tykes, and being the good-hearted woman that she was, she set straight to work in her small upstairs kitchen.

Shad held out the bundle to Poppy.

"What treasures have you brought us, Mr. Petty?" she responded playfully, leaning in his direction as if she was pulled by a magnet. "I can hardly wait to find out."

In the light from the nearby window, he saw her high-set cheeks burst into color. Being she was a proper lady, she stuck to formalities around others.

"Open it and find out." He placed the bundle in Poppy's hands and took a step back, putting a few safe steps between them. His dreams were filled more and more with the unattainable socialite. He didn't want to set himself up for misery.

July lifted his sister down from the bed, and they rushed over to Poppy's side.

She carefully untied the knot and laid aside the red-checked material, noticing a delicious sweet scent. A longing gasp came from July's lips, and his gaze darted first to Poppy and then to him.

Shad smiled and nodded. "There's one dozen. Four for each of you."

Poppy looked like she wanted to jump up and kiss him.

Whoa there, cowboy. That's wishful thinking. You know no such thing.

"Where? How?" she stammered, and then swallowed. "I was just wishing I could bake something for these sweetiekins, and in you walk with cookies. You're a kind and thoughtful man."

"They're from Berta May across the street," he replied quickly.

She let the children each take one. April and May both stuffed the whole thing in their mouths at once, their cheeks bulging out like hungry mice. Sounds came from their throats. No child should be so hungry.

Worried, he cautiously inched closer. "Careful now, don't choke."

Once, when Tanner was just a toddler, he got a piece of an apple stuck in this throat. Those were the most terrifying ten seconds of Shad's life. Amidst his grandmother's screams to spit it out, Shad lifted his little brother, even though Shad wasn't much larger. Losing his balance with the heavy load, he stumbled, and they fell to the floor with a thud. The piece of apple popped out like a bullet, something he had never forgotten.

"Chew the cookie well," Poppy said in a calm voice, looking at him curiously.

She reached out and stroked both the girls' hair, and then smiled at July, who was licking invisible crumbs from his palms. His eyes darted to the remaining cookies in the cloth.

"You may each have another cookie now," Poppy said. "And two more before bedtime." She smiled. "You'll sleep well tonight."

July groaned but didn't object. Surely, the children could down all four now with no effort at all.

Poppy brushed strands of hair from the boy's eyes. "We must write a little thank-you note for Berta May. I'll do the writing. Her kindness will not go unnoticed. She did what I couldn't." She almost looked as if she were tearing up.

"I have some good news," Shad said quickly to ward off her sentimentality.

"More surprises?" she responded, brushing away a tear. "You're a good man to know."

"Yes, I guess I am." Why not play it up? "You'll hear this soon enough from Deputy Wesley, but I think you'd like it now. He visited some ranches today."

"Kathryn?"

He chuckled. "That's right. Everything is fine at the farm. They came through the worst days with few difficulties. She's well and happy, and so are Tobit and Isaiah. No problems there."

Cutting his gaze back to the children, he hoped she wouldn't ask any questions. Harsh winters were not always easy.

"And the animals? Buddy? The hogs? The horses?"

"I didn't get much of the details, but they did lose a few animals." He cringed, knowing how she felt. "As sad as that is, it's not unusual in the kind of cold we've had."

"Which ones?"

Shad shrugged. "Sorry. Don't know."

Poppy was quiet as she carefully wrapped the remaining goodies, and then crossed the room and set the bundle on the dresser. "That Kathryn, Tobit, and Isaiah are fine is a blessing. Thank you for letting me know. At least I don't have to worry about her anymore. I still hope to get out there. Maybe they'll let me stay with them until the stage can make it over to Waterloo."

Little May stepped forward and took Poppy's hand, surprising her—and him too. Had the child understood that Poppy might leave? Her going was unavoidable, but still, he hated to think about it. The place wouldn't be the same at all.

"Have you heard anything from the McCutcheons?" Poppy asked, now standing close. "Has anyone ridden out there, or has any ranch hand ridden in?"

"I haven't heard anything. But they're much farther out than the Holcombs or the Preeces. And in the other direction, where the road is more difficult to navigate. I wouldn't expect them yet. No news is good news, I'd say."

"Yes, of course."

Her tone was sad. She must still be thinking about the farm animals.

He bent down and picked up one of the girls. "How was that cookie?" he asked, tickling her side. He glanced at July. "Who am I holding?"

"That's May. You can tell by the freckle on the end of her nose."

"Freckle on the end of her nose?" Poppy repeated in surprise, gently pulling Shad's arm down so she could see. "I've never seen a freckle." She studied the little girl's face. "You're right, July," she said with a laugh. "I see it now as plain as day."

Shad was glad to hear the spark back in her voice.

She touched the boy's cheek. "Thank you for pointing that out. I'm amazed now that I never noticed it before. That tiny dot will come in handy."

"July," an angry male voice shouted. "Where are you, boy?"

July's gaze flew to the door, and then to Shad. If he wasn't mistaken, the child was scared to death. Anger roiled around inside. He needed to do something to help.

"You'd better go see what your father wants," Poppy said.

Her voice was calm, though Shad could tell she didn't like the man one bit either.

"But keep the cookies a secret. I'll be sure to bring you your other two before bed, all right?"

"July! I'm not calling you again. If I count to five and you're not here, you'll regret it."

Shad hated to set May down, but he did. Both he and Poppy watched as the girls followed their brother out the door.

She waited all of three seconds after they left to grasp his arm. "That man is horrible. He can't be their father."

"You can't take children from their parents, Poppy, even if they don't deserve them. The law says so." He needed to calm her so she didn't do something drastic before he had any proof of the situation.

"Don't tell me you don't see it too," she cried, taking a step into the hallway and looking both ways. "Each day that goes by, they become dearer to me, Shad. I don't see a bit of resemblance between them and *that* man or *that* woman."

"Maybe he's their stepfather."

She went to place her hands on her hips in a defiant move, but stopped short when she looked at her bandages.

"Let's get those dressings off," he said in an attempt to change the subject. For now, in the small confines of the hotel, they needed to keep the peace so nobody lost their head. "I'm sure by now they're healed. How do they feel?" He reached out to take one of her hands.

She pulled back, her brow arched in speculation. "I'm not that easy to distract, Shad. You'll learn that once I set my mind to something, that's it. I follow through, whether the journey is difficult or easy."

Oh, he'd learned that about her already—a few times over. She was a spitfire just waiting to be tamed—or not. He still wasn't sure about anything except he enjoyed her company. And when they were apart, she was all he thought about.

"I'll do my best to remember that, Poppy," he replied, stepping with her back into the bedroom.

She allowed him to unwrap the long white cloths that protected her palms and fingertips.

He lingered over the examination. "They look good. No infection."

She smiled. "I could have told you that," she answered playfully. "I don't have time for more recuperation. I have things to do. Question is, are you helping me or not?"

He knew he would. The moment she asked, he was putty in her hands. "Not. I have things to look after here until these people can get back to their lives."

"Harold's gone, and so is Abe."

He crooked a brow. "I still have you, Scott, Hildy, Lenore, and the Sangers. And don't forget the Grants. Mel and Bonnie are here until they can get home to Pine Grove or on to Waterloo, where they were headed before the storm hit. Wouldn't want nothin' to happen to that nice old couple."

"Sheriff Crawford's back in town," she argued. "And his deputy. They can keep tabs on the hotel well enough. It's just across from their office."

She had a point. He should get back to the ranch as soon as he could. That wasn't quite yet, but soon. "You tryin' to get rid of me?"

She lifted a shoulder and gazed into his eyes. "I'd never do that."

What are you thinking, Miss Poppy Ford? Am I a plaything to you? Are you stringing me along like the fops in Virginia who were falling at your feet for attention? I'm not one of them, and you best remember that. When I decide to play, I play for keeps.

Feeling a bit vindicated, even if it was just to himself, Shad smiled back, making her color. "That's good to know," he said slowly. "I'm banking on your truthful words. Someday, I just may come 'round to collect."

He laughed when her eyes widened.

Two could play cat and mouse.

Chapter Forty-Four

Luke stepped onto the ice-covered porch of the bunkhouse and turned to Shadrack's younger brothers following closely behind. "Remember what I said in the house. The men have just lost a comrade and are in a bad way. They've had a rough go," he said, his mind on other things besides the newcomers.

The Petty brothers had turned up an hour ago and had come straight to the house. Any other time, he'd have sent Hickory to the bunkhouse with a message for Francis to see to their horses. But in light of the recent trouble they'd had with the wolves, he did that himself while Nick and Tanner gobbled down a meal of savory pot roast and fresh bread Esperanza set before them.

Luke preceded them through the door.

Lucky was the first to stand and come forward. The others crowded around behind.

"Men," Luke began, still feeling heavyhearted about Uncle Pete. His unexpected passing felt like a bad dream. Made a man realize that he was mortal, and best be prepared to meet his maker at any given point. "This is Nick and Tanner Petty, Shad's younger brothers. We've known they were on their way, but just didn't know when to expect 'em."

"Howdy." The middle-aged cook held out his hand in welcome. Lucky's face, wan and lined with fatigue, was missing his characteristic smile. Uncle Pete had been a good friend to them all. "Welcome aboard," he added as an afterthought. "You let me know about your birthdays, and I'll bake ya a cake."

Nick and Tanner smiled, their saddlebags still slung over their shoulders.

Luke pointed around the room. "That's Francis. Don't tease him about his name, or he'll take it to fists. That's Jonathan or John, whatever you like, Ike, Smokey, and Lucky. We have a little cowpoke named Hickory, but during these storms, he stays in the big house with my folks. And a hand named Pedro, but I believe he's in the barn."

When Luke glanced at Francis in question, he saw the young man nod. "I explained why Shad isn't here at the moment," Luke went on. "He got recruited by Sheriff Crawford to fill in for a few days at the hotel. We don't really know when to expect him back, so we're playing the situation by ear."

"Howdy," each brother said to the men, looking around the room. Both appeared dirty, unshaven, and heavy-lidded from their long, difficult journey.

"We're real sorry to hear about your friend," Nick said, and Tanner nodded. "That's a real shame."

The ranch hands dipped their chins or mouthed some quiet response, but for the most part, they just stood there.

Luke caught the Petty brothers looking at the fire a few times. They must be frozen all the way through, even after the time spent in the house. Their getting here in the midst of the storm said much about their character and stick-to-it-ness, a quality all the McCutcheons admired in anyone.

"Lucky will show you which bunks are free," Luke said, unable to stop his gaze from tracking over to Uncle Pete's empty bed. The bedcovers had been changed and done up with fresh linens. The rest of the beds around the room were made, but all looked laid upon, or mussed.

Luke remembered the time Uncle Pete had short-sheeted Ike's bed when a tipsy Ike returned after a few too many drinks from his day off visiting the Hitching Post. Luke had heard the story more times than he could count, and it still made him laugh. All the men pretended to be asleep as Ike tried his darnedest to get into his bed, to no avail. Ike mumbled as he fell out the first time, and second, and third, and then let rip a streak of words to make even a cowpuncher blush when he realized he'd been had. They'd ribbed him for a year after that, praising Uncle Pete for the entertainment, all done in good fun.

Enough woolgathering. Luke jerked his attention back to introductions. "Smokey, how far up to Covered Bridge did you and Ike get today?" Best to get everyone's minds back to work. "See anything unusual?"

"Halfway, boss," Smokey replied, looking comfortable with a coffee mug in one hand and his other elbow rested on the fireplace mantel. "Some places the drifts are just too deep to ride, as we suspected. Found following the north fence line helped. We caught a glimpse of some of the cattle."

"And?"

"Some still digging around, trying to find feed, but others seem to have given up."

Sick to heart, Luke nodded. He'd seen the same on his ride from his homestead. "As soon as you can make it the whole way, release all the hay stored in the loft. The amount is not near enough to last the winter. Hell, it won't last more than a couple of weeks, but something is better than nothing. We can hope for a warm wind, or better yet, a long, warm rain." That was what could come to the rescue, if anything at all.

Another look at the Petty brothers told him they were trying to look alert and interested but were dead on their feet. They had a strong family resemblance to Shad.

"As I said before," Luke said to Nick and Tanner, "for now, Shad is stuck in town. Not sure when he'll make it back. Roady Guthrie, our foreman, will be in a bit later to lay out what we'll be doing for the next few days. Normally, we have a routine, but with this weather, we take it day by day."

Seeing the men were still holding their saddlebags, Luke said, "Come on, Lucky, get these men situated. They've had a long, hard ride, and I'm sure they'd like nothing better than to stretch out and get some shut-eye."

"Sure thing, boss." The cook started for the far wall and waved the men over. "These two will do ya fine. Ya don't need ta be right next ta yer big brother, I presume?"

A ripple of laughter moved around the room.

Good. A little humor.

"'Course not," Nick bit out.

Luke hid his smile when Tanner Petty cut a disgusted look at his brother for taking the bait. Maybe their arrival was good timing. The men's attention would turn to a little friendly hazing for the next few days. At least, that activity was something to get their minds off Uncle Pete and the hungry livestock.

Luke pulled his hat down tight and headed toward the door. "You're in good hands, boys," he called behind him. "Get settled in. If you have questions, take 'em to Roady. If he's not around, Smokey can help. Welcome to the Heart of the Mountains. You're now riding for the McCutcheons."

Alone, Luke paused on the bunkhouse porch. The house, the snow-covered pines, and the snowy pastures beyond were all as still as a graveyard.

Tired, he scrubbed a hand over his face and shoved away the gruesome thought. The ranch would get through this. They would survive. As much as he hated to think so, he believed many ranches would not.

Question was, what would the territory look like come spring?

Chapter Forty-Five

Sitting alone in the dining room, Poppy waited for the noon meal, the only true meal she'd have today. Her belly growled. She sipped her watered-down coffee with delight. It was good, and sweet, no matter that the drink looked more like brown dishwater from the sink.

She pulled her tattered cape more closely around her shoulders, thinking about the Sanger children. Three days ago, learning of their birthdays had given her hope. For what, she wasn't quite sure. And today she felt optimistic. Good things were on the horizon.

Her gaze wandered around the dining room and stopped on Oscar sitting alone on the far side of the restaurant, barely seen in the dim light. Since the roof collapse, he'd not said more than four words to her, a fact that didn't make Poppy feel all that bad, if she were honest with herself.

But *that* thought did make her repentant. *Am I really that unforgiving? I've known Oscar all my life. I should feel at least something now that I know his true character doesn't fit what I thought of him. Or perhaps feel sad that our relationship has come to a bad end.*

She wished she could go back to the farm and stay with Kathryn until the snow cleared enough to take a stage to

Waterloo. The town that was a stopping point for all folks who were headed to Y Knot and beyond was much larger than this small cattle-ranching settlement. Waterloo had shops and restaurants aplenty. She and Oscar wouldn't stumble over each other at every turn as they did now, and would continue to do in town once they were allowed to get out some. At the moment, her sullen friend, if she could still call him that, slowly spooned in the watered-down soup Cook had served them preceding the noon meal.

She dropped her gaze to her cup when his regard wandered her way. His words of devotion the other day had hit her like a ton of bricks. She'd never gotten the feeling that he loved her. As children, they were best friends, getting into one situation after the other, sneaking snacks from their family's two kitchens, running off to the Boston docks to watch the ships come in. Then, after being found out, they'd find a way to bail out each other and get on the good side of their parents. The challenge was exciting. Even though Oscar had always been promised to Kathryn, he gravitated to her, his friend. She'd even scolded her sister for turning him down.

His words echoed in her mind. "I've always *loved* you, Poppy. Right from the very start."

Had she been wrong not to recognize that Ossy's feelings for her were warmer than the friendship she felt for him?

Feeling the heavy weight of guilt, she took another sip. How unfairly she'd treated Kathryn—and yet her sister had always been Poppy's most ardent champion. Then and now. *Will I ever make up for the past?* That was a question she didn't have the answer to, but she desperately wanted to try.

She glanced again at Oscar. The man couldn't wait to throw her into the fire at her father's feet. Perhaps he'd ventured out already and sent a telegram. She'd not ask him and risk another dressing-down. For him, everything was either black or white, as she herself used to think. Now she was beginning to see hues of gray in her life, as well as pinks, blues, and yellows.

At her silly thought, she smiled to herself. She'd try to send her own telegram today, if she could get over to the telegraph office. She'd been out of touch with her parents for a few weeks. Maybe she could soften them by explaining that she hadn't had a choice in the matter of the collapse and the situation afterwards.

A shiver of longing trickled down her spine as she remembered being in bed with him, snuggled against his side.

Another daydream. Stick to reality. He's a cowboy, and I'm leaving as soon as travel is possible.

Poppy sighed and took another sip of coffee.

Shad had returned to the hotel last night with a good-sized sack of sugar, a gift from Trent Herrick and his father. Seemed citizens who found themselves with a surplus of a food item shared with the hotel staff since they had so many more mouths to feed.

Mel and Bonnie Grant were at their normal table on the right side of the room in front of the window that looked out back. Lenore hustled back and forth, collecting dirty dishes, and Hildy went about with the coffeepot, topping off cups.

Today was Poppy's day to help with the dishes, an activity she'd found she actually liked to do. Something was comforting about taking a dirty object and washing until it was sparkling clean.

Cook had admonished her for taking so long and using too much water, but she didn't care. She enjoyed her time in the kitchen. She was making up for the days she'd had her hands bandaged and couldn't do a thing.

Miss Aubrey appeared in the restaurant doorway, drawing everyone's attention. She wore a borrowed dress just like Poppy.

The homespun fabric looked out of place on the elegant woman who normally wore fabrics suited for entertainment. The wide cream-colored sash accentuated her small waist, though, and looked pretty. The length, a bit too long, caused her to hold up the skirt as she walked so she wouldn't catch her boot toe in the hem. This was the first time the saloon woman had joined them in the dining room.

After taking stock, she sashayed over to Poppy's table, making the everyday dress look exceptional. "Good afternoon, Miss Ford," she said in a soft, alluring voice.

Poppy wished she could speak like that. "Good afternoon, Miss Aubrey," she replied. Then, without even giving a thought to her already damaged reputation, she put out her hand and gestured to the seat opposite her. "I'd be ever so honored if you'd take this meal with me. I'm starved for conversation. How are you feeling?"

"You sure? Might not be in your best interest, consorting with the likes of me."

Poppy followed the woman's line of sight to see Cook standing in the doorway of the kitchen, watching with curiosity. Behind him, Harold and Lenore stared.

What in the world was wrong with everyone? They knew Miss Aubrey well enough from the saloon. From what she'd heard, Miss Aubrey was friends with Harold. Why was he staring? He gawked as if she'd grown an extra head overnight.

Fiddle-faddle. Let them be offended, if that's the way they wanted to be. By Poppy's way of thinking, they were all in this together.

"Absolutely. I've been wondering about you. Hoping you're doing better. Now I have a chance to find out firsthand." She glanced at Miss Aubrey's forehead. The lump had subsided under a shadowy bruise.

"In that case, thank you, sugar."

As Miss Aubrey sat, Poppy chanced a quick look at Oscar, who gaped, his spoon frozen in midair. *Why, the big two-faced ox. He's known Miss Aubrey in the saloon but won't acknowledge her outside those protective walls. Disgusting.*

Poppy felt like marching over to toss her coffee in his face. If the beverage were in plentiful abundance, she just might. At the mental picture, she began to laugh.

Miss Aubrey, now situated in the seat across from her, looked up.

"I'm sorry," Poppy said. "I couldn't help but notice Oscar Scott is about to burst his seams in indignation. He's such a phony. Some people, I just can't abide. And now, much to my surprise, he's one of them."

Hildy approached. She smiled and poured Miss Aubrey some coffee, giving her a conspiratorial wink. "That's a pretty frock on you," she said quietly.

Poppy waited until Hildy was gone. "Her dress?"

Miss Aubrey nodded. "What I brought is still boarded off on the third floor."

"Mine too," Poppy replied, feeling comfortable with the woman. She wondered where Shad was today, hoping he didn't miss the one meal. She took a sip of coffee, smiling at Miss Aubrey, and then set her cup into its saucer. "I've been making do by the generosity of others, as well."

The saloon woman smiled in response. "I'm going home today, and wanted to thank you before I left. Who knows what would have happened if you hadn't come to my rescue, much to your own detriment." She glanced at Poppy's hands. "I'm indebted now and forever. Not everyone would do what you did for a woman like me."

"Nonsense," Poppy sputtered. Miss Aubrey's acknowledgment was the last thing she was expecting. They'd sent word back and forth during their recoveries, but hadn't spoken in person. "You would have done the same for me, I'm sure. I am just glad I was able to help."

Lenore arrived with a tray. She set it on a stand and served Poppy.

The plate had two small slices of beef, a side bowl of rice covered in something that look like it was meant to be gravy—she didn't want to know what Cook had used to make enough for everyone—and two small biscuits. She'd not look a gift horse in the mouth.

Next, Lenore set a bowl of the soup like Poppy had just finished in front of Miss Aubrey.

"Thank you," Miss Aubrey said, lifting her spoon. She waited for the waitress to walk away before taking a taste.

"Home? Where is that?" Poppy placed the biscuits into her napkin and carefully wrapped them.

Miss Aubrey's eyebrow tented. "For our little darlings?"

Poppy nodded but waited for the answer to the question she'd just asked.

"Why, home is the saloon, of course," she replied in her sultry voice. The woman had two different voices she saved for different situations.

Poppy reached out to touch her arm, but withdrew her hand. "You don't have to go yet, just because the snow has stopped. Stay here where you have some company, and the rooms are warmer."

"I can't. Abe left a week ago. By now, I'm sure some men are back to drinking and playing cards. He'll need my help. Besides, I've been through harsh winters before."

Poppy took a bite of her meat and chewed. The size was small, but the portion was tasty.

"I'm going stir-crazy staying in that room," Miss Aubrey added. "I'll enjoy doing something instead of reading and gathering dust."

What did the saloon girl think about? Where was she from? Poppy wondered if anyone knew. Dare she ask?

Giggling and indistinguishable words marked the Sangers' arrival for lunch. Mrs. Sanger came through the door first, carrying one of the twins. Poppy was too far away to tell who.

July came next, the other twin cuddled in his small arms. They took the table farthest away—as usual—and set each of the girls on a chair of their own, their tiny faces barely peeping over the top of the table. Mr. Sanger was nowhere to be seen.

Poppy waved, and July waved back.

"He's so cute," Miss Aubrey said.

"He is."

Poppy wished she could do something to help the children who seemed so sad when with their parents, but were bright and happy when they were with her. For now, she'd just have to bide her time—even though a niggling down deep told her not to wait too long.

Chapter Forty-Six

With the noon meal over, most of the dining room had cleared. Mr. and Mrs. Grant stood, gave Poppy a polite nod, and tottered out of the room. Miss Aubrey had left several minutes ago.

Poppy slowly sipped the remainder of her coffee, making it last. She was waiting, hoping to see Shad. Even though she'd been embarrassed to do so, she'd asked Hildy if she knew his whereabouts. She actually missed him, or was it just the conversations they shared? The room was quiet except for the clink of utensils at the Sanger table. Poppy was just about to go over and say hello when Mr. Sanger's voice came bellowing from the lobby.

After several angry shouts, he burst through the dining room door, stopped on spread feet like a pirate on his deck, and searched the room.

He's intoxicated. Where did he get the whiskey? Surely, Mrs. Sanger won't let him near the children in that condition.

When he spotted his family, he tramped angrily forward, making July cringe in fear.

The little girls leaned so far away, Poppy was afraid they'd fall off their chairs. Alarmed, she pushed her to her feet. She didn't care if the man was twice her size; she'd not allow him to hurt July or the girls.

"I told you to bring some food back to the room," he slurred.

His angry gaze pinned July to his seat. Faster than Poppy thought possible, Mr. Sanger grasped the back of July's threadbare coat and dragged the boy to his feet.

"You think I was kiddin', lad? I'll show you what kiddin' is. Then you won't never doubt me again." Mr. Sanger pulled back his hand.

"Stop," Poppy screamed, rushing toward their table. Where was everyone else?

At the sound of her voice, Mr. Sanger released July's collar. He scuttled away, grasping May's arm, and he stumbled back with her out of the fool's range. April sat like a frightened rabbit on her chair, too terrified to move.

Mr. Sanger began to chuckle, a low sound that grew into a loud, uncouth belly laugh.

The man was disgusting. Poppy braced herself for what was to come.

"You're butting in where you're not wanted, girl. You best get back to your room and mind your own business."

The menacing tone of the last part of his sentence sent curls of fear down Poppy's spine. She'd never dealt with a drunkard before. She'd argued with her father, who could get very angry indeed, but she was never in any danger of being struck. Would this man actually hit her? She didn't know.

Where on earth was Cook? She'd prefer Shad, but Hildy had said he'd gone off early and wasn't likely to be back anytime soon. She wished one of the men would hear the disturbance and come to their rescue. This man had violence on his mind. If he couldn't hurt the little boy, surely he'd take out his temper on her.

"July, April, and May *are* my business," she said, her voice not nearly as strong and powerful as she'd imagined it would be. She clenched her hands into fists to keep them from shaking.

"Stop your meddling. I'm sick of it. I'll be happy to teach you a few manners on minding your own business. Right after I'm finished with my son."

Shock zipped through Poppy when she saw Mrs. Sanger nod her head. What kind of a woman was she? Didn't she love her children at all?

At Poppy's silence, Mr. Sanger swayed and his attention shifted to April, who'd begun to cry. Still in her chair, the child was frantically searching for her siblings, who were huddled under a table a few feet away. Poppy shook her head, trying to signal the boy to stay put, but he came out for his sister anyway.

Once July was in his range, Mr. Sanger immediately caught July's arm. He screeched in pain as Mr. Sanger pulled him up close.

"Let him go," Poppy shouted, rushing forward. She pushed the man with all her might. "He's only a boy. How can you treat him like that?" She implored Mrs. Sanger with her gaze. "Do something. Stop him."

"He's drunk. I can't stop him, and you can't neither. Not unless ya want to get beat near to death."

"Cook," Poppy screamed, seeing Mr. Sanger unbuckle his belt and pull it off as he smiled at how scared July looked. "Oscar. Help! We need help in the dining room!"

No one is coming. I'll have to take care of this myself. But how?

July tugged to get away but the drunk was strong, and by his joyful, crooked grin she could tell he enjoyed the fear he saw on the boy's face. He reared back to strike July with the belt.

Grasping an empty platter from a tray stand nearby, Poppy hoisted it up and swung, smacking the tall man on the back of his head. Losing his grasp on July, he pitched forward and fell to his knees.

Relief washed through her when July scampered away. At least he was safe. During the commotion, April had snuck over to May and was now out of sight too.

"I'm gonna kill you," Mr. Sanger bellowed as he climbed to his feet. With his left hand, he reached back to feel for damage. "No woman hits me and lives to tell."

He swung around, his eyes blazing with anger. He lunged at Poppy, but she darted behind the nearby table, keeping its round width between them. When he went right, she did too. Ugly, filthy words spewed from his mouth.

If there truly was a devil, Mr. Sanger was him. From the corner of her eye, she saw Mrs. Sanger slink from the room, carrying two plates of food.

"You'll be sorry when I catch you, Miss High and Mighty. I see how you look at everyone. We're mud on your shoes."

What was he blabbering about? Poppy didn't feel that way about anyone in the hotel, except him and his wife. She liked Hildy, and even Lenore. *Shad is who I don't want to leave behind.*

Poppy was now Sanger's only prey. He lunged left, a new tactic, but she was fast too and circled left, keeping out of his range. She'd seen how fast he could move, even drunk. She chanced a quick look behind. Could she dart under the next table and crawl to the door? He looked so vile. Whatever he was thinking was evil.

Mr. Sanger shot forward and she parried, but caught her heel in the hem of her borrowed dress. Crying out in fear, she fell to her hands and knees.

With a laugh of triumph, he leaped forward and pinned her to the floor, leering nastily in her face.

Dear Lord in heaven, I'm in big trouble now.

Chapter Forty-Seven

Shad came down the alley wearing a pair of snowshoes he'd found in the storeroom of the hotel, a couple of turkeys he'd been fortunate to kill slung over his shoulder, and his rifle cradled in his arms. Walking wasn't easy but he labored onward, looking forward to being inside and warming himself by the fire.

Thoughts of Poppy lightened his step, as well. He couldn't wait to show her the feast they'd have tonight. And he wanted to see a smile on the Sanger children's faces.

July rounded the corner and ran smack into him. "H-help," he sputtered, his eyes frantic with fear.

"What?" Shad gasped, steadying the boy on his feet without dropping his gun. "What's happened?"

Not Poppy. Not the children. The boy had come outside without any extra clothing. Something was deadly wrong.

Shad swung the two turkeys to the ground and hunkered down to see into July's face as the boy struggled to breathe. "Tell me."

"Help," he said again, finally able to speak. "Miss Ford needs ya. Now!"

Shad jerked his gaze up to the hotel. Everything looked quiet, blanketed in the freezing white. He didn't hear anything.

"Now. She needs ya now. Ain't time to talk!" July ripped himself out of Shad's grasp, turned, and ran back the way he'd come, his feet postholing in the snow as he went.

Panicked, Shad followed, leaving the turkeys where he'd dropped them. The boy was faster because he didn't have the snowshoes to slow him down. He looked like a rabbit bounding ahead. When Shad reached the front, the boy was waiting, holding the door open wide and pointing the way. Shad proceeded in, snowshoes and all.

Hating to waste one single second, he stopped, ripped them off, then ran through the lobby and into the dining room. The room was dim, except for the lunch lantern near the kitchen door and another on the far side of the area.

Cook was kneeling with an arm holding up Poppy's head as she lay on her back. Fear flashed through Shad as he rushed forward, then fell to his knees.

"What happened?"

He heard Poppy's groan like a gunshot around the room, even though the sound was barely audible. She'd been severely roughed up. Her hair was a shambles, and the collar of her dress was torn.

Shad laid the rifle on the floor and gathered her into his arms. Seeing her wince in pain, he loosened his grip. With a cold finger, he gently pushed a lock of hair out of her face.

"Poppy," he said softly. "Poppy, say something."

"I'm all right," she finally said. Her color was coming back, much to Shad's relief.

July came in close and laid a small hand on her arm.

"That bum Sanger," Cook spat.

At the man's name, Shad felt Poppy tense.

Cook nodded toward July. "When I come in, I saw his pa was struggling with Miss Ford on the floor. They were the only ones here." He shrugged. "So I hit him with this pot to get his attention. He's drunk. And mad as a bull."

Fury shot through Shad's whole being. He scanned the empty room. "Where is he? I'll kill him."

"Not sure. I was helping Miss Ford. Guess he figured he'd have to go through me before he'd have his way with her."

Shad stood with Poppy in his arms and then set her on her feet, still supporting her. He needed to get after that scoundrel but didn't want to leave her. His wrath was a living thing that needed to be fed. Lifting her into his arms, he started for the kitchen.

"I'm leaving her in here with you while I hunt him down," he said to Cook. "He's here somewhere."

"I'm fine now, Shad. Put me down. I just needed a moment to get my bearings."

"Nothing doing. Not until we're in the kitchen." Crossing the room with July and Cook beside him, he set her in the chair by the stove.

Cook cast his gaze to the floor. "Sorry it took me so long ta hear ya, Miss Ford," he said. "I was in the outhouse. Don't know where everyone else is, though. Locked away in their rooms, I'd guess."

"It-it's all right, Cook," Poppy said softly, still shaking. "I'm just glad you finally showed up." She stood and defiantly looked Shad in the eye.

"You'll be okay then?" Shad asked. *That's all I care about.*

At her nod, he turned to go, but she caught his arm.

"What're you going to do?"

Shad pressed a hand to the Colt on his thigh under his coat. *Kill him.* "No one roughs up a woman, child, or his horse, and gets away with it."

"Shad. Be careful. Please."

"I'm going to his room first. You stay here."

She straightened. "I can't. The children scattered. They're scared and hiding." She glanced around. "That woman didn't try to help when Mr. Sanger threatened July with his belt. I don't care if the Sangers *are* their parents. There must be something we can do."

"That's a conversation for later. But I agree with you wholeheartedly."

Chapter Forty-Eight

With nerves strung tight, Poppy waited only a few seconds after Shad entered the Sangers' room before she inched forward in the hallway.

"Come in, why don't ya?" Mrs. Sanger said when Shad barged in, gun drawn.

"Where's your husband?" he demanded.

Behind her, Poppy heard a noise and turned, fearful for an instant it might be Mr. Sanger.

Oscar stood a few feet away in the hallway. Had he heard her calls for help, but ignored them? Cook had been outside, but where was Oscar? Both the Grants were hard of hearing, so them not coming to her defense was understandable—but Oscar?

Disgusted, she turned away and inched into the room.

"What's he gone and done now?" Mrs. Sanger asked, her gaze darting to Poppy when she slipped into the room. "That gun must mean something."

The woman set the plate she held next to an already cleaned dish. She'd eaten all the food, leaving none for July or the girls.

Poppy's resolve hardened all the more. She would do something to help these children. They didn't deserve the life they had.

"Where is he?" Shad asked in a no-nonsense voice.

"How would I know? I left him in the dining room—with her." She sneered at Poppy.

"Attacking me, you mean," Poppy threw out, her outrage growing. "What kind of a woman are you? You should be ashamed of yourself."

Poppy could hardly stand to remain in the same room. Since the Sangers began coming out for meals, Hildy had said the man never allowed her inside the room for any reason. The bedsheets and blankets were heaped in the middle of the bed, and the air was rank. Most likely, the chamber pots under the beds hadn't been emptied for days.

Oh, my poor girls. My poor, poor July. I should have followed my instincts and demanded to come inside.

"Where'd he get the whiskey?" Shad asked.

"Found it in the basement."

Shad turned to Cook, who had arrived with a shotgun. "Make sure she doesn't leave this room. Sanger can't be far. In his drunken state, I doubt he went outside. He's hiding around here somewhere. I'll find him."

Poppy felt empowered. She'd make her stand today. "Why do you keep the children?" she said straight to the woman. "Clearly you don't love or want them. I'll care for them from here on out."

For the first time since they'd entered the room, the woman's face blanched. "W-what? You can't have my babies. That's against the law."

"We'll see about that, won't we? When I find where they're hiding, I'm taking them to my room and keeping them."

Mrs. Sanger's face flamed red. She took a menacing step in Poppy's direction, but Shad cut her off.

"Sh-she ain't our ma."

At the frightened voice, all the adults in the room swung around to see July standing in the doorway. May and April were beside him, and Oscar watched from behind.

"Shut yer mouth, boy," Mrs. Sanger whispered low. "You know what happens when you go telling lies." Her malevolent gaze slid over to May and April, causing July to look at the floor at Poppy's feet.

Poppy dropped to one knee and took one of July's hands into her own. His eyes held fear and trepidation. He was so young, too young to be in such pain. The situation would be difficult for an adult, let alone a child.

"You can tell me, July. You don't have to be frightened. They can't hurt you anymore. Or your sisters. I'm here to help, and so is Mr. Petty." She turned and glanced over her shoulder to find Shad watching. Her heart fluttered at the concerned look in his eyes. "Go on, tell us the truth. Is this woman your mother?"

July's small chest rose and fell several times before he shook his head. "No, she ain't. And the man ain't our pa. He said he'd hurt my sisters if I told anyone. Kill 'em, maybe." He pulled May a little closer by a soft tug on her hand.

I knew it. I should have done something sooner.

"The boy's out of his mind," Mrs. Sanger spat. "Never could believe a word he says. But you can't have our children. It's my word against his—*and* my husband's."

"The same man who attacked Miss Ford?" Shad scowled, pointing a finger. "Go get the sheriff," he said to Cook. "This woman and her husband have kidnapped these children."

"No," she screeched and darted to the other side of the messy bed, her eyes wild. She looked at the girls and held out her arms. "Come to Mama," she crooned.

Her voice was disgusting. A shiver of revulsion ran down Poppy's spine as she thought of the little ones being tended by this couple.

The girls didn't move, and a glare replaced the woman's smile. "Did ya hear me, May? I was talking to you. You too, April. Get over here."

Feeling confident, Poppy stepped forward. "If these are your children, tell me which one is May? You don't even know, do you?"

Mrs. Sanger's eyes bulged, then her gaze flicked between the girls.

"I didn't think so. Well, I know, and you should as well, if you really gave birth to them. But you didn't."

The woman's chin jerked. "Too close to tell. What difference does it make, anyway?"

"And while we're sorting this out," Poppy added, remembering the time she'd watched her father's solicitor question a suspect in the courtroom, "tell us their birthdays? And how you came up with their names?"

A gush of happiness filled Poppy. The revelation that these horrible people really weren't related to the children at all was wonderful. She would take them and raise them, even if she was only eighteen years old. Almost nineteen, she reminded herself. Some women were mothers much younger than that.

Shad put a steadying hand on July's small shoulder, and the child took a deep breath. "Tell us what happened."

"Our ma died last Christmas," the boy whispered. "Got sick. Pa tried to save her, but she passed on before the doctor could come." His voice trailed off.

Shad nodded his encouragement. "Go on, July. We need to hear this before we can help you."

"Since then, I did the best I could when Pa worked. Watched the girls. Fed 'em and made sure they were safe." He glanced over at his sisters, who'd sat on the floor. "Then one day, Pa didn't come home. I was scared. Didn't know why. The next day, her and the man arrived in Pa's buckboard. They said he was dead. Had an accident at the mill—but I didn't believe 'em. I think they killed our pa."

The boy took a deep breath, then let it out slowly. "We had a big wagon in the barn, the one we came here in." He looked at Mrs. Sanger and frowned. "They loaded up everything from our house they could fit. I tried to fight 'em, but the man's too strong. Then I heard 'em whispering about our uncle, and how they could get money out of 'im if they held us for ransom."

In a rush of love, Poppy pulled July into her arms, tears brimming in her eyes. What a nightmare. Poor July had been shouldering such pain.

Shad circled the bed and grasped Mrs. Sanger's arm as she tried to shrink away.

"The man is very dangerous," Poppy said quietly. "I could see in his eyes he'd have liked to kill me. You need to find him before he hurts someone else."

Sheriff Crawford and his deputy arrived with guns drawn. Cook stood behind them, red-faced and shivering.

The broad-shouldered sheriff came into the room, his hawk-like gaze missing nothing. Deputy Wesley came forward and slapped a pair of handcuffs around the woman's wrists.

Shad's face was a stony mask of anger. "July says the children were kidnapped for ransom by these two. Mr. Sanger accosted Miss Ford only moments ago in the dining room."

Justin Wesley led Mrs. Sanger out the door. "I'll lock her up and be back."

"You better stand guard until we have Sanger locked up behind bars." Brandon Crawford holstered his gun. "We have a search to conduct. I'll verify the boy's story after they can't hurt anyone else. Let's get moving."

Chapter Forty-Nine

"Roady, are you sure Flood and Claire won't mind you taking the afternoon off to escort me into town?" Sally asked, excitement zipping through her. She watched from the front window of the bunkhouse as the ranch sleigh and a team of horses were hitched and ready to go.

Outside, Francis stood holding the lines, his back hunched against the wind. He was as thick as a bear from all his clothing, and frosty air issued forth from his lips as he breathed.

"I wouldn't want to overstep their hospitality," Sally went on.

Her layers of clothing, as well as the heavy fur coat Claire had insisted she wear, kept her toasty warm. But they were still inside a building. She knew the ride into Y Knot would be brutal. Roady had cautioned her all morning. They'd have to make good time, as not to be out in the cold too long.

Francis glanced at the window and stomped his feet. When he saw Sally watching, he dipped his chin and turned away.

"Said they didn't." Roady pulled on his thick leather gloves. "But I could see in their eyes they think we're *loco*."

"But Francis, Ike, and Smokey?"

"Mr. and Mrs. McCutcheon insisted we take 'em. They'd not let us venture out without men riding guard after what happened to Uncle Pete." He slugged down the last of his coffee and strode to the kitchen.

Smokey and Ike led their horses from the barn.

"They're ready," she said, turning back to her husband. "Everyone's out there."

Roady came to her side and ran his hand down the arm of the borrowed fur coat. "Then let's get going. This is something we should have taken care of months ago. Waiting any longer isn't an option. A day or two could make all the difference."

Sally breathed a huge sigh of relief. He was right. Too much time had passed already. She needed to make sure her sisters were protected from Eric Greenstein. A little cold and discomfort weren't stopping her now.

She nodded. "Agreed. Once we do this, I won't ask for any more favors."

He chuckled and went to the door. "I'd be disappointed if you didn't. I like makin' you happy, but not when we're risking your life."

"And the lives of the men? Only ten days have passed since—"

He shushed her with a look. "They'll be fine. Doing something will take their minds off him. Don't let 'em fool ya; they like going to town."

At the thick wooden door, she went up on tiptoe and kissed him. "Thank you, Roady." She was aware of Lucky's presence. "I won't forget this."

"All right then, let's get this party started," he said.

Sally pulled her fur hat lower and lifted the wool scarf across her nose and mouth.

Outside, with a firm hand, Roady helped her into the sleigh. "Up you go." He handed her to Francis, who had climbed in when they'd come outside.

She snuggled down into the middle of the front seat, and Roady got in beside her. With several animal skins and a heavy buffalo robe, he tucked in every tuckable place. Finished, he laid one robe across his lap and lifted the rifle off the floorboard. They were ready.

Ike and Smokey mounted, both with their Remingtons cradled in their arms. They wouldn't let anything get close.

"We're off," Francis called out, and she imagined his shy smile behind his wool scarf. He clucked his tongue and slapped the lines.

The sleigh glided forward with ease. They made a wide turn in the yard, taking them past the ranch house where Flood and Claire stood in the window.

When they waved, Sally tried to wave back, but her hands were captured under the robes. All she could do was lift her chin and smile, even though that too was hidden. They smiled back, but she could see the worry in their eyes.

When the sleigh was about twenty feet ahead, she turned to see Smokey and Ike started behind. She felt safe and protected.

Except for the cold, the countryside was gorgeous. White as far as the eye could see. The steel-blue sky overhead said they had a clear day, at least for a while. Filled with eagerness, Sally swiveled again and watched the riders. Smokey and Ike's large ranch horses pushed through the snowfall, a bit easier since the virgin snowpack had already been broken by the sleigh's team.

Roady leaned in. "Warm enough?" His gaze searched hers.

She nodded. "Actually, yes. Everything is so beautiful. I'm glad we came."

But were the poor cold ranch hands? She owed them so much for doing this favor. She'd cook them a nice supper and bake a cake once she was home again in her own cozy cabin.

"Good. At least the snow isn't too deep here. Up in the mountains, the drifts must be ten to fifteen feet." He shook his head.

Emerging from a copse, the sleigh moved forward as if on wings. Off to the right, where the trees thinned, she could see open prairie rolling away to the hills, and farther back were the large mountains. A small grouping of cattle stood with their heads hung low. Only a few looked to see who was approaching. Large lumps of white were scattered around, and she wondered what they were.

When Roady noticed what she was looking at, he put his arm around her and turned her head away.

Feeling his uneasiness, she burrowed closer and focused her gaze forward. They passed a stream where the ice had been broken out, and she could hear the trickle of water over stones. By the ranch hands, she guessed. The snow was trampled around the watering hole where the cattle came to drink.

While she stayed warm in the house each day, the men, including Roady, were outside working to keep the animals alive. Ranchers were tough, but vulnerable too. She stole a glance up at Roady, a dark feeling unsettling her nerves. Uncle Pete's passing had opened her eyes. Montana was not only romantic, but perilous too.

Chapter Fifty

Mr. Tracy glanced up when Sally and Roady entered the telegraph office. "What in tarnation brings the two of you into town?" He gaped at them, his eyes widening at their sudden arrival.

As they hurried for the woodstove in the corner of the room, he said, "I'd think you had more sense. I've seen a few folks from town getting out and about a bit, but no one from the ranches. You must be frozen solid."

He was right; Sally was. By the time they'd reached the halfway point, Sally was seriously rethinking her decision. No wonder Flood and Claire had tried to dissuade her. They'd talked until they ran out of objections, giving in to her decision.

They didn't know the real reason why she needed to get to Y Knot. They knew nothing of the telegram she would send—*if* the lines were still up and working. She'd insisted she needed to check on her sister Heather, out at the mill. That she was homesick for her. Sally hoped she hadn't destroyed the wonderful relationship she'd forged with them, especially Claire.

The McCutcheons considered Roady a fifth son, and in turn treated her like a beloved daughter-in-law. Sally risking so many lives—Roady, the ranch hands, as well as her baby and herself—

could not ingratiate herself to them. They'd think her a spoiled brat. But because of her sisters, that couldn't be helped.

"We'd like to send a telegram," Roady said. "Are the lines clear?"

"You're in luck."

She sought out Roady's gaze. They'd talked about what to say, but hadn't written out anything. Didn't want the note falling into anyone else's hands.

Roady beat his gloves together a few times and then peeled them off, tossing them next to the stove. She left hers on and followed him to the counter, where she noticed a plate of food pushed to the side.

The very small telegraph operator wiped his hands on a cloth and nodded. He put his finger on the telegraph and waited.

"Who's it to?"

"Before we get started, I want to make something perfectly clear," Roady said in a serious tone.

The man's head jerked up, and his gaze met Roady's.

"You have to promise you'll keep every single word to yourself. This is private. Our business only."

Sally glanced at Roady's rock-hard expression.

"Of course," Mr. Tracy said, his brows lowered. "That's part of the job."

That might be so, but the man's gnome-like eyes burned with curiosity. Sally felt a moment of panic. In a few seconds, he'd know her shame.

Roady leaned one arm onto the counter, getting closer. "I mean it, Tracy."

Mr. Tracy straightened. "So do I."

Roady gave her one last glance before saying, "This is to Travis Stanford, St. Louis, Missouri, in a sealed envelope. We want the note delivered to him only."

"Confidentiality will cost ya extra."

"Fine."

Sally looked away. Soon this man would know her baby wasn't Roady's. She'd been sure of this decision, and still was, but that didn't make the truth any easier. Humiliation squeezed her chest. She turned to look out the front window, keeping an ear to hear what Roady would say.

Beware Eric Greenstein STOP He forced himself on Sally STOP Keep him away from your sisters and mother STOP Do not take matters into your own hands STOP He will pay in due time STOP I will see to that STOP Tell no one STOP Sincerely Roady Guthrie STOP Your new brother-in-law END

Sally eased closer. How would Travis handle the situation? She'd been so worried about Anita and Melba; she hadn't given her brother much thought. What if he exacted justice himself? What if he killed Mr. Greenstein? She didn't want her brother to go to prison, or worse, be hung. In a panic, she gripped Roady's coat.

He glanced down and smiled. "No worries, sweetheart. Everything'll be fine."

She felt Mr. Tracy's gaze on her face but didn't look at him. Their secret was out. The attack she'd endured wasn't just between her and Roady any longer. She knew what she'd insisted on was the right thing to do. No taking it back now.

"Back so soon?" Mr. Tracy mumbled when Roady returned alone twenty minutes later. The man laid down the buttered biscuit he was about to shove into his mouth and wiped his hands. "Did ya forget something?" He glanced at the area around the woodstove.

"Sure didn't. Need to send another telegram."

Mr. Tracy's gaze cut to the door. "Where's your wife?"

"Visitin' with her sister out at the mill."

The telegraph operator's brow peaked almost imperceptibly. Over the years, the man had most likely heard his share of revelations.

Roady couldn't tell what he was thinking. Did he believe Sally a loose woman? He didn't know, and actually, he didn't much care. Right now, all he could think about was what he had to do next.

"Today?"

"'Course." Tracy hopped down and went to the telegraph.

"This is confidential too. Send it to Eric Greenstein, *St. Louis News and Events*."

The telegraph operator's head jerked up, his eyes questioning, and then he went to work clicking out the address. "Done. What do you want to say?"

Keep watch over your shoulder STOP I'm not a timid girl STOP You will pay for what you did STOP Don't ever approach my wife's family STOP If you ignore this warning your wife will get the letter you sent STOP Along with the bank note STOP And an explanation STOP I look forward to our meeting STOP You can bank on that STOP Roady Guthrie STOP Sally's cowboy husband END

When Mr. Tracy finished, he didn't look up. His jaw clenched and released several times. "Anything else?" he asked, keeping his attention on his fingers.

"That's all. How much do I owe you?"

Mr. Tracy slowly raised his face and looked him in the eye. "It's on the house."

Chapter Fifty-One

Evelyn groaned and gripped her stomach, and Margaret almost dropped her knitting needles into her lap. She and Evelyn sat by the fire after Chance and Andy had finished the noon meal and the kitchen cleanup was done.

In haste, Margaret set her knitting on the small side table and hurried to Evelyn's side. "What is it?" she asked.

"Just getting ready for labor, I think," Evelyn wheezed out. She panted a couple of times and rubbed her large belly. "These pains shouldn't surprise me. Everyone says how agonizing labor is. I can't expect to be different."

"But you're not due." She still had an entire month to go. Surely, Evelyn wasn't going into labor now.

Evelyn laughed and took one of her hands. "No, no, nothing like that. Dr. Handerhoosen said my body will begin to prepare for labor, softening up. That means bones will begin to move, so when the day arrives, labor will be as easy as possible. I'd guess that's what's been happening the last couple of days."

Last couple of days? "You haven't said as such."

From the very beginning, Margaret had been frightened Evelyn would go into labor early, and she'd have to deliver the baby. She couldn't deal with such thoughts. She'd run a mail-order-bride agency, not dealt with matters that came after the unions were formed, like childbirth.

Evelyn laughed and released Margaret's hand. She lifted the tiny layette gown suitable for a boy or girl. "What do you think?"

Margaret forced a calming breath and settled herself back in her chair. "It's beautiful. You're more talented than I with your knitting needles." Everything would be fine. They still had several weeks to go.

Evelyn glanced at the garment, and then back at Margaret. "Really? That's difficult for me to believe. I've tried to measure up to you, but haven't come close." She laughed softly. "Not by a country mile."

Margaret had been pulling out her last sloppy stitch in the baby blanket she worked on. Evelyn's statement made her glance up. *Is that how she feels?* Margaret hadn't meant to impose such standards onto her goddaughter. Not at all.

"What do you mean?"

Evelyn's smile faded. "Only that I've tried to please you, and I believe I have, for the most part. But you must admit, I've fallen short countless times." She waved a hand in front of her. "Actually, I don't know why I brought that up. I truly need to thank you for raising me after Mama passed on. Without a father, or any relatives, I can't imagine how my life would have turned out."

She hadn't known Evelyn felt inadequate. The thought broke her heart. "Raising you was our pleasure. Our home just wouldn't have been the same without you. It would have been much too quiet. My most wonderful memories are of when you were a baby and a child. You were such a curious little thing. You never stopped asking questions." She laughed, even though she felt like crying. "Ran us all ragged. The colonel, as well. We had to keep several steps ahead of your imagination, or we'd be in trouble."

Evelyn smiled, but the expression didn't reach her eyes. "Yes, I remember."

"Those were good years."

Setting the dainty little garment aside, Evelyn gave her an intent look. "Margaret, do you know who my father is?"

Blindsided, Margaret didn't know how to respond. Instead, she looked at the fire between them, deciding how much she should say. So many years had passed, she'd thought perhaps Evelyn would never ask this question. She'd been wrong.

"I'm sorry, I don't." But I have my ideas.

"You must remember who my mother was seeing at the time. Whenever I'd ask her, she had a way of redirecting the conversation." She placed her hand on her belly and rubbed a slow circle. "As I grew older, I realized that was because the topic brought her pain, so I stopped. She lived with you when she was a teacher at Kirkwood Seminary Women's College. Were you with her when she found out she was carrying me?"

That heartbreaking day was burned into Margaret's brain as deeply as a brand on a steer.

"Margaret? Please?"

She nodded. Maybe the time had come for Evelyn to know something, at least. "I'd just returned from lunch with friends at the Teacup Café. Do you remember the quaint little eatery not far from the house I used to take all the girls to?"

Evelyn nodded.

"The house was quiet, or so I'd thought. Your mother had been staying with us for about six months, renting a room on the second floor." Pausing, Margaret reached for her drink to wet her suddenly parched throat. How much should she tell? What did Estelle want Evelyn to know? "I started up the staircase when I heard a noise in your mother's room. I stopped and listened because usually she'd be teaching at that time of day. I thought perhaps she'd taken sick."

Evelyn listened with large, wonder-filled eyes.

"I knocked, but Estelle didn't answer. I put my ear to the door and heard soft sobs and the sound of her blowing her nose. I was alarmed, fearful something had happened." She gripped the chair arms, remembering that day well. Remembering her feelings of helplessness. "I begged her to open the door. She was alone in the world and very upset. I knew she needed a shoulder to lean on, so I didn't stop asking until she let me inside."

Evelyn nibbled her bottom lip. "What did she say?"

"That she'd had to relinquish her position because she was with child. And that she didn't know how she could go on without a job and with a baby on the way."

Margaret would not share how bitterly Estelle had wept. How giving up all that she'd worked so hard to achieve had broken her heart. How the father of the baby had shut the door in her face when she'd gone to him. No, that would stay wrapped up in Margaret's heart forever.

"I made her an outcast," Evelyn whispered, her eyes brimming.

"No. You didn't. She chose a solitary life. After you were born, I encouraged her to get out and meet people. To let me care for you, and to put you in school, but she wanted to stay inside the Victorian and teach you herself."

Lumbering up, Evelyn went to the stacked firewood and hefted a log onto the fire.

Margaret stood and stepped close. "You're supposed to let me do that," she scolded at her side.

"I'm not an invalid, Margaret. I'm going to have a baby. But thank you. Please, go on. Don't stop now."

"Don't you want to sit again?" Margaret asked, glancing at the vacant chairs.

"Not quite yet. I need to get some blood back into my legs. A little walk around the room will do nicely." Evelyn finally smiled. "I can handle this, Margaret. I want to know more. Please."

Knowing her words had cast a gloom over the day, Margaret hoped she could cheer up Evelyn. "Your mother was not only a beauty, but was delightful to speak with. She had a spark, a love of life that shone through her eyes. People flocked around her like bees to honey. After you were born, that changed a little. She held back and was more reserved. But that was totally understandable, under the circumstances."

"How old was she when she came to live with you?"

Margaret watched Evelyn walk slowly to the kitchen, and then start back. Her mouth pinched as if she were having more pain. "I believe Estelle was twenty-five or twenty-six."

Surprise crossed her face. "That old?"

Margaret laughed. "That's hardly old, dear."

"I mean old for still being single."

"That never seemed important to Estelle; at least, she never spoke about being unmarried with me. She loved to read and learn. She enjoyed teaching very much. She was an extremely happy person."

"You mean, before she had me."

"No, that's not what I mean. She loved you with all her heart. She was always the happiest when the two of you were together. You remember that, don't you? Mother and daughter having a picnic in the backyard under the alders."

"Yes. I remember. We'd sit by the carp pond for hours, just talking and whiling away the time after her work was finished in the house."

"Evelyn," Margaret said in a soft whisper, hoping that her goddaughter would believe her. "I never wanted your mother to be our housekeeper. I wanted her to get another job. I offered to watch you so she could. Told her she could stay with us for as long as she liked—without paying. But she'd have none of that. She kept house to pay for the room and board for the two of you, but I think perhaps her reasons were more than that."

For several long seconds, Evelyn stared at Margaret. "The only places she'd take me were the library or the weekend farmers' market. Why was she so afraid?"

Estelle had never sworn Margaret to secrecy, but it was inferred. "I'm not totally sure, Evelyn, because your mother never said exactly, but I believe your father must have been an important man. Someone of great power. I think she worried he'd try to take you away from her." She shook her head. "I don't really know, but in most matters, your mother was fearless."

"That's why I never went to school?"

Margaret nodded.

Evelyn rubbed her stomach and returned to her chair after several trips to the kitchen and back. Her smile tightened. "She must have wanted more from her life, don't you think? I mean, I know she loved living with you and the colonel. I just think she must have been lonely."

"I don't know. She loved you more than life itself. You made her happy, Evelyn. She was content with that."

That wasn't a lie. If Estelle had wanted more, she'd have moved or found another way. But she'd stayed. Was that because she couldn't bear to be far from Evelyn's father? Or to start anew with someone else? That was an answer they'd never know—not now.

Margaret hoped her responses had been enough for Evelyn. She prayed she hadn't made the situation worse.

Chapter Fifty-Two

Shad pulled the blanket up over his shoulder, seeking comfort in his makeshift bed. The lobby was quiet and the iron stove had been stuffed with wood. He breathed out a deep sigh of fatigue. Running this hotel almost took more out of him than his regular chores on the ranch. Even Hickory's chatter would be a welcome change over Oscar's constant complaints.

He stifled a yawn. Finding and apprehending Sanger had not been difficult. If the man had had a weapon, that would have been a different story. After leaving the woman to Justin, Shad and Brandon conducted a thorough search of the premises. It only took minutes to find Sanger nearly frozen in the basement. He was now locked in the cell opposite the woman, who was not even his wife. Justin had learned that fact since arresting her.

Somewhere in the hotel, a woman shrieked in terror.

Jerked from his sleepy thoughts, Shad sat up. He'd know Poppy's voice anywhere. Reaching for his gun, he bolted toward his old room on the first floor behind the dining room.

He entered and saw Poppy thrashing on the bed as if she'd been dunked in hot oil. Crossing in three strides, he tried to take her shoulders, but she fought him like an angry badger. With nothing left to do, he sat on the edge of the bed and wrapped her into his arms none too gently as he ducked and dodged her flailing limbs.

"Shh, it's just a bad dream. A nightmare. You don't have to worry about Sanger. He's locked up tight. He can't hurt you again."

She stilled.

Did he dare loosen his grip? He didn't want to get smacked in the face. Cautiously, he leaned back.

Her eyelids fluttered as she gradually awakened. She blinked and then turned her head, hiding her face in the folds of his coat.

"What were you fighting?" he asked. "You're strong when you want to be."

Now that she was awake, he silently chastised himself for not taking one more moment to caress her silky hair. The desire had been taunting him for days.

When she didn't answer, he said, "Poppy, you awake? I saw you open your eyes."

With her still clamped against his chest, he felt her nod. He gently tipped her face so he could see into her eyes.

"There you are," he whispered and then smiled. "Would you like me to light the lamp?"

"No. I want you to lie down and hold me. Would that be terrible?"

He didn't care if the action was improper. He realized he'd do anything for Poppy. Anything in the world. "Not at all." He moved without making noise, getting up and closing the open bedroom door.

At the opposite side of the bed, he sat and swung up his legs after kicking off his boots. He gently gathered her into his arms, cradling her onto his chest. He drew the blankets over them both, getting warm and comfortable. Her fire burned low and would need some wood soon. He should have taken care of that before getting situated.

"Tell me about your dream," he whispered. "If you talk about the scariness, maybe it won't come back. Were you dreaming of Sanger?"

She stayed silent, but he could tell she was listening. Her arm tightened over his chest.

"It wasn't Sanger. I was home. In Boston," she said, her voice quavering. "I was alone in the big house."

"That's not so bad."

"I went upstairs to my room, but everything was different. A hay pallet had replaced my bed. Snow was piled high on the walls. Then a large wolf lunged at my throat." She gasped and began to cry, hugging him with force.

"A nightmare is all. No wolf's gonna get you."

"I felt his hot breath on my face. My heart was about to explode because my feet were nailed to the floor and I couldn't run." She sobbed, gripping him all the tighter. "I can't describe the frightening sensation." She panted a few times. "And, the worst of all, Kathryn appeared. She didn't try to help me. But I don't blame her. Not one bit."

"It was a bad dream. Nothing else. I have 'em all the time. And mine never make any sense either." He felt her look up at his face.

"Really?"

"Well, no, not that often."

A sob ripped out. "Shad, stop. The nightmare does make sense. You don't know anything about me. You don't know me at all."

He thought about that as he stared up at the ceiling. What was she talking about? "Hogwash. I know you plenty."

Poppy pushed up on an elbow and glared down in his face. "No, you don't. You only know what I've let you see. I'm a horrible person. Shallow and self-centered. I don't care about anyone's feelings except my own."

His chuckle escaped before he had a chance to fight it back. She was being sincere. Really believed her crazy statements. He didn't want her to think he thought light of what she was saying.

"I'm being serious, Shad. My whole life, I've been cruel to Kathryn—for no reason at all. But she's always been so kind in return." Poppy rolled her face onto her nearest hand, for a moment covering her mouth. "I've been the worst sort of sister, if I can even call myself that. I don't know why she even still speaks to me."

Hearing another sob, he laid a palm on her cheek, admiring the softness. For a moment, she nudged in closer.

She really believes this.

"Poppy, here's what I know to be true. I've seen you care for everyone in this hotel. You saved Fancy by risking your own life. You've looked after April, May, and July as if they were your own. I've seen you wrap up your food and go hungry so you could give it to them. You always have a kind word for the Grants, even when you're bone tired." He gave her a shake. "Stop selling yourself short. Even Harold. You loaned him your cape."

"I'm talking about *Kathryn*." Poppy wiped her wet cheeks and sniffed. "I don't know why I've acted this way, except I've seen my father do it all my life. But that doesn't give me license to follow his horrible example."

"To me, you sound like you're sorry."

She collapsed onto his chest again. Unaware, he was sure, of the torment she caused him.

"I am. With all my heart. I just never really gave my behavior much thought until my eyes were opened while staying at her farm. But now I know. Being stuck in this hotel, my attitude is all that I think about night and day. I wish I could do everything over. Be a better sister. Be exactly like her."

Shad ran his hand up and down her arm. "You can fix that. If you really believe everything you've just said, tell her. Explain the situation just like you told me. That's all an apology will take. We all have regrets, but it's never too late to change a direction. That is, until we die."

Again, she lifted herself up and stared down into his face. The sincerity in her eyes made his heart tremble.

"You're sure?" she whispered.

"Positive. I promise."

Wonderful. Against his better judgment, he'd gone and fallen in love with Poppy. Now they'd both have a heartbreak to get over.

Before he realized her intentions, he felt her lips on his as if she'd never kissed a man in her life.

Am I her first?

She was uncertain, and the kiss was soft. Her lips were incredibly silky in spite of the cold weather. He stayed completely still, fearful she'd pull away.

After a short time, she slipped down to his chest before he could see what she was thinking. No more talk was heard, just feeling, wanting. Her hand on his chest felt like a fiery brand.

He'd never leave her, but he couldn't give her what she deserved. *What every woman deserved.* Half a man could never do that.

Until tonight, he hadn't felt the full weight of his medical condition. Living without her would be unbearable.

Chapter Fifty-Three

Wednesday morning, in a fog of confusion, Poppy stood in the lobby of the hotel, staring out the front window. Everything was still frozen and white. She'd been living here over two weeks. Plenty of time to get to know Shad, to become enamored and mixed up.

Outside, a few people dared the slippery boardwalk or rode a horse through the knee-deep snow. At least in some areas, the wind had reduced the depth. They were all thankful for that. Shad said the conditions weren't that way everywhere.

What should she do? Especially after last night. They'd lain together. They'd kissed.

Poppy dragged her jumbled thoughts back to safer ground. Since being watched by Poppy, Hildy, and Lenore, the three tykes seemed much happier. Sanger's pretend wife had become scared and confessed that the man she'd taken up with learned about the children from someone. He'd heard they had rich relatives somewhere. Locating the farm hadn't been difficult. Out of sight of the children, they'd hit their father over the head and dumped him in the river while unconscious to drown.

What would happen to the children now? As outlandish as the idea sounded, Poppy wanted to keep the three siblings. When she was caring for them, something inside her changed for the better. She wanted to become that person all the time. She supposed Sheriff Crawford was contacting towns now, trying to figure out where they'd lived. As much as July tried, he couldn't remember. Once contact was made and the snow receded enough, someone would arrive to escort them to their new home. They would be out of her life for good. Her heart shuddered at the thought.

She breathed on the windowpane and drew a small heart. *Someday I'll have children of my own*, she thought, the possibility not softening the hurt she felt now. How could she ever forget July, May, and April? That wasn't possible.

A sound made her turn.

Mr. and Mrs. Grant slowly made their way down the stairway. The elderly woman had a bear hold on the stair rail, and her husband had a tight grip on her elbow, making sure she didn't fall.

Poppy hesitated for a moment, recalling Shad's words. Was what he said true? She hadn't noticed her acts of doing for others. Maybe, if she hoped hard enough, the woman he'd pointed out might be real.

She hurried forward and climbed the few remaining stairs. "Here, let me assist you down," she said, taking an arm of each person.

The poor things were cold. Everyone was exhausted from the meager rations. Hunger never left their thoughts. The turkeys Shad brought in two days ago had been a welcome addition, but it hadn't taken long to polish them off. Now they were back to the usual fare.

"Thank you, dear," Mrs. Grant said when her feet were safely on the wooden floor of the lobby. "We came down to sit by the fire."

"You're in luck. The chairs are empty."

Poppy kept her hold on the unstable woman until Mrs. Grant was in the chair only a couple of feet from the warm stove. Her husband took the other chair while Poppy opened the iron door and added more logs. She was rather proud of becoming so self-sufficient. In the old days, she would have rung for a servant to do that chore. Finished, Poppy stood, intent on returning to her post at the window and watching the little doings of the outside world.

Mrs. Grant caught her arm. "One moment, dear."

Startled, Poppy glanced from Mrs. Grant to her husband, who smiled and shrugged. "Yes? What is it? Can I get you both a cup of tea? I know for a fact Cook was warming water a few minutes ago." They were probably as hungry as she was. Hot water helped to dull the ache.

"Oh no." Mrs. Grant patted the arm she still held. "I just wanted to thank you for looking after us as you do. You're like a devoted granddaughter. We appreciate all the care you've showered on us since this ordeal began."

Poppy's face heated. No one had ever thanked her for helping. "I haven't done much."

"You've done everything."

"She's right, young lady," Mr. Grant added. "You've made us feel right at home, as much as one can in these conditions. We won't forget your kindness."

Now released from Mrs. Grant's grasp, Poppy slowly returned to the window, emotions swirling within. Shad's words from the middle of the night kept taunting her.

What did he think—*really think*—of her after she'd shared her heart about Kathryn? Was righting a wrong as easy as he said, just talking with Kathryn and telling her how she felt? Saying she was sorry?

Maybe, maybe not. And certainly not for Tobit. His words would be forever carved on Poppy's heart, and perhaps that was just another mark of her arrogance. Was she more concerned about how he thought of her than how she had treated Kathryn for all these years?

She sighed, and a ring of fog grew on the glass. No way of knowing. *Except to try.*

Across the street, Berta May came out of her shop. The woman was bundled from head to toe. She inched forward and looked up and down the deserted street. Her breath streamed out in a straight line, and her arms wrapped around her substantial figure.

Poppy knocked hard on the glass and waved.

"Wh-what was that?" Mrs. Grant asked, caution in her voice.

Looking over her shoulder, Poppy laughed. "Oh, just an acquaintance across the street. The owner of the fabric store has stepped outside. I was trying to get her attention."

"Ah, I see. You go ahead and pound away then. Just be sure not to break the glass. Since the collapse upstairs, keeping this place warm has been all the more impossible. I can't imagine if Mr. Petty had to board up the window too."

Ah. Mr. Petty. *Shad.* The man was never far from her thoughts.

"Yes, I can imagine. We wouldn't like that very much."

Poppy waved again, and this time Berta May saw her and enthusiastically waved back, a smile wide across her face. Being able to get out and interact with others would be so nice. These walls had closed in on her a long time ago. She needed to get some fresh air. See the sky overhead…

Chapter Fifty-Four

Poppy was still at the window when someone behind her cleared their throat. Shad? She hoped not. What would she say? How would she face him after she'd gone and kissed him like that? Why had she been so stupid?

Someone tapped her shoulder, and she turned.

"Ossy," she said, unable to hide her surprise.

His brow fell. "Don't look so disappointed."

"I'm not," she fibbed. "You're speaking to me today? Why?"

"I thought it time to bury the hatchet." His all-knowing smile appeared. "Plus I have a surprise."

He'd captured her interest. Anything from the ordinary was welcome.

"Don't keep me in suspense."

"I've rented the sleigh from the livery. I thought you'd like to go for a ride."

She glanced at the window. The street was still abandoned. Was an outing safe?

"Really? I thought Mr. Petty said he'd let us know when going out was possible. Everything is still frozen. I'm surprised June Pittman would rent the sleigh."

"I told her I just intended to go up and down Main Street a few times. I'm going stir-crazy in here. I'm sure you are, as well— or at least, the 'old' Poppy I used to know would be."

Oscar had a point. "Yes, I am a bit. At least now, when the children are napping. There's only so much to do. But I'm not sure I want to brave the temperatures. We'll freeze, Ossy. And once we get back inside, warming up will take so long. I don't think it's a good idea."

"That's what I *told* June Pittman, but not what I have planned." He lowered his voice so only she could hear. "How would you like to ride out to see Kathryn? The way you've been moping around, I thought seeing your sister would cheer you up. Quick ride there, visit for an hour, and then quick ride back. We won't even be missed."

"Kathryn?"

Hope jumped in her chest. Maybe she and Kathryn could have that talk. She could tell her how sorry she was. An honest discourse wouldn't fix everything, or pay for Poppy's past, but it might be a start. If Shad was right, maybe Kathryn would understand and forgive her. Maybe then Poppy could start with a clean slate and be the sister she should have been all her life.

"You're being very quiet. I can see I've caught your interest."

His sly smile almost made her say no.

"What do you think?" he asked again. "If you're game, I can have the sleigh out back in fifteen minutes. We can be to the ranch in time for ten o'clock tea, and be back here for the noon meal. But you'll have to decide quickly."

"Why would you go to all this trouble?" she couldn't help asking.

"I told you why, but you didn't believe me. I love you. And I—"

Poppy held up her hand. "Please, Ossy. Don't. Nothing you do or say will change my mind. That's all. Nothing."

He heaved a deep sigh. "Fine. I still want to do this for you, if you want to go. Kathryn will be relieved to see you, as well. I'm sure she's worried about her little sister."

Poppy nibbled her bottom lip. She knew the way and so did he. The farm wasn't that far. If they went directly there, the trip would only take about twenty-five minutes. That wasn't long. The temperature was still cold, but not as bad as during the storm. They could handle that, couldn't they?

"Well?"

She threw caution to the wind. "All right. As long as Hildy agrees to see to the children when they wake."

His lips pulled down in an ugly frown. "The children," he repeated in an irritated tone, "are not your responsibility."

She pointed at his chest. "You hush."

"Fine. I'll knock two times softly on the kitchen door when I'm out there."

Excitement surged inside. Here was her chance. If she could speak with Kathryn today, get some of her feelings, guilt and more, off her chest, Poppy would be able to deal with as many winters as she fancied. Kathryn was who she hurt for, not herself.

The sleigh ride was much slower than Poppy had anticipated. She'd expected to get in, get covered, and arrive at the Preece farm in the same amount of time it took a buggy. And that most likely would have been the case if the road had been traveled. But no other sleighs had been out that way. Their poor horse had to trudge slowly through the virgin snow, breaking a trail.

Poppy scooted closer to Oscar in an attempt to feel a little of his body heat. Minutes ago, her feet had turned to blocks of ice.

"Oscar, I think we should turn back. This is much more difficult than I'd anticipated. I had no idea the road would be this hard going. The poor gelding is already worn out. Look at the animal." She set her gloved hand on Oscar's to get his attention, because he appeared lost in thought. "Oscar, did you hear a word I said? An hour has passed, and the sky has turned dark. I don't like the feel of this at all. We shouldn't have come. I'm getting worried."

"Stop nagging," he retorted in his usual arrogant way. Little ice crystals had formed on his cheeks, and his blue lips looked painful.

"Look. It's beginning to snow." She stretched out a gloved hand and caught a few white flakes.

"We've already passed the Holcombs'," Oscar bit out. "We'll be to the farm soon. Just be patient."

"But the snow, Oscar! We won't be able to get back."

"So we'll stay at Kathryn's. I'd think you'd like that better, anyway."

Under normal circumstances, yes, she would. But now she had the children to think about. If she didn't return, they'd think she'd abandoned them. July was opening up more and more about his family. She'd not let him and the girls down. Doing so would break their hearts. And Shad. What would he think?

"I can't stay away that long. The children depend on me. Staying at the farm isn't fair to Hildy and Lenore."

The children now slept in her room, and they felt like a family. The girls were so affectionate, and July was just a doll. No, her heart said, they should turn around this moment while they still could.

"I've changed my mind. I want to go back."

The snow was now falling in earnest. The flakes were small, but moving fast. Her stomach tightened as warning bells went off in her mind. What was Oscar thinking?

"Ossy, did you hear me?"

"I did," he said, giving her a sideways glance. "And I don't appreciate your tone. You don't care about those children. You want to go back because you're afraid of missing that man."

"Oscar? What's gotten into you?"

He went on as if he hadn't heard her. "Shad Petty. He's mesmerized you. You've lost all sense of reality. You're living in a dime-novel pretend world." He looked at her through narrowed eyes, his mouth pinched tight. "I won't let you do it, Poppy Alexandria Ford. I won't let you throw away your life like Kathryn has."

"You don't have a say in anything I do."

Angry, she grasped his arm and jerked, trying to shake off the hate-filled look he'd just cast her way. The confused horse threw his head.

"Turn around this instant," she shouted, fear sprouting in her chest. "If you don't, you'll regret your decision for the rest of your life."

Oscar laughed. He actually laughed.

This was a serious situation, and he was treating it like it was some silly childhood game. She remembered what a bad loser he was, how he'd pout for days if she bested him at anything. What was going on in that head, to be so mulish at a dangerous time? She had to get through to him fast, but she also needed to be careful not to send him into one of the pouting fits that would keep him silent for hours.

"I know seeing Kathryn would be nice and would calm my nerves after worrying about her, but I'm cold," she said softly, scooting closer to his side. "Really cold. Aren't you, Ossy? Aren't you cold?" When he didn't respond, she shook his arm. "And I'm scared. I'd like to go back—*please.*"

The snowfall was now a dense white wall.

What should she do? How could she make him understand? Something inside said this situation was far different from any she'd encountered in her life.

"Oscar," she yelled. "Look at me."

He turned, displaying the heated wrath in his eyes.

She gasped. Something was wrong with Oscar. He was thinking horrible things. She needed to get through to him or they wouldn't live to see the light of another day. In a swift move, she grasped the right line and hauled back, trying to turn the sleigh around.

Surprised, the horse jerked sideways, making the icy rails of the sleigh slide askew in the crusted snow. A little farther in the turn and the sleigh would be headed back to town.

She and Oscar fought for the lines, him cursing words she'd never heard cross his lips. He yanked the lines from her hands and shoved her to the other side of the seat.

Shocked at his behavior, Poppy then heard a deep, menacing growl.

The horse reared in his harness. When his front hooves landed, he kicked out behind and bolted, taking them down the side of the embankment.

Poppy screamed, grasping for something that would keep her from being thrown out. The sleigh felt like it was flying.

Suddenly, they jolted to a stop, snapping her head forward. Stars danced before her eyes, and pain gripped her.

The sleigh, wedged between two aspens, tipped slightly to one side. The poor horse fought for release, but the harness and underbrush kept him trapped where he stood. After several minutes of frantic struggle, the animal quieted, then stood knee-deep in the snow, quivering in fear.

They weren't going anywhere at all.

Where was Oscar?

Chapter Fifty-Five

"I'd best begin that apple pie, if I want to be finished with it by the time I need to make the noon meal."

Margaret set aside the book she'd been reading on the yellow settee since the breakfast dishes had been washed, dried, and put away. So much waiting gave her plenty of time for worry and speculation.

"In a few hours the men will be back inside, ready to eat a wagonload of food for lunch. Seriously, Evelyn, I don't know how you've done it these last few months without me. When I cooked for the colonel, he was *one* man. One man who ate a lot, yes, but compared to your two ranchers, that was nothing. They eat more than I'd have guessed any two people could."

"The cold weather coupled with ranch chores makes them hungry," Evelyn replied, closing her own book.

"But they ate a whole pie the other day—in one sitting."

Evelyn nodded, glancing at the fire. "I know, Margaret, feeding two men can be daunting at times."

Margaret was sure her dear girl would be happy to finally deliver. She'd washed and fixed her hair, but she was looking quite large these days. She wasn't eating much and her sleep was topsy-turvy.

"I'm glad I'm here to help then. When I go for the pie fixings in the cellar, what do you want me to bring up for supper? I'll need to get that on soon. The pork roast? The leftover meatloaf will do fine for lunch. I believe enough of that is left." She was running off at the mouth, but Margaret couldn't help herself. Two days had elapsed since the conversation about Estelle, and Evelyn had been quiet ever since. "When will Chance and Andy be in? Did Chance say?"

As she smiled and shook her head, Evelyn climbed slowly to her feet. "Actually, this totally slipped my mind. With the weather holding, he and Andy decided to snowshoe over to the Preece farm. He said somehow a heifer got out last night, and they're hoping she ended up there. If she did, Chance wants to make sure Tobit puts her in the barn. Chance is worried about her."

As I'm worried about you.

"By crossing the back pasture, the distance isn't far at all. I'm sure they'll be home before suppertime." Evelyn glanced at the clock and gave her a wide smile. "Nice that we don't have to worry about fixing their lunch." She patted her stomach. "Just ours."

Gone? Chance was gone?

Margaret had thought he was spending the day in the barn, like he did more often than not, working on this or that. He must have told Evelyn his plans when Margaret went to her room to get dressed for the day.

"That's fine," she said calmly. "I look forward to the meatloaf. It was delicious." She went to the cellar door in the hall by her bedroom. "The pork roast? For supper?"

Evelyn smiled and nodded. "Thank you. You're such a help."

"And I'm happy to be so. While I'm down there, what else would you like me to grab? Another jar of strawberry preserves? The one we have is almost gone. Potatoes?"

"Anything that suits your fancy, Margaret, suits me as well." Evelyn was at the sink, working the pump for a glass of water.

"Yes, well then."

Margaret hastened down the steps. Thankfully, Chance hadn't made them as narrow as in most homes. They were steep but manageable. A rush of frigid, musty-smelling air hit her face. At the bottom, she took a moment to light a candle, for the area had no windows. She worked in the light that streamed down from upstairs.

Once she had the candle burning, she went to the back of the room where Chance hung his meat. She sought the medium-sized pork thigh and, going up on tiptoe, hefted the chunk of cloth-covered meat from its high hook. Walking along the wall, she stuck six large potatoes into the oversized pocket on the front of her blue apron, and imagined herself looking much like Evelyn.

Moving slowly, she proceeded to the shelf with cans and jars and lifted her candle close. Finding the preserves, Margaret secured the jar of jam in the crook of the arm that held the meat, hugging it to her body, after which she reached for two jars of canned apples for the filling.

At the stairs, and in the light from above, she stopped and reorganized the items in her arms so she wouldn't lose anything on the trip up. She blew out the candle and left it where it belonged.

Emerging from the hallway, Margaret caught sight of Evelyn and the food dropped from her hands, jars breaking on the floor in a crash.

Evelyn was perched on the edge of a kitchen chair, her forehead resting on her arm stretched across the table. Her other hand clenched her stomach as a puddle of liquid spread on the floor beneath her.

"Evelyn!" Margaret rushed over, gently taking her shoulders. "What happened?"

Evelyn's breath shuddered out in staccato rhythm. "M-my water has broken. I'm having a contraction. Wait a moment until it passes."

Horrified, Margaret stepped back, her mind assessing the situation at hand. Unless Chance came home soon, she would have no help. Evelyn would not deliver in town with the doctor. She'd have her baby here, at home, with an inexperienced woman who'd never had a child of her own.

Snapping herself out of her astonishment, Margaret went to the linen closet and brought out two towels to mop up the floor, and another she tossed over the apples and jam she didn't have time to clean up.

Evelyn sat back, breathing heavily. Her face was white, her eyes large with fear. "It's happening, Margaret. My baby is coming."

"Yes, I know, dear." She gently took hold of her arm. "Let's get you situated. I've heard that once your water breaks, heavy labor is not far away. I want to get you into that large bed while I still can."

Evelyn's smile wobbled. She let Margaret lead her into the bedroom, all the while holding the bottom side of her large belly.

Margaret stripped off Evelyn's clothes over upstretched arms, as she'd done when Evelyn was small, and slipped on a clean nightgown. For the first time in days, the house was on the warm side, as was the bedroom. Again taking Evelyn's arm, she helped her climb the small set of steps Chance had constructed to make getting into the enormous bed easier on his wife. After Evelyn was comfortable, Margaret pulled up the sheet and gently placed the blanket over the top.

She smiled. "There, how's that?"

Evelyn reached out and took her hand. "You've always seen to my needs. Taken good care of me. I'm so relieved you're here. I know you won't let anything happen." She gave a small smile. "That's a good feeling."

With nerves pinging around her body, Margaret gently pulled away her hand. "Yes, I'm glad too, dear. Now, let me light a few lamps. The room is quite dark. And then I'm going to clean the mess off the floor." In the last couple of minutes, dark clouds had moved across the sky, blocking out the sun. "I can barely see my hand in front of my face. I assume we'll need to see what we're doing." She was unable to stop a nervous laugh.

Evelyn relaxed back onto the pillows, a serene smile playing around her lips.

Margaret made a mental picture of the way she looked now. In a few hours, God willing, Evelyn would be a different person. A mother. With a healthy, happy babe at her breast.

Chapter Fifty-Six

God help them! Shivers wracked Poppy's body from head to toe as she strained over the back of the sleigh to see if the wolf she'd heard had followed them down the slope. Was he out there, just waiting to attack?

Her arm ached. She must have hit it on something during the crash. And she tasted blood in her mouth. She spat to the side, the sight of crimson splotches on white snow making her head spin. She struggled to catch her gasping breath. Where was Oscar? She didn't see him anywhere.

Again, the horse struggled to get free. He slipped and fell to his knees but regained his footing. His sides heaved, but soon his energy ran out and he quieted.

There. Oscar. Facedown in the snow.

Poppy climbed out of the contraption and fought the snow to the far side of the sleigh. Taking his shoulders, she heaved with all her might to roll him over, praying he was still alive. He was heavy and wet, and snow continued to fall. His lips, purple from the cold, stood out against his sallow complexion.

"Oscar," she cried, shaking his shoulders, but there was no response.

Poor Oscar. We may have had our differences, but I'd never wish him dead. What should I do?

Peeling off her glove, she shoved her hand under his coat collar, fingering through his layers of clothing as she searched for his skin. She should feel for a pulse, but she didn't know how. Finally, under his coat, scarf, and several shirts, she pushed her fingertips to the base of his neck. She held her breath to stop the sound of her own ragged gasps.

Nothing.

Dazed, she sat back. Her head throbbed with pain.

The frightened horse wriggled once more in his harness, snorting and pawing the snow. He'd be defenseless against wolves—as would they all.

With her thoughts jumbled in her head, she stood and lumbered back to the tilted sleigh where she grasped one of the blankets and covered Oscar from the falling snow. She would like to get him back in the sleigh, to provide him with its protection, but he was much too large. She grasped Oscar's arm and shook him again, but still he gave no response.

As if taunting her, a wolf howled in the distance.

Frantic now, Poppy went back to the sleigh and dug under the backseat, looking for a weapon. She brushed aside the snow accumulating faster than she liked. Had Oscar thought to bring a gun? Was it hidden away? If he had, she could figure out how to shoot, to defend against the wolves. Or to sound an alarm.

She'd grown used to her chattering teeth and hardly noticed anymore. Her thoughts were running like a river. She swept away more snow, still searching, still hoping, still praying. Realization dawned. She stifled the sob that clawed at her throat.

I'm stranded with no weapon, Oscar is dead, and surely, I'll be dead soon too.

The falling snow was blocking out the light.

Their tracks. They had to have left some. If a rider came by now, perhaps they'd see the hoofprints and sleigh marks leading off the road and down the slope. Wouldn't they?

She pushed herself up, ignoring the pain in her arm, and looked over the side the way they'd come. The signs were being erased by the falling snow. Their tracks were nearly gone. Covered. Soon no one would be the wiser to their plight.

Should she go for help? How far back was the Holcomb ranch? How much farther to Kathryn's?

Poppy couldn't remember. Her thoughts felt like scrambled eggs. Right now, the tipped sleigh was the only cover she had.

She pulled the blanket around her shoulders, trying to think. She wouldn't last the night. She'd die, abandoning the children. And never know if her sister forgave her. Her mother and father would be crushed.

And Shad? Her heart quivered, remembering how gently he'd held her last night. How sincere he'd been, trying to sort out her feelings with Kathryn. She sat up, shivers taking over her body.

I'm not dying tonight—at least, not without a fight.

The horse struggled again, longer this time, his sides heaving from the energy he was expending. Perhaps there was some way she could release him and climb aboard. He'd run home to the livery.

Grasping the cold rail, Poppy pulled herself out and stepped down, sinking up to her knees. She pushed through the snow, and the gelding began to struggle again, frightened.

"Whoa, boy, easy now," she crooned softly, thinking of the tall, expensive thoroughbreds she was used to riding.

She placed her gloved hand on his side, and his cold hide twitched. She was careful to stay far away from his hooves. He might be trapped, but that didn't mean he couldn't break her bones with a single kick of his powerful leg.

She inched forward, trying not to think about the cold, how fast she would drift off to sleep and never awaken. But she couldn't do that. Not without freeing the horse. If he stayed here, he'd become a meal for the ravenous wolves. She had to unharness him for his sake, as well as hers.

"Easy now, fella." She put out her glove. Enough slack remained in the lines that he could nuzzle her hand.

His large eyes blinked, and he struggled again.

She stepped back until he stilled. "Easy, now."

She checked the harness, running her hand over the leather until she found a buckle. With both hands, she pulled up on the frozen strap, but it wouldn't budge. The animal had so much weight pressed against the keep, unbuckling would be impossible. If she had a knife, she might be able to cut the leather, but unfortunately, she didn't. Fighting her own rising panic, she felt along the frozen side poles of the rigging. She found another buckle with the same problem.

She couldn't accomplish the rescue. The nice old gelding was stuck—just like her.

"Easy, sweet boy," she said again through chattering teeth as she ran her hand down his sodden neck. He would most likely die here with her and Oscar, if Oscar was still alive. Why had they been so foolish to come out in this weather?

"Aaughhh…"

Poppy glanced over her shoulder to see Oscar moving, lifting his head to look around. He reached from under the blanket and scrubbed snow from his face.

"Ossy!" She hurried to his side and dropped to her knees to help him brush the snow away. "I thought you were dead." Tears clogged her throat and eyes, but they were too frozen to spill out. His image swam before her. "Thank God you're alive."

"Wh-what happened?" he asked, his gloved hand slowly cupping his forehead.

"We had an accident. We're down the hill where nobody will find us."

"Down the hill?" He struggled to sit up but wobbled and flopped back down.

"Yes. Off the side of the road. A wolf spooked the horse. We careened down the embankment. We're stuck. Don't you remember anything?" She refrained from reminding him how they'd fought for the lines.

He stared blankly into the sky, and a new wave of fear blossomed inside.

"Oscar. We don't have long to get out of here. If I help, can you climb the hill?"

Grimacing, he brought his gaze back to hers. "The pain in my head, and my side. I think my ribs are broken." He looked at the climb and then shook his head. "I'd never make it."

"Can you make it back into the sleigh? You'll be warmer, at least a little. In a few hours, the light will be gone. Wolves are everywhere. Do you understand what I'm saying?"

"Yes. We're going to die."

Blood trickled from Oscar's ear. He was seriously injured. Empathy for him pushed away her anger and fright. "After I get you to the sleigh, I'll go for help. Maybe I can reach the farm, or go back to the Holcombs'. Either way, I'd better go soon."

A wolf's howl rent the snowy stillness, causing the gelding to struggle.

She and Oscar stared at each other.

"You wouldn't make fifty feet," he said weakly. "I think they're waiting for nightfall. But you can bet they're out there right now, watching as we speak."

"Did you bring a gun, Ossy? Please say you did. I need to hear you say yes." Her blood pounded in her head. "I've looked everywhere but…"

He didn't answer.

"Ossy?"

"No. Thought we'd be to Kathryn's in a few minutes. Sorry, Poppy, I let you…"

More howls went up as the area closed in from the falling snow.

The horse snorted, and pawed the snow.

Would anyone even come looking? Maybe June would put out word when they didn't return with the sleigh. Would that be soon enough? And Shad? What about him? Anyone riding down the road wouldn't be looking over the side.

"Shhh," she said, "no need for apologies. Let's get you to the sleigh."

Poppy helped him roll to his side, and then dragged him to his feet. The span wasn't far, but he could barely walk, and he leaned most of his weight on her. Once there, he collapsed and she tucked the blankets over him, keeping one for herself.

I must find a weapon. I must find something.

As she reached under the backseat one more time, her fingers touched something cold. She grasped and pulled.

A lantern! Crammed under the seat bench. The kind that's meant to be hooked to the front of the sleigh on a romantic moonlight ride.

With shaking hands, she worked to get the light fixture free. Praying with all her heart, she lifted it to her ear and shook. Fuel, and a lot of it.

"There's a lantern, Ossy," she practically shouted with excitement. "I'll light it and take it to the top of the hill. Maybe someone will come looking and see our signal. The lamp's small, but at least it's something."

"But—the wolves. You can't."

"I must; it's our only chance. I think they'll be frightened of the light and leave me alone." More for her sake than his, she briefly touched his arm.

Or they'll attack and have me for supper. Either way, at least I will have tried.

Chapter Fifty-Seven

In the waning light of day, Shad ran through the semi-trampled snow of the boardwalk, concentrating on what he was doing so he wouldn't hit any icy patches. The snow began falling on his way back from Lichtenstein's and was coming down heavier by the minute. As he approached the livery, the light in the window gave him hope.

Let her be there!

He shouldered open the stiff door. "June," he shouted, wiping the snow from his face. The slot where June parked the sleigh was still empty. He'd hoped Poppy and Oscar would be inside. "June. You here?"

"Coming, Petty. What's up?"

"Where's the sleigh?"

June's gaze cut to the darkened window and then back to his face. Her brows dropped down as she slapped her leg and frowned. "Dad-blasted fool. He said he was only going out for a few minutes. A few runs up and down Main Street. I lost track of the time."

"Yeah, well, so did I. I was helping Brandon hunt for the looter of the mercantile. Turned out to be that fella staying at Lou's. He was so thankful to see us when we showed up, to save his backside, he didn't even resist. He sells what he steals to the miners, who pay him top dollar. Since he hadn't made it out to the river, he hadn't sold anything yet. When I returned to the hotel, Hildy said Poppy had gone out with Oscar, but that was all she knew." He trudged down the barn aisle way. "I need a fresh horse."

"You sure you want to go back out? Looks to be another big storm." She pounded her arms wrapped around her frame. "By now, they're most likely out at the Preece farm with her sister."

"That's what I think, as well, but I won't have a moment's peace unless I make sure. I don't trust Oscar. I wouldn't wager a plug nickel on him."

She gave him a knowing look and nodded.

"Morgan around?"

"He left a few hours ago, and there's no time to waste. I'll ride with you."

"No. You have to stay here in case I don't come back." He'd already finished saddling, so he checked his gun and took the rifle June offered.

"Be careful out there. You hear what happened to Uncle Pete?"

Shad nodded. "Justin will be showing up soon with the horses we rode. I left the chore to him to get back to the hotel. Felt something funny in my bones, and now I know it's not so funny. Tell him what's up. Maybe he can check out at the mill and the other road."

"Will do. Watch for the snowdrifts and wolves."

"You bet I will." With that, he was out the door and on his way to the Preece farm.

Navigating the steep hill, Poppy held the lantern as high as she could, the dim light not helping much at all. Even though she feared the wolves, she knew the temperature was a fiercer enemy, because it kept dropping. The feeling in her hands and feet had long since passed.

In her other hand, she carried the only weapon she could find, a large stick the horse had uncovered from his pawing. Almost as tall as she was, the lance was devoid of branches and had a spear-like point. She could see the weapon belonging to an Indian brave.

She moved by rote force, pushing herself up the long uphill climb and then the short rise of the embankment. Trees and shrubs closed in on her, giving the wolves plenty of places to hide. She remembered the description Shad had given her of the large lead wolf in Y Knot as he walked out onto Main Street. The animal hadn't been the least bit worried about any challenger. The depiction of his long yellow fangs was etched in her mind.

I mustn't think of that *beast.* She felt as if someone tickled down her back with long, frightening fingernails. A shiver, and not from the cold, made her swallow. *I have a mission. I can't be distracted.*

The lance and lantern grew heavy. Poppy halted, resting her arms. She'd only gone twenty feet, but it was becoming more and more difficult to climb in her wet clothing. She needed to get to the top of the ridge before she ran out of energy. Plant the lantern somewhere it would be seen and then get back to protect Oscar.

"Almost there. Keep going," she whispered to herself. A flash of something from the corner of her eye made her start. She stopped, her heart kicking into her throat. She scanned the bushes not fifteen feet away.

"Don't stop," she whispered aloud, her words slipping out in an icy puff of breath. "There's nothing else I can do. Keep going. Keep moving."

She'd gained several yards when the horse neighed in fright. She could barely hear the thrashing of his legs as he panicked in the death trap created by the harness. She shivered so hard, her hands jerked forcefully, and she almost dropped the lantern. What was happening back there? She didn't like to speculate.

Forcing herself to put one frozen foot in front of the other, she heard a sound. She tipped her head and pulled back the scarf wound around her ears, letting the icy snow drop inside her clothing.

A horse! Up on the road. She was sure. Although difficult to hear, the sound of muted hoofbeats moving at a fast pace made her want to cry with joy.

That's what our gelding must have sensed. Why he's struggling. Maybe someone was out searching for them.

"We're here," she called out, her untested voice barely scratching through her frozen throat. "Help!" she tried again. "We're here, down the side. P-please stop."

Whoever it had been was gone. Just that fast. Could be if they were headed to Kathryn's to see if she and Oscar were there, they'd come back this way, since Kathryn's road was a dead end. She had to get the lantern to the top of the embankment. If she didn't go now, this instant, all might be lost.

With a new sense of urgency, Poppy forced herself up the hill. She held the lantern high and used the lance to push with. More movement, in the trees to her left this time. Were the wolves closing in? As she'd hoped, the lantern was keeping them at bay. For now.

Hurry; I must hurry. I have to have the signal out before the rider returns.

The final climb was before her. In her exhausted and frozen condition, the rise looked impossibly far, although the height couldn't be more than twelve feet. She pulled in a strengthening breath. She'd made the fifty-yard trek from the sleigh, and was still alive. She had no option but to try.

Pushing the lance deep in the snow, she struggled upward, almost dropping the lantern when her foot slipped. Poppy gasped but kept going.

Standing at the top, on the road at last, she wanted to laugh and cry with joy. She clutched the lantern and lance close to her chest and slowly turned a circle in the falling snow. A chance existed, albeit a small one, that they'd be discovered.

Her frozen face stung like piercing needles were embedded in every inch as the wind whipped snow against her skin, but that didn't rob her of her joy. With shaking hands, she laid down her lance and pulled the piece of string she'd been so happy to discover earlier out of her pocket, and inched over to a small pine tree. Being careful to find a hearty branch, one that could handle some weight, she fastened the lantern to the bough.

Please, God, send help. I don't want to die.

The lamp swayed in the wind. She stared at the small yellow flame. She'd like to stay up here, to be ready if the rider came back. Anything was better than where she'd come from.

The horse screamed.

And this time she heard Oscar yell too, his words unintelligible, but they were laced with alarm and desperation.

I have to get back. I'm the only one they have.

She didn't want to leave. At least up here, she was closer to Kathryn. Fear sliced through her. Ossy was unprotected. He had no weapon at all, and was still helpless from being thrown from the sleigh.

Choking back her dread, she turned, looking toward Kathryn and Tobit's farm. "Please come, Shad," she cried, her whole heart splitting in two. She felt sure he'd been the one that galloped by. "Please come, before it's too late."

As much as she hated to, Poppy lifted her lance and started down the embankment in what was left of the shadowy light.

Chapter Fifty-Eight

Evelyn cried out, turning her head away from Margaret, who held a damp cloth in one hand and felt totally useless.

Lunchtime had come and gone. The first few hours of Evelyn's labor had been tranquil, with hardly a contraction. After sipping tea and eating a few nibbles of toast, she'd dozed on and off. She hadn't said anything outright, but Margaret could tell she was worried about Chance. Evelyn wasn't the only one who wished her husband would hurry and get home. Now, several hours later, her contractions had kicked in, and perspiration moistened her face.

Turning back, Evelyn grasped Margaret's arm when she reached forward to wipe her brow.

"What?" Margaret sputtered in surprise.

"I want Chance," Evelyn whispered. "Please. I want him here with me." A shriek whistled through her clenched teeth, and her hair clung to her damp skin.

"I know, dear, I know. He'll be here soon." She reached over and wiped Evelyn's forehead, and then moved lower to her cheeks to whisk away her tears. "I'm sure he's on his way and will be coming through the door momentarily."

Evelyn sucked in a breath and hiccupped. "No, he won't." She looked out the window. "He must have stayed at the Preece farm when the snow started. I'm scared. I want him here. With me." After a sob of distress, she rolled away and hid her face in her pillow, her shoulders quivering.

Margaret had yet to check on the baby's progress. She'd been hoping and praying Chance would return. In her mind, his experience with animals made him the better choice to assist his wife.

She glanced at the side table where she'd brought in all the supplies she thought they would need: a stack of soft towels, a pair of scissors that she'd run several times through the flames to cut the cord with, a bottle of iodine, just because she thought she might need it but she didn't know what for, and the baby's small cradle, sitting on the floor nearby. Looking at it now gave her courage to continue. Evelyn needed her, as did the baby. She'd take this one contraction at a time, and they'd get through. Beneath Evelyn's back and legs, she'd layered several towels.

Evelyn rolled and glanced out the window again, her eyes red from crying. The snow was still falling. Pain skittered across her face. The last contraction had only ended four minutes ago. This baby would be born soon.

"Ohhhh. Ohhhh…" Her head thrashed back and forth, unequivocal fear etched on her face.

Over the last hour, the contractions had become longer and much more intense. Evelyn's face turned bright red, and her breath huffed quickly in and out. After what seemed like an eternity, she relaxed back on the pillows.

"Here, drink this while you can." Margaret held up a half-full glass of water.

Evelyn shook her head. "I can't."

"Yes, you can. Take it." Margaret used her no-nonsense voice. "You need to keep liquids in you."

"I want Chance." Evelyn began to whimper. "*Please*, Margaret, I want Chance. I want Chance." She twisted the sheet in her fingers, her eyes wild. Her face was swollen from crying and the onset of labor.

"I know you do, sweetie, I know you do. He's on his way. I promise. He's coming, even through the snow."

"Chance," she cried. "He needs to hurry."

"I don't think so. I've heard first babies take a very long time to be born. We've only been at this a few hours. He'll be here. He wouldn't miss this."

Those words seemed to calm Evelyn, and Margaret prayed they were true. She'd like nothing better than to hand over the reins to Chance. She'd gladly pace the floor in the other room with Andy, waiting for little Holcomb to make his or her entrance into the world.

Evelyn took a breath and lay back on her pillow, closing her eyes.

"That's right, you get a little rest while you can. I'm putting water on in the kitchen. I'm only a step away."

She brushed Evelyn's blond hair off her slick forehead. When her goddaughter didn't respond, Margaret realized she had actually fallen asleep.

Margaret went into the other room but didn't go to the water pump. Instead, she went to the table by the sofa and reached for Evelyn's Bible. Sitting on the settee, she flipped the pages open to a random spot and began reading. The words soothed her, calmed her heart, and quieted her rapid-fire breathing.

Please, Lord, let this baby be born effortlessly, without complication. Give me the wisdom to know what to do and how to do it when the time arrives. Please bring Chance home.

She thought of the wolves he'd mentioned the other day. *That wouldn't happen.* Feeling a little better, she got up and hurried to the kitchen, and began pumping water into a cast-iron pot.

"Margaret!"

Margaret almost dropped the pot. Instead, she set it on the already hot stove and rushed into the bedroom.

Evelyn was panting as if she'd just run ten miles. "I need to push. I c-can't stop myself. It feels good and yet it hurts." She bore down for several long seconds, her face going white.

Chance would not make it back before his child was born. Margaret would have to deliver the baby herself, whether she liked it or not.

Gathering her courage, she pulled back the light sheet covering Evelyn's large belly and assessed the situation. The towels she'd put down were stained with spots of blood. Evelyn pushed, and Margaret thought she saw a tiny crown of light-colored hair, but she couldn't be sure.

"Evelyn," she said sternly. "I think you should sit up higher in the bed and bend your knees. Can we do that?"

The contraction had stopped, and Evelyn collapsed back against her pillows.

"Did you hear me? We must move now, before the next contraction."

Margaret took Evelyn's arm and sat her forward, put Chance's pillow behind her back, and directed her to sit upright. She helped lift one leg into a bent position, and then the other.

Evelyn's breathing picked up and her gaze darted around the room. "It's coming; it's coming?"

"Yes. There's no stopping this birth now." *As if there ever was.* "I want you to stay calm. When the feeling overtakes you, push for all you're worth."

Her lips quivering, Evelyn looked over and she nodded, although Margaret wondered if she'd actually heard anything she'd said. Soon, Evelyn was panting and moaning, and she looked like she was holding back.

"Do you need to push?"

She shook her head. "Almost, almost— Yes, I do now." She grunted loudly, her face squishing, her hand wrapped around Margaret's with a vengeance. She panted louder and then cried out. "Oh, it feels so good to push," she yelled into the room. "So much better than fighting the pain."

"Good girl, just keep doing that. All will be well. All will be well."

Margaret hoped what she said was true. The baby born, with both he—or she—and mommy doing fine. That was the only thing Margaret could think.

Her gaze cut to the window as pain from Evelyn's grip on her hand almost made her cry out. *Please come home, Chance. I don't want to do this by myself.*

Chapter Fifty-Nine

Scott and Poppy never made it to Kathryn's?

The question rolled over and over in Shad's mind as his horse struggled through the snow at a slow lope, giving Shad some speed, although he'd like more. He didn't have a choice on pushing the animal harder than he'd like to. The temperature was dropping. Night wasn't far off. When he found that fool Oscar Scott, he would give him what he should have the very first time the dandy had talked back. The man had no sense—and should have known better than to go out and take Poppy with him.

And Poppy? What of her behavior? They'd spoken often of the dangers. She certainly knew better than to go out, especially with someone like her stupid friend. Scott wasn't all to blame, no, not at all.

As snow smattered Shad in the face, he shoved back his anger and rode on. With the wolves, anything could happen. A fear he hadn't known since he was a young lad responsible for his brothers filled him. He didn't like thinking something could have happened already to Poppy. He'd become fond of her in the past few weeks.

Fond, hah. He'd fallen in love, plain and simple. Because of his injury, he couldn't have her, but he darn well could protect her.

He'd frightened Kathryn and Tobit to death when he'd come out looking for her sister and Scott. And poor Isaiah. The man had almost broken down and cried. Chance Holcomb and the new fella, Andy Lovell, had been there earlier, but had started home moments before he'd arrived. They'd been biding their time, waiting for the snow to stop, but finally they started back overland. Shad hadn't waited for Tobit but mounted up and headed back to Y Knot.

He'd check Chance's on the way, and if he didn't find them, he'd go straight to Klinkner's mill, taking the shortcut behind the Biscuit Barrel. The snow-covered trail would be risky, but that was the quickest route. They'd been gone for some time now. He hoped Morgan and Brandon were searching the town.

The livery horse slipped on a patch of ice and almost went down. Deep in thought and half-frozen, Shad hadn't been ready and was pitched up onto the gelding's neck, clutching the horse's mane with his thick leather gloves. Because of the mishap, he almost missed the flicker of light that caught the corner of his eye. Surprised, he reined to a halt, turned a half circle, and rode back to the side of the road.

A sleigh lantern tied to a Douglas fir?

He sucked in a breath and wanted to shout with happiness. Turning his head, he listened, not hearing anything but the horse's labored breathing and his own. The snow had thickened, closing in around him.

A screech, and a small cry.

"Hyah!" Plunging his mount down the embankment, he rode through the trees and snow. His horse spooked and snorted when the growls of wolves reached his ears. Shad bellowed and pulled his gun from its holster, riding all the harder.

Poppy's shout.

More growling.

A horse whinnying in fear.

Then he saw her and a surge of pride flashed through him. The sleigh was wedged in the trees and the horse stuck tight, still in his harness. Poppy stood at the horse's side with a long stick, lunging at two wolves when either got too close. Scott sat in the tilted sleigh, sobbing with his hands clutching the side.

If the wolves went toward him, Poppy lumbered through the snow and thrust her lance forward, fighting them off. She must have hit her mark at least once, because even in the dim light, Shad could see splotches of crimson marring the snow. With that much blood scent, more wolves would soon arrive.

Aiming, he shot the one closest to the sleigh. The animal fell into the snow and the other darted off into the trees.

"Shad," she cried, turning toward him, her voice ringing with joy. "I knew you'd come."

He rode closer, keeping watch. Wolves were good jumpers and could take him out of the saddle. "You hurt?" he called when he was almost there.

Blood smeared her face, and her clothes were sopping wet.

"No, I'm unhurt, but Oscar hit his head in the fall. He's bleeding from his ear."

Shad chanced a glance at Scott in the seat of the sleigh, wiping at tears. An eerie chorus of howls went up from nearby. Shad drew his rifle from the scabbard and handed it to Poppy before he dismounted, never taking his gaze from the circle of trees.

"Get back in the sleigh," he ordered, pulling back the hammer of his gun. He wanted to be ready if the wolves all rushed at once.

"Do you have a knife?" she asked. "We can cut the harness and ride the horse out."

He turned, meeting her gaze for the first time. A deep longing filled him. Poppy was disheveled, wet, and blood-smeared, but beautiful in her own right. What courage. Not many men would go up against two wolves with a tree branch.

"Yeah, I do. But I know this horse. He's not broke to ride. As wild-eyed as he is, even I wouldn't stay on bareback long before he bucked me off."

Her face crumpled as she looked at the trapped animal. "Let's cut him loose then. So the wolves don't get him."

"Not just yet. Some of the wolves might follow him, but not all. With the horse gone"—he looked at his own flighty animal—"we'd be the prime target. As it is, the horses are a distraction."

"What about your gunshot? Won't others hear?"

"Maybe. Maybe not. We can't count on that." Grasping the cold siding, he tried to rock the sleigh to see if he could unwedge it, but it was stuck tight. "Gunshots are not uncommon. Besides, the snow muffles sound. Waiting to be rescued would be a mistake."

When she went to object, he held up a quieting hand and glanced back the way he'd come. If not for Scott, he'd ride out of here right now with Poppy in his arms. As it was, he wasn't quite sure what they'd do.

Chance and Andy were returning the way they'd previously traveled, cross-country and not on the road. If Tobit missed the lamp, how long until someone else found them? Shad had his rifle and gun, as well as some bullets, but not an overabundance. And he didn't trust he could get all the wolves if more than a handful rushed the sleigh.

He looked at Poppy. "Can you shoot?"

Her teeth chattered as she hugged her arms close to her body, making him wish he could get her out of this cold.

"I never have before, but I can learn."

He kept a close watch on the tree line. What should they do? The snow was coming down heavy. He didn't want to spend the night here. He doubted they'd last until tomorrow.

He turned to Scott, who hadn't looked him in the eye since he'd arrived. "How's the head?"

The man's gaze slowly tracked to him. "Hurts. And I'm dizzy."

Shad assessed the situation. Could he get them to the Holcombs' without Scott falling off the horse? At least here, they had the sleigh for some sort of shelter. If they left and couldn't make it, they all might freeze to death.

"Think you can ride if I help you onto my horse?"

"Shad, what are you planning?" Poppy asked.

He reached out and pulled her to his side, wrapping an arm around her shoulders. "I'll put you both up on my horse and lead you out."

Poppy nudged him. "I'm sorry for being so foolish. Oscar offered to take me to Kathryn's, and after what I told you, I was anxious to speak with her." Sadness burned deep in her eyes. "But that's no excuse. I should have known better."

"You're right. You did know better. I told you more than a few times." Irked, he didn't want to let her so easily off the hook. A Montana winter was nothing to trifle with. Three lives were now at risk because of their senseless decision. "But let's get out of this mess before you go apologizing. We have a lot of work to do. Since I've arrived, the forest has darkened. We don't want to still be here tonight."

A falling pinecone spooked his edgy mount, making the animal snort and shy to the side.

"Easy now," Shad said, reaching out to touch his neck. "Scott, you never answered me. Can you stay in the saddle if the two of you ride double?"

"I don't have any choice. I'll have to."

Poppy shook her head. "Oh, Ossy, can you ever soften up?"

"Never mind that," Shad bit out, "let's get moving." He pulled his horse closer and handed one rein to Poppy, the other still slung over the saddle horn. "Hang on for your life, because your life depends on it."

She nodded, her poor chapped lips bleeding in the wind.

"Come on, Scott," he said, stepping closer and extending a hand.

"Now?"

"Exactly." Shad grasped Scott's wrist and pulled him out of the sleigh. The man's cries reverberated through the trees.

A chorus of growls rippled around the area.

Poppy sucked in a breath. "There're so many. I had no idea."

"That's why we have to move now."

"Shad, look." Poppy pointed at the far tree line where three husky wolves had stepped out, watching.

Shad didn't waste one second. "Once I get you both on my horse, I'm cutting the gelding free. Hopefully, he'll draw away most of the wolves. Scott, can you shoot a rifle?"

"I've hunted pheasants all my life, but now my vision is much too blurry. I don't think I can."

Disgusted, Shad shook his head. "Fine. Come on, Poppy, you go up first where you can shoot if need be. If any wolves come too close, just aim and fire. They'll scatter. Be prepared, because the rifle has a strong kick. With Scott behind you, you should be okay with staying aboard."

She was so light, she went up easily.

He pointed to the saddle horn. "Have you ridden, um—like a man before?"

"A few times, yes."

Behind him, Scott huffed.

She settled her skirt in the saddle, the hem pulling up the middle of her leg and her feet not reaching the long stirrups. Between her shaking hands and clattering teeth, she didn't look very confident.

The same couldn't be said for Oscar Scott. The man was dead weight and wasn't much help. On the third frustrating try, Shad had a thought to leave the troublemaker behind.

Chapter Sixty

"**P**lease, Evelyn, try to push a little harder."

The baby had been crowning for over half an hour. Dread that something was wrong kept rolling around in Margaret's mind. She'd only attended one other birth, and both mother and child had perished. A cold chill of fear threatened to paralyze her.

I can't let that happen. I must do something. Evelyn is counting on me.

From her position at the foot of the bed, Margaret glanced at Evelyn's face. "Did you hear me, dear?" she asked more forcefully. Evelyn's eyes were closed, but Margaret knew she wasn't asleep, just waiting for the next contraction to hit. They were coming every three minutes without enough time in between to fall asleep. "Evelyn?"

"Yes, I hear you. I'm just so tired. Why isn't the baby coming? I—I want Chance…"

Margaret could hear the thickness in her voice and knew her goddaughter was about to resume her tears. Irritation at Chance bubbled up. She would box his ears when he finally returned. How dare he go anywhere today?

The baby isn't due for another month.

"Still. That's no excuse." Margaret wasn't aware she'd spoken aloud until Evelyn lifted her head at Margaret's angry tone.

"What?" She began to pant loudly.

"Oh, nothing, sweetheart. This contraction, I'm telling you to push like you never have before." She drilled Evelyn with an imposing stare. "This is it. Your baby is about to be born."

Evelyn couldn't answer. She was too consumed with the contraction wracking her body. With a loud groan, she bore down. Her breathing stopped and her face turned blue.

Please, God, let this child be born now. Evelyn doesn't have much strength left.

If she weren't so busy, Margaret would have sank to her knees beside the bed with hands folded. But there was no time. She put out her hands in preparation.

With Poppy already seated in the saddle of Shad's skittish mount, all they needed to do was pull Ossy aboard behind and then get up that hill, away from danger.

The horse snorted, sidestepped in the snow, and then flung his head.

"The scent of the wolves," Shad said, almost to himself as he lifted Oscar's leg in an effort to get his boot into the stirrup.

Poppy held the reins with the hand that also supported the rifle, which made controlling the horse's movement near impossible. With her other hand, she grasped Oscar's arm, his bulky coat hampering her hold. He was heavy, unsteady, and still groggy. He wasn't helping the situation in the least.

If that wasn't enough, Poppy kept her gaze fixed on the tree line. Her job was to make sure the wolves didn't take them by surprise. Before Shad had arrived, she'd injured one of the pack with her spear. He'd been bold, slinking up close as another wolf kept her attention. At the last second, she'd spotted him only a few feet away. Plunging forward with a shriek that came out of her mouth in surprise, she'd caught the predator's shoulder. The pointed tip of her branch had driven deep. He'd yipped and pulled back, leaving a trail of blood on the snow.

"We don't have all night, Scott," Shad snapped. "Help me out here."

"I'm trying."

Shad glanced up at her. "Can you keep the horse steady? So far, this isn't working," he added in a calmer tone, but frustration simply seeped from his body.

The storm was so cold now, she couldn't remember what warmth felt like. The gelding's crest, ears, and rump were covered in snow, and she imagined her head was, as well. All she wanted to do was get out of here. The place was a death trap.

Again, the horse stepped sideways, and Oscar slumped to his knees.

"Poppy," Shad bit out.

"I know," she shot back.

His gaze was filled with purpose. She didn't want to be caught here either. She had a life to live, she thought, nodding with determination when Shad looked at her again. Her chest filled with possibilities—possibilities of a life with Shad. The way she felt right now, she didn't ever want to be without him.

"There." Shad shoved Oscar's boot in the stirrup and pushed him from behind.

Poppy, an expert rider, kept pressure with her offside leg, as well as pressing the gelding with her heel—hard. She wouldn't mess this up.

Halfway up, Oscar grasped the back of the saddle with one hand and the saddle horn with the other. Taking what seemed like an eternity to throw his leg over. He was finally aboard.

Deep growls brought her and the men around. Shad stood vulnerable at the horse's side. Six or seven wolves slunk forward, growling and baring their teeth. The gelding still caught in the harness snorted in fear and thrashed with all his strength, kicking out behind at nothing, crazy with a desire to run free.

Poppy sucked in a breath. "The wolves! They're coming!"

"Let's get out of here," Oscar cried. "What're you waiting for, Poppy? Get moving up the hill."

Shad drew his gun and the pack scattered. A few pulled back into the snow-covered brush while others ran to the right and left, essentially surrounding them. They weren't gone for good.

Shad gave her a quick glance. Something in his expression pierced her heart.

"Can you keep him aboard if the two of you ride out of here? I need to cut the horse free."

"I'm not leaving you," she cried.

Behind her, Oscar straightened. She felt his arm tighten around her waist.

"Listen to him, Poppy. He knows what's best. He's protecting you." Oscar grasped for the reins.

Poppy brought the butt of the rifle down on his hand, mashing it between the gun's stock and the saddle horn.

The gelding pranced in fear, and Shad stepped back.

"You witch," Oscar blurted. He jerked away his hand and shook out the pain.

The horse snorted, pawing the snow.

"You've never had any class. What was I thinking to follow you to Y Knot? The worst mistake of my life."

"Just be quiet, Oscar. I swear, I'll dump you before I leave Shad." Poppy glared over her shoulder. "Believe it, or suffer the consequences. I couldn't care less what you think of me." She nodded to Shad. "Cut the horse free." She lifted the rifle to her shoulder as she kept a hold on the reins, pointing it at the last spot they'd seen the wolves. "I'll cover you. I may not hit anything, but I'll scatter them. We're getting out of here together, or not at all."

Withdrawing a pocketknife, Shad trudged over to the injured horse, speaking to the animal in soft tones. First, he cut away the secondary leathers, so the horse would still feel constrained and not struggle, thinking it was free when it wasn't. When Shad pulled off the headpiece, the livery horse tried to surge forward, eager to be away.

"Hold tight to your horse," Shad called over his shoulder. "When this one runs, yours will want to bolt too."

"Go on. I'm ready," she responded.

After two quick slashes with the knife, Shad cleared the lines, and the gelding was finally free. Discovering this, the horse took two testing steps and then snorted, flung his head to the side, and galloped up the hill toward the road.

Just as Shad had predicted, the gelding she rode reared and tried to bolt, but Poppy held him tight.

"Whoa, now," she said in a soothing voice. She felt Oscar's animosity burning from behind, as well as his panicked grip around her waist. Would he really abandon the man who'd come to their rescue?

Shad was again by her side. "Let's go. Maybe we can make it all the way back to the hotel. I'd like to try." He scanned the area again, and then began his climb with the horse prancing by his side.

Poppy kept an extra-sharp watch on the trees, which was difficult through the heavy snowfall. Were the wolves gone, following the sleigh horse? Or were they prowling only a few yards away, waiting to attack?

She shivered, glancing down at Shad, so vulnerable on the ground as he trudged through the snow. He was a prime target.

Steeling her nerves, she hefted the rifle in her arms, determined not to let any more misfortune happen today.

Chapter Sixty-One

The door suddenly opened. A gust of freezing air and a flurry of snow rushed inside the house.

Chance came through the threshold, looking much like a snowman. After closing the door, he bent, unstrapped the snowshoes from his feet, and stepped out of the them. His face was totally crusted with ice. When Margaret didn't rise or say anything, he looked up at her in question, a dark shadow passing over his eyes.

His gaze darted to the bedroom and then back to her. "Margaret?"

So much happiness swirled inside Margaret, she couldn't speak. She just dropped her gaze to the warm bundle in her arms.

For several long seconds, Chance gaped. He took one small step in her direction before stopping. He stripped off his snow-caked coat with trembling hands, let it fall to the floor, and then peeled off his gloves. After scrubbing the snow from his face, he was by her chair next to the fire in three large strides.

Dropping to one knee, Chance slowly lifted the soft blanket that kept the baby concealed. His breath jerked before he raised his anxious gaze up to Margaret's face. "Evie?"

The word held all the sentiment existing in the world. Margaret hadn't meant to be cruel, and now she realized how this looked.

"Sleeping. She did a fine job. You should be proud."

Relief washed over his face, and his eyes instantly filled with moisture. Margaret had never seen the cowboy display such tenderness.

He held out his arms. "May I?"

"Of course. Don't you want to know if you have a son or daughter?"

Margaret couldn't take her eyes off the tiny pink face, eyes closed in slumber after the long first feeding. She was smitten. Bringing this babe into the world had been the most spiritual and joyful moment of her life. She'd never felt so close to God. He'd been there with her every moment, his comforting hand on her shoulder, his wise words whispered into her ear.

Chance's deep chuckle brought a smile to her face.

"I was so surprised by the birth, I forgot about that. Is my child a boy or a girl?"

"You have a handsome son, Mr. Holcomb. As bright and beautiful a baby as I've ever seen." To hand him over, Margaret stood, as did Chance. She carefully transferred the precious bundle into his arms.

For a moment, the baby's eyes opened and he looked up into his father's face, the outer edge of his tiny lips pulling up.

Chance chuckled again before he sought out Margaret's gaze. "He's so small. I can hardly feel him."

"He's early. A month or two will pass before he fits into the cradle you built."

"Can I see Evie?" he asked, his voice rough with emotion. He didn't even flinch when a tear escaped his left eye.

"Absolutely. She's anxious for you to be home. She's been worried about the snow." Margaret frowned and lifted one eyebrow. "And so was I. A fine day you picked to go for a visit."

She led the way to the bedroom door, quietly turned the knob, and peeked inside. Evelyn was awake, staring out the window. Guessing what she was thinking about wasn't difficult. Her hair, still matted from the delivery, was stretched out on the pillow around her sweet, fatigue-lined face.

Margaret must have made a noise, because Evelyn turned to the door.

"Come in," she said softly. "I miss my little man. Where is he? In his cradle?"

Stepping back, Margaret let Chance enter carrying the infant.

Evelyn's eyes widened, and a smile burst onto her face. "Chance," she said on a whispered word of adoration. "You're home."

He came forward and bent to kiss her for several long moments. When they finally parted, he said, "Darlin', I'm so sorry I wasn't here for you."

Excited, Evelyn pushed to a sitting position, and Margaret rushed over to help. Once Evelyn was settled, Chance sat on the edge of the bed, staring down into the blanket he held.

So much love flowed between the couple, Margaret could only stare as tears trickled down her face.

"What do you think?" Evelyn asked, reaching forward to finger the few strands of light brown hair.

"That he's mighty small. I'm afraid he'll break when I hold him."

Evelyn beamed with pride. "He'll grow and be as tall and large as his daddy."

"I'm sure he will," Chance replied, nodding and glancing over at Margaret. "And you delivered him? All alone? The one thing you didn't want to do."

Well, not exactly alone. "That's right. I can say now, the delivery was the most wonderful moment of my life. But at the time, not so much."

The three laughed.

"For now, I've made up a small bed out of one of the drawers in my bedroom," she added. "He gets lost in the cradle. I'm still waiting to hear what you'll call him." She couldn't stop from reaching out to caress the baby's tender cheek with the back of her finger. "He and I have had time to get acquainted, but we haven't been formally introduced. He likes my rocking and singing, though."

Chance looked into Evelyn's eyes. "Are we still set with what we decided? You've changed your mind more times than I can count."

"That's my prerogative as his mother." She laughed. "But yes, I like what we picked."

Leaning forward, Chance kissed the baby's cheek. "His name is Garth Davenport Holcomb."

The dedication to Estelle made Margaret suck in an emotional breath. In a rush of love, she smiled, and her gaze sought out Evelyn.

"Your mother would be very touched you picked her family name." She leaned forward and kissed her goddaughter's forehead, and then she returned her attention to the tiny babe in Chance's arms. "I'm pleased to meet you, Garth Davenport Holcomb," she whispered. "You're a balm to this woman's heart."

Evelyn took Margaret's hand when she began to back away. "I want my mother to be a part of my life." She glanced at

Chance. "Our lives. Always, even if in spirit only. If the baby had been a girl, we intended to name her Estelle Margaret."

Garth interrupted the touching moment by squishing up his face and letting out a very boisterous shriek for someone so small. His small legs pushed out, and his head turned toward Chance.

"I think he's hungry again." Evelyn reached for the bundle Chance willingly held out.

Margaret stepped quietly to the door, extremely moved by Evelyn's acknowledgment. "Now that you're home, Chance, I'll happily see to supper, and the pork roast I meant to put on hours ago. Don't you worry about a thing. I'll have a celebratory dinner whipped up soon."

She didn't think anyone even heard, as both new parents were bent over the bundle held close to Evelyn's chest. Their heads almost touched, and the murmur of soft, inaudible sentiments filled Margaret with love and sent her on her way with a grateful heart.

Chapter Sixty-Two

Relief washed through Shad when they reached the road. He couldn't help a small smile when he glanced at the lantern on the wispy bough, still burning after all this time. He went over, untied the knot, and carried it along. If they kept moving at this rate, they'd make it back to town within an hour. Thankfully, the snow had stopped, at least for now.

"What?" Poppy asked through chattering teeth. She was hunched forward, weighted from behind by Scott's bulky frame. Her whole body shivered, but a sparkle shone in her eyes that he couldn't deny. "I see you smiling at something, Shad Petty. Tell me what."

They made their way slowly down the middle of the road. Night had fallen, and the white snow's reflection was their only light.

"Just thinking how smart you were to hang out the lantern," he replied, lifting it high. "I'd never have found you otherwise." He shook his head in amazement. "And how brave too. Fighting with wolves. You're pretty gutsy, for a girl."

"For a girl, huh?" Her voice was infused with affection.

"For anyone." He gestured to Scott behind, who had his head turned away, as it had been since they'd reached the road and begun the ride to town.

She softly laughed. "Thank you. I'll take that as a compliment. I've never been praised for my courage before."

Scott turned their way and looked down at Shad. "Can you stop the cooing banter until we get back? I'm not feeling so well, and listening is making me sicker than I already am."

Poppy laughed into the still, white countryside.

He looked at her again, liking what he saw. This trip west had set her free from the constraints of her upbringing; that was a fact. The blinders were off her bridle, and she was getting set to run free. If Shad had been a help for that, he was glad.

"Shad, I was thinking," she began, and then jerked back, pulling up the rifle. "Look out!"

She fired, but not before one of the two charging wolves reached him.

The animal knocked him to the ground, its snapping, biting jaws close enough for him to smell its rotted breath. Shad's head hit the ground hard, but he dared not let himself black out. With as much strength as he could muster, he held back the wolf with both hands around the animal's shoulders, his fingers buried deep in the predator's scruff.

He heard shouting in the background but couldn't make out the words. The wolf had the advantage. Sharp fangs tore at his clothes. He kept his arms up, shoving the wolf away as it lunged in again. He couldn't even get to his gun. Desperate, he brought up his legs, placed his feet on his attacker's chest, and pushed with all his might. If he drew fast enough, he'd have one instant to get off a shot. If he missed, he'd be ripped to shreds in front of Poppy.

Crack. Crack.

The wolf fell from his crouched position as he prepared to leap for Shad's throat. He lay motionless not five feet away.

Chapter Sixty-Three

His Poppy had shot straight and true, slaying a hundred-pound wolf before it killed him. She saved his life. Well, not *his* Poppy. Shad knew that. But he was still shaken, which made it difficult to think clearly.

They'd reached Y Knot safely, where Kathryn and Tobit had showed up at the hotel in a panic about Poppy's whereabouts. Amidst all the commotion of the reunion, and feeling antsy from all of Poppy's warm looks, Shad felt it best if he got back to the ranch, where he belonged. He quietly exited the hotel's back door, collected his horse and headed for home.

With a deep sigh of relief and thankfulness to still be alive, Shad limped into the familiar surrounds of the bunkhouse. He was pleased to be there, but nothing would ever feel the same again. Gone were his happy-go-lucky days. Past was his youth. He'd fallen hard for Poppy Ford, even though she was miles above him in social class. Him only half a man, without the ability to give her the life she deserved. He might as well get used to the feel of his battered heart, because the hurt wasn't going away anytime soon, if ever.

"Shad."

Blinking in surprise, he stumbled to a halt at the sight of Tanner and Nick playing cards at the table, a cup of coffee at each spot as if they'd been living here for years. They stood and greeted him with strong hugs.

"Boys," he said, excitement filling his chest. "When did you arrive?"

Tanner looked at Nick. "'Bout six days ago, I reckon."

His brother's crooked smile chased away Shad's sadness over his plight with Poppy. Life would be good again—someday. He'd just take some doing to remember that fact from time to time.

"That's right," Lucky said, ambling over. "These two polecats have been eating me out of house and home." He gave Shad a good up-and-down perusal. "I think you need a bath. You want me to heat some water?"

Shad had never bathed here at the ranch, just now and then in town at the bathhouse. "Where would one do that?" he asked suspiciously.

"In my private quarters. Don't worry; I won't come in."

"In that case, yes, I'd be much obliged."

Both his brothers laughed. "Tell us what you've been doing in town so long. We was getting to think you weren't ever coming home," Tanner, the younger of the two, said.

His brown gaze held mounds of affection, causing a wide smile to break out on Shad's face. He released the worry that had nagged his mind for days.

Nick winked. "Not that we'd mind if you didn't. Leaves more of Lucky's cooking for us."

Shad grasped them both by a shoulder and squeezed. "I see the tide has already turned against me. So much for family loyalty."

Poppy searched her mind for a way to start this conversation with Kathryn. She'd tried yesterday, when Kathryn and Tobit had first showed up at the hotel. But the talk centered on the wolves, of Oscar's bumped head and dizziness, of their daring escape—then that led to the roof collapsing in at the hotel, Miss Aubrey, and the Sangers—and the adorable children. So much had happened in such a short amount of time.

Poppy had even taken her sister into her bedroom, so they could speak in private, but all Kathryn could do was gush about how relieved she was that Poppy was alive, and how much she loved her. The decision was made that Poppy would return to the farm and stay with them there until she could make the trip back to Boston.

Oscar turned down the offer, opting to take a room at the boarding house as he waited for Dr. Handerhoosen to return. He'd said he couldn't stay another night in the hotel.

"Poppy," Kathryn said, sitting at a table in the dining room where they were having tea. "The plight of those poor orphans has been weighing on my mind—heavily." She raised the cup to her lips and took a sip. "I know you expressed your desire to keep them, but you're so young, and not yet married. Would that be a wise decision?"

"At least until their relatives are found and informed. And some decisions have been made," Poppy said a bit defensively. Kathryn doubted she was grown up enough to care for July, May, and April?

"Actually, what I was thinking was we should bring them to the farm. Then, besides you, who would be their primary guardian, I could help too. And Tobit, as well as Isaiah. Between the four of us, how difficult could the task be? Our house has plenty of room."

Here she was again, as usual, being an angel on earth—and Poppy loved her all the more. Still, Poppy couldn't decide a single thing until she confessed, told Kathryn exactly how she felt and why she'd left in the first place.

"Thank you, Kathryn. That's so generous. I don't know what to say."

Kathryn set her cup into its saucer and studied her sister's face. "First, I'd say tell me what's troubling you. You're not yourself. Yesterday I thought the reason was all the life-and-death scenarios you've been thrust into lately, but now I think something more is involved." She reached out and took Poppy's hand. "Remember back when we were girls? You used to tell me everything. You still can. You can trust me."

Heat rushed to Poppy's face. Her eyes pricked as they filled with tears.

"What?" Kathryn asked, alarmed. "What's happened? Oscar? Shad?"

Poppy stared into her lukewarm tea. She'd been wanting this chance, and now it was here.

"Please. You're frightening me."

"The problem concerns me, Kathryn."

Kathryn tipped her head. Her brows inched together as she waited.

"And you. I—I just want to tell you how sorry I am for the way I've treated you over the years."

Kathryn pulled back. "What on earth are you talking about?"

"I've been condescending, critical, and mean. And all the while, you're always kind and forgiving. I've taken a good long look at myself and don't like what I see. I'm spoiled and self-centered. I wish I could be more like you, but I never seem to measure up, even when I try. I just want you to know that I realize my shortcomings now. I'm a horrible person, but I'm trying to change."

Poppy lifted her cup for a sip of tea, but it jiggled so violently that she had to set it back on the table.

Kathryn stood and came around to scoot in close on Poppy's side of the booth. She took both Poppy's hands into hers. "First off, you're not a horrible person. You're spunky. Filled with life. I'm honored to call you my sister."

The tears spilled down Poppy's cheeks.

"Second, if you ever were mean to me, which I'm not saying you were, then you've come by it naturally. You've had a good teacher in Father. He belittles me all the time, or he did, when I lived at home. Mother has told me in some of her letters that he is changing quite a bit." She smiled kindly, took out her handkerchief, and dried Poppy's tears. "But all those hurt feelings from him are in my past, and I don't let them bother me. Ever. I've been given a second chance at happiness. I love my life and wouldn't trade it for all the tea in China."

Poppy swallowed back her misery. "I'm so sorry. Please say you've forgiven me."

"If doing so will make you feel better, then yes, you're forgiven. To tell you the truth, I hardly remember anything but happiness when I think of you. So this is difficult to imagine you feeling this way."

A tidal wave of liberation washed over Poppy. All these weeks had been pure misery, reliving every slight, intended or not, she'd dealt her sister over the years. Joy and happiness filled every inch of her body, and she couldn't stop a huge smile. Shad had been right.

"Thank you," she gushed and flung herself into Kathryn's arms. "Thank you, dear sister. I promise to be the best sister in the world. Starting over feels wonderful. I'm so relieved to finally say I'm sorry."

Only one question remained and it was a puzzling one. She slowly pulled back from Kathryn's arms and looked into her sister's eyes.

"But *why* do you think Father treats you the way he does? I don't understand."

Kathryn blinked and looked away. Poppy couldn't refute the pain she saw there.

"Some things are better off left unsaid."

Kathryn's tone was measured and controlled, but laced with sadness. She knew the answer, but wasn't saying.

"The best thing you can do is say a little prayer for Father, and forgive him with all your heart. Take it from me; I know." Kathryn winked. Her dimples appeared on either side of her beautiful, wide smile.

Everything was going to be all right. Unable to stop herself, Poppy threw herself into her sister's arms again, so thankful for new beginnings. She couldn't wait to share this new beginning with Shad. Tell him he'd been right all along. That moment would be very special indeed.

Chapter Sixty-Four

Four Months Later, May 1887

With a heavy heart, Luke handed down Esperanza from the buggy at the church cemetery as Flood assisted Claire on the other side. Most of the snow had melted, except for a few small patches. The harsh, unforgiving winter months had passed, but a crisp spring wind still had them bundled in coats.

More cattle had perished that winter than anyone could have ever have imagined in their worst nightmares. Some neighbors died too. Handfuls of ranchers had been completely wiped out by the devastating loss.

The Heart of the Mountains had survived because of their early sell-off in November. For that remarkable forethought, Luke was thankful, but the action didn't take the sting out of the thought of all those cattle dying from starvation as well as the fierce temperatures. The tragedy was sickening, at best.

Once the herds of cattle had begun to perish by the tens of thousands, the ranchers' problems with the wolves had abated. But they would still need to take action so they didn't run into the same problem next winter.

At the sound of crunching wheels in mud and dirt, Luke glanced to the road to see the wagon that bore Uncle Pete's coffin slowly making its way toward them. *The other overwhelming loss.* Sadness had prevailed over all the houses on the ranch because of the cowboy's death, as well as the state of the widespread suffering. A hundred years would need to pass before anyone forgot the blizzard of 1887.

Ike sat holding the lines on the buckboard seat, with Lucky at his side. The coffin was draped in a colorful Mexican blanket, one that had been Uncle Pete's favorite. The rest of the hands, as well as the new Petty brothers and Hickory, rode two by two in a long procession behind the rig, all mourning their comrade in their own way, either lost in memory or just plain sad.

Luke glanced back to the spot under several quaking aspens on the far side of the cemetery where other hands from the ranch had been laid to rest.

The preacher waited by Uncle Pete's final resting place with some townsfolk. A somber-faced Mark and Matt, and their wives and children, Amy and Rachel holding their new sons, as well as Faith and Luke's brood. Roady and a very pregnant Sally. Chance and Evie Holcomb, with baby Garth. Evie's friend, Margaret Seymour from St. Louis, was at their side.

Mr. Lichtenstein and Mr. Simpson, his clerk. Brandon and Charity. The new deputy, Justin Wesley, his bullwhip fastened on his hip. Morgan and June. Berta May, as well as Hildy, Lenore, Harold, Lou, and Drit. Trent Herrick held the arm of his ailing father, next to the short Mr. Tracy. All the Klinkners. Abe and Fancy stood on the outer circle, both knowing Uncle Pete well from his time spent at the Hitching Post.

Kathryn and her sister Poppy were there, each holding one of the orphaned twins in their arms. The boy, July, stood near Tobit and Isaiah, kicking his toe at something in the grass.

Judge Harrison Wesley, the deputy's father and also the circuit judge, had come through Y Knot last month, and sentenced the couple to life in the penitentiary for kidnapping the Sanger children and murdering their father. The felons were gone and life was back to normal, as much as it could be.

Today was a sad day for Luke.

For the ranch.

For Y Knot.

Poppy. Shad was riding toward the end of the processional with his brothers and Francis when he spotted her next to her sister and the young'uns. He hadn't seen her since walking out of her life in January. He'd made a point of making the break quick and final.

Every night for three months, he'd dreamed about the kiss they'd shared, the feel of her lips, and the storm of feelings it created. And each time, he'd awaken in a sweat to find he was still in the bunkhouse. Just this last month, he was beginning to feel human again, like maybe his life was still worth living, at least a little. Now here she was to start that familiar ache all over again.

Actually, he was shocked Poppy was still in town. The stage had started service a month or so ago. He'd have figured her long gone by now. What would she say? And how would he answer?

The ranch hands dismounted and tied their horses to any spot they could find. Chance joined them and helped carry the coffin off the wagon bed. With so many helping, the burden was light. From the corner of his eye, Shad noticed Mrs. McCutcheon dabbing her eyes with a white kerchief. Soon other women were doing the same. The men walked slowly, carrying Uncle Pete for his last ride through the churchyard. Ike and John couldn't stop full-force tears.

They set the simple pine box on the ropes that had been laid out, and then lowered Uncle Pete into his grave. The group was silent, as well as the animals and insects. There wasn't a single sound except the gentle clacking of the aspen leaves. The preacher said a few words followed by a prayer, and then Flood McCutcheon stepped forward and gave an accounting of how Uncle Pete had come to the ranch, how he'd stayed on for years. What Uncle Pete's loyalty meant to him and his family. Flood had to stop a few times and get a hold of his emotions.

Halfway through, little baby Garth took to crying. Chance escorted his wife and her friend away toward town, being pressed back by the chilly north wind.

After Flood finished, a handful of the men shared a funny anecdote or a touching good-bye. All in all, the service lasted a good hour.

"May God bless you and keep you," Reverend Crittlestick proclaimed loudly. "Thank you all for coming out to show your respect and say your good-byes to a fine man. I know Uncle Pete would have appreciated every single one of you here."

Casper Slack, the town troubadour, stood a few feet away under the trees. With his nimble fingers, he began a soft rendition of "Amazing Grace" on his mandolin. Ike pulled out his harmonica and softly played along.

Conversation started. People pulled away and began their walk down the road to Y Knot, clutching their coat collars around their necks. Men went for buggies and wagons as the women waited.

Feeling like a coward, Shad stayed with Tanner, Nick, Francis, and Pedro, hoping Poppy and her group would pass them by without stopping. And yet, he wanted to seek her out and talk all night. There was no winning in this situation.

No use. They were headed his way.

"Well, let's get to the Hitching Post," Tanner said, looking at him and then around the group.

Francis nodded. "Sure. Heard the other fellas saying they were gonna drink a few last whiskeys to Uncle Pete. Say good-bye." He started away with Pedro following.

Shad caught sight of Poppy. She and her sister were almost to him and his brothers with the twins in their arms. The young'uns looked healthy, happy, and clean, the girls dressed in matching coats, gloves, and bows. Tobit, Isaiah, and July were still hanging back, speaking with Mr. Lichtenstein.

Feeling like a kid, Shad swallowed nervously.

"Mr. Petty," Kathryn said in her smooth Boston accent. After giving him a smile, she glanced at his brothers. "Gentlemen."

Poppy just looked at him, little May snuggled against her chest like a shield.

He couldn't read her blank expression, but something told him she was steaming mad. "Mrs. Preece," he replied respectfully, forcing a smile onto his lips. "Miss Ford."

For some odd reason, Nick and Tanner exchanged a dubious look.

"Girls." Shad reached forward and gave each little cherub a gentle rub on the head, bringing a swift jolt of melancholy. "I'd like you to meet my brothers, Nick and Tanner." He pointed to each as he said their names. "This is Mrs. Preece and Miss Ford, sisters from Boston."

"We're pleased to meet you," Kathryn said.

Poppy offered a wan smile and nodded. She was being unusually quiet.

Much to Shad's relief, his brothers added to the introductions.

"The pleasure is ours," Tanner finally said.

Nick touched the rim of his hat. "Yeah."

Shoot. This was uncomfortable. Would he ever get over her?

"We'd best be on our way. We don't want to have to wait for a table at the Biscuit Barrel," Kathryn said, glancing down the road where most of the congregation had gone.

Just as they were moving away, Poppy laid a hand on her sister's arm. "Kathryn, would you please take May with you to the Biscuit Barrel? I'll only be a minute. I'd like to speak with Mr. Petty, if he can spare the time."

Her blue eyes glimmered like sapphires in the icy Montana sunlight, bringing a jolt of excitement to his numb insides.

She lifted her chin. "Well?" she asked none too nicely. "Do you have time?"

"Sure," he replied and held out his arm. "We can take a little walk, catch up with each other."

Tanner cuffed Nick on the shoulder. "Come on, brother. We'll see you at the saloon, Shad." The two hurried away.

"Good-bye, ma'am, miss, and, er, girls," one of them mumbled.

Ripples of pleasure moved up Shad's arm from Poppy's small gloved hand. A million memories cascaded through his head, followed by a million warnings.

He couldn't go there. He couldn't. Imagining possibilities wasn't fair to Poppy.

Chapter Sixty-Five

When they started down the street toward the Biscuit Barrel directly behind her sister and the children, Poppy couldn't stop her anger building inside. Shad meant to be rid of her just as fast as possible, without saying a word. Well, she'd not have it.

"Where're you taking me?" she asked. She risked a look up his tall build into his face for clues, but couldn't see any.

"You'll know soon enough. Don't go gettin' mad."

Too late. She'd been mad for months, hurt and confused. She'd thought they had something between them. *We did have something between us.* She could feel the attraction now, zipping around like a flock of hummingbirds on a newly blossomed honeysuckle vine.

To her surprise, they passed the crowded eatery as her sister and girls entered, and continued around back, heading across the expanse of soft spring grass toward the empty gazebo. Fine. He wasn't such a cad, but close.

Shad led her up the two steps, and she pulled her hand away. He went to the far side, brought back a chair, and placed it facing the other.

"Have a seat," he said.

She got comfortable as sounds from the restaurant floated across the field. Things could be so different. They *should* be so different. They should be in the Biscuit Barrel with the children and the rest of her family, enjoying the day. Laughing and loving. She glared at him when he sat.

"Poppy," he said softly. "I'm sorry if I hurt you. That wasn't my intention."

Her anger vanished, replaced with blinding pain. This was the end. Shad didn't love her like she loved him. He was letting her down easy, if you could call the last excruciating months of agony by that description. After all this time spent wondering what he was thinking, she couldn't stop the scalding tears from falling.

"Hey," he said, his voice clogged with emotion. "Don't cry." He dug around inside his coat and pulled out a handkerchief. "Go on; take it. It's clean."

Poppy wiped her eyes, all the while carefully keeping her gaze from his. How could he? After all they'd been through.

He grasped the edges of his chair and hopped it closer until their knees were almost touching. They sat in silence.

She stared down at the cloth clutched in her hands, feeling as if time was standing still. But it wasn't. He'd soon say good-bye for the last time, and she'd never have this chance again. If she wanted to talk, she'd better get started.

"I thought you liked me," she finally whispered. "I believed all those nights talking in the lobby of the hotel meant something to you, as they did to me."

He remained silent, his boot toe tapping the stage.

"And the kiss?" She glanced up. He stared at her with the most agonized look she'd ever seen. "Won't you say anything? Am I that insignificant to you that you can't utter a word?"

He shot to his feet and paced to the far side of the gazebo, looking out at the vista.

"Shad," she called, standing as well, her anger edging out her pain. "Shad? Say *something*. Even if it's, 'You got it all wrong, Poppy. I was just being friendly. That was just a sociable little kiss. And besides—good-bye.'" She huffed loudly. "My gosh, we're not toddlers."

He turned to face her. "You kissed me."

Accepting the fact hurt, but it was the truth. And he flung it at her like the lance she'd thrown at the wolf. The remark sank deep into her chest, and she wanted to die.

Instead, she lifted her chin. She'd had fights before with her father, although compared to the ones he'd had with Kathryn, they'd been small. But still, she was no doormat.

"You're certainly right about that," she replied. "My fault, yes. I could tell by your response, you didn't like it at all. But besides my one blunder when I was overcome with grief, I did have indications you were feeling the same. Many looks, touches here and there, soft-spoken words. Concern for my welfare—you risking your life to save mine." She shrugged. "Alas, those didn't mean a thing."

Shad's face colored. He cut the space between them in half, stabbing his finger at the wooden deck. "Damn it, Poppy. Stop this. You're talking circles around me, but it won't change a thing."

All her bravado fizzled away. He was right. Nothing mattered. She couldn't talk him into loving her. That was something he had to do on his own. And that hadn't happened.

She dropped her gaze to the deck and watched a lumbering beetle trying to get away before it got squished.

"Fine," she whispered. "Just tell me you don't love me, and I'll go away. Stop pestering you. Just say it, Shad, so I can believe it. Because, for some strange reason, I think you do." She sighed and lifted her gaze to his. "I need to hear it from your lips."

He just stood there, but she refused to move.

Why wasn't he saying it? Why wouldn't he put her out of this misery?

Because he does love me.

The truth hit her like a ton of bricks. Shad loves me, but he's afraid to say it. He loves me. His feelings were all right there in his eyes.

Poppy flew into his arms, barely giving him a chance to catch her. She wrapped her arms around his middle and laid her head on his chest, unable to stop her tears. He felt so good, and his scent, so beloved, filled her heart.

Several moments passed before she could pull back and look up into his face, only to see a stony mask of pain.

"Loving you doesn't change a thing," he said. "We can't be together. Period."

She felt her smile freeze in place. What was he going on about now? She'd already decided to stay in Y Knot. Written to her parents with the news. Why couldn't she and Shad be together? That was ridiculous.

"Remember when you saw me with Redbud, the bull, in Virginia?"

What on earth does this have to do with anything? "Yes."

"He butted me with his head, hurting some things inside me. I'm not the man you think I am." He set his hands on her shoulders and gently eased her back. "I'm not the man you need."

Stunned, Poppy stepped away, taking his hands in hers. She blinked back her tears, all her happiness gone, replaced with a chilling fear.

"Tell me."

"I'll never sire any children, Poppy." His deep voice was filled with emotion. "Every woman wants babies, and that includes you. I'd never sentence you to a life like that. It's not fair."

Her mind buzzed with thoughts, and she wanted to figure this out. She loved Shad. Wanted him for her own, and would never love another. But this *was* big news. He was right.

"I see," she replied, just to fill the moment so she had time to go over the possibilities. "I can understand why you'd think these facts would be unfair." She swallowed, dropped one of his hands for a second to wipe her eyes, and then picked it up again. "But I see the situation a bit differently. First of all, can you try making babies?" She knew that was a very unladylike thing to ask, but felt the reality was an important part of the puzzle. "I mean, is all *that* working?"

His forehead crinkled and he actually blushed. "No problems there."

Thank God. She squeezed his hands to dispel his uneasiness with the conversation. "And who gave you this life-altering news?"

With a low voice, he said, "After I was well enough to leave Virginia, I hustled back to Texas. I quit the ranch and rode to Colorado, just for something to do. Things just didn't feel right, so I went to a doc in some town. He asked a lot of questions, did an examination, and gave me a couple bottles of elixir to make me feel better. His opinion was things inside got crushed and would never allow my, uh, seed to get to the desired destination. That's about it."

Poppy made a sound in her throat. "I'm surprised you're taking the word of a Podunk doctor as gospel. Will it hurt anything to try and prove him wrong?" She couldn't stop a smile. "If it's children you're needing so quickly, have you so soon forgotten April, May, and July? Brandon hasn't found out a thing about our sweeties' relatives, so they aren't going anywhere yet, and maybe never. And on the small chance we're not able to conceive on our own after some time, my father knows the best doctors in Boston. You can be sure I'm not allowing a no-account sawbones to ruin my life."

A tiny smile appeared, and he chuckled. "You're not?"

She shook her head. Running her hands up and down his broad chest a few times, she went up on tiptoe and found his lips. At first, he didn't respond. Then, after a moment, he wrapped her up so tight, she thought she would die. She couldn't get close enough. She felt his love and his desire. They would make it, no matter what.

Finally, they parted. Shad's serious brow was back. "And if that no-account sawbones was right?"

"Then I'll still be the happiest woman alive. I love you. I've been so empty until now. Your love fills me up with happiness. I don't want to live without you. However my life plays out, as long as you're in it, I'll never regret a day. I promise you that. Forever and always."

"I think you're forgetting one thing."

"Oh?"

"Your parents. They won't be thrilled with your choice."

If he only knew how right he is. "You let me deal with them."

Chapter Sixty-Six

"Please hurry, Kathryn. Shad's been sitting in the parlor a whole fifteen minutes. I don't want to keep him waiting too long."

Poppy turned back and forth in front of her bedroom mirror examining her reflection. She'd donned one of her best gowns, returned after Morgan Stanford and a few others had begun repairs on the hotel. The dress had a high-waisted bodice, sleeves trimmed in lace, and was a beautiful light shade of violet that complemented her complexion perfectly. The frock felt good, and she knew she looked pretty.

"July is keeping him entertained with magic tricks," Kathryn responded, tying a silk ribbon into a bow. "His hands were bound behind his back last time I peeked in. Besides, you'll benefit by making him wait a little and being unpredictable. You'll see."

This was Poppy and Shad's first time to town together since they'd announced they were officially courting. After several rounds of letters, her mother and father had acquiesced only after insisting they wait at least six months before they got married, even though Poppy wanted to tie the knot immediately.

Kathryn fastened the bow in her sister's hair with a pin. "There, you're done. I don't think I've ever seen you look more beautiful. His heart will burst when he sees you."

Poppy couldn't stop a small, excited laugh. "I hope so. I mean figuratively, of course." She lifted her reticule from the bed, and then followed Kathryn down the stairs.

Shad and Tobit stood when the women entered the room. The twins were jabbering on about something as they looked at Shad's wrists behind his back held firm with a soft piece of rope. July beamed at her, as pleased as a peacock.

"Poppy," Shad said shyly. "You look beautiful." He glanced down. "July, get me untied. Where was the trick, anyway?"

The boy shrugged, quickly released him, and then ran out of the room.

Rubbing his wrists for only a second, Shad took Poppy's hands and kissed her cheek. "You ready to go? I have a nice outing planned." He looked straight at Kathryn. "I'm taking her to town for an early supper and will have her back before seven."

The formality seemed sort of silly after all the time they'd shared together in the hotel, and even in his bed, but Poppy was loving being courted.

"That sounds lovely, Shad," Kathryn said. "You two enjoy yourselves."

"Think about what I said." Tobit smiled and crooked an eyebrow as they shook hands at the door. "It's the way of the future. We'll be one of the first here in our area."

"Thanks, Tobit. I'll let you know."

Once in the rented buggy, after they'd passed the barn for privacy, they shared several chaste kisses.

She couldn't believe this handsome cowboy was hers. Their future was an open book of possibilities. After one last kiss, and several touches of his beloved cheek, Poppy sat back. She couldn't quell her curiosity any longer.

"What was Tobit talking about? He sounded very mysterious."

With a flick of the lines, they started off.

"Just how ranching is changing. So many ranches were wiped out because of their dependence on grazing the open range. Speculation is most ranchers will keep smaller herds, which they'll fence in and feed. Heard talk around the bunkhouse of the same. They'll need hay. Some will grow their own. Some won't want the trouble and will look to buy. Because of that, down the road, the demand will increase, and Tobit aims to cash in. He's planting hay next season."

Poppy hadn't heard any of this. She and Tobit were getting along splendidly. All those other feelings had gone away once she'd had that talk with Kathryn and forgiven herself.

"Sounds like a good idea. Was that all?"

Shad turned and looked at her for a few seconds, then shook his head. "You don't miss a thing, do you? He's been able to work a few fields, but could do so much more with help." He winked at her. "He's asked me to come in as partner."

"Oh, Shad." Unable to stop herself, she reached up and began peppering kisses over his face, cheek, and lips. "That's too wonderful to be true. What did you say?"

"That I'd think about it."

He pulled the buggy to a halt on the deserted country road and again wrapped her in his arms. The weather had warmed, and colorful little birds filled the sky. After another kiss, he nuzzled her neck.

"Mmm, you smell good. Better than sweet molasses cake." He chuckled and sat back. "I'd say we've been pretty blessed, Miss Poppy Ford, soon to be Mrs. Poppy Petty. With everything that's happened, even with all the heartbreak and death, Y Knot's had several new babies, neighbors have come out to help each other like never before, my brothers arrived safely… and I ended up with the prettiest girl in town. I'm still figuring out how that one happened." He fingered a small wisp of hair around her ear. "I love you, sweetheart."

The gesture sent a delightful shiver down her back. She was the happiest girl in the world, and she'd never tire of telling Shad just that.

"I love you too, my wonderful cowboy. I love you too."

Acknowledgments

Thank you to my brilliant team; I would be lost without you. To my editors, Pam Berehulke of Bulletproof Editing and Linda Carroll-Bradd of Lustre Editing. To my husband, Michael, for brainstorming and finding plot holes in the first draft. To my sons, Matthew and Adam, for their help in marketing and social media. To Kelli Ann Morgan for a beautiful cover design. And to my very patient formatter, Bob Houston.

To my dear family for making the seriously long hours I spend at my computer worth every moment. I love you all.

And to my readers, no author could be as blessed to have such wonderful friends, readers, and supporters. *Thank you*.

And to our Awesome God for making my dreams come true.

About The Author

Caroline Fyffe was born in Waco, Texas, the first of many towns she would call home during her father's career with the US Air Force. A horse aficionado from an early age, she earned a Bachelor of Arts in communications from California State University-Chico before launching what would become a twenty-year career as an equine photographer. She began writing fiction to pass the time during long days in the show arena, channeling her love of horses and the Old West into a series of Western historicals. Her debut novel, *Where the Wind Blows*, won the Romance Writers of America's prestigious Golden Heart Award as well as the Wisconsin RWA's Write Touch Readers' Award. She and her husband have two grown sons and live in the Pacific Northwest.

Want news on releases, giveaways, and bonus reads? Sign up for
Caroline's newsletter at: www.carolinefyffe.com
See her Equine Photography: www.carolinefyffephoto.com
LIKE her FaceBook Author Page:
Facebook.com/CarolineFyffe
Twitter: @carolinefyffe
Write to her at: caroline@carolinefyffe.com

Made in the USA
Monee, IL
30 June 2020

35196530R00224